Munshi Premchand's

GODAAN

Masterpiece of Hindi Literature

Munshi Premchand's

GODAAN

Masterpiece of Hindi Literature

Anurag Yadav

Published by:

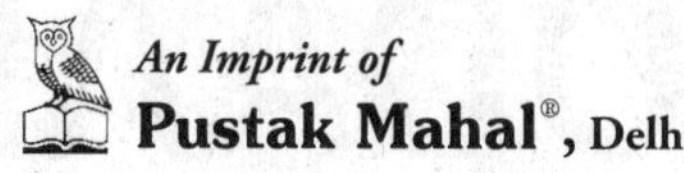

Administrative office and sale centre

J-3/16 , Daryaganj, New Delhi-110002

☎ 23276539, 23272783, 23272784 • *Fax:* 011-23260518

E-mail: info@pustakmahal.com • *Website:* www.pustakmahal.com

Branches

Bengaluru: ☎ 080-22234025 • *Telefax:* 080-22240209

E-mail: *E-mail*: pustakmahalblr@gmail.com

Mumbai: ☎ 022-22010941, 022-22053387

E-mail: unicornbooksmumbai@gmail.com

Patna: ☎ 0612-3294193 • *Telefax:* 0612-2302719

E-mail: rapidexptn@gmail.com

ISBN 978-81-223-1067-2

Edition 2016

Price : ₹ 250/-

Printed at : AR Emm International, Delhi

1

As he finished tending the bulls-giving them their feed, Horiram turned to his wife Dhania, "Send Gobar to cut the sugarcane as I don't know when I'll be back... Pass me my *lathi*."

Dhania held up her soiled hands as she was making the cow dung fuel cakes. "Come on, what's the big hurry? At least have a bite of something before you go."

Hori's furrowed brow wrinkled further. "You are worried about feeding me when I am concerned about getting late for meeting the Master. If he sits down for his prayers, it will be hours before I can see him".

"That's exactly why I am saying, have something before you go. Heavens will not fall if you do not go today. Didn't you go just the day before? "

"Don't butt your nose into things you don't understand. Give me my *lathi* and just do what you are good at. It is only because I meet and humour him regularly that we still survive. Otherwise, you wouldn't know the kind of misfortune that would befall us. Almost everyone in the village is finding the going tough with ejections and attachments orders for their land. When someone powerful can crush you under his heel, it is best to lick his feet and keep him humoured."

Such wisdom was beyond Dhania. Her logical mind told her that they were paying the rent to the landlord for tilling his land and beyond that there was no need to grovel. In her twenty years of married life, it had dawned on her that though she scrounged on food and clothes, saved every *anna,* the landlord's rent would still loom large every month. And if they still somehow managed to pay it why cringe before him? This difference in their thinking led to many quarrels between husband and wife.

Of her six children, only three had survived. Gobar, her son was 16 years old and the girls, Sona and Rupa were 11 and 8 years, respectively. Three of her sons died before they could reach their teens. A dull anger would nudge her occasionally at the injustice of it all. If only she could have afforded better medicines, they would have all lived. But she never had any money for medical care. And look at the toll it had taken on her. The burden of her 36 years lay in deep wrinkles on her face, spreading its grey imprint in her hair. Her limbs dull, the dusky brown complexion sallow, even her eyesight was failing.

Worrying about the next meal cut into even the little joys, life offered her. A lifetime of penury had riddled her self respect with holes and made her almost indifferent to it. Weighed down by the struggles to plan the daily meal, her heart revolted at having to struggle for the next. Why try to please or suck up for something that doesn't seem to come anyway? It was only when she was buffeted a few times by her circumstances and upbraided by her husband that she would grudgingly accept harsh reality.

Defeated and angry, she collected the shoes, turban, *lathi* and the little pouch of tobacco and thrust them in front of Hori.

Hori glared and snapped at her- "You think I am going to your father's house that you brought out all this finery? As it is, there aren't any sizzling sisters–in- law who I would want to impress."

As he spoke, the hint of a soft smile lit up his rather haggard and sunken face. Dhania's cheeks flushed at this, "As if my sisters will fall for a dandy young man like you!"

Hori folded the scruffy *'mirjai'* carefully and put it aside on the cot. "So you think I have grown old, eh? I am not even forty. Men actually begin to bloom into manhood not before they are sixty."

"Hold a mirror to your face! Men like you never really get to that. With no milk, or *ghee* for your body, sustaining your health itself is a feat. Oh Lord! I shudder to imagine what your condition will be, when you actually get old. Whose door shall we go to beg at that time?"

The momentary joviality in his conversation was scalded by the brutality of stark reality. He gripped the *lathi* in his hands, mumbling that such a situation will not arise, as he would wind up and depart this world much before he was sixty.

Dhania looked remorseful. "Now let that pass, will you? There's no need to talk negatively like that. Even if I say something in jest, you start cursing me."

She stood at the door, staring vacantly at him as he propped the *lathi* on his shoulders and left. His comments sent a shiver of foreboding and dread through her saddened heart. In silent dedication of her womanhood, she sent out prayers of forbearance for her husband. A surge of goodwill gushed in her heart and seemed to reach out to him, as if encircling him in a protective shield. In the misery of scarcity, her austerity and wifely devotion was the glimmer of light that she clung to in a drab night of existence. His intemperate words, howsoever close to bitter truth they may be, had tried to snuff out that ray of light, and they stung because they were so close to what might actually come to pass. None except the handicapped can feel the sting that comes with being called an invalid.

Hori was moving in fast strides. On both sides of the path, the lush green of swaying sugarcane fields made him wish that if God was kind, and it rained in time and all went well, he would definitely buy a cow this year. The local breed hardly gave any milk and their calves were no better either. At best, they could be used to dredge the oil mill stone. No, he would get a Western breed. Serve it well and surely she will give at least four or five seers of milk.

His son, Gobar longed for milk and if he did not get it at his young age, would he ever get it when he was past his need? His was the age to eat and drink well. If he got a lot of nourishing milk for a year or so, he would turn into a strapping lad. The calves would also grow into sturdy bulls.

Hori knew that a cow would not be less than 200 rupees. But, so what? A household can never appear prosperous without a cow. How auspicious it is to wake up in the morning to the mooing of your own cow! He wondered when his dream would see the light of day. Like any other householder, the desire to own a cow simmered eternally in his breast. This was his life's greatest dream and ambition. His humble heart did not envision ideas of living off bank generated interests, building a big house or buying real estate.

The June sun rose above the cluster of mango groves, lending a golden glow to a red hue in the sky and the breeze was turning hotter every minute. On both sides of the path, the farmers working in the fields nodded in greeting and waved at him deferentially to come and share a smoke with them but Hori had no time for those civilities. His hunger for social acceptance and respect glowed on his face as he noticed those respectful glances. That's the positive fallout of being in close contact with the masters. Otherwise who would notice him? After all, what is the worth of a farmer with just four or five *bighas* of land? Even tillers owning three to four ploughs, respectfully bowed before him- wasn't that good enough?

He, now, left the pathway through the fields and came to a shallow open area, where collected rainwater had created a damp green cluster of vegetation even in the heat of June. Cows of the neighbouring villages would come here to graze. There was a cool, welcome, freshness in the air at this spot. Hori breathed deeply; once, twice, thrice. He wanted to sit there for sometime, as all day he was destined to run around and burn in the hot summer sun. Many farmers were ready to pay any price to get this piece of land in their name. God bless the Rai sahib, who had bluntly stated that this part of land was for the cattle to graze and would not be sold to anyone for any price. Had it been any other landowner, he would have cared two hoots about the cattle, for why should he let go of an opportunity to make money? But Rai sahib was from the old school who still respected tradition. After all, what worth is a Master who does not care for his subjects?

Suddenly he saw Bhola coming his way with his cows. Bhola was a cowherd, living in the borough, adjacent to the village and had a petty business of milk and butter. He would sometimes sell his cows to the villagers if they offered a good price. Hori felt an intense desire to own one of them. What if Bhola gave him the cow, which was leading the pack? He'd pay him the money in some time, gradually. He was aware there was no money at home. The rent was not paid as yet and Bisesar Sah was also to be paid whose loan was gathering interest at an *anna* a rupee.

Yet the thick-headed lack of vision that usually accompanies deprivation and penury, the shamelessness that survives unmindful of sarcasm, abuse and flogging, nudged him on. His ambition that had gnawed at him for long, made him desperate. He went up to Bhola and said, "*Ram Ram* brother Bhola, what's up? I hear you have bought new cows from the cattle fair?"

Bhola instantly got wind of Hori's intentions, so he replied brusquely and with little reciprocal warmth, "Yes, I've bought two calves and two cows. All of my cows had stopped giving milk. If cows stop giving milk, how will I make both ends meet?"

Hori patted the cow –"She looks like a good milch cow. How much did you get her for?"

Bhola puffed up with pride-"The market was going through the roof; I paid eighty rupees for her. Paid through my nose, the two young ones cost me thirty rupees each. Yet, customers pay only just one rupee for eight seers of milk."

"Wow! You've got some guts, brother! However, what you now possess is unheard of in half a dozen villages in the neighbourhood."

Bhola was on cloud nine. "Rai sahib was giving a hundred for her. For the calves fifty each, but I didn't take it. God willing, I'll make a little fortune this season itself."

Hori continued, "Rai sahib doesn't have the heart to make a deal like that. He'll take it, if it comes as a gift. Only you are brave enough to shell out a handful of notes, trusting your fate. I really can't take my eyes off her. Your life is blessed, as you spend it serving the cows. Our luck does not favour us with even cow dung. It's such a shame, when a householder doesn't have a single cow at home. For ages, we have not tasted the nectar of cow's milk. My wife pesters me to talk to you. I tell her, when I meet you I'll let you know. She is so impressed with your good disposition. She says, she hasn't seen a man like you, who speaks with such decency- barely raising his face to look her in the eye."

Bhola's rising euphoria touched a new high, with this latest boost. He said, "Only a decent man will consider another woman as his mother or sister. Any man who stares insolently at another man's woman should be shot."

"Exactly, that's well said, brother. Only a gentleman respects another's dignity as his own."

Bhola looked enviously at Hori and said, "You are blessed you have a caring wife. My home is ruined, brother and there is no one to help me in my loneliness.'

Last year, Bhola's wife had sunstroke and died because of it- Hori knew that, but what he didn't know was that Bhola's fifty year old toughened frame harboured such sentimentality. The craving for a woman's companionship came alive in his moist eyes.

Hori found an opening there and his farmer's cunning came gushing out to grab the opportunity.

"There's an old saying...Without a wife, a home is as barren as a haunted house. Why do you not get married again?"

"I am on the look out, brother but I am unable to find the right woman. I am willing to spend money but nothing seems to move. Let's see what God wills."

"From now on, I will also be on the look out. God willing very soon things will change for the better for you."

"That will be almost like emancipation for me, brother. God has been benevolent and I have everything at home. Almost a *paseri* of milk comes to my lot everyday but then what's the use?"

"There is a woman in my in-laws' family. A couple of years ago, her husband abandoned her and went off to Calcutta. She somehow ekes out a living by grinding foodstuff. She has no children and is quite an eyeful too. Consider her as some sort of fortune."

Bhola's emaciated face glowed in anticipation. Hope is such an aphrodisiac! He said, "I depend entirely on you brother. If you are not busy, one of these days we can go see her."

"When I line up everything, only then I will let you know. Too much of eagerness can spoil chances at times."

"What eagerness? We go whenever you have time. And you take this mutt if you fancy her."

"This cow is not within my budget or in my destiny, big brother. I do not want to cause a loss to you. It's not for me to take advantage of my friends. Life can go on as it has in the past."

"Now you speak as if we are strangers. You take the cow and give whatever price you want to give. It's the same thing if she lives in your house or mine. Come, I bought her for eighty, you take her away for eighty itself."

"But big brother, I do not have cash, please understand this."

"Brother, who is asking for cash?

Hori's chest swelled with joy. For eighty rupees the cow was a bargain. Such a sleek healthy body, six or seven seers of milk morning and night and so gentle that even a child could milk her. Her calves would sell for a hundred each. Tethered to the doorway, she would make his house glorious. He was under a debt of 400, but Hori considered a loan as something that would come for free if Bhola were to get engaged. Once that was done, he would not open his mouth for at least a year or two. And even if he did what could be worse? The maximum he could do was to come asking for his debt repeatedly, get mad, maybe bad mouth him a bit. Hori was not unduly ashamed of all that. This was something, he was quite used to. Such was a farmer's destiny.

He knew he was tricking Bhola into this deal, yet felt it was well within his moral parameters. For him, any documented or written agreement for a loan was as good or not as good as one done orally. The travails of life had indeed cost him his confidence, as the wrath of God buffeted him at all times. Such trickery was not cheating in his vocabulary. It was a mere self preserving selfishness at best and that was not a bad thing after all. He indulged in such trickery every day. Despite having some money in his pocket, he would always lament his destitution. When the money lender would call on him, he would swear he had not a *paisa* on him. Dampening the hay to increase its weight and adding some *binola* seeds to the cotton for a similar objective, was no cheating by his rules. Definitely not in this case, as here, there was a curious element of entertainment and amusement too. The density of old men is supposed to be amusing and if one filches something off them, there is no harm or ethical turpitude in it.

Bhola handed the animal's leash to Hori, "Oh come now, Hori! As soon as she mates, you can expect to deliver six seers of milk everyday. Come, let me lead her to your place for you. She is not familiar with you yet, and might create problems on the way. Now let me tell you honest to goodness, the Master was ready to pay ninety for her but there's no love lost for cows in his household. He would have passed it on to some government official or another. What do those government people have in them for cows? They just know how to suck people's blood. They would have kept her with them as long as she gave milk, and sold her off as soon as she ran dry. Who knows who would have taken her? Money is not everything brother. After all, piety and faith are more important. If she is at your place, she will live happily. It's not as if, you will let her go hungry while your family eats. You will pet her and tend to her with love. The cow will bless us. Now, how should I put it- there is hardly any fodder left in the house. All money was spent in the market. I thought I will borrow some money from the moneylender for the fodder but I still have not repaid the earlier loan. He has refused. I am worried to death what to feed the cattle. Even if I feed them a pinch daily, it adds up to quite a bit everyday. Only God can help me."

Hori's words dripped with sympathy, "Why did you not let me know earlier brother? We just sold a cartful of fodder!"

Bhola slapped his forehead, "I did not say that earlier as it's futile to tell others about your own problems. No one shares your sorrows, they only laugh at you. I am not worried about the cows that have run dry, somehow or the other, I will feed them leaves from here and there, but the milk-yielding cows can not live without a nutritious feed. If it is possible, give me 20 rupees for some fodder."

A peasant is, without doubt, rather selfish. It is not easy for him to loosen his purse strings, he is always alert while making deals, and he spends hours fawning over the moneylender to write off his debts. Unless he is convinced about it, he rarely falls for anyone's mollycoddling or smooth talk, yet his entire life remains an unswerving symbiosis with nature.

Trees bear fruits only to be eaten by others, the fields grow grains but they are consumed by the world, cows give milk but she doesn't drink it herself---that is left to others. Clouds send rain only to quench the parched earth. In such giving, there is little space for selfishness. Hori was after all just another peasant. It was not in his nature to use someone else's misfortune to his advantage.

On hearing Bhola's tale of woe, his heart underwent a complete transformation. He handed back the animal's leash to him and said, "Brother, money is something that I do not have. But I do have some fodder left which I will give you. Come and take it. I will not let you sell your cow for fodder. Won't my hands fall off my body before I do such a thing?"

There was pain in his voice as Bhola said, "Won't your bulls die of hunger? It's not as if, you have an abundance of fodder with you."

"No brother, this time round I had a good supply," said Hori.

Bhola looked perturbed. "I realise I raised this issue of fodder unnecessarily."

"Had you not told me and if I came to know about this later, it would have hurt me. It would have meant, you do not consider me as your own. If brothers don't help each other in times of need, how do you think life will ever go on?" said Hori.

Bhola handed back the leash to Hori. "Please take this cow with you."

"Not now brother, perhaps later," said Hori magnanimously.

Bhola took his hand and said, "In that case, you must adjust the cost of fodder with the milk I will supply you."

Hori spoke with genuine sorrow in his voice- "Oh come on, this is not about *anna-paisa*. If I break bread with you at your place a few times, will you ask me to pay for it?"

"But won't your bulls starve of hunger?" asked Bhola.

Hori waved his hand and said, "God will provide some solution. Monsoons are knocking at the door. I will sow cumin and get plenty of fodder."

Bhola folded his hands and said, "This cow is yours from now. The day you want, come and take it away."

"It is as much a sin to take this cow, as it is to walk away with the mortgaged bull of a brother," said Hori.

If Hori had the guile to read between the lines, he would have gladly taken the cow. He instinctively knew Bhola was not offering cash for the fodder as he had some other purpose in mind. But Hori was like the proverbial mule that stops dead in its tracks, startled by rustling of leaves, refusing to be coaxed into moving despite being whipped. An ancient sentiment of not accepting any object that has any sort of misfortune attached to it lay deeply entrenched in his subconscious mind.

Gratified, Bhola asked whether he could, in that case, send someone over to collect the fodder. Hori replied he was going to the Rai sahib and would return home in some time. He could send someone later.

Bhola's eyes moistened with tears. He said-"Hori, you have saved me today. I realise now that I am not alone in this world. There is someone who cares for me." Pausing for a moment he added, "...do not forget the other thing we talked about."

When Hori moved on, there was a spring in his step. His heart raced with a sudden newfound energy. Poor Bhola would not have to sell his cow in his hour of crisis. When he was able to secure some more fodder, he'd go and fetch the cow. He prayed that God help him find a match for Bhola .Then everything would be just fine.

Hori turned around and looked back. The cow was swishing its tail, shaking her head and ambling with a sensuous, slow gait---as a queen would stroll with her attendants. He was filled with delight when he thought of the day, when this divine cow would be tethered to his door.

❁❁❁

2

Semri and Belari are two villages of the Awadh province. Hori lived in Belari whereas Rai sahib Amarpal lived in Semri. There was a distance of five miles between the two villages. In the last civil disobedience movement, Rai sahib earned a great name for himself, when he resigned from the membership of the Council and went to jail. Since then, his reputation rose dramatically amongst the common folk of his constituency. Expectedly, the demurrages and taxes were not lessened in any way but Rai sahib managed to blame the tax collectors, and his own glory remained unsullied. After all, wasn't the poor soul also a victim of the system? The attachment of properties would continue as in the past. Thus, despite no concessions coming from the government, Rai sahib's reputation remained intact.

He would talk to the commoners, laugh with them and humour them. It is natural for the lion to roar and hunt small animals, but if he sweet talks them instead, his prey will come and knock at his door. Scouting the forest for prey becomes redundant in that case.

Rai sahib was a nationalist, yet he maintained amiable relations with the authorities. He was a lover of the arts and literature, fond of theatre; he was a good orator and an equally efficient writer and was also skilled in archery. It was a decade since he was widowed but he never remarried, spending his days simply being nice to everyone and jesting with them.

As he reached the gates, Hori saw frenzied preparations were on for the bow and arrow celebrations for the coming Dussehra festival in the month of *Jyestha*. They were setting up dais at one place, guest rooms at another and makeshift shops at yet another. The weather was getting very warm, almost hot, yet Rai sahib was on the job in person.

Along with his estate, Rai sahib had inherited a spiritual devotion to Ram from his father and had transformed the bow and arrow sacrificial ceremony into a dignified theatrical performance. On this occasion; his friends, employees, local officials and other notables were all invited. For a couple of days, the area around his residence was the centre of intense activity.

Rai sahib's extended family was so large, that about a hundred and fifty members would dine at the same time. There were dozens of uncles, a few score cousins, many brothers and a large number of close filial acquaintances. One uncle was a devotee of Radha and lived in the holy town of Vrindavan. He would regularly compose verses in devotion to the goddess, publish them off and on and distribute them to friends and relatives. Another uncle was a devotee of Ram and was translating the Ramayana in Persian. All had some endowment from the property coming to them every month. None of them had any real need to work for a living.

Hori stood at the gate, wondering how he should announce his presence when Rai sahib himself walked right up there and exclaimed, "Hori! Good you came. I was about to send you an invite. Now listen, you have to play the part of King Janak's gardener this time. As soon as Janaki enters the temple to pray, you should be standing close enough and hand over a bouquet of flowers to her. Don't fumble on this one now.... And yes, call on all the people and let them know that they must come to make an auspicious donation." Rai sahib looked at Hori and said "Just come inside with me- I want to talk to you about something."

He moved towards the mansion with Hori at his heels. He sank into a chair under the dense foliage of a tree and motioning Hori to squat on the ground said, "The tax collector is coming within the next six or seven days and I have to arrange about 20,000 rupees. How will I ever do that? You might wonder, why I am lamenting about all this to a miserable chap like you. But then, I do not know who else will listen to my heart's woes. I don't know why, but I seem to trust you. I have a feeling you will not laugh at me and if you do, at least I can handle it. I cannot tolerate the jibes of those who are my equals in status; since their scorn is laced with jealousy, sarcasm and envy. And why shouldn't they laugh? Do I not do the same---relish at their misfortune, wholeheartedly? Wealth and compassion are opposites.

"You know why we give alms and do charities? It is merely to show others in a poor light. It is a sheer ego trip. If any of us has his property attached, mortgaged or is issued summons, is put in jail for reneging on loans, if anyone's young son dies, his widowed wife runs off with another, if someone's house goes up in smoke in an accident, if a harlot cheats any of us or if subjects beat up their masters, it pleases us to no end. We joke about it, celebrate it, yet when we meet up, we act as if we are ready to shed our blood for the other. What's more; my cousins, uncles and other distant relatives from both sides of the family, who enjoy the fruits of this inheritance, who mouth poetry, gamble, drink and revel in indulgence, are all jealous of me. They will light lamps in celebration if I were to die today. There is no one who will empathise with me in my sorrow. According to them, I have no reason or right to be sad. If I cry or am unwell, they say I am trying to gain sympathy. If I did not marry and save myself from unnecessary strife of family life, I am a selfish soul; if I do it, I am blinded by lust. If I am a teetotaler I am miserly. If I drink, it is akin to drinking their blood. If I do not indulge in life's base pleasures, they will call me a moron and if I do, I will be termed- a dirty old man. These people have tried their best to lure me into extravagant indulgences. They are still working on it. Their only desire is that I turn blind, so they rob me of everything. They assume it is my bounden duty to be oblivious of all that happens. That I see everything and remain an ass forever."

Rai sahib reached out for betel leaves, taking a momentary break before he resumed his tirade, pausing to stare at Hori's face, seemingly searching his expressions.

Hori gathered courage before he spoke- "I thought such things happen only amongst my kind, but it appears sophisticates also have such people amongst them."

Rai sahib stuffed his mouth with *paan* as he spoke, "You think we are sophisticates? We are just puffed up empty balloons. If poor people are envious or inimical to each other, it is because they have issues of hunger or self preservation. Their jealousy and ill feelings can be forgiven. If their daily bread is snatched, they take it as their right to scrape it off the offender's palm or reach into the snatcher's gullet and pull it out. But the rich man's envy and enmity is for pleasure and entertainment. We have become so exalted that for us, pettiness and stealth are the source of selfless and ethereal bliss. We have reached that stage of divine greatness, where we revel in the sorrows of others. Now don't you ever consider this any mean accomplishment! We have fewer ailments. What worth is a rich man, if he suffers a common illness for a prolonged period? He must be instantly administered medicine if he has fever. A pimple for him is always a blemish. All varieties of surgeons are summoned by wires and telegrams. A man is dispatched to Delhi to fetch a faith healer, another is sent to Calcutta to get the *Ayurved*. Durga incantations are chanted even as astrologers ponder over his charts, the *tantrics* get on with their ceremonies. Ah! There's a race to save his lordship from the jaws of death. Doctors and *vaids,* expectantly look for signs of a headache as it means a shower of gold for them. And that money is extracted from the likes of you, with a dagger on your neck.

"I am surprised why the fire of your agony does not reduce us to ashes. You people are slowly but surely burning us in installments, tortuously, one little finger after another. And to save ourselves from that prolonged suffering, we seek refuge in the police, the officials, courts and lawyers. The world assumes that we are very happy with high mansions, fine carriages, servants and attendants, huge investments, and concubines. But he, who is without the honour and strength of the soul, can be anything but happy. I will not call that person happy, who knows no rest because of his enemies, who is the butt of fun by all and for whom no one has any empathy, who is as if held on a leash by others, who has lost himself in hedonistic pursuits, who preys on those weaker to him and wags his tail for his superiors. For me, that man is the most unfortunate in the world.

"When superiors come; either on an official tour or hunting for game, my calling is merely to tag along like a tail. If they as much as frown, people like us begin to whimper. We go to any extent to please them. Gift hampers and sundry bribe is probably understandable, but many of us are ready to prostrate ourselves before them. Freeloading has crippled us; we do not trust our capacity for work. We somehow perfect the art of wagging our tails to ensure remaining in their good books, so that we are left at will to exercise our tyranny over the masses. Kowtowing to these sycophants has turned us so haughty and short tempered, that we have lost all humility and sense of service. I often feel if the government usurps all our land, forcing us to work for a living, it might actually do us a favour. However, it's evident that the government is not going to bother about us. It does not require us any more. The symptoms of our extinction are on the wall. I am ready to welcome that day when it finally happens. May the Lord hasten that day, for it will be the day of our redemption. We are victims of our circumstances and these circumstances are the fettering on our feet. It is destroying us. As long as the shackles of wealth and property bind us, we will remain accursed forever and never attain the altar of humanity which is life's ultimate goal."

Rai sahib reached out for the box and stuffed a few more betel leaves in his mouth. Before he could speak further, a servant came up to him, "Sir, the labourers have struck work. They say they will not work unless they are given something to eat. When I got mad at them, they dropped everything and moved away."

Lines of worry formed on Rai sahib's forehead. With fire in his eyes he snapped, "Let me set these no-gooders right. We have never given them food earlier, why should they raise this issue now? They will get their wages of an *anna* a day as always, and this is how they will have to work, whether they like it or not."

Turning to Hori he said, "Now you go and get started on what you have to do. Remember what I told you. I expect at least 500 rupees from your village."

Grimacing, he walked away. Hori wondered how after mouthing all those lofty ideals of ethics and morality, he had suddenly lost his cool.

The sun was up in the fullness of the day. Overpowered by its brilliance and heat, the trees gathered their shadows around them. The sky was covered in a muddy haze as the earth seemed to tremble before it.

Hori picked up his *lathi* and started trudging home. The worry of arranging the money for the auspicious donations, weighing heavy on his mind.

❁❁❁

3

As Hori reached his village, he saw Gobar-still in the sugarcane field along with his two sisters. A small windstorm rose from the earth, already smouldering with heat. It seemed as if nature had poured a ladle of fire in the air. Why were they still in the field? Did they want to die working in this manner? He walked into the field and shouted at them from a distance; "Gobar, why have you not gone back yet? Will you keep working forever? It's late afternoon, don't you realise that?"

As soon as they saw him, the trio picked up their sickles and started after him. Gobar was a dark, tall and thin-framed young lad who appeared barely interested in anything around him. Instead of joy, his face bore an expression of discontent and rebellion. The elder girl Sona was a bashful gentle maiden--supple, dusky, pleasant and full of vivacious energy. Her red *saree* of coarse cloth which she wore folded at her knees, seemed large for her slight frame, lending her a graceful maturity. The younger one, Rupa, was a kid of five or six years--muddied, with hair like a ruffled nest, wearing a loin cloth tied like a diaper, very obstinate and quick to tears.

Wrapping her slight body around his legs, she said- *"Kaka,* see, I broke every clump of mud despite Sona telling me to go sit under the tree. *Kaka,* if the clumps are not broken, how will the earth ever be levelled?" Hori swept her up in his arms and spoke to her lovingly, "You did well, my little baby. Let's go home now."

Suppressing his rebellious streak, Gobar finally spoke up-"Why do you go to the Rai sahib every day and suck up to him? If we default on payment, his henchmen turn up to swear at us, we have to work without wages for that, the money he pays as bribes to grease his way through, is also extracted from us eventually. Why do we have to salute anyone?"

At this moment, Hori's mind was swirling with similar emotions but it was necessary to suppress his son's radical thinking. He said, "If we do not go to offer salutations where do you think we should go? When God has made us slaves; is it in our power to do things different? It is all due to these salutations that we managed to build a fence at our doorstep and no one raised as much as a squeak. Ghura had fixed a peg for his cows outside his door and the Rai sahib's men made him pay a fine of two rupees. You remember how much sand we dug up from the river bank? No one raised an objection. Anyone else would have had to pay up for that transgression. I walk all the way to salute him because it is good for us. My feet are not possessed nor am I very pleased doing it. I have to keep waiting for hours, before the Rai sahib gets to know that I have come. Sometimes he comes out and at other times, he sends word he is busy."

Gobar's reply was laced in sarcasm, "There must definitely be some pleasure in sycophancy, otherwise, why will people ever indulge in it?"

"When you face it son, only then you'll realise. Now you can say whatever you want. I also harboured such thoughts when I was young but now they have me by the collar-- haughtiness serves no purpose."

Having transferred his frustration onto his father, Gobar felt slightly relieved and walked on quietly. Sona noticed that Rupa was still in her father's lap and was envious. Snapping at her she said, "Why don't you step down from his arms and use your feet? Your legs are not broken."

Rupa put her arms around Hori's neck firmly and replied with pronounced obstinacy, "I won't! You buzz off! *Kaka,* she teases me everyday saying she is like gold because she is Sona and I am not as precious as I am Rupa which means silver. Give me another name."

Hori turned to Sona in mock anger. "Why do you tease her so, Sona? Gold is just for admiring from afar, it is silver that is actually used. If it weren't for Rupa, how would money be minted?'

Sona sprang to defend herself, "If it were not for Sona, where would gold coins come from? Or nose rings? Or necklaces?"

Gobar joined this lighthearted banter and prompted Rupa, "You tell her that Sona is yellow like a dried up leaf. Rupa is bright like the white sun."

Sona retorted, "In weddings, they wear yellow sarees. Nobody likes a pale silver *sarees*."

Rupa was hurt by this. It weighed down the arguments of Hori and Gobar. She looked at Hori with sad and frustrated eyes. Hori quickly offered another explanation. "Sona is for rich people. It's Rupa for us poor folks. Just as barley is known as 'king' and is like Sona for the rich, and wheat- the low caste *'chamar'* is like Rupa for poor people like us."

Sona was outwitted by this statement. Miffed, she said, "Both of you sided with Rupa or else I would have taught her a lesson till she cried."

Rupa cocked her thumb at Sona teasingly, "Yeechh! Sona - low caste, Sona-low caste!"

She could not contain her sense of victory and leapt out of her father's arms and pranced around with the same refrain..." Rupa--king, Sona--low caste! Rupa-king, Sona-low caste!"

When they reached home Dhania was standing at the door, waiting. Peeved, she said, "Why so late today, Gobar? No one gives up his life for a job."

Angrily she addressed her husband, "And when you return with some earnings you march straight to the fields as though the fields will disappear the next morning."

There was a well near the entrance. Hori and Gobar poured water over their heads, bathed Rupa and sat down to have their meal. The *rotis* were of barley, but white and smooth like those of wheat. The lentil was cooked with freshly cut green baby mangoes. Rupa sat down to eat from her father's plate. Sona glanced at her with envious eyes that seemed to ridicule this loving exchange of filial attachment.

"So what did you discuss with the Rai Sahib?" asked Dhania.

Hori downed a glass full of water and said, "We just discussed tax collections, what else? We think these big people are very happy, but the truth is they are worse than us. We are just worried about one thing--hunger, they have a thousand worries."

Hori did not remember the other things Rai sahib had talked about. All those revelations were embedded loosely in his memories.

Gobar threw a jibe, "Then why doesn't he hand over his estate to us? We are willing to give him our fields, bulls, spades, sickles--everything. Will he do a barter with us? This is sheer hypocrisy. A man who owns a dozen cars, lives in a palace, gorges on *halwa puri,* remains absorbed in frivolous entertainment, can never be unhappy. Rai sahib enjoys the pleasures of royalty and yet calls himself miserable!"

Hori was irritated-"Now who can argue with you? Is it easy for anyone to go ahead and relinquish his property? Why should you expect him to do the same? What do we get out of our fields? Not even wages that are worth an *anna*. The servant, who earns a mere ten rupees is better dressed and fed than us. But does that mean we will let go of our fields? If we give up our fields what else can we do? Are jobs available for the asking? And of course, there is the issue of one's honour and prestige. The respect that comes with working in the fields is not there in a job or in service. The *zamindaars* are in a similar predicament, they have a hundred problems to contend with. Transport the produce to the authorities, bribe people in power, and keep their workers happy. If the duty is not paid in time; there is jail, their property can be confiscated. Nobody ever takes us to jail. The maximum we have to confront is a few expletives and some threats."

Gobar tried to counter this, "All this is mere talk. We hanker for every grain of food, not a single cloth on our body is in one piece, we sweat our guts out yet are not able to make both ends meet. What do they know? They are content resting their behinds on comfortable cushions; they have a hundred servants to look after them, thousands of people over whom they exercise their authority. They enjoy all sorts of pleasures. What else will anyone do with money?"

"Does your intelligence say we are equal to them?"

"God has made everyone equal," said Gobar in his youthful defiance.

"That is not correct my son. Differences between people are providential. It takes a lot of austerity and sacrifice to earn a good fortune. They are reaping the benefits of their karma in a previous life. We have not earned any good karma in our past, so how can we enjoy its benefits?"

"All this is said only to fool people like us. God makes everyone equal. Here, whoever is powerful goes ahead and tramples the poor to become richer," said Gobar getting angry.

"That is your illusion. Even today Rai sahib prays for four hours daily," defended Hori.

Gobar snapped back, "He does all this prayer and devotional stuff at the cost of the farmers and the workers like us. He conducts all this charity and austerity so that he can digest his ill gotten wealth. That is why he is singing these *bhajans*. We would love to see him carry on with his spiritual songs, if he were a starving destitute. If someone ensures us two square meals a day, we will sing and pray all our waking hours. If one has to hoe sugarcane all day, devotion to God vanishes like smoke."

Exasperated, Hori said, "There is no use arguing with you. You question even the ways of God."

In the evening when Gobar picked up the sickle and was leaving for the fields, Hori called out to him. "Wait, my son, I am also coming. Just take some fodder and put it aside. Bhola will come and take it. The poor man is in deep trouble these days."

Gobar looked at him with a surprised expression. "We do not have that much fodder that we should start selling it."

"I am not selling it, simply giving it to him. He is in a crisis. We have to help him."

Gobar's eyes flashed with anger. "Well, he has never given us a cow, has he?"

"Actually he was giving me one but I didn't take it."

Dhania made a face as she piped in. "Oh really? He says he was giving him a cow. The man, who has never sent us a spoonful of milk, will give us a cow!"

Hori protested, "No, no I swear on my word. He was giving me his western cow. He is in a tight position, doesn't have enough hay or fodder. Now he wants to sell a cow for fodder. I thought how can I take away the cow from a man who is in trouble? I will give him some fodder and when I come into some money I will take his cow and pay for it in small installments. She is for eighty rupees but is worth much more."

Gobar was getting angrier. "Your saintliness is the reason for our misery. The deal is very simple--his cow is for eighty rupees, he takes fodder worth twenty rupees from us and hands us the cow. We'll pay the remaining sixty rupees gradually over time."

Hori smiled mysteriously. "I have a plan by which this cow will come to us for free. I will find a woman whom Bhola can marry. Then I'll get the cow free. The little fodder I am giving is merely to impress him."

Gobar began getting hot under his collar. "So now you are going around fixing people's marriages as well."

Hori tried to explain, "If by a little effort from my side, someone is able to get a good life and home, what is wrong with that?"

Gobar picked up his *chillum* and went to light it up. He was completely furious with the idea of his father finding a bride for Bhola. His mother Dhania shook her head, "Whoever helps him set up home will not be content with just a cow; he should get some money as well."

Hori tried to appease her. "I know this but why don't you see how gentlemanly he is? Whenever he meets me he starts singing your glories, 'she is such a Goddess, she is so dignified'..."

Though Dhania's face lit up with pride, she rose to express her disinterest, "I am not hungry for his praise. He can keep it with him."

An affectionate smile played on Hori's lips. "I told him that you don't let a fly come within swatting distance and when you are angry you can shower the choicest expletives, but he kept saying 'she isn't a woman, she is a Goddess'. He says, whenever he sees your face in the morning, he earns some good money that day. I told him that he was lucky. I see your face everyday but never get to see a single *paisa*."

"If your luck is bad what can I do about it," said Dhania undecided whether to feel happy or angry.

Hori continued, "Bhola's wife was very sharp-tongued. The poor man ran scared of her all his life. That's why even after her death, he keeps bad mouthing her. He complains she never gave alms to any beggar, used to chase them out with her broom, she was so miserly that she would even borrow salt from her neighbours."

"One should not criticise the dead but the fact is she was always jealous of me," said Dhania with a smile playing on her lips.

"Bhola is very patient and only he could manage to live with her. Any other man would have committed suicide. Bhola is really decent. Though he must be ten years elder to me but he greets me with a *Ram-Ram* even before I do."

Vanity was now creeping into Dhania. "So what was it he said about me when he sees my face in the morning? What happens?"

"That day God gives him something good."

"His daughters-in-law are such greedy women. That day they ate melons worth two rupees on credit. Once they get anything on loan, they forget that they have to re-pay it someday," said Dhania.

At that moment Gobar walked in and announced, "Bhola is at the door. Go give him one or two mounds of fodder and then proceed to hunt for a bride for him."

Dhania didn't like Gobar's tone. "There's a man at the door. Instead of asking him to come in and sit, you have started grumbling. At least learn some basic manners, take the water jug so he can wash his hands and feet, give him something to drink. Only in extreme distress will a man come asking for a little fodder."

Hori said that it was not necessary to pamper Bhola. After all he had not come as a guest.

Dhania didn't agree. "He doesn't come to your doorstep everyday. He's come to our house in such terrible weather, surely he must be thirsty. Hey, Rupiya, go see if there is any tobacco in the box. With Gobar around, I doubt if there is any left. Run to the Sahuain and buy some for a *paisa*."

The welcome and hospitality extended to Bhola this day was the first of its kind. Gobar threw down a cot for him, Sona brought the *sherbet*, Rupa came in with the tobacco pack. Dhania stood behind the door with rising eagerness to hear her glories with her own ears.

Bhola took the *chillum* in his hands and said, "When a good wife comes to your home, you can assume that the Gods have been kind to you. Dhania knows how to welcome a guest, regardless of how big or small he is."

In her heart, Dhania felt a subtle delight. Her soul-burdened by worry, despair and scarcity was relishing the tender touch of those words.

When Hori picked up Bhola's bag to fill it up with fodder, Dhania followed him. He muttered, "Don't know from where he got such a large bag. Must have taken it from the wholesale granary. It will need at least a mound to fill it up. If he takes two bags it means two mounds of fodder gone."

Dhania, meanwhile, was floating on air. Staring at her husband with accusing eyes she said, "When you invite someone for dinner then it is your duty to give him enough to eat. He hasn't come to collect flowers from your garden that he should have brought a small basket. He has come to take fodder and for that he requires a big bag. Give him at least three bagsful. Poor man, how will he carry it home? Why didn't he bring some boys with him?"

Hori couldn't comprehend why Dhania was in such a generous mood. "I will certainly not give him three bags full of fodder."

"I forbid you to send him off with just one bag. Tell Gobar to get his bag too and go with him."

"Gobar is going to hoe the sugarcane."

"Sugarcane will not shrivel up if not attended for a day," said Dhania in anger.

"Is it not his responsibility to organise to take the stuff with him? God has blessed him with two sons. He could very well have brought them," said Hori puzzled at his wife's support for Bhola.

"They might not be home. They could be in the market, peddling milk."

Hori did not like his wife's insistence. "You mean I should not only give the fodder for free but also deliver it to his doorstep like a postman!"

But Dhania would not give up. "OK, enough. No one needs to go. I will deliver it myself. There is no shame in doing some service for those elder to us."

"And if I give him three bagfuls, what will be left for my bulls to eat?"

"You should have considered this before extending your generosity."

"Generosity has its limits. It does not imply you gift away your dwelling."

"If the *zamindaar's* man were to knock, you will gladly load the hay on your head and carry it there. And while at it, you would have also cut a few mounds of firewood for him."

"The *zamindaar* is a different issue."

"Yes, because he gets things done forcefully with his clout."

"We till fields that belong to him. Don't we?"

"If we till his fields, we pay him the rent for it."

"Ok, don't irritate me further. Both of us will go. You are impossible. It's so difficult to stop you once you get going."

As he saw the three bags being filled with fodder, Gobar scowled and was livid with his father. He was convinced that his father was a loser and was frittering away whatever little they had. Dhania was happy. As for Hori, he was bobbing up and down in a flow of both righteousness and anger at having to give Bhola three bags.

Hori and Gobar dragged out one of the bags. Bhola rolled his *angocha* into a headrest, putting it on his head, he said, "I'll take it and come back fast for the second one."

Hori said, "Not one, there are two more bags. You do not have to come again. Gobar and I are coming with you along with the bags."

Bhola was stunned. He had not expected so much kindness from Hori whom he now started considering as his very own brother, probably much more intimate and closer.

The trio left with the fodder bags and struck a conversation on the way. Bhola said, "Dussehra festival is fast approaching, I bet there's a lot of activity at the Rai sahib's house."

"Yes, the tents and stage are already set up. This year Rai sahib wants me to enact the role of a gardener of King Janak."

"The Rai sahib is mighty pleased with you."

"He's merciful."

After a momentary pause Bhola enquired, "Have you arranged the amount for the auspicious donation? Just playing the role of a gardener will not suffice, you know."

Hori wiped the sweat off his face with his *angocha*. "I am worried to death about it, brother. The grains were disposed of in the granary itself. The *Zamindaar* took his share and the money lender took his. I was left with just five seers. I had removed and hidden the hay for this fodder on the sly at night, otherwise not a straw would have been left. There is one *Zamindaar* but there are three moneylenders, is Sahuain, Mangru and Datadin Pandit. Even the interest on their loan could not be met fully. Half of *Zamindaar's* amount still remains to be paid. I borrowed some more from Sahuain and that helped a bit. I have tried saving whatever I can but things don't seem to be working. We are accursed by birth to toil and fill the coffers of big people. I have paid twice the amount of the principal as interest but it still remains unchanged. People advise us that we should spend wisely but no one comes forward to explain how. Rai sahib squandered 20,000 rupees on his son's wedding. No one questioned him. Mangru blew up 5,000 rupees on his father's funeral. No one questioned him. But if we spend a meagre amount on our daily needs, people question us as if we have no prestige or honour."

Bhola's voice cracked with sympathy- "How can you compare yourself with these big people?"

"We are also 'people', remember."

Bhola looked at him in sympathy and said, "Who says we are human beings? Where is our human-ness? Only those who have money, education, pelf and power are human. We are born to be tied as beasts of burden. To top it all, we do not have any unity amongst us. We are constantly trying to pull each other down. Love and affection are dead in the world."

For the old and wizened there is no topic more entertaining than joys, that are past and future that is uncertain. Both friends narrated their miseries to each other. Bhola complained about the doings of his sons, Hori carped about his brothers as they set their load next to a well and sat to quench their thirst. Gobar went across to a grocer to request for a vessel to draw water and started pulling on the rope promptly.

Bhola asked with concern, "When the division took place, you must have been heartbroken? You brought up your brothers, Sobha and Heera like your sons."

In a pained tone Hori said, "Don't remind me of that, friend. I wanted to drown myself. I wish I had not lived to see it happen. Those for whom I laid down the years of my youth, stood before me as my accusers. And what was the cause of the disagreement? That my wife does not go to work in the market. Somebody should ask them; do we not need someone to look after the home? Managing the house, taking care of it, is a full time job. So, who will do it? Was she sitting at home doing nothing? Sweeping, mopping, cooking, washing dishes, cleaning the kitchen, looking after the children...Isn't that enough work? Could Sobha's wife manage the house or did Heera's wife have the efficiency for it? Since we've had the division, they cook food once a day in their homes. Before the separation, everyone was eating four times a day. My wife's health was ruined because of the responsibilities around the house. She wore the hand-me-downs of her sisters-in-law, used to sleep empty stomach but would always provide refreshments and snacks for them. She did not have a single thread that could pass off as adornment on her body while she bought not one but a couple of jewellery items for each of them. Okay, they were not of gold, but at least they were made of silver. They were jealous only because she was the one who ran the household as the mistress of the house. Good, they moved away. It was a great burden off my back."

Bhola took a sip of water and said, "It's the same story everywhere brother. In my case, it's not an issue among brothers, but the problem is with my sons who do not see eye to eye with me as I stop them from straying from the straight and narrow path. They want to gamble, smoke marijuana, and drink liquor. But where will all the money come from? If they want to spend on vices, why don't they go and earn the money themselves? When the elder one, Kamta, goes to get provisions for the house, he never returns the money that is left over. Ask him where it vanished and he has no answers.

"The younger son Jangi has befriended some singing minstrels and keeps playing on drums and cymbals the whole day. I don't say that singing minstrels are bad company. Devotional singing isn't bad but it should be done in your spare time. But he is into music all the time and does nothing for the household. I have to do everything—prepare the feed for the cows, milk them and then take the milk to the market. As a householder, you have a golden hook stuck in your throat—you can neither spit it out nor swallow it. My daughter Jhuniya, is extremely unlucky. You came for her wedding, didn't you? The family was so good and well to do. Her husband had a small business of vending milk in Bombay. But during the Hindu Muslim riots, someone stabbed and killed him. That ruined everything. She could not survive in that house anymore, I went and brought her back thinking I will get her married again but she does not agree. Both her sisters-in-law trouble her day in day out. There's constant bickering in the house. Poor girl, she came here to live in peace but misery has followed her here as well."

Sharing their sob stories, they reached their destination. Bhola's neighbourhood was small but pretty alive and vibrant. It was predominantly inhabited by *Ahirs*. Compared to other farmers, their condition was not all that bad. Bhola was the village headman.

There was a courtyard at the gate and a dozen or so cows stood there chewing their feed off it. A musical drum hung from one nail in the wall and a pair of cymbals from another. On a niche, wrapped inside a bag, lay a book-possibly the holy Ramayana. The sons' wives sat in the courtyard, making cow dung fuel cakes as Jhuniya stood in the doorway. Her eyes were bloodshot and the tip of her nose had a pink flush to it. It appeared as if she had just woken up from a slumber. Her body was well formed and her blooming health pulsated with a budding youthfulness. Her face was large with full lips and small deep set eyes. Her forehead was small but the fullness of her breasts and cheeks had a magnetic appeal. A pink *saree* completed the picture of her all-encompassing attractiveness.

As soon as she saw Bhola, she reached out and leaned to relieve him of the load on his head. Bhola took off the bags from Gobar and Hori's head and told Jhuniya to organise a *chillum* and get *sherbet* for the visitors. "If you do not have fresh water, get me the vessel, I will pull some from the well. You recognise Hori, don't you?"

Turning to Hori resignedly he said, "No life without a wife. There's an old saying that goes 'Shorties in the field, daughters-in-law at home.' It means that dwarf bulls cannot plough the field and daughters-in-law cannot manage your household. Ever since Jhuniya's mother passed away, there is no charm left in this house. My daughters-in-law cannot run the house, they can only run havoc with their tongue. Their husbands are wasting away their lives. Work shirkers, lazy louts! As long as I am alive, I'll try to do something for them. When I am dead, they will realise too late and lament. My grand-daughter also starts grumbling, even if she has to do minor odd jobs around the house. I tolerate it, but will her husband do the same?

Jhuniya arrived briskly with a *chillum* in one hand and a pitcher of *sherbet* in the other. Picking up a rope and vessel, she made a move towards the well. Gobar crept up to her bashfully, “Give that to me. I will draw the water.”

Jhuniya didn't oblige. Smilingly, she went up to the well and said, “You are our guest. You will complain we did not offer a glass of water to you.”

“What guest? I am a neighbour.”

“The neighbour who is seen barely once a year, is as good as a guest.”

“But dropping by every other day is not dignified.”

Glancing sideways, Jhuniya laughed, “Come once a month, I will offer a glass of water. Come every fortnight, you will be served a *chillum*. Come weekly and I will give you a special chair to sit.”

“Not even a glimpse?”

“A glimpse comes with propitiation.”

As she spoke her face fell, as if she was reminded of the fact that she was a widow. At one time, her husband stood as the protector of her womanhood and that gave her confidence. Now she felt unprotected and hence cut herself from outside contact. Sick of her loneliness, sometimes she would casually saunter to the doorway but immediately bolt the door if she heard or saw anyone approaching.

Bhola told Gobar to come and take the cow the next day, as she was feeding at that moment. Gobar's eyes were transfixed. He had no idea the cow was so beautiful and supple.

Hori suppressed his mounting excitement and said, “What's the hurry? We will send for her soon enough.”

“You might not be in a hurry but I am. When you see her tied to your door, she will be a constant reminder to you of our friendship. So send Gobar tomorrow.”

Both father and son adjusted the bags on their heads and moved on. They were as happy as if they were returning from their weddings. Hori was delighted, expecting the fulfillment of a long felt desire of his heart and that too without spending a *paisa*. Gobar, however, had discovered something more precious. A yearning had awoken in his mind.

He took a chance and looked back. Jhuniya was still standing at the door---frisky and restless, like an inebriated hope.

❁❁❁

4

Hori was not able to sleep that night. Lying on his cot under the *neem* tree, he kept gazing at the stars. There was so much to do. He had to hammer a tether for the cow. For sometime she could remain outside, but not for long. Soon another place would have to be found to shield her from the evil eyes of jealous people; whose spells could sometimes make the cow's milk run dry. Moreover, the *Zamindaar's* men would surely create a fuss and demand bribes.

Hori plunged deep into his thoughts. "I'll tie her inside. It's a small courtyard but I'll build a fence. Surely she will deliver more than five seers of milk. Gobar needs a seer just for himself. Little Rupa must also drink milk. I think, off and on I will gift one or two seers to the higher-ups too. Mollycoddling always pays dividends. Besides, I must repay some part of the money to Bhola and should not delude him just with promises of getting him re-married. It is petty of me to try and hoodwink a man who is so trusting. He handed me his cow worth eighty rupees, simply because he had faith in me. Otherwise, no one parts even with a single *paisa*. If I am able to return him even twenty-five rupees of the total sum, Bhola will feel relieved. I should not have told Dhania about the cow beforehand. I should have surprised her. That would have been so much fun. But I can't keep a secret. I can't hide even the extra money, I earn at times. Though in a way, that is a good habit.

"It's a pity Gobar is so lazy. I wish he had been more responsible. But then, he's just a young boy and a bit carefree. Even I fooled around when my father was alive. Poor man, he'd start chopping the hay before dawn, sweeping the floor and spreading manure in the fields. I slept through it all. If I was woken up, I would throw a tantrum and threaten to run away from home. If boys do not enjoy a life of fun when their parents are around, they can never do it when they have to face responsibilities. Did I not take over responsibilities as soon as my father died? Everyone in the village would say Hori will ruin the house. But I turned a new leaf and everyone was surprised into silence. My brothers Sobha and Heera have separated but if they had not, our home would have been exemplary. What was Dhania's fault? Poor women, ever since she has come to this house, she hasn't had a moment of rest. Even as a new bride, she was burdened with responsibilities of the household. First she slogged for my brothers' families, now she labours for her children. If she were not so patient and free of malice, Sobha and Heera, who strut around twirling their moustaches in pride, would be starving and begging on the streets. People are so selfish. Those you help are the ones who turn against you."

Hori looked towards the east once again. Dawn was about to break. He wondered if Gobar would wake up early as he had promised to. "I can go and nail the tether on the ground but on second thoughts, I think I should let the cow arrive first. If Bhola reneges on his promise or is not able to part with the cow for any reason, the whole village would make fun of us. They'd say that I was in such a hurry, that I nailed the tether before the cow arrived! Though Bhola is the head of his household and can do what he wants to, but he has grown up sons, who can tell him not to give away the cow.

Gobar woke up with a start. Rubbing his eyes he exclaimed, "Oh! It's already dawn. *Dada,* did you nail the tether?"

Hori looked at the toned body of his son with pride and thought, what a fine man he would turn out if he were to get a regular supply of the cow's milk. "No, not yet. If we do not get the cow, we will become a laughing stock needlessly."

Gobar raised his eyebrows angrily. "Why will we not get it?"

"Suppose Bhola has a rethink?"

"Rethink or not- the cow is coming to us now,"

Without a word Gobar got up, propped his *lathi* on his shoulders and set off. Hori saw him leave with a quiet pride in his heart. It was time the boy was married. He was already seventeen. But where was the money? Since the partition in the household, the family's name had been sullied and most people from the community did not want any matrimonial connections with them. Those who agreed, wanted money as collateral as also the wedding expenses. Where would the money come from? There was barely enough to eat. Marriage was unthinkable. Sona was also reaching a marriageable age. She would have to be married first and everything else would come later.

Chaudhry Damri Bentsar greeted Hori with *Ram Ram* and said, "Do you have any bamboo growing in your house, Hori?" Chaudhry was short, fat, very dark, with large eyes and a huge moustache, a scythe for cutting bamboo dangling by his waist. He came by once or twice a year, and cut bamboo from which he made chairs, stools and baskets.

Hori was glad to see him. Hopeful of making a quick buck, he took Chaudhry around and after negotiating a bit, struck a deal for rupees twenty. Hori offered him a puff from his *Chillum* and said in a conspiratorial tone. "My bamboos do not go for less than thirty but you are like family, there is no need to haggle with you. But half the money has to go to my brothers. So tell them the deal is for fifteen rupees. By the way, your son who was engaged, is he back yet?"

Chaudhry took a deep puff from the *Chillum* and coughed. "Hori, I have died a thousand deaths for that lout. Leaving his young wife at home, he went away to some distant land to fool around with other women. My daughter-in-law eloped with someone else. I tell you, such good for nothing women are faithful to none. I tried my best to tell her that she could eat, dress and live in my house whichever way she wanted to and not bring disrepute to the family, but would she listen? God should give everything but beauty to women. They just can't handle it." Then he turned to Hori and enquired, "So what about you? Was your house divided in three parts when both your brothers separated?"

Hori looked up at the sky and seemed to float in its vastness, "Everything was divided. These boys, whom I brought up as my sons, are now equal claimants."

Chaudhry started hacking at the bamboos. But as ill luck would have it, Heera's wife Punia came out of the house with a lunch box that she was taking for her husband. When she saw Chaudhry cutting the bamboo, she called out from behind her veil, "Why are you cutting our bamboo?"

Chaudhry paused for a moment-"They are not for free. I have bought them from Hori for fifteen rupees." Heera's wife was an aggressive woman. It was because of her, there was division amongst the brothers. Sometimes Heera would thrash her. But despite that, in normal circumstances, he danced to her tunes much like the horse, who kicks its owner occasionally but remains under his yoke.

Settling the lunch on the ground, she said "Our bamboos will not be sold so cheaply." It was against Chaudhry's policy to get into a discussion with any woman. He said, "Go send your man. If there is anything to be said, let him say it."

Punia reached up to Chaudhry and trying to hold him by the hand, she snorted "Why should I send my man? If you have to say anything, then talk to me. Haven't I made it clear that bamboos shall not be cut?"

Chaudhry wrested his hand away from her grip but she pounced upon him again. This scuffle continued till Chaudhry shoved her back in self-defence. Thrown off balance, she fell on the ground but gathered herself quickly and taking the slipper off her feet attacked Chaudhry, slapping him on his face, head, arms, wherever she could. A mere bamboo seller and he dare push her? She kept on hitting and screaming loudly. Chaudhry had pushed her – used force on a woman. He was already contrite. He had no option but to stand helplessly and get beaten up.

Hearing Punia's loud wails, Hori came running out. Seeing him, Punia's wails grew shriller. Hori thought Chaudhry had hit Punia. He was furious. Jumping over the fence, he ran towards Chaudhry and began kicking him saying, "Just get out of here if you value your life. Who do you think you are? How dare you raise a hand against my daughter-in-law?"

Chaudhry swore repeatedly to plead his innocence. Chastened by the hurt of the incessant rain of slippers, his conscience was numbed into meekness. He was kicked for no fault of his and his swollen cheeks were wet with tears. He had not laid a finger on her. He was not such a moron that he would raise his hand against a woman of Hori's family.

Hori glared at him unbelievingly "Don't try and fool me. If you haven't done anything, why is she crying? I will set you right. I and my brothers may be separated but we have the same blood running in our veins. Anyone who dares cast an evil eye will have his eyes gouged out."

Punia was the incarnation of an infuriated Goddess. She hollered at the top of her voice. "Swear by your son that you didn't throw me to the ground?" The news of a fight between Punia and Chaudhry travelled fast. Heera heard that Chaudhry had pushed Punia and she had beaten him with slippers. He dumped everything and made a beeline to his house.

Heera was known for his fiery temper. He had a short muscular body. His eyes bulged out like cowries and the veins on his neck stood out. However, his ire today was directed not at Chaudhry but Punia. Why did she pick up a fight with a man? She should have come and told him about it and he would have handled the situation. If brother Hori had settled the bamboo deal, who was she to jump in and raise an issue?

He caught her by the hand and dragging her aside, started raining blows on her. Ill begotten wretch! You are intent on shaming me. You go around trifling with low class men. Here, I am waiting for my lunch and there you pick up a fight. Such utter shamelessness, you have no dignity at all."

Despite the thrashing and her stream of tears, Punia's curses came out like a torrent "May you be devoured by wild ants! May you be struck with influenza! May God curse you with leprosy and your hands and feet wither and drop away!"

Heera heard every abuse hurled at him, in silence. Yet the last epithet cut to his core. There was no pain in influenza---ill one day and up the next. But, leprosy? Such a miserable death and such a horrid life! Riled beyond measure, he lunged towards Punia once more, gnashing his teeth as he grabbed her hair and dragged her face to the ground, "What use will you be to me if my hands and feet wither away? Probably, you'll find another husband and drop out of sight, you wretch!"

Chaudhry spoke to Heera assuringly, "Let bygones be bygones, that's enough. What if your wife hit me? I have forgiven her."

Heera barked at Chaudhry, "You keep quiet, Chaudhry. Keep out of this lest you also get a piece of my mind. Today she has fought with you; tomorrow she'll fight with someone else. You want to let this pass; someone else might not be so kind. If he thrashes her, what will happen to my reputation?"

As he imagined the scenario, his anger flared up again. He moved towards her threateningly but Hori caught him and taking his arm, shoved him aside. "Enough! You've proved to the world what a brave man you are. Do you want to kill her?"

Heera regarded his brother with respect. He never argued or fought with him directly. If he wanted, he could have easily brushed him aside and freed his hand. He looked at Chaudhry and said, "Now don't stand there staring at me. Cut the bamboo and pay the fifteen rupees. I have set everything right. The deal is done."

Punia was sobbing quietly before she heard that. She got up dramatically and beat her head. "Go, set the house on fire. I have nothing to do with it any more. My accursed luck, I have a butcher like you as my husband." She left the basket of his lunch on the road and made straight for home. Heera thundered at her, "Where are you off to? Return to the well or I will come and kill you!" Punia stopped dead in her tracks. She did not want an encore of the act. Quietly, she picked up the basket and amidst sniffles, went to the well.

Hori said to Heera, "Don't start bashing her again. Women become shameless if you hit them all the time." At this point, Dhania appeared at the door and shouted at Hori, "What are you doing there watching this drama? Does anyone pay heed to what you say? Remember, this same woman hurled abuses at you from behind her veil when there was a division. She's in the habit of picking up fights with men and she deserves to be soundly thrashed."

Hori ambled over to the door and spoke with an indulgent mischief in his tone, "If I beat you like that, what will happen then?"

"You are talking as if you have never hit me."

"Had I beaten you so mercilessly, you would have left me and gone. Punia tolerates quite a bit."

"As if, you are a very concerned husband? I still have a mark where you hit me once. (Heera beats her but he also cares for her and indulges her whims.) You know only how to raise your hand, you have no sense of loving or caring. Only I could have tolerated you for so long."

"Oh come on, don't praise yourself like that. You ran away to your parents on a trivial issue. I pleaded for months before you returned."

"My dear man, you came to mollify me for your own selfish reasons and not for love."

"That is why I sing your glories to everyone."

The dawn of marital life unfolds with a pink euphoria and covers the heart with its golden rays. Then comes the scorching afternoon with its intense heat and hot currents, rising from the burning earth. That's when love and longing give way to stark reality. Later comes the restful evening, peaceful and mild, when we sit ourselves down like tired travellers who talk to each other, sharing incidents of the day as if we are seated atop a distant peak, removed miles from the humdrum and noise, raging at the foothills.

Chaudhry walked in, all sweaty, "Hori, come and count the bamboos. I will come tomorrow and cart them away." Hori considered it unnecessary to count the bamboos. Chaudhry was not that sort of person. And even if he took a few extra bamboos, it was no big deal. People came and asked for a bamboo or two for free. When there was a girl's wedding, people would walk away with dozens of them.

Chaudhry took out seven and a half rupees and handed them over to Hori, who counted them and said, "Give me more. The deal was for twenty rupees of which I was to get twelve and a half and my brothers seven and a half."

Chaudhry spoke without batting an eyelid. "The deal was for fifteen, wasn't it?"

"Not fifteen, it was for twenty rupees."

"Didn't even Heera say it was fifteen and right in your presence. Do you want me to call him and confirm?"

"The deal was struck for twenty, Chaudhry but you hold the aces at this moment and you can say what you want. Five and a half rupees remain to be paid to me."

Chaudhry was a seasoned player. He was totally bereft of qualms at that moment. Hori's tongue was tied. He was helpless and left squirming, cursing his fate, barely managing to say, "This is not fair, Chaudhry. You will not turn rich if you filch five and a half rupees from me."

Chaudhry was caustic in his reply "Neither will you turn rich filching some money from the share of your brothers. You are ready to sell your soul for five and a half rupees and dare to lecture me on honesty? If I start talking you will lose face."

It was as if a hundred blows had rained on Hori in one go. Chaudhry left the money on the ground and walked away nonchalantly leaving Hori rooted to the spot where he stood under the neem tree, utterly apologetic and contrite. The extent of his greed and selfishness dawned on him. A pittance of two and half rupees was enough to warm the cockles of his heart and make him feel proud of his cunning. Shaken, he realised his folly.

Dhania had gone inside the house. When she came out, she noticed the money lying on the ground. She counted it and said, "Where's the remaining amount? It should be twelve and a half, shouldn't it?"

Hori made a long face and lied, "Heera sold it for fifteen rupees, what can I do?" He allowed himself to nurse defeat in his heart. He was like a thief who falls from a tree while trying to steal mangoes from someone's orchard. Success justifies everything. The shame of defeat has to be borne in silence.

Righteously, Dhania gave a piece of her mind to her husband. Such opportunities were rare. Hori was smarter than her but today the odds were stacked in her favour. Gesticulating with her hands she scoffed at him, "Oh yeah, why not? If your brother says fifteen, how could you ever say twenty? Wouldn't Heera be crestfallen, will he not?"

Hori listened to the tirade quietly. He did not wince. He felt irritated and angry, his blood boiled and eyes flashed. He gritted his teeth but did not utter a word. Silently, he picked up the sickle and stood up to leave to hoe sugarcane. Dhania snatched the sickle from his hands. "Is it early morning that you are setting out to hoe the sugarcane? The sun is in the sky. Go, get refreshed and bathe. Food is ready."

Hori mumbled "I am not hungry."

Dhania again rubbed it in. "Why should you be hungry? Your brother has fed you delicious *laddoos,* has he not? May God bless everyone with such brothers."

Hori was livid, his anger straining at its leash. "You are pushing your luck too far today."

Dhania gestured dramatically in mock humility "I am helpless. Your pampering has made me so haughty and rude."

"Will you let me exist in this house or not?"

"It's your house, you are the lord and master. Who am I to send you packing from your home?"

Hori that day had no shield to deflect those barbs of sarcasm. Timidly he put the spade away, picked up the towel and went to have a bath. He returned half an hour later but there was no sign of Gobar yet. How could he have lunch all alone without him? The lout must be joking and giggling with that waif, Jhuniya. Yesterday too, he was getting quite carried away with her. If he did not get the cow, what was the point in staying on for such a long time?

Dhania said, "What are you waiting for? Gobar will not be back before sundown." Hori did not utter a single word, to avoid another barrage of comments from Dhania. He finished his meal and lay under the shade of the *neem* tree.

Rupa came in running, her bare body draped in a loin cloth, unkempt hair flying in all directions. She threw herself on Hori's chest. She complained that her elder sister Sona told her that when the new cow arrives, she alone will make the dung cakes and Rupa will have nothing of it. "Why should she alone make the cakes? I am as good as her in everything. If she cooks, don't I wash the utensils? If Sona draws water from the well, don't I take the rope to the well? And if Sona returns carrying the pitcher, I gather the rope and bring it back. If Sona goes to till the fields, don't I go to graze the goats? I will not tolerate such injustice."

Enamoured by Rupa's innocence, Hori said, "No, you will make the cow dung cakes. If Sona as much as goes near the cow, you shoo her away."

Rupa wrapped her arms around her father's neck- "And only I will milk the cow."

"Yes of course, who else but you will milk the cow?"

"She will be my cow."

"Yes, all yours!"

Delighted, Rupa scampered to convey the news to Sona.

Sona had the built of a young woman but had a childlike nature. Her face was long and dry with a pointed chin and she bore a happy expression. Her eyes glinted with a quaint peaceful aura. Her hair was un-oiled, with no kohl in her eyes or ornaments on her body – as if the burden of the household had dwarfed her youthfulness. She shook her head and said, "Okay, go and make the cow dung cakes. When you milk the cow I'll drink all the milk."

"I will keep it under lock and key."

Warning that she will break all locks and keys, she got up and walked away to the mango orchard. The mangoes had ripened. As the breeze rocked the boughs, a few fell to the ground. They were yellowed by the hot winds but for kids, they were *tapkas*---the fruit that falls on its own and which kids could eat without fear of upbraiding. A ragtag bunch of urchins hovered around the groves expectantly. Rupa followed her sister there. Whatever Sona did Rupa had to emulate.

It was evening and Hori, tired as he was, was in no mood to go to the sugarcane fields. He tethered the bulls, fed them, lit a *chillum* and retired to a corner, puffing on it. After selling off all the crops of the season in his granary, he was still under a debt of three hundred rupees of which a hundred would accrue as interest every year. Five years ago, Mangru Sah had loaned him sixty rupees for buying a pair of bulls of which he had paid back sixty as interest but the principal stayed put. He had borrowed thirty from Datadin Pundit to sow potatoes. Thieves dug out the potatoes and bolted but the thirty rupees grew to a hundred in three years. Dulari was the widow who owned a shop selling oil, salt, tobacco and other groceries. During the family partition, he had taken a loan of forty rupees from her to pay his brothers. That too was now hundred since the interest was an anna per rupee. Twenty-five rupees had to be paid for the local excise and he was yet to arrange the money for donation for the Dussehra festival. The payment from the bamboo sale had come not a day too soon. It would solve the problem of the donation.

The whole village would be agog even if a piddling amount came his way and it attracted creditors like predators smelling blood. But he decided to pay those five rupees as donation come what may, though there were other pressing issues like the marriages of Gobar and Sona. However hard he scrounged, the expenses were a minimum of three hundred. Where would he get that from? He did not want to take a single *paisa* as loan and repay every *paisa* he owed but despite bearing all sorts of hardships, debt clung to his neck with a vice-like grip. Interest would pile on gradually, and one day his home and hearth would be auctioned. Deprived of shelter, his children would beg on the streets. Whenever Hori finished his tasks for the day and lit up his *chillum,* such thoughts came to haunt him. His only relief was in the knowledge that he was not the only one. Almost every farmer was in the same predicament. In fact, many others were worse off. His brothers Sobha and Heera had separated from him three years ago but were already burdened with loans of four hundred each. Jhingur worked with two ploughs but had a debt of a thousand. Jiyavan was penniless. Everyone was buried under debts.

Suddenly Sona and Rupa came running in and shrieking almost simultaneously- "Gobar is coming with the cow." After delivering the news both ran towards the orchard to welcome the cow.

Hori said, "Let's nail the tether fast." There was a youthful glow on Dhania's face. "No, let me first give her a drink of flour and jaggery. Poor thing has come trudging in this heat. She must be thirsty. You go and nail the tether. I will make the drink."

"There is a bell lying somewhere. Find it. We'll tie it around her neck."

"Where's Sona? Send her to the Sahuain's shop and get a black thread. Cows get the evil eye very fast."

"Today my heart's greatest desire has been fulfilled," said Hori with pride

Dhania suppressed the joy in her heart. The fear of any obstacle to their newfound fortune sent a shiver down her spine. Looking heavenwards she said, "The real happiness of the cow's arrival will come when she bears a healthy calf. It's all in God's hands."

She had hardly made the watery flour mix when Gobar appeared at the gate with an exuberant procession of kids in tow. Hori ran and hugged the cow's neck. Dhania tore a piece off an old *saree* and tied it around the cow's neck.

Hori gaped awestruck at the cow as if a goddess had incarnated herself at his door. Lord had mercifully granted him the day when his house was sanctified by a cow. He wondered what pious deeds were responsible for it.

Dhania spoke with a fearful apprehension "Why are you just standing there? Nail a tether in the courtyard."

"Where in the courtyard? There's no space here."

"There is enough space."

"I will nail it outside."

"Don't be stupid. You know all about our village and yet act ignorant."

"But where can we tie a cow in this teeny weenie courtyard?"

"If you do not understand some things, don't act as if you do. You are not the sole repository of all worldly wisdom."

For Hori, the cow wasn't simply an object of faith and devotion but also a living fortune that he wanted to show to the village by tying her outside. That would surely enhance his prestige. He visualised people passing by and pointing at his house and saying what a lucky guy he was to possess a cow. It would also suitably impress those coming with marriage proposals. But if she remained inside the courtyard, who would notice her?

On the contrary, Dhania was not sure of the wisdom of keeping the cow outside. If she had her way, she'd never let the cow out. Usually, Hori had his say in everything. He would stick to his guns and Dhania would have to finally bow to his wishes. But today, none of Hori's wiles mattered. Gobar, Sona and Rupa all sided with Hori but Dhania stood her ground. An unusual self assurance overtook her that she would stand her ground.

But there was no stopping the spectacle. It was impossible for an event of such magnitude to not cause a buzz in the village. Buying a cow worth fifty or sixty rupees was a major happening. But a cow for eighty? That was too much to stomach. How could Hori afford it? A steady stream of spectators and critics crowded the doorway as Hori ran up and down, greeting all and sundry. He was never so happy and humble.

Seventy year old Datadin arrived, wobbling on his stick and spoke in a toothless mumble, "Hori may I see your cow? I hear it's beautiful."

Hori hurried up to him, bending down to touch his feet in deference to his age and brought him into the courtyard respectfully. He gave the cow an experienced appraising look, examining her horns, udder and hump. Eyes shining with a youthful fire under his bushy white eyebrows, he said "She's impeccable. God willing, your good days are here. Just ensure, you give her good nutrition. Each of her calf will fetch a hundred rupees." Datadin spat a spittle of tobacco from his mouth and said, "This is God's grace. Did you pay cash for her?"

How could Hori let go an opportunity to show off his prosperity, even if it was to his creditor. He lied with a beaming smile, "Bhola is not such a considerate soul, Sir. I paid cash. Crisp notes." The falsity in that statement did not escape Datadin's aged eyes, which had more experience than sight in them.

Happily he exclaimed, "No worries, son. She will give you five seers milk daily."

Dhania corrected him instantly, "Sir, there won't be so much milk. She is old and where's the nutrition?"

Datadin looked at her with soft eyes, acknowledging her alertness, accepting that after all it's a housewife's responsibility to cover up her husband's garrulousness. Then he whispered to her conspiratorially, "Do not keep her outside the home. Take that from me."

Dhania flashed a look at her husband with an I-told-you-so air and then turned to Datadin "No Sir, we will not tie her outside. If God is kind, we will soon have three more in the courtyard."

The conversation was lost to Hori whose eyes were searching someone in the crowd. Then he turned to Dhania, "It's surprising that neither Sobha nor Heera have dropped by."

Dhania said in disdain, "Not that we are falling over to welcome your brothers and their families."

"All you want is to pick up a fight. If God has blessed us with a day like this, we must learn to be humble. There is more joy in sharing the good tidings with those who are close to us. Moreover, the bond between brothers always remains strong despite occasional quarrels. Every one fights for their rights and share. But that doesn't mean we are not of the same blood. We must call them over and show them our cow or they will say we have become arrogant."

Dhania drew back her lips in distaste, "I have told you a hundred times not to praise your brothers to me. The entire village knows we have a new cow and only they seem to be ignorant despite the fact they live next door. The fact is they are burning with jealousy that we have a cow."

It was time to light the evening lamps. There was no kerosene in the house so Dhania picked up the empty bottle and went to get oil.

Hori called out to Rupa and lovingly sat her on his lap and said, "Run across and see if Sobha *Kaka* and Heera *Kaka* are at home. Tell them I want them to come. If they refuse hold their hands and drag them here."

Rupa made a face and said, "*Amma* forbids us from going to their house."

"Are you *Amma's* baby or mine?"

"Amma's," she chirruped and wrapped her arms around him, laughing.

"In that case, please get off my lap and stop eating from my plate."

There was one brass alloy dish in the house. Hori ate in that plate. Rupa ate with him. She was in no mood to give up that honour therefore she acquiesced with a 'yes'.

"So go and bring in Heera and Sobha."

"And if *Amma* gets mad?"

"No one will tell *Amma*."

With a hop, skip and jump Rupa ran across to Heera's house.

The net of envy snares big fish. The tiny ones never get entangled in it and if they do, they escape real fast. For them the dangerous net is not an object of fear but a playground which they traverse at leisure.

As she stepped out of the house she was confronted by Dhania, coming back with the bottle of kerosene. She ticked her off brusquely to turn home and asked where she was off to so late in the day. Rupa lost no opportunity to get into her mother's good books and obeyed instantly.

Dhania chastised her, "Go back, you do not have to go and call anyone."

Holding her by the hand, she trooped in and said to Hori, "I have repeated a thousand times, do not send my children to anyone's home. What if somebody casts an evil eye or does something worse? If your heart is so overflowing with love, why don't you go there yourself? It seems you have not had enough of them."

Hori was nailing the tether. His hands were muddied. Feigning ignorance, he muttered, "What are you so miffed about? Don't bark at the wind, like a dog."

Dhania had to pour oil in the lantern. Rupa went in to the other children.

The night wore on. The tether was fixed to the ground. The feed -mix, water and fodder were poured into the cow's bin. The animal crouched quietly in a corner, morose, like a newlywed bride, recently arrived at her in-laws home. She did not move her snout to the feed bin. Gobar and Hori brought half a *roti* for her but she turned her head away. That was nothing strange, animals get scared and saddened if they are moved out of familiar surroundings to a new place.

Hori sat on the cot outside and puffed on his *chillum* and thought about his brothers. He missed them in his moment of pride and happiness. Achieving what he considered a fortune has made him grow benevolent with humility. What if they had separated, they were not enemies. If this cow had arrived three years ago, it would have also belonged to them. When the cow gives milk or they make curd from its milk, he would surely give some to his brothers. They might harbour ill will against him, but giving back in the same coin was not in his code of ethics.

He got up from his cot and walked towards the home of Heera and Sobha. Both were sitting on a *charpoy* and discussing something. Neither saw Hori sidle up close. Hori stopped and listened. Heera was saying, "When we were together, he never bought a measly goat, now he gets a western cow. I have not seen anyone thrive after depriving a brother of his share."

Sobha was more circumspect "Now that's not fair. Hori accounted for every single paisa. I will never accept that he ever hid any assets from us."

"Believe it or not, this cow is from the money that should have come our way."

"You should not level baseless charges against anyone."

"Oh? So did this money fall from the skies? We have as many fields, we have a similar yield of crops. Why is it that we can't raise enough for our funeral pyre while they can afford a new cow?

"Hori must have got a loan."

"Bhola is not one to offer loans."

"You may say whatever you like, the fact is she's a beautiful cow. I saw her when Gobar was taking her through the fields."

"Ill begotten wealth never lasts long. God is witness, the cow will not be with them for long."

Hori could not stand it any longer and a surge of anger swept through him. He wanted to respond to the allegations right then and there but he controlled his outburst, sensing that it could spiral out of control. His intentions were honest, he had committed no sin and God was witness. He turned back as soundlessly as he had come. When he entered his house, he tried to puff on the burnt out tobacco in his *chillum* but the poison spread steadily through his veins. He tried to sleep but in vain. Just as a person is numbed by intoxication, his furious mind was working overtime. He crept inside the house, dazed. The door was ajar. Dhania was lying on the mat on the floor as Sona massaged her feet while Rupa, who usually slept by this hour, stood near the cow, stroking her muzzle. Hori unfettered the cow and walked towards the door with her leash. In his mind, he had firmed up the decision to take her back to Bhola that very instant. He had no desire to retain her in his house in the face of such wicked allegations.

Dhania asked him where he was taking the cow so late at night.

Hori stepped forward and said, "Back to Bhola. She has got to be returned."

Flummoxed, Dhania sat up, "Why are you returning her back?"

"Yes, it is necessary for her to go back."

"Why? What happened? You brought her with such earnestness and now you want to return her? Did Bhola ask for money?"

"No, he didn't."

"Then what happened?"

"Why do you want to ask?"

She lunged forward and snatched the leash from his hands. Her nimble mind was quick to sense the reason. "If you are afraid of your brothers, go and fall at their feet. I am not scared of anyone. If they are burning with jealousy so be it."

Hori's voice was very subdued and humble, "Speak softly. If anyone hears us they will say we are quarreling in the middle of the night. You have no idea of what I have heard. They are accusing me of cheating them at the time of the division, and stashing away what was justly theirs. Now they are suspecting I bought this cow from that money."

"Are Heera and Sobha saying that?"

"Not just them. The entire village is saying it.?"

"It's not the village, it's just Heera who says so. I will go and ask him how much his father left him, before he died? We wasted our lives after these vermin. We brought them up and the monsters say we are the ones who are dishonest? Let me warn you, if the cow as much as steps out of this home, the world will fall apart. Let Heera and Sobha and the whole world say whatever they want."

Hori was taken aback. Dhania grabbed the leash and tied it back and took menacing steps towards the door. He tried to stop her but she was already out in an instant. He slumped down holding his head, not wanting to create a scene by going out to stop her in the open. He was well accustomed to her temper. She turned wild when enraged. She would not be stopped by words or fear of a thrashing but Heera had an equally inflammable temperament. If he hit her, it would be doomsday for all. Perhaps, Heera was not so stupid. Why did he have to needlessly rake this fire? He felt extremely angry at himself. If he had locked the anger in his heart, it would not have exploded so badly.

He heard the sharp voice of Dhania shouting, followed by the thundering bellow of Heera. He also heard the stinging cries of Punia. All at once he thought of Gobar. He leapt outside and saw Gobar was not on his cot. That was terrible! Gobar had gone there too. His volatile temper could cause havoc. The cacophony rose by the second. The entire village was jolted out of sleep. It appeared there was a fire and people leapt out of their cots, running to douse it.

For some seconds he sat slumped, stunned into silence, then his mind raged against Dhania. Why did she go out to pick up a fight? Unless something is said in one's presence, it should not be taken seriously. In private, people say so many things about others.

Hori's peasant mind-set avoided unpleasantness and strife. It was better to ignore and let it pass than pick up cudgels over a few hot words. If there was a scuffle or worse, then one would have to go to the police, plead and beg, waste time at the courts while the fields and crops got neglected. He had no control over Heera. But he could pull Dhania back. At worst she would abuse him, not speak with him for a few days but at least it would save trips to the police station.

He strode briskly across to Heera's house and hid himself behind the furthest wall. Like a clever commandant of a war unit, he wanted to understand the ground situation completely before venturing into it. If his side was winning, there was no point in disturbing the course of events but if it was weakening, then he would jump into the fray right away. He observed that *Thakur,* the village chief and many others were already there. The scales were tilting and Dhania's aggressiveness was turning the public sentiment away from her. So foul was the barrage of her angry epithets that the crowd was slowly turning against her.

She was screaming- "Why are you so jealous of us? Why does your heart burn when you see us prosper? Is this the reward we get for raising you? If it were not for us, you would be begging on the streets."

Hori felt such harsh words were totally uncalled for. Bringing up his brothers was his rightful duty. He was the custodian of their share of property. It was natural and obligatory for him to bring them up or else he would have lost face in society.

Heera retorted, "We worked like dogs in your house and ate what you threw at us. We never knew what it is to be a child or what it means to be young and carefree. We spent full days sifting through dried cow dung. Yet, you never gave us a morsel without an earful of abuses. Our lives were ruined because of you, you witch."

Dhania's anger shot up, "Hold your tongue or I pull it out. Witch is what your wife is. Who do you think you are? You headless devil, you petty thief, backstabber!"

Datadin cut her short, "Why do you utter such bitter words, Dhania? A woman should be patient and tolerant. He is an uncouth lout; you don't have to get into a war of words with him."

Lala Pateshwari, the *patwari,* agreed, "An argument is countered with an argument, not foul words. You nursed him since he was a child, but you should not forget that you were in control of his property."

Dhania misread him and assumed the whole village wanted to put her down. She geared to take up the fight on many fronts, "You don't say that! I can see through everyone. I have lived in this village for twenty years, I know everyone through everyone. So you think, I am using foul words and he is showering petals on me?"

Dulari Sahuain poured oil on the raging fire, "She is such a foul mouthed woman! The way she fights with a man! Only a mild man like Hori can tolerate her. Any other would beat her every day."

Had Heera displayed a minor sense of civility at this juncture, victory was his for the asking but he was bristling with the abuses Dhania had hurled at him. He lost all composure. Sensing others in his favour, he turned more aggressive. Shouting at the top of his voice, he hollered, "Go away from my doorstep or I will beat you with my shoe! I will pull your hair and throw you out. You dare abuse me, witch? Perhaps, you are too proud of your son, bloody...."

That turned the tables. Hori's blood boiled much as a spark would ignite an ammunition dump. He stepped out of the shadows and said, "Stop it Heera, you've said enough. What can I say about this woman? Every time I am cut to shame because of her. I don't know why she cannot hold her tongue."

Heera was deluged from all sides. Datadin called him shameless; Jhinguri Singh said he was a scoundrel. Dulari Sahuain labelled him the family's rotten apple. One loose word from him had swung the scales in Dhania's favour. Hori's conciliatory and subdued words further consolidated her victory.

Heera gathered his wits. The entire village was turning against him, leaving him with no option but to retreat silently. This wisdom dawned on him despite the fury.

Dhania felt doubly vindicated and said to Hori, "Now see for yourself, listen carefully. He wants to beat me with his shoes. We brought him up..."

Hori snapped at her- "Why are you jabbering again? Just go home."

Dhania planted herself on the ground and wailed, "Let him come and beat me with his shoes. I want to see how he does that? Where is Gobar? Why isn't he coming to defend me? I want him to come and see how his mother is being humiliated."

Her loud wails kept the embers of her anger alight and fanned Hori's temper at the same time. Her consistent harangue built his irritation into a gnawing anger. Tearing herself away from Hori's grip, she ran towards Heera and threw him off balance, shouting, "Hit me, hit me, let me see how you hit me with your shoes?"

Hori lunged forward, and catching her by the hand, dragged her back all the way to the house.

❁❁❁

5

That day, Gobar had a long conversation with Bhola's widowed daughter, Jhuniya. When he left for home with the cow, she came halfway across the distance with him. It was not easy for him to walk the cow alone, as it would certainly have resisted going with a stranger. Jhuniya looked at him tenderly and said, "After taking the cow, I don't think you have any reason to come this way again."

Gobar was a pubescent boy. All young girls and women in his village were akin to his sisters or sisters-in-law. Thus, there was no scope of flirting with the girls. Though the married women,in his village, did indulge in mild teasing but all in good humour. They treated him with an indulgence prompted by his young age. For want of any real female attention, his adolescence was stuck in a frozen pre-teen limbo.

Constantly hurt by her sister-in-law's jibes, Jhuniya's deprived heart fell for Gobar's childish youth. The somnolent animal that lurked in the boy's heart too was alerted, startled as if by a slight rustle of interest.

Gobar spoke with ill concealed eagerness- "Of course I'll come. If a beggar is hopeful of alms, he will stand at the door of the donor all day and all night."

Testily, Jhuniya waded into deeper waters, "Beggars knock at ten doors before they feel satiated, such beggars come dime a dozen. Moreover, what does a beggar give in return? Thanks? Blessings? Neither is of any benefit to the giver."

Gobar was slow on the uptake and failed to catch the import of Jhuniya's words. As a young girl, she had to go to customers' homes where her family supplied milk. She continued to do that at her husband's home. Now, after her husband's death, she was back to her father's home and the responsibility of delivering milk fell on her again. This job exposed her to a wide range of people and she managed to spend her time in an interesting manner. However, she pined for lasting love and her desire for domesticity overcame overtures of romantic opportunism from men.

Gobar stared at her with an expression steeped in desire, "If a beggar gets enough to satisfy his hunger, at one place, why will he go door to door?"

Jhuniya gave him a compassionate look and thought to herself, 'He is such a simpleton; he has no idea of such things.'

"A beggar never gets enough from one door--never more than a pinch. To get everything you desire you have to be ready to offer everything you possess."

"What do I have, Jhuniya?"

"You think you have nothing to offer me? I'd say you have what even millionaires don't possess. You don't have to beg at my door. You can buy me off!"

Gobar stared at her, awestruck.

Jhuniya went on, "And you know the price that you have to pay for me? You will just have to be mine. And after that if I ever see you beg at any door, I will throw you out of the house."

Gobar was ecstatic. A joy mixed with fear coursed through his body as if he had accidentally bumped into an object, he was searching for long. But how could he go ahead with this? If he eloped with Jhuniya, how could she live with him in his home as a kept woman? The entire village would bristle with loose talk. Everyone would turn against him. His mother would not allow her to enter the house. But he realised she was a bold woman and was not afraid, so why should he be scared as a man? At worse, everybody would forsake him. He could stay alone. Indeed there was no woman like her in the village. She was so understanding and loving. If they excommunicated the two of them, it was not as if this was the only village in the world. But why should he leave the village at all? Matadin brought a low-caste woman home and people could not do more than gnash their teeth in vain. Jhinguri Singh got a Brahmin woman for himself. Was any one able to do anything about it? In fact his status went up. Earlier, he ran around searching for jobs but now he has become a money lender with the money she brought with her. Abruptly, Gobar checked himself. What if Jhuniya was simply talking to him in jest and not serious about him? He decided he wanted to be convinced of her seriousness.

He asked her point blank if she really meant what she had said, or she was merely showing him visions? He said, "I am all yours, Jhuniya but do you feel the same?"

Jhuniya replied, "Yes, but how do I check whether you actually want me?

"If it comes to that, I'll die for you."

"Do you know what it means to die for someone?"

"You tell me."

"To die for someone means to live for someone. To take someone's hand and vow to stay together, unmindful of what the world says. Even if it means forsaking your parents, kith and kin, house, hearth, everything. There are umpteen men, who talk about dying for others. Will you also fly away like the rest?"

Gobar held the leash in one hand. With the other he clasped Jhuniya's hand. As he did so, he felt a bolt of lightening coursing through him. His body trembled with the first touch of a woman. She had such a soft, silky hand.

Jhuniya didn't pull her hand away. When a few seconds elapsed, she said, "Today you have held my hand. Don't forget this."

"I'll remember it to my dying day."

Jhuniya gave him a disbelieving look, "Everybody says that Gobar. But I am always on guard. I have been selling milk and curd since ages and meet all sorts of moneyed men, advocates and government officers, who try to entrap me with honey laden words. Some big officer-types ogle at me with lovelorn eyes as though they are completely besotted with me. Some offer money and jewellery.

They promise to be my slaves all through this life and the next, but I know better. They are fickle bees, flitting from flower to flower, in their quest for nectar. I play along, leading them on with sidelong coquettish glances. They try to fool me and I try to fool them. If I die, they would barely bother and if they die, I wouldn't shed a tear. I will belong to someone who wants to be with me through fortune and calamity. I don't hanker after money or good clothes. I need the company of a decent man who loves me and whom I can love."

Jhuniya went on to narrate an episode. "I know a *pundit,* who has great pretensions of piety. He buys half a seer of milk from me. Once when I went to deliver milk, I discovered his wife was away. I was not aware of that and went right inside the house as on other days. Suddenly I found the *pundit* striding in, after bolting the front door. I instantly knew he meant no good. I asked him angrily why he bolted the main door and why the house was so quiet and if his wife was not home. He said, 'She has gone somewhere,' and took meaningful steps towards me. I told him to take the milk if he wanted to otherwise I was going immediately. To which he said, 'No, you are not going anywhere Jhuniya; I have been smitten by your looks, today is my chance.' I broke into a cold sweat."

Gobar spoke with mounting disgust "If I lay my hands on him, I will bury that scoundrel alive. Just tell me who he is."

"Relax, I can handle such louts on my own. However, I panicked wondering what I would do if he touched me. I knew my screams would go unheard but I decided in my mind that if he tried to molest me, I would break the pot of milk on his head. It would mean a loss of five seers of milk but he would learn a lesson for a lifetime. I gathered my wits and warned him I was the daughter of a cowherd, and he had better watch out as I would pull out every hair from his moustache. I asked him if that was what he learnt from his holy books. He began pleading, falling at my feet, telling me how he loved me. He went on to say that if God were to ask me if I had helped satisfy a poor Brahmin's needs, I should not cut a sorry figure. God would blame me for not putting my beauty to right use by denying my body to a Brahmin. It would be an act of great piety and God would be happy.

"On an impulse I tried to search his mind and said, 'I will charge fifty rupees for that.' You will be surprised Gobar, that miserable man went inside the room and came out with five ten-rupee notes. When I threw down the money and marched angrily to the door, he came up and caught my hand. I was prepared for such an eventuality and hit his face hard with the pot. He was drenched in milk from top to toe. He was hurt bad and sat down on the floor groaning and holding his head. I opened the door latch and ran out."

Gobar guffawed in delight. "You did well! So he was anointed with milk! The vermillion must have washed off his holiness' forehead! Why didn't you also pull out his moustaches?"

"The next day, I went to his place again when his wife was home. He sat in the living room with a bandage around his head. I asked him if I should disclose his antics to his wife, and he fell at my feet with folded hands. I told him that his wife would kill him. I felt pity and didn't say a word."

Her pardon did not go down well with Gobar. "Why did you do that? You should have told his wife. She would have beaten him black and blue. Such charlatans need no mercy. Point him out to me tomorrow and I will pound him to dust."

Jhuniya glanced at his wiry adolescent frame. "You can't beat him. He is quite a stud, living off freebies has done him good."

Gobar was affronted by this slight to his manliness, "A big build is not everything," he boasted, "there is steel in my bones. I do three hundred push-ups in one go everyday. I do not get milk and ghee in my diet or else my chest would be something to look at."

Saying so, he blew his chest to whatever level it could rise.

Jhuniya assured him, "Okay, I'll show you who he is. But there are so many like him. How many will you set right? Men have this trait of staring at women and ogling at their breasts. And that, despite the fact I am not good looking."

Gobar objected, "You are not good looking? One look at you and I want to hide you away in my heart."

Jhuniya boxed him playfully on his back. "There you go... like the others....trying to praise me. One should seek good qualities and not good looks in a person you are going to spend a lifetime with. Most men need just a woman's body to entertain them. Near my in-laws place, there lived a rich Kashmiri family who bought five seers of milk every day. They had three daughters, all within the ages of twenty and twenty five and extremely beautiful. They studied in a big college – perhaps one of them taught in the same college. They were talented girls and played the sitar and harmonium. They knew dancing, singing, but none of them was married. God knows whether they rejected men or men rejected them but they seemed very happy. Once I asked the eldest one about it and she laughed it off saying, 'We don't want to get into that rut.' They seemed to be enjoying life and boys keep hovering around them. They wore shirts and trousers and went horse riding with men. The city was abuzz with rumours of their activities. Their father was embarrassed and ashamed of their activities and wore a forlorn expression. He got mad at them but they openly rebuked him, telling him to mind his own business. It was not possible for him to lock them up or give them a sound thrashing; one never knows the ways of big people. They have no fear of any village council or society. But why should I talk ill of anyone? The mind becomes what you teach it to become. I have known people, who savour *halwa-poori* after a fortnight of *dal-roti*. There are others, who are quite happy with simple meals and never hanker after fancy foods."

This was a whole new world for Gobar. Fascinated by its novelty, he heard everything in rapt attention. Every now and then he would stop in his tracks involuntarily, become conscious of it and resume walking again. First, Jhuniya charmed him with her beauty and today she cast a spell with her knowledge, experience and suggestions of her chastity. If such an exquisite basket of beauty, good qualities and wisdom fell in his lap, Gobar decided it would be worth taking the village elders' council and the objections by the community, head-on.

When it was amply clear to Jhuniya she had made a good impact, she put her hand to her breast, bit her lip delicately and said, "Oh, we are so close to your village! You are very clever! You did not tell me to turn back when we were half way."

Having made her point, she turned to leave.

Gobar said, "Oh come on home for a moment. *Amma* must see you as well."

Jhuniya blushed and looked away. "I am not going to your home like this. I am surprised how I travelled all this distance. Tell me, when will you come again? There's a musical show near my house at night. Why don't you come? I'll see you at the backdoor."

"And if I do not find you there?"

"Then you go back."

"... Never to return."

"No, you must return, you have to. Let me make this clear, I insist."

"You must swear you will meet me."

"I do not swear on anything..."

"Then I am also not coming."

"Whatever!"

Jhuniya made a teasing gesture with her thumbs and walked off. In their very first meeting, both had claimed some sort of right over the other. Jhuniya knew he'd come. Gobar also knew there was no reason why she would not be waiting.

He herded the cow and walked on. As he took the first few steps alone, Gobar felt he had just stumbled out of heaven.

❁❁❁

6

June evenings in Semri are scorching and listless. This particular evening, water was sprayed in every street and the town appeared cheerful. Rows of flower pots and green plants surrounded the stage as electric pedestal fans whirred noisily. Rai sahib had an electricity generation unit in his workshop. His guards strutted in smart yellow uniforms and bright deep blue turbans, snorting haughtily at the commoners. The servants wearing white tunics and saffron turbans scurried around, greeting guests.

A motor car screeched to a halt and three persons emerged from it. The gentleman in slippers and a *khadi kurta* was Pandit Onkarnath, the editor of the daily newspaper Bijli. He was extremely concerned about the state of the nation. The second in the coat and trousers was a lawyer Shyam Behari Tankha but since his law practice was not doing well, he had turned into an insurance agent. The third man in the tight pajamas and silken *achkan,* B. Mehta, was a philosophy professor. The three were school friends of Rai sahib and had come to attend the festivities.

Today the laity would come to offer ceremonial donations. Late night, there would be the 'bow and arrow' sacrifice followed by a banquet. Hori had offered his five rupees donation already. With a pink turban, pink waist-jacket and knee length dress, he stood with a shovel in hand in the role of King Janak's gardener. His powdered face glowed with a pride that seemed to suggest, he was responsible for the entire evening's programme.

Rai sahib was a broad shouldered man. His forehead was wide and his face shone, and the crimson shawl on him looked resplendent. Pandit Onkarnath enquired of him, "Which play are you enacting this time?"

Rai sahib seated the three gentlemen next to him and said, "First we will have the bow-arrow sacrificial ceremony. That will be followed by a stage performance. Of a play I have scripted myself which can easily conclude in two hours."

Onkarnath had grave doubts about Rai sahib's literary talents. He believed staunchly that real talent lay with the poor and impoverished much like a lamp, the light of which can only be seen, if it is dark. He turned his face away with an indifference, which he barely tried to mask.

Tankha was not interested in what he considered useless stuff but wanted Rai sahib to know he did have an opinion on the subject. He said, "Any play can be good if it has a cast of fine actors. The best of plays turn insipid for lack of good performances. Our theatre scene will continue to be in a pathetic state unless educated ladies step in to take up acting as a career. By the way, you created a stir in the Council with your questions. I bet no member has a better record than you."

Mehta, the philosophy professor, could not tolerate this praise. He wanted to object but decided to camouflage his feelings in a salvo of righteous principles.

He had recently completed a book after many years of uninterrupted toil. Unfortunately, since it did not receive a fraction of the accolades he anticipated, he was deeply hurt and disappointed. He said, "Now, now- I am not concerned about the number of questions raised in the Council. I am of the opinion that our lives should be consonant with our ideals. You are a well wisher of the peasants and want to secure concessions for them. You consider *Zamindaars* as the scourge of society and want to clip their wings, take away their rights. But you are yourself one of them. If you want peasants to have equal rights, you can make a beginning with yourself- give rights to them, put an end to labour without wages, abolish penal taxes and don't lay claim to grazing land. I have little sympathy for those who talk like Communists but live a bourgeois life that spills over with selfishness."

Rai sahib was devastated. The lawyer frowned and the editor was speechless. He was also a supporter of equality but did not want to upset the party so abruptly.

Tankha spoke up for Rai sahib, "Rai sahib is very sympathetic to peasants. If all *Zamindaars* were like him, these issues would have no meaning."

Undeterred, Mehta delivered another punch, "Agreed, you have a warm relationship with the hoi polloi but isn't it prompted by selfishness? Is it so, since according to you a soft blow doesn't hurt as much? The one who kills softly is more successful than the one who kills savagely. You see, either one is an egalitarian or he is not. And if one claims to be so, he better start acting like one and stop mouthing drivel. I am against a life of pseudo ideals. If someone likes eating meat, then he should eat openly. But to suggest privately, that's it is fine to eat meat and yet hide the fact that you do – I find that totally unacceptable. This is cowardice and chicanery."

Rai sahib was adept in public posturing. He knew how to handle insult and injury with patience and forbearance. He spoke with the right measure of self-doubt, "You are absolutely right, Mehtaji. I am sure you are aware how much I respect your plain speak. But you seem to forget that like any other journey, in the progression of ideas, there are halts and stops and nobody can abruptly leapfrog from one level to another, out of the blues. I was brought up in an environment where the king was considered God and the *Zamindaar*, his minister.

"My father was so considerate to the people that at times of drought or extreme winter, he would forego half and at times, all taxes levied on the peasants. He would open his granaries and distribute food amongst them. He would sell off the family silver to pay for the marriage of poor girls. But this he did as long as it was his bounden duty. He refused to part with a single *anna* if he was forced to give it away as the farmer's right. I was born and bred in this environment but I am proud to say that I have gone beyond such notions and believe that the lot of the peasants will improve only by according those rights and not mere sympathy and good will.

"Giving up selfishness voluntarily is an exceptional act. Despite all the concern and sympathy I nurse in my heart, I admit to selfishness yet would like the government to exert its power and influence through its policies and force us to give up on our ways. You may call it cowardice; I say it is helplessness. It is not right to profit on the labours of another. It's shameful to be a parasite. A social system that inculcates such capitalist ideas is a fortress that must be breached.

"It's such a shame, so deplorable that while workers are deprived of two square meals a day, their officials and handlers happily pocket five thousand and more. I am well aware of the extent to which crass licentiousness, hedonism, consumerism and timidity has seeped into us. But I do not oppose the system for these reasons alone. Actually, it cannot be endorsed even for the sake of selfishness. We are so worried about preserving these indulgences, that we trash our self respect and grind it beyond existence. We are helplessly forced to exploit the masses. If we do not send expensive gift hampers to the officials we are considered rebels and if we do not live in style, we are considered miserly. The mere suggestion of progressiveness is sufficient to make us quake in fear and go bleating to the officials asking for succour. We have faith neither in ourselves nor in our capacity for work. We are no different from sick spoon-fed children, who might appear plump but are weak, listless, dependent and without substance."

Mehta clapped his hands and applauded, "Hear! Hear! How I wish your intelligence had half the refinement of your speech. It's so tragic. You realise it completely but are so afraid to put it to practice."

Editor Onkarnath chipped in, "One swallow will not make a summer, Mr. Mehta! We have not only to march in step with the times but also see that it is in tune with our requirements. We need as much understanding for our positive aspects as for our shortcomings. Why do you pocket eight hundred rupees every month when millions of your poor brethren scrape through with barely eight?"

Rai sahib turned to the editor with an apparently disapproving look but with a deep sense of satisfied vindication in his heart "Please do not resort to personal criticism. Here we are simply discussing the social system of our milieu."

Mehta retorted in an equally cold fashion, "Oh no, not at all. I do not take it personally. Society is composed of individuals and it cannot be studied in isolation. I accept such a salary because I have faith in the system."

The editor was surprised, "So are you a supporter of the present system?"

"I am of the view that in society, there are always two classes--the higher and the lower--that is how they exist and that is how they shall continue to be. Any attempt to bridge this divide will lead to the annihilation of mankind."

This switched the duelling partners. Rai sahib moved out of the ring as the editor entered the fray, "You believe in class divisions in the twentieth century?"

"Yes, I strongly believe in it. The dogma you endorse isn't any modern in outlook. It has its roots in human greed. Buddha, Plato and Jesus all were proponents of equality. Ancient Greece, Assyria and Rome experimented with it and discovered that it failed because it was unnatural and against the grain of human nature."

"Your views astound me."

"Astonishment indicates ignorance."

"I am indebted to you! You should start a syndicated column on this topic."

"I am not a jackass. I will consider it only if you pay well."

"The principles you propound are amazing. You can make a killing writing about them."

"The distinction between you and me is that I follow what I preach. Your actions are different from your words. You can impose some sort of an equitable distribution of wealth but it is beyond you to distribute intelligence, character, beauty and talent in a similar fashion. The difference between classes is not material. We have seen the rich prostrate themselves at the feet of humble mendicants. Eminent personalities grovel before the beautiful-- is that not another form of social inequality? I am sure you will quote Russia when the only difference there is that the mill owner takes on the position of the government official. It is intelligence that is in control in both situations."

Betel leaves were brought in a tray. Rai sahib offered them along with cardamoms to his guests and said, "We have no objection in accepting the superiority of intellect if it is free of selfish motivations. This is the socialist ideal. The reason we bow our heads before mendicants and holy people is because they carry the aura of renunciation. We do want to offer respect and leadership to the intelligent but definitely do not want to give them rights over material wealth. A man's intellectual competence departs with his death but his property stays back with its potential to sow seeds of hatred and mistrust. We agree no society can be managed without intelligence; we simply want to defang the scorpion."

Another motor car arrived with Khanna, who was a bank manager and managing director of a sugar mill. He was accompanied by two ladies. The one wearing a khadi saree and a soulful expression was his wife, Kamini. The other ever smiling lady in high heels and spirits was Malti, recently returned from England with a medical degree and was now practicing medicine. She had easy access to the homes of the influential. She was modernity incarnate. Her demeanour was calm but she was bursting with energy. Not unduly shy, perfectly coiffeured, with ready wit, well versed with the sunny side of life, fairly aware of male psyche and quite conversant with the art of restrained flirting.

She extended her hand to Mehta and remarked, "I must admit, you have a very philosophical face. I wanted to seriously pick on you after going through your new book. You have ripped apart the metaphysicists to shreds. Do philosophers have to be so devoid of compassion?"

Mehta blushed. He was unmarried and mighty nervous with modern young women. He was chirpy in the company of his kind but no sooner was he confronted by smart woman, his wit and intelligence would freeze and stall, making him forget to extend even common courtesies to the fair sex.

Khanna asked her, "What's so unique about a philosopher's face, my lady?"

Malti looked at Mehta piteously, "Should I tell you, Mr. Mehta? If you do not mind, that is?"

Khanna was one of Miss Malti's fans. He would follow her wherever she went, hovering around her constantly. He wanted to monopolise her time and constantly thirsted for her attention.

Khanna gave a sly wink and said "Philosophers do not mind anything. This is their special virtue."

"In that case, please take this from me. Philosophers are as alive as stone– completely absorbed in themselves all the time. They would look at you but never notice your presence; you may speak to them but they are forever on their own trip as if floating in space."

Everyone guffawed loudly. Mr. Mehta seemed to shrink into the earth.

"My professor of philosophy in Oxford was a Mr. Husband..."

Khanna interjected, "Now that is a one-in-a-million name."

"Yes, and he was a bachelor..."

"Mr. Mehta is also a bachelor...."

"Bachelorhood is a philosophical affliction."

Mehta grabbed this opportunity, "Aren't you suffering from the same disease?"

"I have vowed to marry none but a philosopher but this species is mortally scared of marriage. My professor, Mr. Husband, would scurry for cover when he saw a woman coming. Most of his students were girls and if any of them approached him in his study, he would be petrified as if he was being stalked by a lion. We used to needle him quite a bit but actually he was quite a simpleton. His salary ran in a few thousands but I always saw him in one suit. He had a widowed sister, who managed his house and he hardly bothered to eat. Mortified of meeting people, he kept himself closeted in his room, studying most of the time. When it was time for his meals, his sister would enter through the inner door and quietly close his book and ask him to eat. His dinner time was predetermined and his sister turned on the lights to announce it. Once, when she wanted to close the book, he clamped his hands on it and a tug of war began between the brother and sister. Finally, she wheeled his chair into the dining room."

Rai sahib interjected, "Our Mehtaji is quite amiable and pleasant. I am sure he will never get into such a fracas."

"In that case, you are not a philosopher. How can we be happy worrying about the problems of the world, if we are already burdened by our own?"

Meanwhile, the editor was narrating the economic woes of his profession to Mrs. Khanna, "Ma'am, an editor's life is an unending wail to which no one lends an ear. On the contrary, they try to stifle it. The poor guy can neither resolve his own issues nor mitigate the sufferings of others. The public expects him to be in the forefront of all campaigns, go to jail, get flogged, and have his belongings attached all as part of his duty. But no one bothers about his problems. They expect him to be well versed in all subjects under the sun, but do not grant him the right to be a normal, living, breathing person. By the way, you do not pen anything these days. Why do you deprive me of an opportunity to be of help to you?"

Mrs. Khanna was fond of writing poetry. The editor would visit her on that count pretty often but lately, caught up as she was in domesticity, she was not able to write for a long time. Actually, it was more of the editor's encouragement than any real literary talent which prompted her to compose poetry.

"I really can't think of a subject to write on. Have you ever asked Miss Malti to write for you?"

The editor spoke with an air of indifference, "Her time is so precious. Only those with love, pain and dedication in their hearts can compose literature. Those who are too engrossed in money matters and the high life; cannot be serious writers?"

Kamini spoke with a delight that had shades of envy, "If you can coax her to write something, it will do wonders for your publication. The glitterati of Lucknow will scramble to subscribe to your paper."

"If wealth was my ambition, I would not be in the situation I am today. It's not that I am a stranger to the art of making money. If I want, I can be very rich but I rate literature above wealth. The sole aim of my life is to serve the cause of literature."

"That's fine but please add my name to your list of subscribers."

"Your name will be included amongst patrons, not subscribers."

"Keep that for the royals who can be of some use to you."

"You are my royalty. There is none more regal than you. I think one is royal if one possesses the virtues of kindness and wisdom. I hate sycophancy."

Kamini spoke mischievously, "Now isn't that sycophantic?"

The editor replied gravely, "This is not sycophancy. This is truth emanating from my heart."

Rai sahib called out "Mr. Editor, please, will you step this way? Miss Malti wants to have a word with you."

The editor's haughty composure vapourised in an instant. He sidled up to her a picture of humility and grace. Malti looked at him kindly, "I was just mentioning to them that editors are the only people, who actually scare me. You guys can make or break anyone any time. Once the Chief Secretary mentioned to me that he would consider himself fortunate if he could personally lock you up in jail."

Onkarnath's moustaches seemed to twirl up with pride. His eyes lit up with a proud gleam. Though he was quite sedate by nature, a challenge never failed to ignite his fighting spirit. His voice was stern when he spoke. "I am grateful for these mercies. At least I am talked about in such exalted circles, for whatever reasons. Please let the Chief Secretary know that Onkarnath is not one to be cowed down by threats. His writings will cease only when he dies. He has taken upon himself to uproot foul ethics and unbridled attitudes."

Miss Malti nudged him further, "I fail to understand your policy of not buying peace with the authorities, when all it takes is plain courtesy. You simply have to dilute a bit of the fire and brimstone in your writings and I can assure you, the government will be very helpful to you in many ways. You have experienced how little common people can do for you. You appealed to them, banked on their good sense, expressed your difficulties to them but to no avail. Why don't you give a chance to the government officials to prove themselves? Just try it and I guarantee you will be driving a motor car within three months or start receiving invites to all official programmes. The nationalists and the rich gentry, who presently appear least concerned, will beat a path to your door."

Onkarnath gathered himself with pride, "This is exactly what I will never do, my lady! I have always held my principles sacrosanct and will stand by them as long as I live. The world is teeming with those who lust for wealth but I am one of those few who stand for ideals."

"I think it is sheer egotism."

"That is your individual opinion."

"You say you have no attachment to wealth?"

"Not at the cost of my principles."

"If that is so, why does your paper carry advertisements of foreign goods? I do not find as many advertisements of foreign products in any other newspaper. You claim to be an idealist, a man of principles, but have no qualms in squandering the nation's wealth to promote foreign goods."

Onkarnath was left speechless. Finding him fumbling for words, Rai sahib spoke in his defence, "What is it that you want? That he should lose out on all fronts? How will he run the publication otherwise?"

Miss Malti knew no mercy. "If it is difficult to run the press, shut it down. No one has the right to promote foreign goods to finance his or her whims. If you feel the economic pinch so badly, why this song and dance about principles? These idealist papers annoy me no end. I want to set them on fire. A person, who cannot strike a balance between ideals and deeds, can never be an idealist."

Mehta perked up at this. He had expressed a similar sentiment minutes ago. When he realised this beautiful damsel had a likewise commitment and she was not merely a pretty socialite, his inherent hesitation gave way. "That's exactly what I was saying. A divide between precept and practice is sheer chicanery. It is deceit."

Miss Malti beamed "So we both think alike on this issue! Now I can also claim to be a philosopher."

Not willing to be a mute witness, Khanna was itching to put in his word. "Every pore of your being is imbued with philosophy," he exclaimed.

Malti reined him in promptly, "Oh! You mean you are also familiar with philosophical stuff? I thought you had dumped all philosophy in the river. How else can you come to control and manage so many companies and banks?"

Rai sahib leapt to his rescue, "Are you implying all philosophers must necessarily be bankrupt?"

"Of course, unless they conquer attachments, they can't claim to be philosophers."

"If that were so perhaps Mr. Mehta will also fit in that category."

Mehta jumped in almost combatively, "I have never claimed anything like that, Rai sahib. I believe that the tools of a blacksmith can never be the tools of a goldsmith. Would you like your scented garden to bloom like a thorny cactus? For me, wealth means merely those conveniences that make my life comfortable and meaningful. For me, money is not a stepping stone for my ego, it is simply an object of utility. I have no desire for money. You provide me with the things I need to survive and I will forego all money."

Onkarnath was an inclusivist. It was tough for him to digest the exclusivity of the individual. "If that were true, every worker will say he needs a thousand rupees to provide for appropriate conveniences to work."

"If you are convinced you can't do without that worker, you will have to provide him with those conveniences. And if another can do that work for less, you don't have to appease him at all," said Tankha.

"If workers had power and authority, wine and women would be as essential a need for them as it is for philosophers," added Onkarnath.

"Trust me; I would not envy them at all," said Mehta.

"If a woman is so important for a meaningful life, why don't you get married?" asked Onkarnath.

Mehta spoke without batting an eyelid- "Because I believe indulgence does not hamper the development of the soul. Marriage actually puts shackles on ones' life and imprisons the soul."

Khanna supported this viewpoint. "Ties and attachments are the old school. The new school of thought stands for unfettered indulgence."

Malti tried to trap him in, "Mrs. Khanna should be ready for a divorce."

"Let the divorce laws be framed first."

"Guess, you will be the first to utilise its provisions?"

Kamini scowled indifferently at Malti, as if to convey she was barely concerned.

Malti looked at Mehta and asked, "What are your views on the subject Mehta?

Mehta turned grave. Whenever he was called upon to comment on an issue, he did it with all the intensity at his command. "Marriage is a social contract and neither men nor women have a right to break that contract. They are free before they sign it; once done they are bound by its laws."

"Does it mean you oppose divorce?" asked Malti.

"Certainly."

"And what about the idea of unrestricted indulgence?"

"It is for those who are not interested in matrimony."

"Well, everyone is interested in the realisation of his or her soul. Why should anybody marry at all?" asked Malti

"Because everyone wants realisation of the soul but few are willing to forsake their pleasures," said Mehta.

"Which do you think is superior? Marriage or the single life?" asked Malti.

"From the point of view of society, it is married life. From the individual's viewpoint, definitely the unattached life," said Mehta in all his wisdom.

It was time for the bow and arrow ceremony that would be followed by the theatrical performance and dinner afterwards. Preparations for dinner were in full swing. The guests had separate living quarters. The Khannas had two rooms for themselves and other guests had occupied the remaining rooms. All had gone to their quarters to change and were gradually trooping into the dining hall. There was no discrimination of caste in this gathering and everyone sat and ate in a common undemarcated group. Except for the editor Onkarnath, who went to his room where he was served his refreshments, the whole gathering was present in the main dining hall. Kamini Khanna had a headache so she excused herself from the dinner table. There were no less than twenty five guests in the hall. Meat and liquor was served among other food specialties. Rai Sahib had managed to procure the choicest brands of liquor under the label of 'life saving medicines'. There were a number of meat dishes on the menu--fowl, mutton, quail, deer and peacocks.

As dinner was about to be served, Miss Malti queried, "Where is the editor, SahibRai sahib? Please send someone to call him here."

Rai sahib said, "He is a *Vaishnav* and a pure vegetarian. Why do you want to call him here and hurt his religious sensitivities?"

"Oh Come on, it will be an entertaining spectacle, if nothing!"

She spied a certain gentleman and called out to him grandly, "Welcome, Khurshid sahib; I entrust this assignment to you. You will be tested for your capabilities."

Mirza Khurshid was a very fair man with light coloured eyes, a rather rotund frame and shining bald pate. He was attired in a smart tunic and tight pajamas. A hat adorned his head as a final accessory to his sartorial make-up. He voted for the nationalists and was a Sufi Muslim. He had gone for the holy Haj pilgrimage twice but had a passion for liquor. He would often joke about not getting too worried about faith, since he was quite lax on proscribed habits and other regulations of religion. A great entertainer, he was a lively person without a care in the world. He was a contractor and earned a neat sum every month.

Mirza's travails began when he fell for a certain socialite lady. He was in all sorts of trouble. There were litigations, threats of imprisonment and a directive to leave the city within twenty four hours. He left everything and bolted with only fifty thousand in his pocket. His agents lived in Bombay. He assumed he would negotiate all that they owed him and settle for an amount, which would suffice for a comfortable existence in banishment but they turned the tables and he ended up losing his fifty thousand to them.

Crestfallen, Mirza went straight to Lucknow. Enroute, he came across another charlatan on the train who robbed him of his gold ring, watch and whatever money he carried on his person. When he arrived at Lucknow, he had nothing with him other than the clothes he wore. Rai sahib was an old acquaintance. With some help from him and other friends, he opened a shoe shop which was now the most flourishing showroom in the city, with a daily turnover of five hundred rupees. He garnered such public confidence that he earned a place in the Council.

Without budging from his seat, he replied- "Oh no, please. I will not offer myself to disturb someone's faith. You should do that. The challenge should be that you make him drink liquor too. It will be a test of your beauty and wiles."

A number of voices rose in unison from all sides of the room-"Yes, yes, Miss Malti, show us what you can do!"

Malti challenged Mirza, "Will you reward me for that?"

"A bagful of hundred rupees will await your victory."

"Hah," she clicked her tongue, "I will not ruin his faith for a mere hundred."

"OK, you name your price."

"One thousand, not an *anna* less."

"Ok. Done!"

"Not so fast - get that amount and put it in Mr. Mehta's safekeeping right now."

Mirzaji fished out a hundred rupee note from his pocket and waving it around the assembly, said, "Brothers! Now this is a matter of prestige. If we are not able to meet Miss Malti's challenge, we will be shamed. Had I that sort of money, I would have gladly showered a million on her beauty. A poet once confessed he would forsake the vistas of Bukhara and Samarkand for the beauty spot on his beloved's cheeks. Now, today come up and offer whatever amount you have at the moment. Such a spectacle is going cheap even for a million rupees. Behold how the imperial beauty queen of Lucknow plays out her magic on an unsuspecting prey."

As soon he concluded his speech, Mirza began searching the pockets of the men present in the room. The first to be searched was Mr. Khanna, he had five rupees.

Mirza made a face and said, "Oh Mr. Khanna! Fie on you! You are the director of so many companies, earn so much but yet you carry a mere five rupees? Kindly go to Mrs. Khanna and get at least a hundred from her."

Khanna muttered sheepishly, "She won't have anything with her. No one knew there will be a search campaign in this party? But in any case let me go and ask."

"Oh no Mr. Khanna, you are not moving an inch from here. Mr. Mehta, you are a philosopher, an expert in human behaviour. Please see to it that your reputation is not tarnished."

Mehta would get high after downing a few drinks. His philosophical muse would evaporate in alcohol and be replaced by a jovial exuberance. He went to Mrs. Khanna's room at once but returned almost immediately with a glum expression.

But soon he broke into peals of laughter and brandished five hundred rupee notes.

A chorus of 'wows' echoed in the room.

Mirza leapt and hugged Mehta. "Mehta you are wonderful. Now tell us how you worked this magic?"

Mehta stood very straight and spoke with heavy red eyes, "It was no big deal! I went up, knocked and asked permission to enter. She said, 'Oh, Mehtaji, come right in'. I went in and told her that we were playing Bridge and Miss Malti had lost five hundred rupees in the game. Though no one had the courage to ask her for the amount, she herself volunteered to give away her ring which was worth a thousand. When Mrs. Khanna heard this, she smiled and dipped into her purse and handed me these five beauties and told me she does not leave home without some real money. 'You never know when you might need it'- that's what she said."

Khanna spoke with visible irritation, "If this is what our professors are like, God save our universities."

Mirza rubbed salt on the wound. "Oh come on! It is not such a big amount that you have to feel so low. I am sure this is equal to your day's earning. Just imagine you fell ill and had to spend so much money on your treatment. Moreover, this is for Miss Malti, the lady who has a cure for your aching heart."

Malti swung a hook, "Careful, Mirzaji! There is no need to get personal."

Mirza was contrite, "Pardon me, lady."

Tankha was searched next. He had ten in his pocket. Mehta came up with eight *annas* in his. A few men came up and gave one or two rupees on their own. When the collection was counted it was still short of three hundred rupees.

Rai sahib volunteered to chip in with that amount.

The editor had nibbled at nuts and some fruits and lay in his room, resting his back when Rai sahib walked in and told him that Miss Malti was looking for him.

Quite pleased that she remembered him, he got up and came back with Rai sahib and took a seat in the hall.

Meanwhile, the tables were cleared and Malti stepped up to greet him.

The editor was humble- "No formalities please! Kindly don't rise for me. I am not such a great person."

Malti spoke in a humble tone, "Perhaps you consider this formality; I think it a rightful honour. You might not think too high of yourself and its good that you are not haughty, but everyone present here is well acquainted with your service to the cause of literature and the nation. Perhaps, no one recognises the true value of your contribution to society but in my opinion the time is not far when it will be so. In fact, I think the time is well on us that streets will be named after you; your pictures will adorn the walls of town halls across the state. All stirrings of awakening in society are due to the untiring efforts made by your publication. You will be glad to know that your supporters share your vision of village transformation and upliftment and want to chip in. They have an intense desire to launch an initiative called the Village Upliftment Trust and make you its Chairman."

This was the first time Omkarnath had an opportunity to rub shoulders with such eminent people. He did speak at sundry events and was the member of a few clubs and associations but was more or less never included in the inner circle of the educated elite. Since he was unable to enter their charmed circle, he blasted them for their introverted selfish attitudes. His writings were pithy, sharp, bent towards exaggeration, thus creating the impression of an irrepressible loudmouth.

And today that same audience was honoring him! He wondered whether the editors of Swaraj, Independent India and Hunter were aware of his achievements and how providence was shining on him this day. Honest effort never goes waste- this was the wisdom of the sages. His worth appreciated in his own eyes as he pondered over this.

Gratified, he said –"My lady, you are pulling me onto a thorny path. Whatever work I've done was my duty towards society. I think the credit should go to the ideal for which I have devoted my life. My humble submission is that the Chairman's position should go to some other worthy person. I do not believe in decorated positions. I am a servant and that is how I want to remain."

Miss Malti was determined not to accept his contention. She insisted that he must accept that position. She said she did not consider any other person more suited for the honour and added, "A person who wields a magic pen, has such proficiency with words and whose personality is equally attractive, how can he claim to be unworthy? The time has come when talent must finally come to the forefront. The editor must accept this responsibility."

Miss Malti would be the Secretary of the organisation and a fund of one thousand rupees was already raised by the assembled enthusiasts - and all this when the drive to raise funds was yet to take off! A pleasant sensation took over Onkarnath's mind. The initial faint tremor of joy in his heart assumed the dimensions of grave responsibility. He said-"I hope you realise, Miss Malti, this is a very serious undertaking and you will have to devote a lot of time to it. On my part, I can assure you that you will never find me slack in my duties."

"Your worst critic will not say that you have ever hedged your responsibilities", said Mirza, encouragingly.

Miss Malti noticed the headiness of liquor rising amongst the gathering and hence spoke with urgency, "If we were not serious, we would not have formed this association and elected you as its Chairman. We could easily have selected some rich person and raised enough funds in the bargain. That is not our motive; we are for serious positive work and the biggest vehicle for our objectives is your publication. We have decided that it should be publicised in every town and village and its subscribers' list should be increased to a minimum of twenty thousand as soon as possible. The chairmen of most municipalities and district boards are our close friends. In fact, a few are present in this room. Even if they take five hundred copies each, the figure will touch twenty five thousand. Besides Rai sahib and Mirzaji are of the opinion that a proposal should be placed in the Council to make it obligatory for all villages to be either supplied a copy of Bijli officially, or some government help be extended to the publication. They are quite confident this proposal will be accepted."

Onkarnath was dizzy with headiness – "We will have to take a delegation to the Governor."

Mirza Khurshid seconded him "Sure, most certainly."

Miss Malti went on, "Our association has also decided that when the next seat is vacated in the Council, we will propose your name as a candidate. We will take care of all the details. You simply have to say yes. You do not have to bother about expenses, publicity and any running around."

Onkarnath's eyes shone brightly. He spoke with measured humility, "I am your servant. Your order is my command."

"We expected this from you. So far, we had backed false gods and gained nothing. We have found a true guide and guru in you and on this special occasion, we must be united in committing our collective faith and pledge to douse our egos and pride. From today, there is none amongst us who is a Brahmin or low caste. There are no Hindus and Muslims amongst us, there are no divisions of class amongst us, we are all progeny of one mother and we share a common life of dedication. Those who believe in distinctions of caste, class or creed have no place in our midst. An organisation headed by a noble chairman like Onkarnath has to be bereft of all differences based on class and caste. Anybody who has any objections to these rules or has any sort of reservation is welcome to dissociate himself right now."

Rai sahib expressed his doubts-"I don't think unity in principle implies we give up our food habits and preferences. For example I do not drink. Does that mean I should dissociate myself from the association?"

There was little softness in her tone when Malti spoke, "Definitely. You will have to go. You cannot be a part of this group and exercise any sort of discrimination."

Mehta said testily, "I am afraid I am not sure if our chairman shares the same views regarding food habits."

Onkarnath's face took on a sallow pallor. Why did this idiot have to pipe in with this discordant note? The rascal was unnecessarily digging up ghosts to shatter this dream before it took off.

Malti looked steadily at him with a quizzical glance as she responded to Mehta confidently, "Your doubts are unfounded, Mr. Mehta. You assume such a devoted advocate of national unity, a poet of such sensitivity and a man with such a generous heart will have anything to do with this shameful discrimination? Such a doubt is an insult to his national commitment."

Onkarnath's visage lit up all over again. A shadow of contented happiness spread like a soft glow over him.

Malti went on in the same breath, "And more than that, it will be an affront to his chivalry. Is there any decent man who will refuse a glass offered by a lady? That will be an insult to all womanhood at whose altar the greatest warriors kneel in chivalrous respect. Come, let's bring on the drinks, we will first raise a toast to our chairman."

Ice, liquor and soda kept ready on the sidelines, were brought in immediately. Malti presented a glass of the amber coloured liquid to Onkarnath with her own hands with such a comely look that his entire determination and ideas of superiority vapourised in an instant. His mind worked differently. He thought to himself that it was perfectly fine if his forefathers never tasted liquor. When did they ever get an opportunity to do so? They were content with reading and reciting holy books. Where would they get liquor from and if they did, where would sit and drink it? They were different people. They did not travel by train, did not drink water if it was not drawn the same day and refused to learn English, considering it a sin to do so. Times had changed. Unless you kept in step with them, you would be thrown by the wayside. If such a beautiful lady offered poison, one should be obliged to take it without questions. Even kings and princes seldom got such an opportunity that stood in front of him that moment. How could he reject it?

He took the glass from her and lowering his eyes in mute gratitude, raised it to his lips, drained it in one go and turned a confident look at his audience as if asking them whether this was enough proof of his credibility.

No sooner had the drink travelled down Onkarnath's gullet that the whole assembly broke into a roar of applause. It was as if a caged beast was let out of a limiting barricade. 'Bravo, Lady!' 'That was great!' 'Simply amazing, Miss Malti', 'The fortress of religion has been breached'!

The liquor down his gullet released the romantic aspect of Onkarnath. He smiled and said, "I placed my faith on a platter in Miss Malti's delicate hands. I have a firm conviction that it is safe in her possession. May a hundred such faiths be sacrificed at her altar!"

The hall resounded with laughter.

The editor's face was bloated and there was already a heaviness in his eyes. He filled another glass and said, "This one is for Miss Malti's health. Please drink and bless her."

Everyone downed their glasses immediately.

At that moment, Khurshid came in with a garland and placed it around the editor's neck and said "Gentlemen, I have composed a few lines in honour of our chairman. If you permit, may I recite them?"

A roar of 'Hear! Hear!' reverberated across the room.

Onkarnath did take a bit of cannabis off and on but this was his first experience of liquor. The intoxication of cannabis would creep on him softly, in gentle waves, much like a dream and gradually envelope him like clouds gathering in the sky. He remained conscious of it every moment. He would be aware of the fluency of his words as well as the flow of conversation. But the headiness of liquor pounced on him like a lion and held him firmly in its jaws. Awareness was fast deserting him. He was totally oblivious of what he was saying. This was no romantic fantasy of a dream; it was a state of wakeful existence in which forms merged into formlessness.

Somehow his mind told him that reciting a tome in his honour was totally uncalled for. He banged his hand on the table and slurred - "No, never. There will not be any recitation here at all. Not at all! I am the chairman. I order this. I can dissolve this assembly right now. I can throw everyone out. No one can do anything to me. There is no other chairman except me."

Mirza folded his hands and said "Sir, this citation is full of nothing except your praise."

The editor blinked at him with bloodshot but dull eyes, "Why do you praise me? Why? Come on, speak up. Why do you praise me? I am nobody's slave. Is there any idiot who provides for me? I am the editor of Bijli. I am everybody's slave. Yes, everybody's slave. I am the dust of your feet. Malti is a goddess, she is Laxmi, she is Sarasvati...."

As he blurted senselessly, he lurched towards Malti, stumbled and fell on his face on the floor. Mirza Khurshid ran forward to hold him. He lay him down on the floor and whispered for all to hear- "May your soul rest in peace! If you permit, may we bury you?"

Rai sahib cautioned, "Just you watch out. He will be really furious tomorrow. He will roast everyone in his publication. And you will rue what you did to him. He is one rascal who never forgets an insult. It's really surprising how such an ass can write so well."

A couple of men lifted the editor and took him to his room where they settled him on his bed. Meanwhile, in the pavilion the bow and arrow ceremony was on. Quite a few junior level officials had reached the venue and were engrossed in the activities when all of a sudden an Afghan strode into the hall. Tall and well built with a huge moustache, he had a broad chest and eyes that burnt with a fearless passion. He wore a loose tunic above baggy pajamas with a waistcoat lined with fine embroidery, a fabulous turban on his head and on his shoulders he carried a leather bag and a gun, and a sword which was tied around his waist. He appeared seemingly out of nowhere and thundered angrily, "Halt! No one leaves this place. One of my men has been robbed. Whoever is the headman of this place has robbed my man. You must pay up for that. You will have to return every single *paisa*. Where is your headman? Get him here fast!"

Rai sahib stepped forward- "What loot and robbery are you talking about? It's men like you who are experts at those things not gentile people like us. What is it that you want?"

The Afghan glowered and hit the floor with the butt of his rifle- "You dare to talk to me like that? You looted my man. I am the chief of the Afghans in this area. There are fifty of us. Our man was on a collection spree and you stole one thousand rupees that he had. First you robbed him and now you act as if you don't know. Let me show you what it is to loot people. My men will be here any moment. We will take everything from your village. We'll see how you stop us."

Sensing the Afghan's mood, Khanna tried to slip out of the room quietly. The man yelled at him, "Where do you think you are going? I will kill anyone who tries to leave this hall. I will not let anyone escape from here. You have stolen one thousand from us. You rob people and sit here drinking with your concubines."

Miss Malti avoided his eyes and tried to sidle past him. He pounced on her like a hawk and stood before her, "You tell these men to return my money or else I will take you away with me to my camp. I like you, beautiful woman. Tell them to pay up now or you are coming with me. You are so charming!" Turning to the rest he said, "I have fifty of my men around this place. I am the chief of my tribe of ten thousand men. I can take on the Emir of Kabul. The British government pays me ten thousand to buy peace with me. If you do not return my thousand rupees, I will plunder your village and take away your women. There will be rivers of blood. Now it's for you to decide."

There was terror writ large on everyone's face. Miss Malti was not her usual chirpy self any more. Khanna was shivering. The poor man lived in a single storey house because he was afraid of falling off the stairs. Despite the heat, he slept indoors. Rai sahib prided himself as the headman of village. He considered it extremely embarrassing to be scared of a *Pathan* on his own turf but who could argue with a gun? These men might be fat headed but they were quick on the trigger. Had there been no gun, Rai sahib was in a mood to lock horns with the man. The problem was the scoundrel was not allowing anyone to leave the hall. If somehow news could be sent out, the whole village could band together and beat the hell out of him or his men.

Finally, he mustered up courage and confronted him, "We are not petty thieves and robbers here. I am a Member of the Council and this lady is a well known medical practitioner from Lucknow. We are all respectable people. We are totally unaware who robbed your men. Kindly go and report the matter to the police."

Khan stomped his foot and slung the gun off his shoulders, changed his stance and roared, "Stop this nonsense." He then ground his shoes on the floor and said, "This is how I treat Members of the Council. I fear no one except Allah. If you don't give me back my money right now, I will kill all of you."

Rai sahib almost fell on the table when he saw the barrel of the gun pointed at him. This was a strange predicament. The scoundrel stuck to the refrain that he had stolen his money. He wasn't open to reason and did not allow anyone to leave the hall. The servants and the guards were occupied with the bow and arrow ceremony. In any case, these people were slow to respond; they had to be pushed a dozen times before they reacted to any instructions. If only one guard would glance in this direction or come this way, Khan would never know what hit him.

Mirza stared with blank eyes at the scene before him. "What a shame! Just the day I didn't get my pistol along or I would have shown him what it takes."

Khanna appeared as if he was about to burst into tears. "Throw some money at him and get rid of him."

Rai sahib turned to Malti, "What do you say?"

Malti was livid. "Well, the worse is already happening. I am being insulted with disgusting impunity and all you do is watch. There are so many men here but none has the courage to dash out and raise an alarm. Why don't try and snatch his gun? At worst, he can open fire and a few will get hurt. So be it!"

The opinion in the assembly on getting hurt was very different from hers. If some foolhardy person did step forward to challenge him and in a fit of anger the Afghan shot him, the repercussions would be terrible. At best, the police would send the killer to the gallows though that was also not guaranteed. He was the chief of a big tribe. The government would think twice before hanging him. There would be extraneous pressures. Where does justice stand when confronted by the pulls of politics? It would be no surprise, if a counter case was filed against them and they are taken into protective custody. What a mess! Everything was going so well, there was so much laughter and mirth; by now everyone would have been happily enjoying the theatrical performance. This man had come and spoilt it all.

Khanna reprimanded Malti, "You rile at us as if it is a crime to try to be cautious. It is normal for anyone to worry about saving his life. There's no shame in it. It pains us to observe how cheaply you value our lives. It is an issue of merely a thousand rupees then you have a thousand right now and it has come to you for nothing. Why don't you pay him off with it? You are inviting ridicule on yourself, what can we do about it?"

Rai sahib bristled agitatedly, "This lout dare make a move towards Malti and I will take him head on. He is just another man after all."

Mirza sahib shook his head apprehensively "Rai sahib, you have no idea how hellish such men can be. If he starts shooting, he will cut down everybody. They are sharp shooters, all of their kind."

Tankha had arrived in the village with visions of adding to his political clout. He wanted to have a good time and drive back home in peace and here he was involved in these sordid goings-on. "The easiest way out is what Khanna has suggested. It's an issue of a thousand rupees. The money is with us. Where's the problem? Just give it to him. Where is the need to discuss this endlessly?"

Miss Malti looked at Tankha with hate and scorn.

"I was not aware you are all such cowards"

"Neither was I aware that you have so much lust for money. Especially for that which is not your own."

"If you can see me insulted, I am sure you can let your women be insulted as well."

"I am sure you will also not mind sacrificing men folk from your household for a few measly rupees."

Khan was listening to their altercations in irritated silence. He spoke menacingly- "That's enough! I am standing here for such a long time and you are not able to decide one way or another." He took out a whistle from his pocket and said, "I am giving you one final chance. If you don't hand over the money, I will blow this whistle and this place will be swarming with my men. Understand?"

As he said so he gave a leering look at Malti

"You come with me, sweetie! I think you are a lovely woman. I will be ready to die for you. So many men here seem to have a soft corner for you but none has the courage to protect you. They are cowards. I will show to you what real love is. One command from you and I will drive a knife in my heart. Come with me."

Mirza pleaded with her, "Malti, for god's sake, give him the thousand rupees."

Khanna folded his hands, "Have mercy on us Malti."

Rai sahib was furious. "Not on my life! Tonight either we die or teach him a lesson he won't forget in his life."

Tankha was mad at Rai sahib. "That is foolhardiness. Why do you want to walk into the jaws of death."

But Malti was on another plane of existence. The lust in Khan's eyes had assured her and she had started relishing a strange fantasy. Her heart was responding to the raw appeal of his earthiness in contrast to the wimps, who surrounded her. She'd seen through the listlessness of sophisticated people and her instincts drew her towards this Afghan's fatal attraction. Her mind gravitated towards his raw animal-like pull as one would run to watch a mad elephant fight immediately after sitting through a concert of classical music.

She walked up to him and stated without a trace of fear. "You will not get any money."

Khan stretched his hand in front of him "I will grab you even as you stand here and whisk you away"

"You dare not do this in the presence of so many men."

"I can take you away from the midst of one thousand men."

"You will die."

"To have you as my beloved, I am ready to die a hundred times."

He caught hold of Malti and pulled her to him.

In that very instant, the door opened and Hori stepped into the room.

In the play he was enacting the role of King Janak's gardener. His performance had the villagers in splits. He was wondering why Rai sahib had not arrived to watch him enact his role. As he walked in, he was dumbstruck by the scene. Everyone inside the hall was standing still, absolutely quiet and trembling, watching the Afghan intently with pleading eyes; full of fear and foreboding, as he was moving to pull Malti towards himself. Within seconds, his peasant brain interpreted the situation.

Rai sahib's voice cracked through the silence, "Hori! Run! Call the police!"

Hori turned to bolt but Khan swung before him and pointed the rifle at his chest "Where do you think you are going, you swine? I'll kill you."

Hori was an uneducated fellow. Though the sight of a policeman's red turban was sufficient to send a shiver down his spine but he could take on a mad bull with just his stick. He was not a coward and was ready to deal aggression with aggression. And when the master called out for help, he wouldn't blink before jumping into the open jaws of death.

He sprang forward and held the Khan's waist and gaive him a cross tackle that floored him in a flash even as he cursed loudly in Persian. Hori jumped on him, straddling his chest and pulled wildly at his beard. The beard tore off his face and came into Hori's hands. Khan threw off his startled opponent and stood up very straight.

Oh, this was Mehta! Our very own Mehta!

Benumbed at first, everyone surrounded him. A few hugged him, some patted his back but there was no hint of a smile or trace of pride on Mehta's face. He stood there, quietly; as if nothing had happened at all. Malti pouted at him in mock anger, "Where did you learn to masquerade so well? I am still trembling in panic."

Finally, he smiled and spoke "I was simply testing the bravado of these gentlemen. If it has caused any distress, I appeal for forgiveness."

❁❁❁

7

By the time the masquerade came to an end in the hall, religious ceremonies had concluded in the pavilion and theatrical performances were about to begin. However, the people in the hall had absolutely no interest in it. The only person to attend the performances was Mehta and he was there till the very end. He enjoyed himself thoroughly applauding profusely with cries of 'Once more, once more' whenever they delivered a pithy dialogue.

Rai sahib had scripted a satire on a rural *Zamindaar,* who went overboard with litigation on the slightest pretext. The audience was entertained by the comical character of the *Zamindaar,* especially when he delivered commonplace dialogues littered with legalese. The villagers loved the plot and the fact that he filed a case against his wife for not serving his meals on time. The manner in which the *Zamindaar* brought fake witnesses and how they goofed up in front of the magistrate, brought the house down.

Everything about the play was so energetic and full of sparkling witticisms that when it was over, Mehta went up and embraced the main actor on the stage and announced individual medals for the entire cast. His opinion about Rai sahib's literary worth went up many notches. Rai sahib was backstage, directing and supporting the cast. Mehta ran up and hugged him profusely and spoke as if mesmerised, "I had no idea you had such sharp wit and vision."

The next day, they decided to go on a hunt. The plan was to drive to the riverside, cook food outdoors, swim and frolic around in the water, and return by the evening.

Mrs. Khanna's head was still aching so she stayed back and editor Onkarnath fuming over last night's incident, was busy planning a series of articles to get back at his tormentors. He was furious. All of them were seasoned scoundrels; they flaunted ill begotten wealth and were downright arrogant. They were not bothered about anything outside their world. Their sole interest was self aggrandisement and sensory pleasures.

Of what use was Mehta's philosophic ideas to a man, whose wife was ill and he was unable to raise money for her treatment? Of what use was his philosophy to a man, whose only concern was to somehow pay the next month's rent. These self-proclaimed philosophers like Mehta, would only wake up the day when the revolutionaries punched them between the eyes and compelled them to plough the field with their manicured hands.

And Malti, who was so experienced in most things, had the gall to let people address her as 'Miss'. She refused to marry 'because it would constrict her life'. Her motto seemed to be to enjoy endlessly, demolish every ideal and break every spiritual rule of life. For people like her, if parents were a bother, she would dump them. If marriage was restrictive, she would break it.

The hunting party departed at 8 A.M. Malti was very excited at the prospects of having a gaggle of admirers at her side. Khanna had never been on a hunt and gunfire made him tremble but if Malti was going, he would not be left behind. Tankha was angling for an opportunity to talk about the impending elections. The hunt was a good opportunity to raise the topic. Rai sahib had not visited that part of his constituency so this was the perfect opportunity to reach out. It was important to visit the area, occasionally, to forge personal contact with the people.

Mirza Khurshid loved adventure, especially if it involved unknown thrills. Mehta was the sole person actually excited about the real hunt. Rai sahib wanted to bring along food stuff, cooks, servants, porters and palanquin bearers but Mr. Mehta firmly shot the idea down.

Khanna protested, "Won't we eat there? Or do you want us to starve?"

Mehta replied, "Yes, we will eat, of course. But today we will try to do everything on our own. We should try to see if we can survive without attendants. Miss Malti will cook for us. We can borrow utensils and leaf plates from locals in the jungle and there is absolutely no dearth of firewood. And we will have to hunt for food."

Malti said, "Please keep me out of this. You twisted my wrist so badly last evening that it still hurts."

"We will do the cooking. You merely give instructions," Mehta corrected himself.

Mirza Khurshid said, "Okay we will hunt a deer, roast it, eat it and enjoy a jungle siesta afterwards."

This proposal had many takers and ultimately they left in two cars, one driven by Malti and the other by Rai sahib. After a 20 mile drive, they entered hilly terrain with rows of hills on both sides of the road. The road turned serpentine around a sudden steep decline and brought the river in view clearly. It appeared as a thin ribbon, emaciated like a sickly patient. They drove the cars towards a clearing below a dense spread of banyan foliage and stepped out into the bracing breeze. They decided to split in three groups of two's and proceed for the hunt, promising to return to the same spot by twelve noon. Malti went with Mehta as Khanna fumed silently. This negated the very basis for his joining the trip. Had he known Malti would ditch him, he might have turned back on the way. Tankha and Khurshid did not have any opinion or preferences. The three pairs of hunters went in different directions.

Walking some distance with Mehta on the rough forest path, Malti paused for breath and said, "You walk so fast. Can't you wait a while?"

"We have not walked a mile yet. You are tired already?" said Mehta with a smile.

"I am not tired but we can still stop for a while."

"It is not right to halt unless we complete our business."

"I have not come on a hunting expedition."

Mehta looked at her with a puzzled expression, "Oh? I wasn't aware of this. What was your motivation other than hunting?"

"What should I say?"

They spied a flock of deer, grazing in the distance. Both hid behind a rock and taking aim, Mehta fired at them. He missed. Alerted, the deer bounded gracefully out of sight.

Malti looked at him, "Now what?"

"Nothing. We keep walking. There will be more."

They walked in silence. Malti paused again and said, "The heat is killing. Let us sit under this tree for a moment."

"Not now. If you want, you may rest here. I am not sitting down."

"You are merciless."

"I cannot rest till I find game."

"You may kill me in that case. Anyway, tell me, why did you annoy me so much last night? I was terribly mad at you. Remember what you said to me - 'Sweetie, why don't you come with me'? I didn't know you could be so mischievous. Tell me truthfully; could you have actually nabbed me away like that?"

Mehta ignored the question as if he had not heard it.

Both continued walking. With the cruel June sun above their heads and a stony rough path below their feet, it was a tough walk. Malti sat down on the ground.

Mehta looked back and said, "OK, you sit right there. I will soon come back."

"You will leave me all alone?"

"I know you can protect yourself."

"How do you know that?"

"That is how all modern women are. They do not want a man's protective company. They want to walk as equals."

Malti blushed and said, "You are nothing but a philosopher, Mehta."

There was a peacock sitting on a tree nearby. Mehta aimed and fired. The peacock flapped its wings and flew away.

"Good. My curses are working."

"You have not cursed me. You have cursed yourself. Had we hit the bird, we could have had a break for ten minutes. Now you have to walk."

Malti stretched out her hand to hold Mehta's and heaved herself up, "Philosophers are heartless creatures. Good you didn't marry. Your attitude would have killed her. But I will not let you off so easy. You can't walk away from me."

In one brisk movement, Mehta loosened her grip on his hand and moved on.

Malti's eyes misted. "I say stop this instant or I'll hit my head on this rock."

Mehta walked faster. When he had gone twenty steps or so she got up and ran after him. There was no joy in resting all alone. When she caught up with him she snapped, "I didn't realise you are such a beast."

"I will present the deerskin to you when I get my quarry."

"Deerskin be damned. I am not talking to you any more today."

"If we do not hunt an animal and others come up with a decent game, I will be very embarrassed."

As the road bent forward, they came across a wide riverine chasm. Craggy rocks surrounded it. The water current was swift and made waves as the river splashed around the rocks. The sun was above their heads and sunlight sparkled merrily in a blinding dance over the waves.

Malti spoke in a relieved voice, "Now we have to turn back."

"Why? We have to go across to the other side. We will find game on that side."

"The current is so swift. I will be washed away."

"Fine! You sit here. I am going."

"You go if you insist. I am not so reckless."

Mehta stepped into the water and moved step by step, balancing himself carefully in the gushing water. With every step he took, the water level rose perilously higher till it almost reached his chest.

As she saw Mehta wading through the water, Malti panicked. She was surprised at how concerned she had become about this man. Her voice was on an edge as she spoke, "Don't go further. You will fall and lose balance. The water is deep. Wait, I am also coming."

"No, you keep away. The current is swift. You will be swept away."

"You don't worry about that. I am coming."

Malti raised her saree above her knees and waded into the river. The water rose up to her waist in barely a couple of steps.

It was Mehta's turn to panic. He waved at her frantically, signalling her to turn back to the shore. "Malti, don't go further. The water level is up to your neck."

Malti took another step. "So be it! If you want me to die, I'd rather die with you."

She stood her ground, swaying perilously in the current as it threatened to dislodge her any moment. Mehta turned back and coming up to her, held her hand firmly in a strong grip.

Malti looked at him drunkenly with eyes that flashed with anger, "I have never seen a more uncaring and callous person than you. You are totally insensitive.

Anyway, it's your day, do what you like. One day I will get back at you."

Malti felt her feet lose their balance against the strong current. She grabbed Mehta's gun and clung to him dangerously. He gave her an assuring look and said, "The flow is very fast. Let me lift you."

Malti raised an eyebrow, "Is it so necessary to go to the other side?"

Mehta didn't say a word. He hooked the gun in the crick of his neck and lifted her on his shoulder with both hands.

Malti could barely hide her excitement, "What if somebody sees us like this?

It does look a bit improper."

A few steps later she spoke once again, "Tell me, if I were to drown, would you feel any remorse? I bet you won't."

Mehta spoke with hurt in his voice, "You think I am not human?"

"To tell you the truth, frankly that is how I feel."

"You really mean it?"

"What do you think?"

"What do I think? Huh? Will tell you someday..."

The water rose menacingly around Mehta's neck. Malti's heart hammered furiously against her breast. "Mehta, for the love of God, please do not go further. Don't take another step or else I will jump into the water."

In that precarious moment of panic Malti remembered God, who she ridiculed at every opportunity. She knew there was no God in attendance watching over her and would never come to save her but there was no other source from where she could glean courage and fortitude, which she needed desperately at that moment.

The water level started dipping. Malti felt relieved and told him to set her down.

"No. Keep quiet and stay there. What if there is a dip ahead?"

"You must think how selfish I am?

"Then pay me for this favour."

"What remuneration do you want?"

"A promise, that if you are in a similar predicament in life, you will call me again."

They came ashore. Malti wrung and squeezed her *saree* quietly. She upturned her shoes to dry them and washed her hands and feet afresh. The cryptic and uncertain import of what he had just said continued to play on her mind.

Crossing the river was an adventurous experience and she remarked, "I will always remember this day."

Mehta asked her if she was scared at any point.

"Initially I was scared but soon realised you could take care of both of us."

Mehta looked at Malti proudly.

"Will you ever realise how delightful it is for me to hear this?"

"You never made any efforts to make me realise it. Instead, all you do is drag me through jungles and forests, and now we have to go back through this river again.

You've pushed us in such a perilous situation. If I were to ever live with you, I bet it won't last for a day."

Mehta smiled. He was quite aware what the words implied.

"You think I am such a rascal? And if I say I love you and want to marry you- how would you react to that?"

"Who will marry an insensitive person like you? Your indifference will kill whoever dares to do so."

The look in her eyes conveyed a different story that said she knew he wasn't as dumb as he wanted her to believe.

Mehta spoke as if alerted to the gravity of the conversation, "You are right, Malti. I'll not be able to please any lady. No woman can carry on a charade of love with me. I will reach into the core of her being and soon become disinterested in her."

Malti shivered at the harsh reality that was hidden in those words.

"What sort of life will satisfy you?"

"The one that is same inside out. For me appearances, beauty and sophisticated bearing are significant but only to a certain degree. I need food that provides nutrition to the soul. I have no desire for saucy and spicy stuff."

Malti drew herself up with a deep breath, "You are impossible! Such a crafty man! Now tell me, what do you think of me?"

Mehta smiled and said in a playful accent, "You are intelligent, talented, kind and full of life. You can make sacrifices but I am afraid you are incapable of love."

Malti threw him a sharp glance, "You are a liar. Every bit a liar! I am highly sceptical about your claims of understanding or reaching into a woman's heart."

It was twelve o'clock but Malti was not tired anymore and was in no hurry to get back. Today's conversation perked her up with an entirely new energy. She had floored innumerable intellectuals and political types with her conversational brilliance or merely by raising a coquettish eyebrow. It was impossible for her to build a stable foundation on those shifting sands. Today she had come upon a steady, hard, rock-like base that sent sparks of fire when hit by a shovel. Its firmness attracted her with growing intensity.

A shot rang out in the air. A partridge flying across the crevice was hit, yet it flew awkwardly but finally fell into the water, bobbing up and down with the waves.

"Now?"

"Now what? I will go and get it. It can't go far."

With these words, he ran on the sands and throwing down the rifle, took a leap into the water and started stroking wildly towards the bird that was being swept in the fast current. He swam quite some distance but never seemed to come within its reach. The dead bird was flowing away from him.

Then he noticed a young girl step out of a hut on the bank. Rolling up her saree, she swiftly entered the river and in one motion caught the bird and raising it high above her head, called out to him "Come out of the water, *babuji,* I have your bird." The girl's courage and energy impressed Mehta immensely. He swam towards the other shore and was with her in less than a minute.

The young girl was dark-complexioned and wore scruffy clothes with only two bangles on her wrists as ornaments. Her hair was ruffled and unkempt. Not a single feature of her face was striking, but the natural surroundings in which she lived had lent a rare freshness to her complexion. Nursed in the lap of nature, her body had a well toned suppleness which she carried with an unconscious grace. Her frank youth had the effect of an electric current on Mehta's senses.

He thanked her and said she came well in time or he would have had to swim quite a long distance.

"I saw you swimming frantically so I came out to see what was happening. You are here on a hunt, I presume?"

"Yes, we did come on a hunt but it's already noon and this bird is the only thing we got."

"If you want a leopard I can lead you to its lair. It comes here every night to drink water by the river. Sometimes it also comes in the day time." She added with some hesitation, "but you will have to give us its skin. Come up here; there's a peepul tree nearby, you can rest in its shade. Your clothes are all wet."

Mehta stared at the clothes clinging to her body, "your clothes are wet too."

She tossed her head with a laugh, "Oh, what about them? We live here. We are either in the sun or in the water. You aren't like us."

Mehta marvelled at the quaint mix of common sense and simplicity in the girl. "What will you do with the leopard skin"? He asked.

"My father sells it in the bazaar. That is our business."

"But if we rest here in the afternoon, will you give us something to eat?"

The girl blushed slightly, "We don't have anything that you may be used to. I have *rotis* ready at home. I can cook the bird. There is milk in the house."

"But I am not alone. There is a lady with me."

"Your wife?"

"No, she isn't my wife yet. Just an acquaintance."

"I'll run up and call her. You wait in the shade."

"No, I'll call her."

"You must be tired. I will get her here, in a jiffy." Before Mehta could say anything she was gone like the wind.

Mehta climbed up the knoll to the tree and sprawled on the ground under its shade. His heart responded pleasantly to the sense of freedom in the atmosphere.

The row of hills that greeted his eyes was vast, continuous and pregnant with meaning, almost like a philosophical treatise. Far, on a hill top, there was a small temple. The sight seemed to expand his consciousness and awareness, as if his soul was beholding infinite knowledge and enlightenment...

While he was still contemplating the scene, he saw the girl coming with Malti beside her. One appeared bright and blooming like a flower growing in the wilderness, while the other was forlorn and wilting like a finely designed bouquet that has been kept in the sun for long.

Malti spoke sternly, "I see you find the *peepul* shade rather alluring while I am dying of hunger."

The girl went inside and brought two large pots, "I'll run and draw fresh water from the well. I'll light a fire when I come back and make fresh *rotis* for you."

Malti vent her frustration on Mehta, "Why did you have to come here and sprawl like this?"

Mehta teased her. "Why don't you try to enjoy this bohemian life for a day? Why don't you also discover the sweet taste of maize-cob *rotis*?"

"I can't eat that stuff. Even if I push it down my throat, I'll never be able to digest it. I regret coming with you. You dragged me through hell all the way and now you have dragged me in this godforsaken place."

Mehta had stripped off his clothes and sat in just his blue underwear. When he saw the girl going with the pots, he took them from her and followed her to the well. Despite his devotion to the study of philosophy, he was quite conscious of his health and spent considerable time looking after his body. As he strode with the two pots in each hand, his muscled pectorals and sinewy thighs made his body appear like a Grecian sculpture in motion. The girl stared at him with curious eyes. For her, he was no more an object for sympathy but one of attraction.

The well was around sixty feet deep. The pots were heavy and despite his athletic body and strength, he felt exhausted as he strained at the ropes. The girl grabbed it from his hands and said, "You go sit. This is not your job let me do it."

Mehta could not accept this affront to his masculinity. He snatched the rope back and did not stop till he filled the other pot too, lifted both in his hands and walked back with them right up to her door. The girl lit a fire, burnt the partridge's feathers, chopped it with a knife and put it in a utensil to cook.

All this while Malti lay on the string cot, angry and watching the scene with the expression of a reluctant patient awaiting surgery.

Mehta stood at the door watching the girl move with easy grace, pottering around with her usual domestic chores. Admiring her skills as she went about her work he said, "Give me something to do. How can I be of help?"

The girl chided him pleasantly, "You do not have to do anything. Go and sit with the lady- she looks tired and hungry. Give her some milk." She took a fistful of flour from a canister and began to knead it. Fascinated, Mehta watched every movement of her body. The girl looked at him sideways and returned her gaze to the job at hand.

Malti called out to him, "What are you doing standing there? I am having a bad headache."

Mehta came up to her. "It's the harsh sun that has got you."

"You brought me here to kill me."

"Too bad, you do not have medicines with you."

"Why should I have carried my medicine bag? It is at Semri in my room. Oh God! My head is bursting."

Mehta sat down on his knees beside her and began to rub and massage her head. Malti closed her eyes.

The girl walked up to them, her hair dishevelled, hands caked with dough, eyes red with smoke from the oven, her clothes sweaty; clearly revealing the rise of her bosom. "What's wrong with ma'am?"

Mehta said, "She has a bad headache."

"I'll go and get her the medicine. Rub it on her head and she will be fine."

"Where will you go in this terrible heat?"

The girl did not wait to hear that. She was off like an arrow, climbing the rocks till she vanished from sight. Half hour later, he saw her high on the hill. She appeared like a clockwork doll. He marvelled at the helpfulness of this girl of the forest. She was going right up to the sky in this strong sunshine and blistering heat.

Malti opened her eyes. "Where's that black mutt gone? She looks so awful, like the backside of a kettle. Send her off to inform Rai sahib where we are, so he can bring the car here. Another hour in this dreadful place and I'll dehydrate."

"She's gone to get some medicine. She says it relieves migraine real fast."

"Their medicines suit them best. It won't work for me. Why are you so fascinated with her?"

Without mincing words Mehta said, "There are some qualities in her which could make you a perfect angel provided you emulate them."

"Let her live with her greatness. I don't desire to be great."

"If you insist I will go to get the car, though I have my doubts if it can be driven to this place at all."

"Oh! So you plan to be her guest for a longer time? I presume there are better chances of finding game at night."

Mehta was stung by her words and said, "I can never have such feelings for this girl but she is a wonderful human being. I will never dream of climbing a hill in this heat even for my best friend. We are merely passersby and she knows it but still she runs up to get you medicines and cook food for us. I can write essays and columns on world peace and brotherhood, I can deliver lectures on compassion but she actually lives that life. Deeds are sometimes so much better than words."

Malti laughed softly and derisively, "Indeed she's an angel, I agree. Her breasts are full and her behind is well formed what else does one need to be an angel?"

Her words cut into Mehta like a sharp knife. He got up in silence, put on his clothes which had dried by then, picked up his gun and was all set to leave. Malti hissed at him, "You cannot go like that, leaving me alone."

"Then who will go and call Rai sahib?"

"Your angel, who else?"

Mehta stood there, numb and transfixed. It was his first realisation of the ease, with which women exert their power over men.

She came in, running and panting with a clutch of bushy twigs in her hands. When she came close, she noticed Mehta was dressed and ready to go. She said, "I've got the herb and I'll grind and apply it to her forehead in a moment. But where are you off to? The meat should be ready now. I'll make the *rotis*. Ma'am can have milk. Stay on. You can leave when the heat eases a bit."

She walked up to Mehta and without batting an eyelid, started unbuttoning his tunic.

It took quite an effort for Mehta to restrain himself. He wanted to kneel down and kiss this unlettered nymph of the forest.

Malti said to her, "Don't worry about your medicine. Our car is parked under a large tree just down the river bank. You will find others there. Tell them where we are and they should send the car here. Go, make a dash for it."

The girl looked at Mehta piteously. She had toiled hard to procure the herb. If they did not like the cure brought by her they could at least make a pretence of using it, if only for her sake.

She put the plants on the floor and said, "By the time I am back, the fire will die down. If you want I'll make the *rotis* first. You can eat and drink the milk and then rest after that. Meanwhile, I will run down and try to find your car."

She went inside the hut and rekindled the fire. The meat was ready, though slightly burnt. She made the *rotis* hurriedly. The milk was scalding so she poured it in a wide brimmed bowl and took it to Malti, who raised an eyebrow in disgust at the shabby utensil. However, she was too starved to refuse it. Mehta sat down on the ground right in front of the hut and began to eat. The girl stood beside him and started fanning him with a handmade leaf fan. Malti called out to her, "Let him eat. He won't run away. You go find the car."

The girl looked at Malti with questioning eyes. What did she want? What was going on in her mind? Madam's face did not reflect the meek submissiveness of a person who was ill. Instead, the girl noticed a pronounced superiority that sneered at her. She was an unlettered simpleton but had a primal flair for reading the mind. She retorted, "I am nobody's errand girl, ma'am. You may be a big lady but I am not begging you for anything. I won't go."

Malti snapped at her, "Oh, so you are being impudent? Tell me who owns these forest lands where you live?"

"This is Rai sahib's jurisdiction."

"Then I will see to it that you are flogged by the same Rai sahib himself."

"If it gives you any pleasure, go ahead and get me flogged. I am no great princess that he will have to send in an army to capture me."

Mehta had eaten a few morsels when he heard Malti's voice and the sharp exchange of words. The food stuck like a thorn in his throat. He got up immediately, washed his hands and announced, "She's not going. I am going."

Malti stood up, challenging him, "I'll see to it that she does."

Mehta spoke to her in clipped English, "You are not covering yourself in glory by insulting her."

Malti snapped back, "Men find only those women interesting, who may have nothing worthwhile about them but who run errands for them and wait on them like menials. I was mistaken about you, I thought you didn't have that sort of wicked male chauvinism but you are like any other man. Totally uncivilised, utterly barbaric."

Mehta had immense knowledge of human psychology. He was able to fathom Malti's emotions but had never come across an instance of jealousy like this. It shocked him to see that a comely, soft spoken and pleasant lady like Malti had such a blazing fire of envy simmering in her heart!

He said, "Say what you may, she is not going. I will fall in my own esteem, if I reward her goodness and kindness in this manner."

There was a certain power in Mehta's words which forced Malti to rise silently and prepare to leave. Miffed, she said to him, "Fine, I m going. You stay back and worship her feet."

When she had gone a few steps, Mehta turned towards the girl and said- "I too must go. Your affection and your selfless nature will remain in my heart forever."

The girl folded her hands tearfully, turned back and disappeared into the hut.

Rai sahib was dressed in his usual silken finery, whereas Khanna was in a hunter's attire which was possibly stitched specifically for the occasion. Khanna was short, slim and good looking. He had wide eyes; a tanned face spotted with marks of an old attack of chicken pox and was a smooth talker.

A few minutes into the walk and he led the conversation to Mehta, who had dominated his thoughts since last evening.

He said, "This Mehta is a strange chap. I think he is rather weird."

Rai sahib had respect for Mehta and thought he was a dignified man. However, he had business dealings with Khanna and he avoided controversies. Without challenging Khanna's contention he said, "I think he is good entertainment. I never argue with him. Even if I wanted to I would not be able to match his verbal sophistry. He makes around a thousand rupees a month. He has no worries, no nagging wife and no irritating kids to tug at his sleeves. If he doesn't mouth philosophies, then who will?"

Khanna shot back, "I have heard he has a dubious character."

"When you have nothing to worry about, preserving character is tough. Unless you live in society and follow its rules you cannot realise its limitations. I don't know what Malti sees in him. She is getting so besotted with him. I am not jealous but I think she's treating him like a plaything."

Khanna laughed at the comment that had nothing in it to provoke such mirth and said, "Apparently you have not understood that woman. The more you gravitate towards her, the more she moves away. The further you run from her, the closer she will want to get to you."

"Then she must be in love with you."

"Me? I am nowhere in that charmed circle of romantics, trust me. All my energies are spent managing the affairs of this estate. All members of my household are busy in their own affairs. I am attached to my country and its people. When the Satyagraha movement began I took part in it. I was sent to jail and was fined heavily and am still reeling under its impact but I don't regret it. On the contrary, it makes me proud as I have always wanted to be of use to the nation or society. I don't relish exploiting peasants to procure luxuries for myself. The tragedy is that I am unable to break away from the system in which I have been brought up. I am stuck in the same grind, trying desperately to salvage my soul from this quicksand. A person in my situation cannot afford to run after Malti or any other lady and if he does, his doom is imminent. At best such an involvement can be momentary."

Khanna was an equally valiant man, committed to the freedom movement. He was fearless and was jailed twice for the same reason. He did not wear *khadi* and was quite fond of French wine but was also capable of tolerating extreme discomfort, if necessary. He abstained from liquor while in jail and despite being eligible for 'A' class facilities, he ate food served to 'C' class prisoners. But for him an element of romance was a minor indulgence which did not encroach on his serious demeanour. "I can't be a mendicant. In my opinion, a person who isn't a romantic will lack the enthusiasm for the freedom struggle. I seriously wonder if a person incapable of loving a beautiful woman will ever love his country."

Rai sahib smiled, "Now you are making fun of me."

"I am not making fun of you. These are facts of life."

"Possibly."

"You look inside your heart and you'll discover for yourself."

"I have delved deep in my heart and let me assure you there could be a hundred faults in me but lust is not one of them."

"If that is so, I feel sorry for you. If you are a bit disappointed with life then it is due to abstinence and asceticism. I am a willing actor in this theatre of the absurd. I know she leads me on yet acts as if she is not interested. I don't lose easy but I must admit I am unable to fathom her intentions. It is so difficult to know what she wants or what she will do next."

"I doubt if you'll ever discover the answer key to that. Mehta will beat you to it."

They came across a flock of deer grazing nearby. Rai sahib took aim with his gun but Khanna made a disapproving gesture, "Why do you have to kill it, brother? The poor animal is grazing, leave it alone. Let's just sit under a shade and talk. There is plenty to discuss with you."

Rai sahib fired the gun but the deer fled away. He said ruefully, "I come upon a game and that too is lost."

Khanna changed the topic. "You grow sugarcane in your plantations. Why don't you join our sugar mill? Its shares are soaring. Buy one thousand, if not more."

"That's too much! Where do I get the money?"

"You are such a famous *zamindaar* and you say you have no money? In all, you have to pay fifty thousand but initially you give only twenty-five."

"No, brother, I do not have that amount."

"You know I am also a bank manager and you can borrow as much money from my bank as you want and start dabbling in the speculative market as well. All these neo-rich upstarts in the city have made their fortunes from the market. You can trade in cotton, sugar, wheat, rubber and other commodities. Speculation is risky but not for the educated and intelligent. With your expertise and pragmatism, I am sure you will be extremely successful. The rise and fall of the share market is not whimsical, it's a science. Once you have your finger on the pulse of the market, there is no stopping you."

Khanna also advised Rai sahib to have his life insured through him as he was an insurance agent as well. "Put in a few hundred rupees and you will get almost fifty thousand at the end of the term. That's not a small sum to leave for your heirs," said Khanna temptingly.

Rai sahib had little faith in speculative investments. He had burnt his fingers a few times in similar pursuits. But the rise of Khanna's fortunes was real and he had witnessed it firsthand. An ordinary clerk in a bank, who had risen to such heights in merely ten years; his advice could not be taken lightly. If Khanna were to guide him, he could make a lot of money in the stock market.

Suddenly they came upon a villager carrying a basket of roots, leaves, herbs and a few fruits. Khanna stopped him. The villager was apprehensive and taken by surprise. Afraid he might be compelled to cough up his belongings for a pittance, he said, "Nothing at all just a few leaves and herbs."

"What will you do with them?"

"I will sell them, sir."

"What herbs? Let's see them."

The villager revealed his wares. They were ordinary leaves and roots found in abundance in the forest. The villagers gathered them from the forest and sold them for a few *annas*. The basket had a variety of plants with local names which he rattled off in a typical salesman's monotonous voice, picking up each as he narrated their medicinal values. "This is *makoy,* sir and it is excellent for fever, nausea, cough, palpitations. One dosage provides instant relief. This one here is a wild mushroom which is good for joint pains..."

Khanna cut him short, "How much will you charge for all of it?"

"Eight *annas*."

Khanna tossed him a rupee and told him to deliver the herbs to their camp. The man was ecstatic as he had got double of what he had asked for. He went off blessing Khanna for his generosity.

Rai sahib inquired, "What will you do with all these plants."

Khanna smiled and said, "I will mint silver from them. Perhaps you are not aware- I am an alchemist."

"Please teach me your skills and secrets."

"Why not? You're welcome. I will impart my knowledge gladly but before that, you must pamper me with *laddoos* and other sweets!"

Rai sahib was confused so Khanna said, "No, no, I was just joking. The fact is that I buy herbs all the time and earn the goodwill of my friends by telling them these are charmed herbs that I have procured from a *fakir* especially for them. I earn their immense gratitude just by spending one rupee. So it's not a bad bargain at all. They remember the favour and are ready to do anything for me."

Rai sahib was curious, "But how do you remember the qualities and names of each herb?"

Khanna laughed, "Rai sahib, you are very naïve! I can call any herb any name and ascribe it any kind of qualities and people believe me. The truth is that most diseases are cured not as much by medicine but by faith. But even the wise old men and senior officers fall for my so called miracle herbs."

From herbs the conversation veered to holy men. Khanna said, "Did I tell you about my *Swamiji*? You must seek his blessings, when he comes visiting me next. In fact, whenever he drops by at my place, there is a queue of people waiting to meet him. He is a holy man, untouched by materialism and I have yet to come across a wiser person than him. He has lived and meditated in the Himalayas for a very long time and is a realised soul. I am confident that he will help you rid yourself of all problems. He will tell you all about your past and future as soon he meets you. The amazing thing is despite being such a realised man, he is scathing in his criticism of holy men and religious institutions. He says all temples, sects, cults are bundles of falsehoods. He exhorts everyone to break shackles of the past and become better human beings and not hanker after ethereal goals."

Rai sahib found it difficult to accept all that he said. Like other wealthy people he also believed in holy men. He sought solace in them. He had often contemplated giving up everything and take to meditation. He considered worldly attachments as impediments to inner peace. But how could anyone cut through these snares without renunciation and monastic discipline?

"When he has himself renunciated everything, why does he castigate renunciation?" asked Rai sahib.

"He has not given up anything. On the contrary, he enjoys all to continue on the path of positive involvement with life. He speaks of the freedom of the intellect as the basis of his teachings."

"I don't get it. What does he mean by 'freedom of the intellect'?"

"Well, to tell you the truth, that is not very clear to me either. When he is here next you must meet him. He says love is truth and truth is love."

"Have you introduced Malti to him?"

"Don't make me laugh. What's Malti got to do ....?"

Before he could complete the sentence, a rustling sound came from behind the bushes. Instinctively, he jumped and cowered behind Rai sahib as a leopard emerged from the foliage and walked away majestically.

When Rai sahib took aim with his gun, Khanna hissed under his breath, "Have you lost your mind? Why do you have to shoot that animal? What if he survives and comes back to kill us?"

"It won't come back, I will kill it."

"Then let me climb that hillock first. I am not so passionate about hunting."

"Why did you come on the hunt?"

"Because I am crazy, that's why."

Rai sahib lowered the gun. "Again I have lost a good game. It was such a rare opportunity."

"I can't stay here anymore. This is a dangerous place."

"Let me hunt something. It will be embarrassing to return empty handed."

"Kindly take me to the car. After that you can hunt leopard or tiger or whatever you please."

"You have feet of clay, Khanna."

"Putting oneself in the face of danger is not bravery."

"You can go back on your own if you want to."

"Alone...?"

"The trail is clear."

"Nothing doing. You come with me."

Rai sahib tried to convince him, but Khanna would have nothing of it. He was pale with fear. At that point even if a squirrel had suddenly come running down a tree, he would have screamed and fainted. He was sweating profusely and shivering with fear. Rai sahib was compelled to turn back against his wishes.

Khanna regained his composure after moving quite some distance from that place.

He said, "I am not scared of taking risks, but walking into a lion's den is not about taking a risk, it is committing suicide."

"Oh, come on. The very sight of a leopard and you start shivering in your pants."

"I consider hunting a tradition of the times when man was an animal. Civilisation has moved much ahead since then," said Khanna defensively.

"I will tell Malti about this."

"Non- violence is nothing to be ashamed of."

"Okay! So that was supposed to be your non-violence at work? Bravo!" Rai sahib mocked.

"Yes that was non-violence. You revere Buddha and Shankar but kill animals. It is you who should be ashamed not me."

Both walked quietly for some time. After a considerable interval, Khanna spoke up-"So when will you come? I suggest you fill the form for the policy and the sugar mill today itself. I am carrying both forms with me."

❁❁❁

8

The cow was a symbol of pride for Hori and his family. Ever since he had bought it, all members of his household walked with their heads held high and it was their main topic of conversation. The cow needed lots of nutrition and so the chaff was set aside and rows of fodder grass were sown in the sugarcane fields.

It was monsoon time and the peasants watched the sky patiently for signs of rain clouds, awaiting the showers that energise the seedlings and help fresh grass burst forth from the earth. One morning, when the village woke up, the torrent rain was lashing at the windows. The peasants made a scramble to their fields with ploughs in tow.

But a shock awaited them. Within no time, Rai sahib's men arrived and firmly announced that farmers would not be allowed to plough the land till they had paid all dues of the past season. The diktat came like a bolt from the blue. Such harshness was unheard of and unprecedented. It was an unwritten law that no one defaulted on the dues but unless they tilled the fields, how could they generate money to clear their past levy?

Hori was perplexed. During Dussehra festivities, Rai sahib had been all grace and kindliness but now he was showing his evil side by issuing such a cruel diktat. He was completely nonplussed but refrained from confronting him as he knew that Rai sahib would not rescind his order. Thus, there was little reason why he should stick his neck out alone. It would be prudent to wait and watch what others did before rushing into things.

With this new order, chaos reigned amongst peasants. They went knocking at the doors of moneylenders. In such a scenario, it was but natural that Mangru Sah's stock should shoot up. Pandit Datadin and Sahuain too were agents of big loan sharks from the city. Besides them, a number of sub agents operated in villages who disbursed loans at one *anna* per rupee without pressing for any documentation. Smelling easy money, a number of people hankered to become loan-givers, so much so that anyone with even twenty rupees in his pocket tried his hand at the game. At some time in the past Hori too had done the same, as a result of which rumours started doing the rounds that he had stashed up money secretly.

People in the village fell over each other to seek loans at whatever interest they could procure them. Hori was in a bind. He could not approach those whom he already owed money. Other than Jhinguri Singh he could think of no one to turn to. He was sure Jhinguri would give him the loan but he was a stickler for paperwork and always insisted on making proper legal documents before he granted a loan to anyone. And he charged them through the nose for these. There were separate charges for preparing the papers, for writing the deed and for appeasement money to petty officials who supervised the process. Sometimes an amount of seventeen rupees would be given for a loan of fifty rupees after deducting all fees and the first year's interest. This was gross injustice but there was little Hori could do. In this hour of crisis, he had no one else to turn to.

Jhinguri Singh squatted on his haunches. Cleaning his teeth with a *neem* twig, he resembled a clown with his short plump body, thick-set, wide eyes and a comical moustache. He was quite an amusing character in that he called himself the son-in-law of the village and addressed all men elder to him either as uncles or brothers-in-law and joked with the women as if they were his sisters-in-law. When he walked on the road, young boys would mockingly greet him with elaborate obeisance. Jhinguri Singh would respond immediately with the choicest curses. 'May you break your leg', 'may you become blind', 'hope you are stricken with epilepsy,' 'may you burn in hell's fire'. But his expletives spread more mirth and the boys had a great laugh at his expense. Yet he was a strict money lender, who never gave any concessions.

Hori saluted him and narrated his tale of woe.

Jhinguri Singh smiled wickedly and asked what he had done with his secret money.

"If I had secret funds wouldn't I have paid back my creditors? Who likes to live under the yoke and cough up interest regularly?"

"I know you will never spend the money you have stashed up. This is typical of people like you."

"What stashed money, *Thakur?* We barely have enough to eat. My son is maturing into an adult and I can't afford his marriage. My daughter is also reaching a marriageable age. If I had money stashed away, why would I waste my time and not do what is so necessary?"

Jhinguri had set his eyes on Hori's cow the day it came to the village. It was a healthy animal and definitely worth five seers milk a day. He had made up his mind to take it from Hori one way or the other. This seemed to be that Godsend moment.

He said, "Well, I accept what you say that you really don't have anything. You can take as much money as you want but you must deposit some jewellery or ornaments as collateral otherwise if you get into the bother of legal documentation, you will stand to lose a lot and will be ultimately trapped by high interest rates."

Hori swore there was absolutely no jewellery in his house. Dhania did not have a scrap of cotton thread that could pass off as an ornament. The bangles she wore were not silver, merely brushed copper.

Jhinguri was full of sympathy and concern, "In that case, just sell me that new cow you bought recently. You will avoid the hassle of heavy interest and stamp paper expenses. Let a neutral person decide how much it is worth and take that amount from me. I know you bought it with so much love but this crisis has got to be handled somehow, isn't it?"

Hori was aghast at the suggestion; it was preposterous. He didn't want to consider it at all but the money lender explained to him the pros and cons so convincingly that ultimately he fell for his guile. Jhinguri Singh was right, Hori tried to convince himself. Legal documentation would drastically reduce the loan amount and if he was unable to return it within two or three years, it would grow to a hundred. Prior experience had taught him that loans are like unwanted guests who refuse to leave once they step in the house.

He said, "Let me go home and discuss with others"

"You don't have to take anyone's advice. You should just inform them that not taking a loan at this juncture is like opening the floodgates of misfortune."

"I understand, *Thakur*, but I must discuss it with my family. I will be back in no time."

When he reached home, he told his family members about Jhinguri Singh's suggestion. Expectedly, all hell broke loose. The two girls started wailing. A shocked Dhania shot down the suggestion immediately. "We won't give away our cow. You raise the money from wherever you want." An emotional Sona suggested that instead of the cow, the father should sell her. "Once you sell me you will also save the money you spend on me." Rupa said she would stop eating if the cow was sold.

Hori convinced Dhania after much cajoling and brought her around to his way of thinking. He said he realised it wasn't proper to sell a cow obtained on a loan from a friend, but these were difficult times and one had to compromise in such circumstances. Otherwise, why would anyone dread adverse situations so much? Gobar also did not raise many objections. He was on a different trip these days. It was ultimately decided that when the girls were asleep, the cow would be taken to Jhinguri Singh's residence and handed over to him.

The day wore on and evening crept over the village. By eight the girls had eaten and gone to bed. Gobar left the house saying he would not be able to bear the pain of seeing the cow leave. Hori maintained an outward semblance of calm but was quite shaken inside. It was such a shame that no one would lend him fifty rupees in his moment of need. As he stood before the cow, he thought her large dark eyes looked at him accusingly, questioning his commitment and love as he was giving her away barely days after he brought her in. He thought her look conveyed pain and disappointment at his claims of caring for her and nurturing her. She would happily chew whatever little he provided her without complaining. Was this the reward for her goodness?

Dhania said, "The girls are asleep. Take her away now. If it's got to be done, do it as quickly as possible."

Hori mumbled mournfully, "I can't do this Dhania. Just look at her face! Let's drop this. I will pick up a loan on interest. God willing, we will pay it off soon. We just have to wait for another good harvest."

Dhania looked at him with love and a distinct feeling of pride, "We got the cow after such hardship; I know it's difficult to give her away like this. Go and pick up that loan. We will clear it just as we are trying to pay back the rest."

The air was humid inside the house. Not a leaf shook as there was stillness in the air. The sky was overcast but didn't convey portents of a shower. Hori led the cow outside and tied her leash to the door. Dhania protested saying it wasn't proper to take her outside but Hori would have nothing of it. He said humidity was for everyone, cow included. Fresh air would do her good.

Leaving her in the open space in front of the house, Hori went to look up his brother Sobha, who was down with a bad bout of asthma for many months. Sobha could barely afford two square meals a day. Proper medication was a far cry yet he was loaded with backbreaking physical work. His condition was worsening by the day. Sobha was a patient man and avoided arguments and strife as much as he could. He kept to himself most of the time and treated Hori with a great deal of respect. Hori was also very fond of him. They discussed the new directive which had become the favourite topic of Rai sahib's critics and now there were many.

Hori took leave of his brother around eleven at night and left for home. As he entered, he thought he saw a shadow lurking in the courtyard next to the cow. "Who's it?" he called.

It was his other brother Heera who spoke, "It's me *Dada*. I have come to take fire from your kiln."

Hori was pleased to note that his brother had come to pick up smouldering embers from his kiln to light his own fire at home. After all, there were innumerable such kilns in the village. He could have gone anywhere but was taking it from his kiln because he considered him as one of his own. Heera's coming was something special, more so after the recent unpleasantness. He was relieved to know Heera might be a temperamental and edgy man but his heart was in the right place.

He asked affectionately if he would also care for some tobacco.

"No, I have enough of it."

"Sobha is in bad shape, Heera."

"He won't take any medicine; that's the problem. He never listens to any advice? According to him all doctors, *vaids* and *hakims* are ignorant fools. He thinks he and his wife are the wisest of all."

Hori was concerned, "This is his biggest shortcoming. Illness has made him still more irritable. But I suppose that happens to all of us. Don't you remember how when you were down with influenza, you would throw away the bottle of medicine and I had to catch hold of both your hands while Dhania forcibly poured the medicine down your throat? And you would swear a hundred times as she did so?"

"Yes *Dada,* I remember all that. How else would I have survived to torment you so?"

Hori thought he perceived a hint of pain in Heera's voice, as if it was choking with tears. Hori was overwhelmed.

"Listen, my child, arguments and disagreements are a part of life. They should not make enemies out of those who are our own. Only those who have near ones to share life with are the ones who can afford to fight. The lonely and forsaken will never have disagreements with anyone."

Both shared a *chillum* and after a few puffs Heera left for his home as Hori went inside. He was hungry and wanted something to eat.

Dhania was in a very cross mood, "Hope you know what your dear son is up to? It is so late in the night and he is still not home. It's not that I don't know. It is that girl Jhuniya, Bhola's daughter. He is besotted with her."

Hori had heard these rumours but did not give them much credence. He asked Dhania from where she picked up such malicious gossip.

That provoked her further. "You must be the only one who isn't aware of it. The entire village is abuzz with this news. He's a dumb simpleton and she's a past master at this game- she is spinning him like a top in her hands. He is under the illusion she loves him. You better talk to him because if anything adverse happens, we will have nowhere to hide."

Hori was in a playful mood. He said, "Jhuniya is not such a bad looking girl after all. Why doesn't he get engaged to her? Where else will he get a bride for so little?"

His impish manner touched her to the quick, "If that wretch comes to this house I will break her legs with my own hands. If Gobar is so fond of her he can take her wherever he wishes."

"But if he insists on bringing her home?"

"Then where will you dump our daughters? None in the community will look at you with respect; we will be such social outcasts."

"I don't think he will bother about this."

"I won't let go this easy. I have burnt my guts bringing him up; I won't let that slut walk away with him. I will stuff her mouth with hot coals if she as much as dares think about it."

At that moment Gobar rushed in, all panicky and worried. "*Dada,* what's happened to the cow? Is she under some evil spell? Look how she is thrashing her legs."

Hori looked up in alarm, "Don't talk rubbish. I just saw her. She was sitting peacefully."

The trio rushed out together. Lifting up the lantern they peered at her in the dim light. The cow's mouth was frothing. Her eyes were dilated in pain, hooves stretched out erect and her stomach was swollen. Dhania broke down as Hori rushed to *Pandit* Datadin's residence. He was the only person with some knowledge of veterinary diseases. *Panditji* was about to retire to bed when Hori came screaming. The two hurried back but it was too late. Within minutes, almost the entire village was at their door. The cow had been poisoned- the symptoms were quite evident. There was no doubt she was fed some dangerous substance. But who could have committed such a terrible sin? Nothing so heinous had ever happened in the village, was it an outsider who could have done this misdeed?

Hori had no enemy in the village. He did have an argument with his brother but that was just another usual tiff between the two. Heera was most hurt by this development. He went around swearing that he would skin the person alive if he could lay his hands on him. The common impression was that Heera might be bad and ill tempered but this was beyond him.

The crowd hung around their place till late night. Everyone was with Hori in his hour of crisis and cursed the killer at the top of their voices. If that person were to be caught at that moment, he would have been lynched; such was the public ire at that mysterious criminal. Such a crime had never occurred in the village as people always tied their animals outside their homes in the open. But this incident would surely change perceptions drastically. A new fear had raised its spectre over the villagers. They spoke in hushed tones praising the 'beautiful' cow with such wide innocent eyes. Almost divine! It yielded no less than five seers of milk a day and if she had had calves, they would have been worth a hundred each. This was a terrible tragedy and to think it had struck so mercilessly within a few weeks of her arrival.

When the crowds receded Dhania pointed her finger at Hori. "You will never listen to what others say. You are such a stubborn man. The moment you walked out from the courtyard with the cow I cautioned you not to take her out. I told you we are going through a bad patch and anything could happen but would you pay any heed? No, it's so humid inside. Now see how pleasant it has become. Jhinguri Singh had asked for her. Had you handed her over to him, perhaps, it would have eased some of our debts. But we are doomed to suffer. When calamities arrive they first rob people of their sense. She was inside the house and there were no problems. She had become so familiar with the family. Who would say she had just arrived in the household? The kids would swing from her horns and she was so patient with them. She lapped up whatever little we threw at her. She was such a Goddess of fortune- Alas!"

Sona and Rupa were jolted out of their sleep with the commotion and were inconsolable. It was they who looked after the cow. It was their duty to feed her and generally tend to her. She was like their playmate. They wouldn't finish their meal without feeding her a *roti* with their hands. Their world now lay in tatters.

Gobar too cried bitterly till he was exhausted.

That night when Dhania came to place the usual glass of water at his bedside, Hori looked up at her and spoke as if in a whisper, "I am going to tell you something in confidence. I warn you not to go singing about it all over the village."

"Oh come on," said Dhania. "Have I ever done something like this? You blame me for nothing and everything."

"Ok, so tell me- do you suspect anyone?" asked Hori

"I don't suspect anyone. It must be some stranger in the village."

"You swear you won't blabber what I am about to tell you?"

"Yes, why should I not shout it from the rooftops? The villagers buy me gold necklaces for providing them information, don't they?" mocked Dhania in anger.

"If you as much as breathe about this to anyone, I will slaughter you."

"Slaughtering me will be of no use to you. It's not easy to get another woman. As long as I am around, I take care of your household. The day I am no more you will weep buckets. You blame me for everything today; then you will regret and repent."

"I suspect Heera."

For a moment, Dhania was shocked into silence. Regaining her composure she said, "What nonsense. That's utter rubbish. Heera will not stoop so low. He merely has a foul tongue, nothing like this."

"I saw it with my eyes. I swear on you."

"You saw what? Where?"

"When I returned from Sobha's house, he was standing in the dark near the cow's tether. When I enquired who it was, he said it was him and he had come to borrow some embers from the kiln. We spoke for some time. He gave me his *chillum* to smoke. Probably he came and fed something to the cow while I was away at Sobha's and had returned to check if the poison was working or not when I saw him."

Dhania took a deep breath and when she spoke there was fire on her tongue. "What a crying shame! To think a brother would fall so low. My goodness! I didn't know Heera was such a rotten man. And to think I brought him up as my own son!"

"Anyway, now go and sleep and don't you dare mention this to anyone."

"That's what you think! Just wait for morning if I don't drag him to the police, I am not my father's daughter. You think that murderer is fit to be called a brother? Is this what you call brotherly conduct? He is an enemy and a murderer. There is no sin in crushing an enemy, letting him go is."

Hori said threateningly, "I must warn you, Dhania. I am cautioning you."

Dhania spoke vehemently, "I don't care if thunderbolts strike me from the skies. I will not rest till I send him to jail. He will go to jail for no less than three years. Three years he will toil in hard labour. He will repent this action of his. And yes, I will call you as witness to his crime and make you swear on the name of your son."

She went in and bolted the door from inside. Hori remained outside, cursing himself for his stupidity. When he could not keep the secret how did he expect her to keep quiet. Now there was no holding back this wretch. When she was bent on doing something it was impossible to keep her down. He thought he had just committed the biggest blunder of his life.

It was pitch dark outside. The only sound was the occasional jingling of bells around the necks of the bulls tethered nearby. The dead cow lay barely ten feet away from Hori who tossed and turned on his string cot all night. All around him was a wall of impregnable inkiness with not a single ray of light.

❁❁❁

9

The next morning there was mayhem in the house. Livid at Dhania's threat to confront Heera over the cow's death, Hori began thrashing his wife and she in turn showered the choicest abuses on him. Daughters, Rupa and Sona clung to their father's feet and were crying loudly as Gobar tried to shield his mother from his father's blows. He would hold Hori's wrists and take him away but as soon as Dhania hurled another expletive at him, he would lunge forward and assault her again. A senile frustration seemed to be giving vent with a suppressed energy that had built up over the years.

The village was shocked. Yet, secretly, everyone relished watching this spectacle at close quarters under the guise of acting as peace brokers between the two. Hori's brother Sobha arrived wobbling on his stick. Datadin chastised Hori, "What is all this, Hori? Have you lost your senses? Is this how you treat your wife? I thought Heera suffered from this madness but now you exhibit the same symptoms."

Hori paused and bowing respectfully in his direction, said, *"Maharaj,* today you keep out of this. I am going to settle her impudence once and for all. The more I tolerate her rudeness the more she gets out of hand."

Teary eyed, Dhania spoke angrily, *"Maharaj,* you be my witness. Today I will send this man and his murdering brother Heera to jail. Heera has poisoned the cow and killed her but when I say I'll report it to the police, he starts beating me up. Is this the reward I get for wasting my life on this lout?"

Hori gritted his teeth and hissed angrily, "Don't insist on this falsehood? Did you see him poisoning the cow?"

"You swear you didn't see him lurking near the cow's trough."

"Yes, I will swear on it – I did not see him there."

"Put your hand on your son's head and then swear."

Hori put a trembling hand on Gobar's head and said, "I swear I did not see him standing near the cows' trough."

Dhania grimaced and spat on the floor, "Shame on you! You told me yourself you had seen him lurking around like a thief and now you lie to shield your brother. How disgusting! If any harm befalls my son, I will set this house on fire! I will burn down the world. How can a man lie so shamelessly through his teeth?"

Hori stomped his foot and glared at her, "Dhania, don't provoke me."

"Why? What more can you do except beat me? You are doing that already, aren't you? You have beaten and kicked me and yet you are not done. You must feel really brave hitting me so, but in front of your brothers you are a whimpering mongrel!"

She wept copiously and ranted loudly about her misfortune of being married to him, how she had toiled for him all her life, how she had scrounged to make ends meet. As for herself, she lived in utter penury with no decent clothes to wear, how she went hungry while she fed the family and how thankless he was to treat her in this manner. She cried out to God for not descending to deliver her from her predicament and lamented His lack of compassion in not hastening to save a poor woman from such distress and misery.

There was a distinct shift and public opinion was gradually tilting in her favour. Everybody was convinced that Heera had poisoned the cow and Hori had sworn falsely by swearing on his son's head. The fear of an impending calamity to his health pushed Gobar firmly into the opposing camp. Datadin's scathing verbal assault dealt the final blow and a crushed Hori made a quiet exit from the scene.

Datadin asked Sobha if he had any idea what had transpired between Hori and Heera. Sobha squatted on the floor and said weakly, *"Maharaj,* I am bedridden for the last eight days. Hori *dada* comes over to help us along. He was here last night but I am totally unaware of what happened between the two today. I do remember Heera came to borrow a spade. He wanted to dig up some root but I didn't see him after that."

Dhania grabbed this straw in the wind, *"Dada,* trust me, this is his doing. He borrowed that spade to dig out some poison root and fed it to our cow. He was simmering with anger and jealousy ever since we got the cow."

Datadin's forehead furrowed and he said, "If this is proven, he will be charged with murder. If the police don't take cognisance, rules of piety will hit him hard. Rupa, run down to Heera's place and call him here. Say *Dada* wants to see him. If he is innocent he should come forward and announce it in public, holding the holy Ganga water in his hands."

Dhania said, *"Maharaj,* we can't rely on what he says. He lies without batting an eyelid. When this man who claims to be so pious can swear falsely on his own son's head, what can be expected of a scoundrel like Heera?"

Now it was Gobar's turn to speak. "Let him swear falsely on our names. Let the entire generation be wiped out."

Rupa came running back. *"Kaka* is not at home. *Kaki* says he has gone out."

Datadin caressed his flowing beard and said, "Didn't you ask her where he has gone? He might as well be hiding at home. Sona, you go and take a look if he is inside."

Dhania interrupted him, "No *Dada,* don't send her. Heera is in a murderous mood; who knows what he might do."

Datadin got up and went himself plodding on his stick. But he returned soon after having confirmed Heera was actually not at home. Puniya told him he had gone with the rope, a pitcher and his *lathi* all set for a journey. When she asked him where he was going he snapped back at her, telling her to mind her own business. She had kept five rupees hidden in a niche in the wall and they weren't there now--- possibly he had taken them as well.

Dhania spoke with an air of certainty and an all-knowing calm, "He is guilty and has run away."

Sobha was circumspect, "Where can he run away? He might have merely gone for a dip in the river."

Dhania doubted it, "You don't take money with you if you go for a dip in the river. Moreover, there isn't any auspicious event on the calendar that calls for a holy dip."

On that fateful day, no meals were cooked at Hori's house. Nobody ventured to feed the bulls or give them water. There was an air of despondency all over the village as people talked in hushed tones. Wherever two or three men met they discussed the same event and expressed critical views about the turn of events. They were now pretty certain Heera was absconding. He must have realised his secret was out. They were quite sure, he knew he would be arrested and taken to prison and had bolted in panic. Meanwhile, at her home, Heera's wife Puniya kept up a relentless wail, she didn't know where he had gone without as much a by-your-leave.

In the evening, the police inspector came and laid the foundation for the final scene of the script. The watchman had reported the day's incident—the death of the cow and the ensuing quarrel---as a matter of duty to the police. Now the custodian of the law was in the village. Datadin, Jhinguri Singh, Lala Pateshwari, Nokhe Ram and Mangru Sah all stood in front of the cop with folded hands. Hori was summoned. It was the first time he was thus called to appear before a police inspector. He was trembling as if a sentence of hanging was about to be handed to him. When he was flogging Dhania, his body crackled with energy but now he was shrinking like a turtle withdrawing into a shell. The cop gave him a searching look that pierced right through to the core of his being. That man had immense knowledge of human nature. He was convinced it was his day and all he needed was an angry snort to make Hori quake in fear.

He asked him, "You suspect anyone?"

Hori touched the ground with his fingers and swore his cow had died a natural death of old age.

Dhania was standing right behind him. She interjected immediately, "The cow has been killed by your brother Heera. Sire is no fool to be taken in by whatever you say. He is here on an investigative mission."

The inspector enquired, "Who's this woman?"

Many in the crowd fell over each other to get an opportunity to address the inspector. They spoke simultaneously, each gratified by the thought that perhaps they were the first to speak, "She is Hori's wife, sir."

"Bring her forward. Let me note her statement first. Where is this man Heera whom she mentions?"

The respectable ones of the village replied in one voice, "He is not to be seen since morning. It seems he has gone somewhere, sir."

"Then I will have to search his house."

A search? Hori gasped. He was short of breath. His brother Heera's house was to be searched when he was not at home! Hori would certainly not allow such a disgrace. As far as Dhania was concerned, he would have nothing to do with her henceforth. She could go wherever she wished to. If she was so hell bent on ruining the reputation of his family, she need not stay at his place any longer. When she'd be buffeted about in the streets, sense would be knocked into her.

The village seniors also went into a huddle to overcome this great shame.

Datadin shook his bald head and whispered, "This is simply a ploy to make money. Tell me, what can he expect to find in Heera's house after all?"

Pateshwari was a tall man and did not convey a dumb look at all. He shook his long face and said, "Exactly! Why else do you think he is here? And since he has come, he will not be shaken off unless his palms are greased."

Jhinguri Singh whispered to Hori, "Now cough up whatever you have. There's no other way to save yourself."

At his end the inspector growled in his throat, purposefully, "I will search Heera's house."

Hori's was ashen. He felt drained of all blood in his veins. A search at his brother's house was as good as a search at his own. Heera had partitioned the house and separated from him but the world knew him as Hori's brother. If he had money he would have readily placed fifty rupees at the inspector's feet and begged him to spare the ignominy of a search. But Hori didn't even have money to buy poison to end his life. Dhania might have a few rupees stashed up somewhere but that woman would never volunteer for this. Like a man sentenced to the gallows and awaiting his death, he stood motionless with his head bowed.

Datadin cautioned him, "Standing silently like that won't help, Hori. Try to organise money to pay him off."

Hori looked up and spoke in a pleading voice, "Now what can I say, gentlemen? I am already weighed down with debts. I am ashamed to ask for more but please get me out of this crisis, I beg you. If I live I will pay back every *paisa*. And if I die Gobar is here to take the responsibility."

They started murmuring amongst themselves, discussing animatedly the amount of bribe to be given to the inspector. Datadin suggested it should be fifty rupees. According to Jhinguri Singh, the inspector would accept nothing less than a hundred rupees. Nokhe Ram concurred with him.

Hori wasn't concerned if the amount was fifty or a hundred. He simply wanted this crisis resolved, whatever be the cost. Whether it was cremated with one mound of firewood or ten – how did it make any difference to a corpse?

However, Pateshwari found it totally unjustified. This wasn't a case of dacoity or manslaughter; the issue was of preventing a search, so his contention was that twenty rupees should suffice.

The other leading lights frowned and chided him, "In that case you should be the interlocutor. We do not want to appear cheap nor are we willing to get in his line of fire."

Hori almost knelt down at Pateshwari's feet. "Brother, only you can deliver me. I shall serve you as long as I live."

The policeman stretched his back menacingly and announced, "Show me Heera's house. I must make a search."

Pateshwari moved close to him and spoke softly into his ear, "Is there such a hurry to make the search, sir? Heera's brother is here; ready and willing to be of some service."

They moved aside and started talking.

"What sort of a man is he?"

"Utterly poor, sir! He barely has enough to eat."

"Oh, really?"

"Yes sir. I swear on my honour, sir."

"You mean he's not worth even a fifty?"

"It's a far cry sir. A tenner is like a thousand for him. He won't be able to raise fifty in as many lives, sir!

The ponderous weight of responsibility bore on the policeman's mind as he chewed on the information for a minute. "If that is so I don't want to burden him any further. It's not in me to punish someone who is already suffering."

Pateshwari realised that he had pleaded the case with more efficiency than he intended. He said, "Oh no, sir. Don't say that - where will we go otherwise?" and added, "It's not that we ourselves have a lot of money."

"What do you mean? You are the local headman and you talk like this?"

"It is only on occasions like these that we are also able to get a small share. If not, who bothers about us, sir?"

"Okay, go and get thirty rupees from him. I will take twenty, you keep ten."

"We are four village elders here; please bear that in mind, sir."

"Very well, halve it. I keep one half you take the other half for the rest."

Pateshwari gave this information to Jhinguri Singh who in turn gestured to Hori to follow him to his house where he expansively handed him three ten rupee notes. "You are a good man Hori. That's why I am giving this to you. But you sign the loan document today itself."

Hori took the money and bundling it in his shawl, went straight to the policeman, smiling confidently.

He was a few steps away when in a flash Dhania pounced on him and snatched away the shawl in one swift movement. The knot in the shawl was loose and opened in the scuffle and the money fell and scattered on the ground. She hissed like a ruffled snake, "Where did you get this money from and where do you think you are taking it? Let me warn you return it from wherever you got it. Your wife and kids die every miserable moment of their lives, they have nothing to eat or wear and you take this fistful of money to save your family name? You think your prestige is such an important thing? We all have some honour to call our own even if we are poor and penniless. What can the inspector do? At worst, he can make a search. Let him do it. Let him make as many searches as he wants to. We lost a cow worth a hundred and now you add this to our losses? Shame on you and your prestige!"

Hori controlled the rage as her words sliced into his heart like a sharp dagger. The village elders bowed their heads, embarrassed and shame-faced. The cop's face turned red. This was the first time in his life he had received such a severe and verbal lashing in public.

But he was a hardcore policeman and unaccustomed to taking things lying down. He said, "I have a feeling this scoundrel's woman has poisoned the cow herself so she can lay the blame on Heera."

Dhania turned to him and gestured provocatively with her hands, "Yes, I poisoned the cow. It was my cow, I killed her. If this is how you conduct your investigations go ahead and file your report. Bring out the handcuffs and tie them around my wrists. Let the whole world see your law and your great investigative skills. Bleeding the poor is one thing; ensuring justice is quite another."

Hori moved towards Dhania with eyes blazing like fire but this time Gobar stood before him and spoke menacingly, "Enough! There is a limit to everything. Step back or you would see me dead? I am not such a depraved son that I will raise my hand against my father but for sure, I will hang myself right here."

Hori retreated as Dhania; emboldened by support from her son turned to him and admonished him to lay off as she wanted to see to what extent her husband could go this day. "I want to see what he will do to me. I want to see how brave he is. He loses prestige and honour in the village because his brother's house is searched, but beating his wife on the street before a crowd is no shame for him. Is this the honour and prestige of the brave? Perhaps, for him, bravery is to kick the one whose hand you vowed to hold for life. From this day onwards you manage your house yourself. I will show you I can survive better away from you. Eat better, wear better I will do it all; alone and without you."

Hori was demolished. He realised how weak and clueless a man can be when faced with a woman's ire.

The village elders had picked up the fallen notes and were gesturing to the inspector to move on from that place. Relentlessly, Dhania delivered another punch. "Give back that money to whomsoever it belongs to. We are not interested in any loan. If money has to be paid, it should be given by the one responsible for all this. I am not parting with a single paisa even if it means being summoned in court or jailed. Some days ago, we wanted twenty five rupees to pay off earlier debts and no one came forward to help us. Now see how fast they dish out a bunch of notes today! I am sure there are kickbacks involved in this. Everyone was benefitting from our misery. These murderous men are not our village elders, they are blood suckers! Whether it is bribes, loans, greasing palms, it is the poor who are ripped off every time. And they talk of *Swaraj,* self governance and independence! Is this how they want to usher in their new order?"

The leaders' faces were ashen, smitten in embarrassment. The policeman had a whipped look about him. They moved swiftly towards Heera's place to stave off the guilt and wash off the shame.

On the way, the cop admitted, "There is no doubt; this woman is quite bold and courageous."

Pateshwari said, "Bold and courageous? She is a total twerp. Such women should be shot dead."

"She deprived you of the money you could have made from this deal."

"Fifteen rupees is a good sum which you would have got from your share."

"When did I lose my share? If that man will not pay up, then the village elders will deliver. And they will come up with not fifteen but fifty. Please get cracking and organise it right away."

Thinking it to be a joke, Pateshwari laughed aloud and said, "Sire has such an amazing sense of humour!"

Datadin added, "A sense of humour is the exclusive quality of great men and such a magnanimous person like you is rare on earth."

The cop's voice was harsh and grating, "Keep this sugary stuff for a later day. Just arrange fifty rupees for me right now in cash. And if you try to play around with me I will search the houses of all four of you. There is a distinct possibility that the four of you might have conspired to gang up to trap both Hori and Heera so that you can make a quick buck from their misery."

The leaders were still under the illusion this was an amusing charade which the cop was playing out with them.

Jhinguri Singh winked at Pateshwari, "Come on *Patwariji,* cough up a fifty!"

Nokhe Ram seconded him as usual, "Yes, why not? This area is *Patwariji's* jurisdiction. He should definitely be hospitable to you sir!"

They had reached Nokhe Ram's courtyard. The cop pulled up a cot and sprawled on it. "So what have you decided? You'll bring the money or do you want me to search your place?"

Datadin made a feeble attempt to raise an objection, "But...sir..?"

"I will not hear any ifs and buts."

Jhinguri Singh mustered more courage, "But sire, this is sheer..."

"I give you exactly fifteen minutes. If you do not come here with fifty rupees, within that time your houses will be searched right away. I hope you are aware of my assistant Ganda Singh? When he gets to work there's no stopping him."

Pateshwari spoke up in a shrill voice, "You have the right to do anything. You can conduct a search. But this is atrocious. Someone commits a crime and others have to pay for it."

"I have been a cop for twenty five years. Do you know that or not?"

"But I have never seen such a travesty of law."

"If you have never seen such a travesty I hope you are not too keen to see it today. I will pack each one of you for five years in prison. It is so easy; I can do it whenever I want to. I can seal the whole village and quarantine every resident under suspicion of dacoity. Don't have any doubts about it, please."

They all went into another huddle on the other side of the courtyard. No one knows what exactly transpired but the end of it all was that the cop was beaming from ear to ear and these gentlemen wore a nightmarish expression.

The policeman mounted his horse and kicked its side and cantered off as the four of them ran some way after him. When the horse had vanished into the distance they returned home with the expression of those returning after cremating a dear one.

Datadin broke the silence. "May I be accursed if my curses don't destroy him?"

Nokhe Ram supported him, "I have never seen anyone flourish so much with ill begotten wealth."

Pateshwari made a prediction, "Evil earnings will go the evil way."

Jhinguri Singh had developed grave doubts about God's fair play and justice. He wondered how the good Lord could allow such injustice and not send thunderbolts to strike perpetrators of evil.

Had someone photographed them at that instant, it would have presented a pretty mirth-provoking sight indeed.

❋❋❋

10

There was no trace of Heera even as days rolled by relentlessly. Hori ran from pillar to post in search of his missing brother. Finally having spent his energies in vain, he gave up in sheer desperation. It was tough to manage things on his own and as time wore on, he discovered that the crops demanded a lot of attention as now he also had to assume the responsibility of his brother's fields. Left on her own, Heera's wife Punia was becoming increasingly aggressive and Hori had to spend most of his time trying to appease her and keep her in good humour.

Hori might have had an axe to grind with Heera but for him Punia was a family member in distress. She was well aware of this and took full advantage of the situation to corner Hori and exploit his kind nature in every possible way she could. Fortunately, the *Zamindaar's* henchmen took pity on her and did not press for recovering taxes. For a petty consideration, they agreed not to pester her. That was a lucky break as Hori was actually planning to take another loan to pay off her taxes along with his own.

Hori automatically assumed the role of Punia and her family's supporter. He worked himself weary sowing her part of the fields and at times at the cost of his own crop. As a result, in the next harvest, it was Punia's granary that overflowed with grains whereas Hori's sill was starkly empty.

Since that unfortunate day, Dhania and Hori nursed bitterness in their hearts and barely spoke to each other. Hori hardly shared more than cursory pleasantries with Gobar. Apparently, the mother-son duo had edged him out of their inner circle. He was a stranger in his own family and his situation was as unenviable as that of a homeless mongrel. His prestige amongst the villagers had nose-dived and Dhania's image went up in equal proportion amongst the women of the village.

For months, the tale was narrated with awe even as her story got exaggerated with every narration and finally took on a divine hue. "Her name is Dhania and she has the blessings of the Mother Goddess herself! When the policeman tried to arrest her husband she went into a trance, praying to the Mother, who promptly manifested Herself in Dhania's body. So great was the power that coursed through her frame that in one slash of her hands she broke the cuffs around her husband's wrists and wrenched the policeman's moustaches from its roots. Then she pounced and sat on his chest, pinning him down. When he pleaded with her, she had mercy on him and let him go." This story was told and re-told and Dhania's reputation went up steadily. She was attributed with immense courage which gave her the power to bring men to heel, if necessary.

But in real life Dhania was undergoing a slow, steady and subtle change. She did not object when she saw Hori working so diligently in Punia's fields. It was not due to her indifference to Hori but out of concern for Punia, who had no one else to fall back upon. Heera's flight and abdication had been enough to snuff the fire of revenge that smouldered in her heart.

Meanwhile Hori suddenly took ill. It was a seasonal disease that struck during harvesting season. Hori had caught it after ages but its severity weakened whatever resistance his body had acquired over the years. For one full month, he was totally bed ridden. Though the disease crushed him, on the other hand it brought about a profound change in Dhania's thought processes. 'When the husband is so weak and perhaps dying, it is futile to nurse anger and hatred towards him,' thought Dhania. 'After all he's my husband who has lived with me, for better or worse, for over twenty five years. He might be obstinate and mean but he has been the companion through difficult and happy times. At this time, it means little whether he was good or bad; he is your own and that's the simple truth. He beat me in the presence of the village folk shaming me before all; but hasn't he been so full of remorse ever since? He avoids looking directly into my eyes and does not utter a word at meal times. Poor man, he is perpetually afraid of precipitating a crisis or risk seeing me fly into a rage again.'

By the time Hori recovered from his illness both husband and wife had made up and things on the surface were almost normal between the two.

One day Dhania raised the topic again. "How could you get so angry? Howsoever mad you might make me, I can never raise my hand against you – what came over you that day?"

Hori was embarrassed, "Don't talk about it, Dhania. It was as if I was possessed. You don't know how deeply I regret doing what I did."

"What if I had killed myself in anger and shame?"

"If that were so do you think I would have remained alive to cry over your dead body? I would have thrown myself on your funeral pyre."

"Ok, now shut up. Don't utter such things."

"When the cow died, she must have cursed me. I am so worried about Punia."

"You're right. Being the eldest in the family is such a responsibility. No one scorns the junior member; all duties are dumped on the eldest."

It was late January and the skies were overcast with rain clouds. The night was dark and hard rain had lashed the trees that now stood motionless in deathly silence. Not a leaf stirred as Hori lay on his string cot next to the hedges near the pea fields. Having finished his dinner, he tried to lie still in order to stave off the biting cold weather but his blanket had worn thin and there were too many holes in it for comfort. The flimsy straw mattress was damp with the moist wind and his scruffy tunic did not offer any relief either. With so many nasty elements, sleep became elusive and Hori lay shivering. Worse! He seemed to have lost his pouch of tobacco and even the cauldron of smouldering coals could not spread any warmth. Tucking his cracked heels close to his body, he wrapped his arms around his knees and made valiant efforts to warm himself with his own breath under the blanket.

The tunic on his body was five years old. Dhania had insisted and got it made for him despite his protestations. She had bought the fabric from an Afghani who travelled from Kabul every year. He had raised a fuss over this purchase but Dhania obstinately stuck to her decision to buy it. The blanket was much older than the tunic; probably it had been around even before he was born. He used to sleep with his father in the same blanket as a child. In his youth, Gobar had slept snuggled close to him during winter nights under the same covering and now in his advancing age, it was still a companion though a feeble one. It was more like his teeth with which he could crack the toughest nuts in his youth but not any more.

In all his life there wasn't a day when he felt free and unencumbered by taxes, duties and pressures from moneylenders breathing down his back. The new burden of Heera's household responsibilities was nothing he could wish away. But despite his best effort, he still felt like a loser. When he was kind to Punia everybody assumed he was planning to cheat her of her share, when he kept away they blamed him for not doing anything to help her. It was rumoured he was filching all her crops. Recognition for selfless work was a far cry; instead, he got a bad name in the bargain. He shrugged his shoulders as he decided he had to fulfill his responsibility towards his brother's wife whether anyone was comfortable with it or not.

Though Dhania had forgiven him she nursed a certain resentment in her heart. He also regretted thrashing her in public and could not fathom what got over him that day to make him stoop so low. To have spent a quarter of a century with a woman and then hit her in public was a very low act. He thought to himself, 'I shouldn't have done it. But didn't she push me to it? She was determined to strip me of all dignity before others.'

Even now Dhania avoided talking to him directly. She'd often tell Sona or Rupa to convey whatever she wanted to tell Hori. He noticed her *saree* was in tatters, but just the other day on a rare occasion when she spoke to him, it was about getting a new one for Sona and not for herself. He looked at Dhania and thought to himself, 'Sona's *saree* can last a few more months with a few patches sewn at strategic places but her own is so patched up already that there isn't any left of the original. I have not been nice to her in any way. I have never tried to find out what she desires; I have never bought her any presents. I am growing old but none too wise for it. Thankfully my recent illness has softened her up a bit; otherwise who knows she might have remained indifferent forever.' Hori went over this repeatedly in his mind as he ruminated over the scant conversation, they had this morning savouring it like fistfuls of food thrown at a starving man.

Hori was completely overwhelmed. He wanted to bend down and rest his head at her feet and plead with her, 'come, hit me if you want to, I won't say a word.' Thus absorbed in her thoughts, he tried to stave off the cold that stalked him menacingly.

All at once he heard the soft clinking of someone's bangles from near the hedges. He strained his ears. Yes, there was definitely someone out there. Must be *Patwari's* daughter or it could also be the *pundit's* wife, come to steal a basketful of pea pods from his fields. He wondered why they stooped to such petty thieving. They made enough money for themselves, were better dressed than any in the village, ate well, ripped off their debtors, took bribes as well as gratification money and constantly picked up issues that helped them derive financial benefits from all and sundry, yet such pettiness was beyond his comprehension. Hori wondered how they would face up to it if he went ahead and caught them thieving. The so called respectable people can be as low as the shallow and mean ones. His scruples prevented him from nabbing a lady and insulting her in this manner. He cursed under his breath- 'go ahead, steal them all. Just assume I am not here.' He thought if the respectable people have no shame, it is the duty of the meek ones to at least help them preserve their dignity.

But he was soon to discover it was Dhania he had heard behind the bushes. She called out to him, 'Are you asleep or awake?"

Hori scrambled up and stepped out into the open field behind the hedges. He felt a strange delight tingle through his body. The Gods must be happy. He smiled to himself joyfully despite the foreboding that crept into his mind at her late night visit in such cold. She must have something important to talk about, he thought.

He said, "Can anyone sleep in this bitter cold? What brings you here in this weather- I hope all's well at home?"

"Yes, everything's fine."

"You should have sent Gobar to call me."

Dhania did not reply and coming up to him, she sat down on the damp straw mattress and sighed, "What do I say about him, it is Gobar who has shamed us all. My worst fears have come true."

"What happened? Did he pick up a fight with someone?"

"How do I know what he has been up to? Why don't you come and ask this of that slut."

"What slut? What are you muttering? Have you gone out of your mind?"

"Yes, I have actually gone out of my mind. Whatever has happened will surely make us very proud," she said, sarcastically.

A distinct ray of light lit up Hori's understanding of the situation.

"Why don't you speak upfront; who are you talking about?"

"It's about that Jhuniya, who else?"

"Is Jhuniya here with you?"

"Where else could she have gone?"

"Isn't Gobar at home?"

"Gobar is untraceable. He has run away God knows where. That girl is five months pregnant."

Everything immediately fell in place in Hori's mind. He had a vague inkling of what was going on when he noticed Gobar's frequent trips to the cowherd's colony but he didn't realise the boy was upto no good. He knew that some sort of romantic inclination was natural for a boy but he was surprised to note that the little wisp of a floating cloud that he had admired indulgently had grown so big to completely cover the sky, bringing a dismal darkness into his life.

How could Gobar be so callous and depraved? That simple lad whom he had always considered a child; wasn't he worried about the consequences of his actions, had he no fear of the village elders, the laws and rituals? Didn't he once consider what would happen to Jhuniya, where she would stay? But presently Hori's concern was not Jhuniya but Gobar. Hori thought to himself that Gobar was a very self respecting boy and having made this mistake, he might take some drastic step out of fear and confusion.

Hori panicked and asked Dhania if Gobar had left any message where he was going.

Irritated, Dhania snapped at him, "What's wrong with your head? His sweetheart is sitting at our doorstep; he won't run off like that. He is hiding someplace nearby. You think he is a little baby that he will lose his way in the forest? My worry is what to make of this wretch who has parked herself at our house. They have been seeing each other ever since he went to fetch the cow from her house. Had she not conceived, the affair would still be under wraps. Once she got pregnant, Jhuniya started losing her nerve. She suggested that the two should elope but Gobar kept putting it off. How would he know where to hide with a pregnant woman in tow? She says that today she put her foot down and insisted he take her somewhere and threatened to end her life if he didn't. He told her to come along with him, saying he will bring us around to accept her and take care of everything. This dumb girl trusted his word and came along with him. He came half way with her and all of a sudden just bolted and ran off. She kept calling for him but he didn't look back. When it turned dark and he didn't return, she came knocking at our door. I have given her a piece of my mind; now she must reap what she has sown.

"The miserable wretch has ruined my son's life and now she is sitting at my door crying her eyes out. She isn't budging an inch, she says she can't face her folks like this. This is a terrible situation. It's better to be barren than have a child like this. As soon as it's light, the village will be feasting on the latest gossip that has landed on their plate. I just want to get out and consume some poison. Let me be very clear to you. I am not having that runt in my house. I hate such slimy characters. And if you try to mediate or act very wise, let me warn you, it will be either you or I who remains in the house."

Hori said she should not have allowed her into the house in the first instance.

"I tried to dissuade her in every way but she wouldn't budge."

"Ok, let me come with you. Let's see how she doesn't leave. I will drag her out forcibly."

Dhania was unrelenting. "That rascal Bhola was well aware of the goings on between the two but he kept quiet. To think a father could be so low!"

"How could he know what was cooking between the two?"

"Of course he knew! Gobar hovered around his house day in day out. Do you think he is so dumb not to understand what's going on."

"Let me ask Jhuniya about this."

They left the fields and started towards the village. It was well past midnight, almost the hour before dawn. A deathly quiet greeted them in the sleeping village, "If a thief were to come by, he will clean out every house and no one would ever know."

"Thieves do not come to such villages. They go to rich men's homes."

Dhania paused in her tracks and turning around gripped his hand, "Now listen to me. Don't make a scene at home and wake up the village unnecessarily. There is no point in making a hue and cry about what has happened."

Hori's tone had a sharp edge to it, "I will not promise anything. I am going to drag her and leave her outside the village. This news is going to be out one day; what difference does it make if it's today or weeks later? Why did she have to come to our place at all? She should go wherever Gobar has gone. Did she consult us before cosying up to him?"

Dhania gripped his wrist again and spoke softly, "If you try to hold her hand, she will raise hell."

"Let her do whatever she likes."

"Why don't you realise she can't go anywhere in a dark night like this?"

"She can go wherever she wants to. What do we have to do with her?"

"That's fine but it is not advisable to send her away at this unearthly hour. She is carrying a child; if anything happens to her, it will make things worse. As it is her condition is such that not much can be done about it."

"I don't care whether she lives or dies. Actually, when Gobar comes back home I will throw him out as well."

Dhania spoke cautiously, "The harm has already been done. Our name is besmirched and we cannot wash off the stigma as long as we live. Gobar has ruined us."

"It is not Gobar. It's this wretch - she is responsible for everything. Gobar is a kid, she led him into the snare."

"Whoever might be responsible the fact is we are doomed."

They reached their house. As they stood in the alley before their door, all of a sudden Dhania turned to him and put her arms around his neck and said, "Swear on me, you will not raise your hand against her. She is already broken and hurt. If it were not for her miserable fate would she have seen such bad times?"

Hori looked at her intently for sometime. He knew Dhania's concern was prompted by a maternal instinct that shone like a lamp in the dark night. Her frame wracked by worry and suffering, softened in its tender glow. A long forgotten youthful ardour rippled through their bodies. As he stared at the haggard woman, who was looking at him with worried eyes, he saw a familiar young girl who had stepped into his life twenty five years ago. In her slight embrace, he felt a deep affection that was above all material wealth in the world.

They went up and peeped through the crack in the door. An oil lamp was burning on a niche in the wall. Bathed in its dull light, Jhuniya sat with her head resting between her knees, her eyes expectantly turned towards the door, anxiously waiting for Gobar, the man who had come into her life like a ray of happiness, but had disappeared when she needed him the most. Tossed around by her circumstances she had survived consistent verbal volleys, barbs and sarcasm in a fervent hope of ultimately finding a restful succour. She was not expecting much but what she got was more than her wildest dreams. Gobar made her feel safe, loved and secure. Today that refuge had vanished and a dark future stared at her, eager to swallow her in its wide open jaws.

When she heard the latch open and saw Hori step into the room, her body convulsed with fear and she threw herself at his feet and wept. "*Dada,* I have no one to turn to except you. Kill me, kick me as much you want but please don't turn me away from your door."

Hori bent down, patting her head and stroking her back affectionately, he said, "Don't be afraid, little girl. This is your home; you can live here without any fear. You are as much my daughter as you are Bhola's. With us around, you have nothing to fear. Nobody can harm you; we are there for you. We will manage everything, all the rituals and social obligations. You keep your peace."

Hearing those reassuring words, she held him tighter than ever and said, "*Dada,* you are my mother, father, everything. I am an orphan. Please save me or my father and brothers will skin me alive."

Dhania could not rein in her emotions any longer. She said, "You sit tight. Let me deal with your father and brothers. They do not own the world; what worse can they do. They might try to take back the ornaments you wear? Throw them off, let them take those away."

Barely hours ago she had called her a slut, a sinner and a whole lot of other names. She had said she would beat her with a broom and sweep her out into the streets. When Jhuniya heard such comforting words from her, she left Hori and fell at Dhania's feet. The chaste woman, who had never dreamt of a man other than her own husband, warmly hugged this frightened girl whom the world might despise as a sinner. She took her in her arms, assuring her, wiping her tears and nursing her wounded heart with gentle words, cradling her in her arms.

She signalled to Hori to get her something to eat and asked Jhuniya if she had even a vague idea where Gobar could have gone.

Jhuniya said amidst tears that she did not have the faintest idea where he could be. She said, "He didn't tell me anything. And now because of me you..." Her words trailed off as her body shook with hysterical sobbing.

Hori couldn't hide his rising panic either. "When you met him today, did you find him uneasy or worried?"

"No. Infact, he sounded quite jovial but God knows what was brewing in his mind."

"What is your gut feeling? Would you say he is in the village or he has gone somewhere else?"

"I have a nagging doubt he has left for some other place."

"That's what is worrying me too. How can he be so naïve? We are not his enemies; if he commits a mistake, we will not dump or forsake him. By running away like this he has landed us in deep trouble."

Dhania took Jhuniya by the hand and took her inside the house. "Such a coward! When he chose to be with someone he should have stayed put with her and not run away in shame. Let him return, I will give him a piece of my mind."

Hori lay down on the hay in a corner. Where was Gobar? The question preyed on his mind like a persistent hawk circling above him in the sky.

11

The furore expected due to a development of such magnitude raged not for a few days but months at a stretch. Jhuniya's brothers scoured the village flashing their *lathis,* looking everywhere for Gobar to teach him a lesson for violating their honour. Bhola vowed not to see Jhuniya nor step into the village where she had holed up. All talk of arranging for his engagement had come to a grinding halt and he decided to insist on cash payment for the cow he had given to Hori. If Hori did not cough up the money, he was determined to get his property confiscated and auctioned. The village treated Hori as an outcaste and boycotted him socially. No one shared a *chillum* with him anymore and considered it a sacrilege to share his drinking water. There was a move to deny them water from the village well but Dhania's fury and temperament was fresh in their memory, hence none could muster enough courage to come forward to press for it.

Dhania had already proclaimed loudly that if any attempt was made to ban their access to the well, rivers of blood would flow through the streets. This open challenge had shaken them up. However, Jhuniya was hit the hardest. She was full of regret and remorse as she considered herself as the cause of all the mess. Lack of information of Gobar's whereabouts compounded this misery twice over. All through the day she remained at home, hiding herself from the world. If she stepped out for a moment, verbal volleys and darts aimed at her cut hard and deep. She toiled at odd jobs around the house throughout the day and cried bitterly when she had nothing else to keep herself occupied. Since no one would eat food cooked by her, she could not prepare meals and had therefore taken up the responsibility of every other odd job around the house. As for the village, wherever there was a gathering of more than two people, she was severely criticised.

One day when Dhania was returning from the local mart, she came across Datadin coming from the other end of the road. Dhania lowered her gaze, avoiding him, but Datadin was in no mood to be thus ignored. He said, "Any news of Gobar? Such a horrible boy he is! He has made life so difficult for you."

Dhania subscribed to similar views on the subject. In a sad tone she spoke, agreeing with him, "When bad luck strikes, it first robs one of all discretion and commonsense. What else can explain his behaviour?"

Datadin spoke up. "You should not have allowed that bad woman in your house. If a fly falls in a glass of milk, it has to be fished out. You don't throw away the pot of milk with it. Do you know what a laughing stock you have made of yourself? If she were not living at your place, they would not have targeted you so badly. Boys commit such mistakes at times. How will you absolve yourself of this stigma unless you organise a community feast and give away alms to Brahmins? All this could have been avoided, had you kept that girl at an arm's distance. Hori is crazy, he is a dimwit; how did you get yourself into this?"

Datadin's son was involved with a low caste *Chamarin*. The entire village was aware of it; yet he wore his caste marks, dabbled in scriptures, gave sermons from the religious books and attended to all holy duties. There was barely a stain on his spotless reputation. He washed away his sins each day with resolute attention to ritual, almost ceremoniously. Dhania was aware that Jhuniya was the cause of her problems. Had she turned her away right then, such scorn would not have been heaped on her every day. At the same time, she was concerned that Jhuniya might attempt suicide by jumping in the well or the river. Dhania had no intention of buying peace at the cost of Jhuniya's life; no, it was actually two lives now. All said and done, the baby in Jhuniya's womb was no outsider but a part of Dhania's own soul. She could not dream of killing her own grandchild merely to protect notions of respectability. Moreover, Jhuniya's humility in the face of her helplessness disarmed her completely. Every evening when she would return from her chores tired, Jhuniya would come to her offer a pitcher of water and press her feet. Her seething resentment would vanish to be replaced by a caring empathy for her. Poor girl! She was already groaning under the weight of such shame and suffering; she didn't deserve any more of it. It was unfair to inflict insult to injury on someone who was already down and out.

She looked back at Datadin and spoke with an edge to her voice, "We are not so bothered about our reputation that we would be ready to snuff out an innocent life. She might not be married to him; but she is someone whom my son has loved as his own. How could I ever throw her out on the streets? When rich people do such things there is no talk of shame, respect or damage to their image- no one casts aspersions on them. When a poor person does something like that, it becomes a sin or a loss of face for them. Perhaps, the reputation of the rich is more precious but as far as I am concerned, there is a life at stake here and respectability be damned."

Datadin was not one to give up that easy. He was the original busybody of the village. He would never attempt a robbery, since it involved risk to life and limb but he would be the first to carve out the spoils of such misadventures. He was utterly mindful of not allowing any sort of taint to sully his image from a yard. He never paid a single *paisa* as duties to the *zamindaar*. When his henchmen came to attach his properties he would march straight to the village well to attempt an elaborate public suicide. He had no money to pay off his loans but had enough to give to his minions on heavy interest. Any woman desirous of buying jewellery could always bank on Datadin's assistance. He loved arranging marriages through deft negotiations; it was enjoyable and added immensely to his popularity, not to mention his profits as well. In illnesses he was ever present to offer medicines, or if the patient desired, a slight dose of traditional mumbo jumbo as well. His social skills were amazing. With young lads, he was one of their kinds yet he was equally at ease with older men. He was a friend to both petty thieves and rich neighbours. None in the village trusted him but there was such magic in his words that despite falling into his trap, repeatedly, they could not resist but to walk in willingly to seek shelter in the honeyed web, he wove with such dexterity.

One day in much the same fashion, Lala Pateshwari caught up with Hori as well. He was known as the kind-hearted good man of the village. Every fortnight, he would religiously conduct ceremonies to propitiate the Gods but would have his fields irrigated without paying for the labour, since he didn't charge interest from his poor debtors. Many in the village were in awe of him and he had built up a sizeable fortune in land through collections of interest from loans he distributed to poor peasants. The produce from the farms, which he took from those who owed him favours, was dispatched regularly in the service of the police and junior officials from local courts. This gave him a special edge over his peers and his clout spread far and wide; the only one who had not fallen for his charms as yet was petty constable Ganda Singh who was posted recently in that area. Pateshwari was also some sort of a philanthropist. During epidemics, he earned undying admiration of all and sundry by distributing quinine tablets supplied free by the government. When anyone fell ill, he never forgot to enquire about his health and welfare. He was known to amicably settle minor disputes between people and volunteered to lend his carriage, carpets and other decorative stuff to people for weddings and other ceremonies and was amply rewarded by their gratitude in return. He was not one to let an opportunity slip by if he could extort some benefit out of it but at the same time had built up a reputation that he delivered promptly on his word.

He called out to Hori as he was walking on the road, "What's this new blight you have invited into your home, Hori?"

Hori looked back and said, "What was that? I didn't hear you."

Pateshwari quickened his pace and caught up with him, "Hori, I merely wanted to know if you are as dense as Dhania? Why don't you send Jhuniya back to her father's house? You are unnecessarily giving everyone an opportunity to make fun of you. Who knows where she conceived that child, yet you promptly let herself into your home. You have two daughters who have to be married shortly; did you spare a thought for their future?"

Hori had enough of such complaints, suggestions and wisecracks. He responded with a fair amount of irritation, "I know all that, brother. But do you think Bhola will welcome that girl back into his house even if I throw her out? If he agrees to accept her I will send her back this very day. If you can make him see reason and accept her back, I will be deeply indebted to you. But aren't you aware his sons are in such a murderous mood? How can I turn her away like that? On the one hand she meets a fellow who ditches her after promising her the world and on the other she is in no position to eke out a living on her own. If she kills herself in desperation I will only blame myself and as far as my daughters are concerned I have faith in God. He knows best what's good for them and He will help me at the right time. No girl remains unmarried for long in our community and moreover. I can't act like a murderer just because I am scared of social pressures."

Hori was a humble man and preferred to be patient with insults rather than retaliate to such attacks with vehemence. Other than his own brother there was not a soul in the entire village who bore ill feelings towards him but how could they accept such a damaging blow to the social structure? Hori's insistence on challenging prevalent norms ended whatever chance there was to salvage the situation. Hori and Dhania threw a challenge at the face of the villagers- daring them to take any step to bend their will or tweak their independence. It was now imperative for the society to make a definitive statement to assert its complex hold on the individual, who dared to break free of its iron grip.

That night a special meeting of village elders was called to thrash out this issue once and for all.

Datadin said, "I don't intend to malign anybody. The world is teeming with sin so why should I be bother at all? But Dhania – such a wretch! - is spoiling for a fight. When one is drunk with ill-begotten money siphoned from a brother's share, it is so easy to be swept away by moral turpitude. These low classes! The moment they come into some wealth, they completely lose their sense of balance. No wonder, the scriptures warn against giving them too much independence."

Pateshwari took another puff from the smouldering *chillum*. "This is the real problem; they are unable to handle money. As soon as they get some money, they lose all sense of proportion and discretion. Today Hori glowered at me with such haughtiness that I felt humiliated. He thinks too much of himself. Just imagine the fallout of these immoral developments in the village. Other widows will take a leaf out of Jhuniya's book and try to emulate her ways. This can happen anywhere---in my house, yours or every other house in the village. Society works best under fear. The day society loses moral control all hell will break lose in the world."

Jhinguri Singh had two wives. His first wife died when he was thirty five years old and left behind two children. Since the second one was childless; he married a third time. He was touching sixty and had two young wives at home. The village gossip mills worked overtime lending grist to rumours and inspiring racy comments about both women but his ample clout kept the rumours and innuendoes in relative control. As it is, quite a fair bit of transgressions can be swept under the garb of marital respectability. The going is tough only for those outside the sanctimony of the protective shield of a husband. He kept his wives on a tight leash and often boasted about their inaccessibility to prying eyes. However, he had little idea of what went on under their staid veils.

Self righteously he thundered, "Such a low woman should be flogged in public. By sheltering her in his home, Hori is sowing seeds of poison in society. Such a man's presence will do little other than corrupt the village. I suggest Rai sahib be informed about this matter. He must be informed in no uncertain terms that if such licentiousness is permitted, there will be utter chaos."

Pandit Nokhe Ram traced his origins from a noble, high caste Brahmin lineage. His grandfather was a minister at the court of some king, who in a sudden change of heart had offered all his wealth in the service of God and had turned into a wandering mendicant. His father had spent his life in a similar pursuit. Nokhe

Ram had inherited this strong inclination towards matters of the spirit from his father and grandfather. He would sit himself down to prayer early in the morning and get up from the devotional exercise not earlier than ten in the day. As a matter of routine, he scribbled the word 'Ram' at least a thousand times as he prayed to the deity. But wrenching himself away from his devotional labour was so painful for his material existence that the trauma dried up all the warmth and poisoned all kindness in his heart. The proposal regarding Hori's misdeeds which was drafted for Rai sahib's consideration struck him as a slight to his power and importance. With his lips barely moving in the folds of his sunken face, he spoke in a harsh voice, "There is no need to consult Rai sahib on this account. I am fully competent and can decide as I please in this case. This man should be fined two hundred rupees for his transgressions; that itself will send him packing from the village. I will also file extermination proceedings on him to ensure his final exit from the village."

Pateshwari had his doubts, "But hasn't he already paid his taxes to the *zamindaar*?"

Jhinguri Singh seconded him, "Indeed he has paid the tax. Actually, he took a loan of thirty rupees from me specifically for that purpose."

Nokhe Ram sneered conspiratorially, "He has not been issued a receipt. Does he have any proof that he has paid it?"

Ultimately, after a spirited discussion the consensus was to fine him a hundred rupees. However, a semblance of formal endorsement by the village assembly was necessary so they decided to call a public meeting and push the proposal through but a drawback to this plan came up rather unexpectedly. At least four to five days were needed to organise this meeting and while the honourable members worked on the logistics, news arrived that a baby boy was born to Jhuniya that same night. This altered everything dramatically, lending a new urgency to the plan. The very next day, all legalities were set in place and the villlage *panchayat* was called to order. Hori and Dhania were summoned to hear the judgement passed by the *panchayat* heads. The village square was packed to capacity with people falling over each other to get a better view. The members of the *panchayat* grandly announced a fine of one hundred rupees on Hori along with another thirty mounds of grains as punitive damages which was to be deposited in the community granary.

Dhania's voice choked as she addressed the village elders after hearing their decision. "Honourable elders, I hope you realise you too will find no peace if you hurt the poor. We will be annihilated; who knows whether we stay in the village or perish somewhere else but our suffering will come to haunt you sooner or later. I am being penalised and forced to pay such a heavy fine simply because I decided to shelter my daughter-in-law in my dwelling and not kick her out to beg on the streets. Is this what you call justice, eh?"

"She is not your daughter-in-law. She is a bloody whore", said Pateshwari.

Hori turned to Dhania and glowered at her, "Shut up, Dhania! This is no way to talk. Village elders are considered living divinity on earth. If that is what providence throws at us we have to accept it with grace and humility. If God wants us to abandon this village and go away who are we to question His ways?" Turning to the men he said, "Honourable Elders, whatever we have is not in our home yet but still lying in the granary in the fields. Not a grain has been transferred to our house. Take away whatever you want. If you want the entire produce, you can have it. We trust in God and believe in His mercy. If you think what we have isn't enough, you can take my bulls to compensate for it."

Dhania gnashed her teeth and spluttered in anger, "I will not part with a single grain and won't pay a single *paisa* as fine. Let me see who dares to take it from me? This is atrocious! Perhaps, you think you can walk away with all our property by imposing this monstrous fine. Don't assume for a moment that you can rob us and we will sit tight or watch helplessly. Not as long as I live! Your evil desires will stew in your heart forever for we are no more interested to remain within your community. Living with you means nothing to us anymore. We live off our hard labour and sweat and shall do so in future as well. We don't need you."

Hori turned to her and folded his hands. "Dhania, should I fall at your feet? Please keep quiet. We are humble members of the community; we have no existence outside it. Whatever fine the community imposes on us we have to accept with humility. It is better to hang ourselves than live a life of shame as an outcast. If we die today who else but the community will deliver us from earthly bondage? Honourable elders, I swear on the life of my son, I have nothing other than what I have spelt out before you. I own little except the grains locked up in my granary. I have no intention of deceiving the community. If your justice has any mercy for my children, please consider how I will fend for them. As for me, I am duty bound to heed your advice and orders, your decisions will not influence my commitment to you."

Dhania got up and left the meeting in a huff. Hori spent the entire afternoon, right into the late evening transferring sacks of grain from his granary to Jhinguri Singh's courtyard all by himself. He had twenty mounds of barley, five mounds of wheat and an equivalent amount of pea pods with a few mounds of grams and oil seeds. He had to single handedly attend to the needs of two households. Dhania had also contributed immensely to whatever assets he had stored in the granary. Jhuniya looked after the house, giving Dhania enough space to attend to the fields with her two daughters. They had planned to pay off an installment of the loan they had taken for the taxes besides clearing up some dues of interest that was growing steadily over time. The barley stocks would have fed them through four or five months till the time the next maize crop would be ready.

This sudden bolt from the blue blew their plans to smithereens. Not only did they lose all the grains but were saddled with a fresh burden of a hundred rupees. There was absolutely nothing left to eat and to make matters worse, Gobar was nowhere to be found. Where could he have gone? There was no news; not even a squeak from him. Why did he get into such a fix if he did not have the spine for it? The state of Hori's mind presented a story that wasn't very different either. The fear of being ostracised by the community gripped him like a demon, whipping him to transport sacks of grain on his head, forcing him to dig his own grave. The money lender, the *zamindaar,* even the government did not invoke such dread. He could not imagine a life divorced from the comforting yet dreadful embrace of the society in which he lived. The community ruled over every stage of his existence- whether it was marriage, death, birth or the long list of ceremonies and rituals attached to daily life. The community surrounded him like a massive tree with roots that entwined into every nerve and pore of his body. If he was rejected by it his life was a waste; shorn bare and bereft of any meaning, support or sustenance.

When he had transferred all but the last few remaining mounds of grain, Dhania ran up to him and caught hold of his hand, "That will be enough. Hold your hand now. You have done enough to abide by your community's bidding. Will you leave something for your children or throw it all in the community dump? I give up! I must have been cursed with rotten fate to have married a man like you."

Hori pried his hand away from her grip and said, "Nothing doing, Dhania. It is a sin to smuggle even a grain and hide it from the Elder's committee. I am going to put all that I have before them. If they are merciful, they will give back something for my children and if not, God will certainly help us."

Dhania was irritated beyond words but she managed to express her indignation. "They are not village Elders. They are demons. They want to somehow swindle all that we have; fine and punishment is merely an excuse. I am trying to make you understand but you are blind. Do you think these demons will have any mercy for you? You think they will let you keep five or ten mounds for your children? You must be really dumb if you think like that. It isn't going to happen."

When Hori did not pay any heed, she held the bag with her hands and pulled it away from him with all the strength she could muster. "I will not let you take this last bag even if you kill me. We sweated our guts out and struggled for this-toiling night and day with our sweat and tears. Did we strain ourselves so hard so that you hand it over to those good-for-nothings on a platter while our children starve for every morsel? You are not the only one who has toiled for it. I have also worked equally with you and have suffered for it along with my daughters. I warn you, put this bag down or today we will part ways for ever. I have had enough and I will not take more!"

Hori paused for a moment. Dhania's words struck a chord in his heart. What right did he have to deprive his children of their earnings to pay his dues? He was the head of his family and it was his duty to care for his dependents and not use their earnings, simply, to appease the community and preserve his image. He told her to take the last bag home and he would let the Elders know about it.

Dhania carried the bag home and put it away in a corner. She settled herself purposefully on the floor and in a voice loud enough to carry across to neighbours' homes, sang songs - auspicious melodies; celebrating the birth of a baby as her two daughters joined her in a musical yet lonesome celebration. This was the first time that on a happy occasion like the birth of a baby, no woman from the community had visited them or joined them in their songs. Jhuniya sent message from inside the house that the occasion did not warrant such loud singing but there was no stopping Dhania. If the community was going to ignore her she was least bothered and would sing all alone, if need be.

As the singing rose from his house, Hori sat in another part of the village, signing a deed, pledging his house in the name of Jhinguri Singh for eighty rupees. There was no other way to raise the amount for the fine he had to pay up on the morrow. He had got twenty rupees in exchange of the oilseeds, wheat and pea pods; the remaining eighty had to be raised by pledging the house. Nokhe Ram wanted to sell off his bulls too but Pateshwari cautioned him, saying Hori needed them to plough the fields. Datadin saw the logic and agreed with the idea that his property could be utilised to raise the fine but some cushion was needed so that he was not pushed to the brink and abandoned the village for good. Thus, the bulls were spared and they remained at Hori's house.

Hori returned home around eleven o' clock late that night after all the papers were prepared, signed and sealed. Dhania asked him why he was so late.

Hori transferred his frustration of the evening to a likely source. "I was busy reaping the sins of that scoundrel. He ran away but ignited a spark to burn down my house and now I am trying to douse the fire. I had to pledge the house for eighty rupees. Now they have lifted the social boycott of eating and smoking together. The community has forgiven us."

Dhania was unimpressed. "How would it hurt us if they had continued with the social boycott? If we don't sit and eat with them or share a smoke, does it make it any worse? I am surprised why you are so naïve. This house is the only thing that remains of our forefathers and you have not spared it either. The few *bighas* of land that's left will also slip away like this and we will be out on the streets. Why didn't you speak up and question those elders? Ask them what sort of holy divinity do they represent. You should have told them that the real sin is that they are living in this world."

Hori told her to pipe down and not make a spectacle in front of the neighbours. She was touched to the quick- "What have I done to be so scared of your precious community? Have I robbed someone or filched someone's property? Taking a woman is no sin; not facing upto it and dumping her definitely is. The biggest sin is to be too simple. Even stray mongrels raise their tail and pee on those who are simple and meek. Today they will be singing your glories...'O what a great man'; and here I am- miserable unlucky woman tied to you by my accursed fate. Not once have I had a day's respite ever since you came into my life."

"I didn't go begging to your father nor did I fall at his feet to give me his daughter's hand. If anyone is to blame it is him for he pushed you into my life."

"What can I say? His commonsense took leave of him for a moment when he took that decision. I just don't know what he saw in you that impressed him so much; you were not even a handsome man."

A subtle shift transported the argument from viciousness to joviality. Eighty rupees were down the drain but a bonny baby worth a million and more, was chortling in their arms. Who could take him away from them? Now if Gobar should return home; Dhania would be perfectly happy to stay in a small hut, if it came to it.

Hori asked, "Who does he resemble?"

Dhania's face lit up with a bright smile, "He looks exactly like Gobar. Believe me!"

"I hope he's healthy?"

"Perfectly."

❁❁❁

12

That fateful night when Gobar left for his home with Jhuniya, his body trembled as though he was about to be demeaned in public. He visualised the turmoil and noisy name-calling, following the revelation of why he brought that girl home. He pictured Dhania hurling abuses at him and quaked in fear, at the thought. Hori was not his major concern; he would holler and raise a storm but nonetheless cool down in no time. His worry was Dhania, who, he feared might attempt to swallow something poisonous or maybe try to set the house on fire. With every passing moment, he grew convinced it was not the opportune moment to go home with Jhuniya.

At the same time he was disturbed about the consequences if Dhania did not allow Jhuniya in the house. She could not go back to her home since she had stepped out surreptitiously. He sweated profusely, worried that she might hang herself or jump into a well. He took a deep breath; there was no one he could turn to in his moment of distress.

He thought about it again and tried to convince himself that his mother was not so heartless. At her worst, she would give her a piece of her mind wrapped in choicest abuse. He knew if Jhuniya fell at her feet and cried, his mother would definitely relent; certainly she would. Till that time, he must lie low and wait for the storm to subside after which he would return quietly and everything would be normal once again. Meanwhile, if he got a job and came back with good earnings Dhania would not say anything to him.

Jhuniya tugged at Gobar's arm, "My heart is beating fast. How was I to know you will land me in such a mess? Woe to the day I met you! I wish you had never come to my house for the cow. I suggest you go ahead and tell your folks about us and face whatever they have to say about it. I will come in a little later."

"No, first you go in and say you had gone to the mart and were delayed. Tell them since it's getting late you came to our place instead of going home. By that time I will also walk in."

Jhuniya was not convinced, "Your mother has a quick temper; she scares me. What will I do if she starts beating me?"

Gobar assured her, "That's not like my mother. She has never slapped us; why should she beat you up? She might get mad at me but she won't say anything to you."

They reached very close to the village. Gobar halted in his tracks, "This is it. Now you go from here."

"Please don't be late," Jhuniya bleated.

"Don't worry. I will be there in a moment. You go ahead."

"I feel so mad at you. I don't know what's going on in my mind."

"Why are you so afraid? I will be there right behind you."

"I think it would be better if we run away someplace else."

"When we have our home why should we run someplace else?"

"You sure you will follow right after me?"

"Yes. I am right behind you."

"You aren't planning to dump me, are you?"

"Jhuniya, do you think I am that low? I have taken your hand in mine and am not one to let go of it till my last breath."

Jhuniya turned and left for his house while Gobar stood rooted at the spot, transfixed for a few minutes. In that fleeting interval the anticipation of disgrace and ridicule, which hovered over his head for the better part of the day, all of a sudden grew into a monstrous entity that threatened him menacingly. What if his mother actually beat her up? His legs felt like lead. From where he stood, there was just a small orchard of mango trees between him and his house. He could see Jhuniya, a black shadow moving reluctantly towards his door. His senses were keen and alerted to the slightest sound. His ears almost heard his mother shout at her. The state of his mind was like that of a condemned man expecting the blade of the guillotine to fall on his neck, any instant. His blood froze as he saw Dhania emerge from the house in a hurry and take purposeful strides towards the dark road. She must be going to his father! Probably, he had gone to watch over the fields after dinner.

Gobar began walking towards the pea fields. He trod on wheat and barley shrubs, scrambling over the field as if he was pursued by a mob. He could see the hedge behind which his father rested at night. Slowing down, he tip-toed to the edge lying well within the darkness. He was right – within seconds he heard Dhania's voice. This was terrible, thought to himself. "She was so hard hearted; she had no pity for a poor orphan girl! How would she feel if I come up and give her an earful? If I am equally rude and tell her to keep off Jhuniya then all her bravado would go up in smoke. Oh goodness! It seems my father too is angry. I am obedient and mindful of their age that is why they are emboldened to say whatever they please. Father is following her back to the house. Now if they get violent with Jhuniya, it will be too much for me to tolerate. O Lord, I trust you. How could I have guessed I would get into such a mess? Jhuniya must be thinking I am a low, scheming, cowardly man. But if anyone as much as touches Jhuniya all hell will break loose today. I'll see to it. Parents are to be respected as long as they care for their children. If they have no love for them, they have no right to exist at all."

As soon as Hori left with Dhania, Gobar crept up behind them, following at a discreet distance. He saw a light streaming out of the open door and sank deeper into the shadows. He dare not step into the circle of light falling outside his house. He leaned flat against the wall and strained his neck to see if he could hear anything as his courage evaporated in thin air. These people were turning the heat on Jhuniya and he was too helpless to check it. He regretted playing with fire. He had no idea that the little spark he had tossed around so carelessly would turn into a blazing inferno, threatening to engulf his life. He was discovering that he did not have the courage to stand up, face up to it or accept that it was all his doing. All the strength and emotional props he had built for himself were badly shaken in this tremor and crumbling down all around him. He turned back. He could not face Jhuniya anymore.

He scurried about a hundred steps- as a soldier fleeing the battleground. The words of love, assurance and commitment he spoke to her came crowding into his mind. The moments of intimacy he spent with her returned to haunt his mind with their sweet memories; how he would pour the affection surging in his heart at her feet. He remembered how he watched her with drunken eyes, heady with an all consuming passion.

Jhuniya lived in her solitary nest like a pining bird. Her world had none of the outgoing energy of male insistence, there was no expectant fluttering of joyful wings and hardly any chirrup of familial tenderness. Untouched by webs of deceit, she was insulated from the reach of wily hunters. Gobar had intruded into her space. Whether he offered any respite from her morbid existence, howsoever momentary, was debatable but it was amply clear to him that he was certainly instrumental in thrusting her into an unenviable predicament. He paused to steady himself. The fleeing warrior heard the exhortation of a fellow soldier and turned back into the thick of battle.

When he came up to the door he found it bolted from inside. Rays of light fell through cracks in the door. He pressed his eye to one and peered in. Dhania and Jhuniya were sitting on the floor and Hori stood nearby. He heard Jhuniya's sobs and his mother's calming sounds of assurance. "You sit tight, my child. Let me deal with your father and brothers. As long as we live, no harm will ever befall you. No one dare cast an evil eye on you." Gobar was overwhelmed! If he was rich enough, he would have right then and there anointed his parents with gold and told them to sit back and relax, not worry about the daily grind, eat and drink to their heart's desire and offer as much as they want towards holy causes. There was no reason to worry about Jhuniya anymore. She had found the shelter he wanted for her. If she now thought of him as a cheating crook, so be it. He would return home when he had enough money to silence wagging tongues in the village so that his mother and father felt proud of their son instead of considering him a blot on their name.

The emotional reaction to hurt is often as profound and deep as the wound that caused it. From feelings of shame and dread, an unlikely and unseen aspect emerged within Gobar's personality. For the first time in his life he awoke to his responsibilities and a quiet determination firmed up inside his mind. So far his objective was to avoid work as much as he could and gorge on food. Not once did it cross his mind that he had also had some responsibility towards his parents. Their kind act of forgiveness revealed his life in an entirely new light in his eyes. When Jhuniya and Dhania went inside into another room, Gobar turned back silently and strode up to the spot where his father rested next to the pea fields and started building on dreams for the future.

He had heard it mentioned that common labourers were paid five to six *annas* per day in the city. Supposed if he earned six *annas* per day and spent just one *anna,* he could save a substantial amount daily and around ten rupees a month or a hundred and twenty a year. If he returned home with a purse of a hundred and twenty rupees, would anyone dare question him about anything? Pateshwari and Datadin would grin sheepishly and nod smilingly at him. Jhuniya would be beside herself with joy and pride. If he continued working like that for another two or three years, his family would come out from penury to extravagance. Today the total income of the household was barely a hundred rupees; then he would earn as much all by himself. What would people say at worse--that he was a common labourer in the city? It didn't make a difference; honest work was nothing to be ashamed of and moreover it was not that he would never get more than six *annas*. As time went by and if he worked diligently his wages would go up. Then he would tell his father to put up his feet and relax or if he wanted, get involved in spiritual activities like any other retired man. Tilling fields was such a cumbersome job. He would rather buy a high breed Jersey cow that yielded five or six seers of milk a day. His parents can take care of her. That would be such a good thing for him---it would spell good fortune for their present and take care of his thereafter as well. Of course, one *anna* should suffice for him; he didn't need a load of stuff. Who needed a house? He could live in someone's barn. Besides, there were innumerable temples and charity houses in the city and maybe his employers offered him some shelter?

But hold on, thought Gobar, wheat flour alone cost a rupee for ten seers--in other words one *anna* for two hundred fifty grams! Did that mean he would have to spend an *anna* just for flour? What about wood, salt, vegetables, edible oil? Goodness! At this rate, it would become very expensive. Or maybe food should not be such a big deal. A fistful of grams was all a man needed to survive. He would definitely manage with half a seer of flour and as for cooking fuel; he could easily pick up itsy-bitsy dung cakes from here and there and use them as firewood. He would buy lentils for one *paisa* and at times procure potatoes for a similar amount. It would be easy and convenient, not to say economical, to bake potatoes or roast them for a meal now and then. To be sure, survival in the city was not going to be a problem.

And then, another doubt crept in his mind. What if he didn't get a job there? But if he worked with total sincerity and dedication, there would be many who'd come looking for him. Employers needed a worker not a shirker. Impediments and obstacles could appear anywhere. Don't hail storms destroy standing crops; don't untimely rains play havoc with them? Don't termites attack fields of sugarcane? In the city he would labour hard; perhaps work nights as well. A watchman's job at night would fetch him another two *annas*. That would be really wonderful – when he returns, he would get new sarees and bangles for his mother and Jhuniya and a new jacket for his father.

He dozed off, relishing the taste of these pies in the sky but the cold made his sleep fitful and restive. He dozed cautiously and at the crack of dawn, took the road to Lucknow. He calculated that he would be in the city by evening. No one from the village visited the city and he was definitely not informing anyone his whereabouts or else his father would arrive the next day and pester him to return immediately. His only regret was that he had not told Jhuniya in as many words not to worry and remain calm as he was only venturing to a distant city to seek his fortune and would be back soon. Perhaps, he did right because she would have insisted on accompanying him and that would have made matters so much more difficult.

The sun rose high in the sky as the day wore on. He had not eaten anything and hunger gnawed at his insides. Famished, his legs gave way a few times as he stumbled in bouts of dizziness. He decided to take a break and rest for a few moments. His body demanded nourishment but he had no money to soothe his hunger pangs. On the roadside he spied some shrubs with wild berries. He ate a few and moved on rubbing his hands on his stomach, as if the gesture would silence its growling protests. Further down the road as he passed by a village, the delicious aroma of jaggery assailed his nostrils. It was too much for him to bear. He borrowed a pitcher and rope from a man by the road and drew water at a nearby well. As he poured water from the pitcher into his cupped palm, a farmer came up to him, “Hey brother, why do you drink water straight off in this manner? You must have something sweet before that. This is probably the last season that we work on our churn and produce our own jaggery. By next year, the sugar mill coming up here will be ready and white sugar will be available at the same rates as our crude jaggery. I don’t think anyone will buy from us any longer.” He smiled and added wryly, “Here, have some of it while it lasts.”

He brought a bowl of jaggery and thrust it before him. Gobar polished off the bowl and drank water from the pitcher. The man asked if he smoked tobacco. When Gobar replied in the negative the old man was pleased, “You’ve done good, son. Tobacco is a disease; if you catch it you are stuck with it for the rest of your life.”

With fuel in its tank, the engine revved up full throttle. Gobar’s strides were faster and much brisker. It was late afternoon and as on all winter days, it was difficult to fathom how time flew so fast and it was evening already. A little way down ahead, he saw a young girl sitting under a tree in what was obviously a protest against her husband who stood close by, cajoling and pleading with her. A few passersby had stopped to watch. Gobar joined the spectators. There are few things more publicly entertaining than an episode of matrimonial acrimony.

The girl glared at the man and repeated, “I am not going. I am not going. I am just not going with you.”

The man delivered her an ultimatum- “So you won’t come with me?”

“No.”

“No?”

“Yes. I have already said no.”

The man caught her by the hair and began pulling her away. She sprawled full length on the road. Defeated, the man relaxed his grip and pleaded with her once more. "Let me make myself very clear. You will have to come with me."

The girl replied with the same firmness, "And I have made myself very clear. I will not come with you- even if you chop off my limbs."

"I will slit your throat, woman."

"You will be hanged for it."

The man let go of her hair and sat down, holding his head in his hands. There was little he could do beyond what he had done to make her see reason.

In an instant he stood up again but this time he spoke to her in a dejected tone, "OK, tell me. What do you want from me?"

The girl straightened up and said, "I just want you to leave me. Simply leave me and go away."

"Will you talk properly and let me know what's wrong?"

"Why should anyone abuse my father and brother?"

"Who abused your father and brother?"

"Why don't you ask your people at home about it?"

"OK, I promise to ask them but I can do it only if you come with me, isn't it?"

"Oh come on! Do you have the guts to ask anyone about it? Go and hide in your mother's apron. Go ahead and listen to her abuse. Why should I tolerate it? She gives me one *roti* and makes me work like a slave. Why should I be treated like this? She is no one to boss over me. Now I am not bothered and I don't care."

The passersby, perceiving elements of a comical play in the domestic squabble, were enjoying it thoroughly and from the look of it, there was quite some time for curtains yet. But the show soon became repetitive and lost out on its novelty. The crowd dispersed one by one. Gobar did not like that man's obstinacy. He was silent in the presence of the crowd but when it thinned considerably, he addressed him directly, "Brother, pardon me for butting in between you two; I know it's not my business – but I must tell you, it is not right for you to be so harsh with her."

The man glowered at him and scowled, "And who are you?"

Gobar spoke calmly, "I could be anybody but no one likes to see a wrong committed in public."

The man shook his head and said, "I don't think you have a wife yet; that's why you are dripping with sympathy."

"When I have a wife, I will not drag her by the hair."

"Fine! Now be gone on your way, man. She is my woman. I can do anything with her. I can kill her, kick her- you keep out of this. Now get going. Run along!"

Gobar was simmering; this rude dismissal brought his blood to a boil. Why should he run along? The road belongs to the government. It isn't anyone's personal property; he would stand there as long he wanted to. No one had the right to order him about.

The man bit his lip. "So you won't scram? Want me to come and show you out?"

Gobar tightened his *angoccha* like a belt around his waist in preparation for battle, "I don't care whether you come here or not. I am not going unless I myself decide that I want to."

"I see you want your bones and limbs broken."

"Time will tell whose limbs are broken."

"So you aren't leaving?"

"No."

The man clenched his fists and sprang towards Gobar. Instantly the young girl caught hold of him and as she pulled him back, looked at Gobar and said, "Hey, why are you itching for a fight? Just go your way, man. You think this is some entertainment show? It's our personal argument- sometimes he hits me, sometimes I get mad at him. What is it to you? It's none of your business."

Thus chastised, Gobar went on his way. He swore under his breath that a woman who talked like this actually deserved to be beaten.

When Gobar turned to leave things calmed down and the young woman turned to her husband and scolded him, "First you pull my hair and are then ready to pick up a fight with a stranger on the roadside! What was so wrong about what he said that it hurt you so much? People will definitely point out your mistakes if you are in the wrong." Softening up on an impulse, she added as an after-thought, "That boy seems to be from a decent background; possibly from our own community. Why don't you consider him for your sister?"

Her husband contemplated for a moment, "I don't think he will be unmarried at his age."

"There is no harm asking him."

The man sprinted a few steps and called out to him, waving his hand as he did so. Gobar looked back. This man was mad and he would not rest till he got a sound thrashing. Perhaps, he was challenging Gobar because this was his home turf. No worries, he would be set right.

But the man's demeanour conveyed nothing like a challenge. On the contrary, his expression was friendly and welcoming. He asked Gobar the name of his village and his caste. Gobar told him and learnt that the man's name was Kodai. Gobar told him he owned five *bighas* of farmland.

"Please forgive me for calling you names; anger does make a man blind. My woman is a decent, obedient lady though she loses her mind, at times. I have no control over my mother. I am her son, she has brought me up – If there is a tiff I can only talk to my wife about it. I can exercise control over her, not over my mother. Yes, I agree I should not have dragged her by the hair but I hope you understand that women fall in line, only if you are tough with them. She wants I should separate from my mother and live elsewhere. Do you think it's possible? How can I hurt the woman, who has brought me up and done so much for me? I'd rather dump this one."

Gobar had to revise his opinion. He said, "True, no one can ever repay a mother for being who she is."

Kodai extended him an invitation to come to his house. Gobar had a fair idea he would not reach Lucknow before dark. He would have to shack up someplace by evening.

He asked, "Has she agreed to go back?"

'Does she have a choice?'

"Well, she gave me quite a mouthful – it was so embarrassing!"

"She realises it now. She regrets it and is feeling sorry. Why don't you come with me and try to make my mother see reason. She must realise it's not proper to abuse her daughter-in-law's father and brother. My wife is not the only one at fault – my mother is equally to blame. My wife has her good points too. She will fret and threaten to leave me but never retorts with foul words. She always remains respectful towards my mother."

Gobar needed a place to put up for the night. He readily agreed to go with Kodai. They walked up to where the woman sat, looking very demure and every inch a proper housewife. She had pulled a veil over her face and was almost bashful.

Kodai smiled at her, "He was not ready to come along. He was saying it is embarrassing for him to go with us after the dressing down you gave him." The woman looked at Gobar from the folds of her veil, "So you run scared from such a minor dose of the medicine? Where will you run to hide once you bring a woman to your home?"

Their village was not far. In fact it was barely a village. Just a cluster of a few houses half of them straw huts and the other half with tiles on the roof. Kodai brought out a cot and threw a cotton mat on it. He ordered a sweet *sherbet* for Gobar and got a *chillum* for himself.

The woman returned with a small pitcher of *sherbet* and in a smiling gesture of letting bygones be bygones, sprinkled a few drops of it on his face. He might soon become her brother-in-law; so why not tease him and initiate some pranks!

❁❁❁

13

It was dark and still some time before dawn when Gobar woke and begged leave of Kodai. By then, everyone had come to know that he was married hence; nobody broached the subject with him. His pleasant manner had won their hearts. Kodai's mother was especially very impressed. He had sermonised to her in such sweet words, all the while so mindful of her exalted motherly status, that she blessed him profusely in sheer delight.

"You are the senior most in the family, mother, you are someone to be worshiped. A son can never repay his mother's love in a hundred lives. Perhaps not even in ten thousand; I guess maybe not even in a hundred thousand..."

The old woman was floored by his adulatory style that overflowed with fulsome praise for her eminence. After such soothing words, everything he spoke was music to her ears and seemed crafted solely for her welfare. Once the physician's credentials are established by the efficacy of his medication, a patient will gladly accept poison from his hands if he declares it is for his benefit.

Gobar looked at her and said, "Just consider what happened today. When your daughter-in-law marched out of the house in a huff; whose prestige suffered? Whose reputation did it damage? Not the daughter-in-law's, for who knows her? Who knows her parents or her grandparents or what lineage she descends from? Her father could be a good for nothing idler, does anyone care?

The old woman shook her head sagely with an all knowing expression, "That is exactly what he is, son. A good for nothing idler, a perfect waste- that's what he is. If you see his face in the morning, rest assured, calamity will stalk you all day."

Gobar put on a surprised expression, "Oh really? So you can see for yourself that such a man's reputation will not be damaged because it is of no consequence whatsoever. The only one to suffer will be you and your son. Everybody wants to know whose daughter-in-law she is. You must bear that in mind, she is merely a chit of a girl – a foolish daughter of a stupid father. It is too much to expect intelligence from her. Getting mad at her will do no good. As the most patient and knowledgeable person of the family, you can only try to be good to her and see if she responds to the language of love and patience. Screaming at her neither covers you in glory nor brings her around to see reason. It lowers your dignity unnecessarily." When Gobar got up to leave the old woman gave a bundle of jaggery and crushed gram flour for him to eat on the road.

On his way to Lucknow, Gobar met some other men and they began chatting and gossiping. By nine at night, they had reached Aminabad market in the city where a large number of other people from nearby villages hung around, waiting to be picked up by labour contractors. Gobar was taken aback by the multitudes that milled around in the market place. There were men swarming all over the place; he wondered where so many people came from.

There were no less than five hundred labourers in the market that evening. There were masons, woodcutters, carpenters, blacksmiths, weavers and ordinary labourers, who merely transported loads on their heads. Gobar felt depressed in the face of such competition. He had no skills to speak of and had no instrument in his hand either, which could identify him as a specialist of one or the other craft. How could all of them find work? Many would be left out and he shuddered to think he was going to be one of them.

As time went by, the crowd of men thinned as most were picked up by employers and contractors looking for workers for their projects. Those not fortunate enough to be selected comprised mostly older ones or those who appeared obviously weak, emaciated or generally good for nothing. Gobar was one of them. But he had the old woman's packet of coarse meal for the night. He wasn't too worried.

A commotion in the market caught his attention. There was a man calling out in a loud voice, telling all those who wanted to earn six *annas* per day to fall in line and follow him. It was Mirza Khurshid and he announced six *annas* for a job that would not go beyond 5 P.M. Other than a few masons and carpenters who stayed back, the entire congregation was ready to follow him. It was a veritable army of almost four hundred poorly clad, haggard and scrawny men who fell in line with Mirza Khurshid in the forefront brandishing a huge baton like a shepherd leading his flock.

An old man asked him, "What's the job, sir? What do we have to do?"

When Mirza told him it took everyone by surprise. They were expected to play *kabaddi*. It was crazy! They had to play a game loved by young lads in villages and be paid for just that? Was he some kind of a madcap? Wealth can drive people crazy; perhaps this man had flipped his lid. A few men voiced their doubts openly; some thought it was a joke. Many were quite circumspect. Well, he could tell them to play *kabaddi* or *gulli danda* or any game he wanted; an advance payment would be an absolute necessity in this case. How could they trust a silly man like him?

Gobar mustered courage and going up to Mirza Khurshid; spoke rather hesitantly, "Sir, I don't have any money. If you will kindly give me some advance, I will go and eat something before we leave."

Mirza drove his hands into his pocket and placed six *annas* on his palm. He looked around at all present and announced, "Everyone will be paid his wages in advance. No one should worry on that count."

Mirza sahib had purchased a plot of land on the outskirts of the city. What the labourers saw when they reached there was a large field, walled on all four sides with a small gate that led to a tiny hut, covered with overgrowth and a few rickety chairs that lay strewn around it. Creepers and wild flowers lent a quiet charm to the hamlet as it stood in its stark loneliness amongst lemon and guava trees that grew next to the boundary wall. Other than a small bed of flowers on one side of the hut, the land was flat and barren.

Mirza ordered all the men to queue up and promptly distributed the promised wages to each one of them. No one had any doubts anymore. They were totally convinced the man was completely crazy but they had no regrets.

Gobar had already received his payment before they left the market place so Mirza told him to water the plants. He was quite disappointed not to be included in the game of *kabaddi*. He wanted to lift those old men and push them around in the sport but he consoled himself with the thought that he had enjoyed the game enough as a child and what's more, he had received his full payment in advance and that was what mattered most.

The large group of wiry men braced to play *kabaddi*. A large number of them had vague memories of the game. They had little time from their daily grind in the city to indulge in such frivolous pursuits. They reached home late and crashed into bed after eating whatever was available that day. Not for them any pleasant diversions as they trudged back on their monotonous routine every morning. Life was a listless humdrum existence; hence, this sudden break in routine perked up their weather-beaten scrawny frames as if their lost youthfulness had suddenly come alive and burst out of their bones.

Folding up their *dhotis,* they pranced about and many old men cackled in toothless delight as if they had stumbled once again into their lost childhood. They formed two teams, captains were selected and team members were picked from the crowd with much deliberation and consideration of their abilities. By twelve noon the game began in right earnest. The afternoon sun in winter is just right for such a sport.

Mirza sahib stood at the small gate, distributing tickets to the show he had organised. Such cynical pursuits held a strong fascination for him. He loved to collect money from the elite for such spectacles and delighted in distributing it amongst the poor who helped set it up and participated in it with the same joy. This *kabaddi* contest had been publicised by him for quite some time. He had pasted huge posters and sent out a number of reminders to friends in his circle and many outside it as well. This was to be a unique spectacle, quite a one of its kind. It was to showcase the vibrancy of India's poor people. All those who wanted to see it for themselves were welcome and those who missed it, would live to regret it. It was such a rare occasion. It wasn't an everyday occurrence-and tickets ranged from as high as ten rupees to as low as two *annas*. By three in the afternoon, there was hardly any space left for more spectators. Motor cars and carriages lined the approach road to Mirza's plot of land. The crowd was well over two thousand. The rich were seated on chairs and benches while the general public stood in the recently swept and cleaned field.

Miss Malti, Mehta, Tankha and Rai sahib – all were seated in the front row.

When the game began, Mirza invited Mehta to place a bet against him on whichever team he thought would win the match.

Miss Malti said, "Only a philosopher can bet on another philosopher."

Mirza stroked his luxuriant moustaches and said, "So you assume I am not one?

Well, I agree I do not have a following but I am still a philosopher. If you want I am ready to submit myself to a test. What do you say, Mehtaji?"

Malti asked him, "Then tell me - are you a materialist or an idealist?"

"I am both."

"How come?"

"I swing with the times. I adapt myself to the role suitable for the moment."

"That means you have no opinion or stand of your own."

"Since nothing can ever be concluded in a philosophical line of thought, how can you expect me of all people to have firm convictions? See, I have already arrived at conclusions which people derive after so much study and back breaking intellectual acrobatics. Do you know of any philosopher who has done anything better than shadow boxing or smoking a pipe?"

Mehta began unbuttoning his shirt and said, "Fine. Let's have a game ourselves. Trust me, I don't know about others but I do believe you are a good philosopher."

Mirza turned to Mr. Khanna and asked him, "Should I find a team and a partner for you too, Mr. Khanna?"

Malti egged him on, "Sure thing! You must take him with you. He could partner with Mr. Tankha."

Khanna blushed, "No, please, keep me out of this."

Mirza turned to Rai sahib, "Should I arrange a match for you as well?"

Rai sahib said, "My ideal match partner will be no other than Onkarnath. But I don't see him here today."

Mirza and Mehta entered the ground and joined the opposing teams, bare-chested and stripped to their underwear. The game began. The band of old men spiritedly got into the thick of the game.

The crowds roared in approval tickled by the antics of the elderly sportsmen; cajoling, shouting words of encouragement, booing, making snide comments, laughing and betting on one over the other. What a sight it was! Their commitment was amazing---the earnest manner in which they tackled their opponents, the seriousness with which they contemplated their holds as if the match was an international event in which they were contenders for a prize trophy! The opposing team would approach their rivals with a keen sense of competition to get the better of their tactics. The audience responded wholeheartedly to the old men's antics. The purity of nutrients of olden days on which they fed was what spurred their strengths; unlike the weak young yokels of the present day and age.

Their attention focused on the ground, the spectators commented loudly on the exciting sport that presented before them. Completely engrossed in the tussles of the players the crowd relished their attacks, counter attacks, tackles and leaps. At times there was a roar of applause from the audience, sometimes a foul brought out boos and hisses. Some spectators were so carried away by the game that they attempted to jump into the field but those holding the higher priced tickets, sitting under the shaded *shamiana*, did not seem to exhibit similar enthusiasm. They had other things to discuss.

Khanna drained the glass of ginger ale to its last drop and lit a cigar as he addressed Rai sahib, "Please understand that the bank will not agree on a lesser rate of interest. I have already talked to the concerned officials and whatever concessions have been made are solely because I presented your case as family."

Rai sahib hid a smile under his bushy moustaches, "Does that mean family is easy meat? You can hang them as a matter of course, no questions asked?"

"What do you mean by that?"

"I mean exactly what I say. You charged seven percent from Surya Pratap for a similar loan. You want me to pay nine percent and expect me to be grateful for it!"

"If you agree to the terms set for him we will charge the same rates from you. We have mortgaged his property with us and there is little possibility of it going back to him."

"I will also pledge one of my properties. It's better to throw away a useless property than pay nine percent. Please sell off my mansion on Jackson Road; you can also keep the commission from its sale."

"It's not so easy to palm off that property. You know it's on the outskirts of the city; the location is nothing to write home about. But let me see, I will try to work out something. How much do you expect for it?"

Rai sahib gave a figure of a hundred and twenty five thousand rupees. He said the mansion came with fifteen *bighas* of extra surrounding acreage. Khanna was astounded.

"You must be dreaming! You are quoting inflated rates, Rai sahib. You should know property prices have plummeted to half in recent times."

Rai sahib felt slighted and made no secret of his displeasure, "Not at all! A decade ago it was evaluated at one hundred and fifty thousand."

"Whatever! I will look out for a buyer. My commission will be five percent on the total sale price."

"Now go on and tell me you charge ten percent from others! What will you do with such hefty profits?"

"You give me whatever you want. Does that sound fine to you? You have also not bothered to pick up shares in the sugar mill; there are hardly any left as it is. You will regret not acting when there was still time. You haven't taken the insurance policy either. You have such a bad habit of dilly dallying over things. When you are so slow to act for your own good, how will you inspire confidence in others that you will work for their welfare? No wonder they say vast estates blunt the senses of those who inherit them. If I had my way, I would confiscate all properties of the landed gentry."

At another corner, Tankha was trying hard to entrap Miss Malti in his web. She had flatly refused to have anything to do with electioneering but Tankha was not one to accept no for an answer in the first instance. Propping his elbows on the table he said, "Kindly reconsider what you just stated. Let me assure you this is once-in-a-lifetime opportunity. Rani Chanda doesn't stand a chance if you jump in the fray. I want those who enter the assembly to be people of character and who have done some real social service unlike that woman whose only achievement in life has been to host the maximum number of social events and parties which she regularly throws for Secretaries and Governors. She should have no place in the Council. The new Council will divest a lot of power into the hands of its members; I don't want that power to fall in the hands of the undeserving."

Malti tried to wriggle out of the situation, "But my dear man, where is the twenty or thirty thousand that will be needed to fund election expenses? I don't have it and Rani Chanda will open her coffers and let money flow. I get four to five hundred annually from her as consultation fees; I have no desire to lose that as well."

"You must first say if you are willing to contest or not?"

"I am willing provided I get a free pass."

"Fine! Now that's my responsibility. You will get your free pass."

"Just a minute, not so fast! Thank you so much anyway for I have no intention of tasting defeat. When Rani Chanda loosens her purse strings it is a gold coin per vote. I bet you will be one of the first to line up!"

"Do you think money power is the sole factor in influencing election results?" asked Tankha.

"Not at all," replied Malti. "Personalities do make a difference. But I have been to jail just once and to be honest, that was more to do with my selfish intentions than commitment to a cause – just like Rai sahib and Khanna. The foundation of this new culture is built on wealth. Knowldge, education, noble lineage, caste and class are of little consequence when compared to money. I can speak for myself as an example. If a poor woman comes to my clinic, I don't attend to her for hours; if a rich lady drives up in her car, I greet her at the door and treat like her a special guest, not a patient. Don't equate me with Rani Chanda; she is a perfect candidate for the Council."

Meanwhile out in the field, Mehta's team was crumbling and losing out points and men to Mirza's. About half of Mehta's team was 'out'. Mehta had never played *kabaddi* in his life; Mirza was a past master at the game. Mehta's expertise lay in dramatics and literature; none could excel him in theatrical performances. Mirza's entire interest was centered on trying to match his strengths with wrestlers in the ring and his wits with dainty women in the social party circuit.

Malti was watching the match with keen interest. She turned around to Rai sahib and said, "Poor Mr. Mehta's team is getting such a drubbing!"

Rai sahib and Khanna were discussing the benefits of insurance. Rai sahib appeared eminently bored of the subject. He grabbed Malti's interjection as a God sent opportunity and promptly turned to her, all ears, eager to hear what she was saying, "Oh yes, to be sure! Why did he get into it at all? Mirza is an expert at the sport."

"Yes, he's shaming himself for no reason. Any member of Mehta's team who ventures into Mirza's court, is 'out' in an instant," Malti bemoaned.

She paused for a moment and enquired if there was a half- time or break in this game?

Khanna made a jab, "The game will be over within a few minutes. It will be fun to watch Mirza tackle Mehta and pin him down till he admits defeat."

"I am not asking you. I am asking Rai sahib."

Rai sahib said, "A half time in this game? No way- here the entire team doesn't play simultaneously; its one man pitted against another from the opposing team."

Khanna continued with his needling, "Just you wait, Mehta's team will be annihilated one by one and he will fall in the end!"

Malti fumed and burnt crisp, "Well, you didn't dare to venture out and play, did you?"

"I don't like these rustic games. It's tennis for me."

"I have won so many sets from you in tennis. I have defeated you so many times."

"I don't intend to win games when I play with you."

"If you do, I am ready for a match any day." Malti snapped at him and settled in her seat again. She was furious. No one had any sympathy for Mehta. Nobody came forward to call the game off. Mehta was such a fool himself; why didn't he play foul and try to win one way or the other? Perhaps, he was trying to prove his dedication to fair play. When he came back defeated, they would clap and humiliate him and he would smile tolerantly. Stupid man!

As the game drew to a close, the crowd's excitement and impatience grew to a crescendo. The rope strung around the ring gave way and volunteers had a tough time keeping the milling spectators from falling into the pit. Finally, the excitement reached a feverish pitch as Mehta's team was ousted completely and he was the lone surviving member in his court and the last pawn in the game. The result of the game now rested entirely on his shoulders. If he could return back to his court after a run around the opposing team's court, he could still salvage the situation. If he succeeded in touching base in his own zone, the number of men who tried to hold him back in the opposing side would be 'out' and an equal number would turn 'live' on his side and return to the arena. If not, he would have to bear the shame and ignominy of defeat as all eyes were on him now.

Mehta moved calmly into the enemy terrain. The crowd roared in delight, observing every move, marvelling at the placid expression on his face, completely devoid of tension of imminent defeat. Every move that he made drew a reaction from the crowd. Some cocked their heads, straining to catch a view; some leaned forward, not wanting to miss a single moment of the nail biting final moments. The tension was palpable as the mercury shot up. Mehta dived into the phalanx of the enemy soldiers. They moved back in a unit inviting him, daring him to enter deeper in their territory. Their formation was impeccable; Mehta was unable to mark a single man as they moved back with surprising agility as he struck out to touch them. Quite a few Mehta supporters amongst the spectators thought he would be able to bring at least four or five of his men to 'life' by escaping back into his area from the other side. They were losing hope and had fallen silent.

All of a sudden Mirza took a leap and grappled Mehta by the waist. Mehta strained to free himself. He was pulling Mirza slowly and steadily to his zone. The audience yelled in excitement and anticipation. Quite a few of Mirza's team of old men leapt and piled on Mehta's back, grabbing him tightly. Mehta was lying silent and prostrate on the ground, holding in his breath, trying to inch slowly towards the line dividing his area from the other camp. If he could touch the line, a host of his men would come 'alive' and the tables would turn dramatically but he was unable to move an inch. Mirza was straddling his back, pinning his neck in a tackle. Mehta's face was red, his eyes wide and bulging from their sockets. He was sweating profusely and Mirza was still astride his back, pinning him down along with a swarm of others.

Suddenly Malti stepped into the cordon and went right up to Mirza and said, "This is not fair, Mirzaji. The game is drawn."

Mirza cuffed Mehta's neck and said, "I am not letting go till he says 'I give up'. That's how it's done. Why doesn't he say those words?"

Malti came closer to the men lying prone on the ground. "You can't force him to say that."

"Of course I can and I will. Why don't you advise him to say those words? I will release him at once."

Mehta tried to raise his head to struggle free but Mirza cuffed him yet again and bore down on his neck.

Malti tried to pry open Mirza's grip and said, "This is not a sport any more. It's an ego game."

"So be it."

At that moment something happened that took everyone completely by surprise. In a sudden jerk, Mehta pushed Mirza sahib to the ground and ran like a hare towards his side of the ring. Spectators went crazy with excitement cheering wildly. No one could fathom how it happened. There were celebrations all around!

Mirza lifted Mehta on his shoulders and carried him in a boisterous procession to the *shamiana*. On everybody's lips there was just one exclamation – what an amazing climax! The surprising reversal of fortunes as Mehta snatched victory from the jaws of defeat had enthused the assembled guests and they praised Mehta's fighting spirit to the skies.

Baskets of fruits were brought for the labourers and each was given a bagful as they were sent off. For the guests, there was a special arrangement for refreshments in the tented *shamiana*. Mehta and Mirza sat across the table facing each other. Malti was seated next to Mehta.

Mehta said, "I had a new experience today. I discovered for the first time how a lady's encouragement and sympathy can help win a lost battle."

Mirza looked at Malti as he responded to him, "Is that so? No wonder I failed to understand how all of a sudden you got the better of me."

Malti blushed furiously. She said, "I also learnt that when push comes to shove, you don't give an inch, Mirzaji."

"It was entirely his fault. He should have said-'I give up'."

"I was in no mood to submit even if you killed me."

The two friends gossiped for some time. A few minutes later, there were farewells and a thanksgiving speech following which the guests left for their homes. Malti had to visit a patient so she also left shortly thereafter. Mehta and Mirza were the only ones left. They were covered with mud and still had their soiled clothes on. They had to take a bath. Gobar drew water from the well and both friends took a refreshing bath.

Mirza asked him as they splashed water over their body. "So when is the wedding?"

Mehta was surprised, "Whose wedding?"

"Yours."

"My wedding? Who's marrying me?"

"Oh come on! Don't act as if it is a state secret and nobody knows about it," laughed Mirza.

"No, not at all. I really don't know anything about it. What is this about my marriage?"

"Well, what do you think? Miss Malti will agree to be your live-in companion?"

Mehta turned grave. "You are totally mistaken, Mirzaji. Miss Malti is beautiful, pleasant, intelligent, and bright and has a hundred other positive qualities but she lacks the attributes I seek in a life partner and it doesn't seem she will ever have them. According to me a woman is an epitome of faith, who becomes an inseparable part of her husband's existence through self denial and sacrifice. Physical body is a masculine concept; the soul is eternally a feminine entity. You can question why a man isn't called upon to sacrifice and sublimate his life and why such things are expected only from women. The reason is it is beyond the capacity of men; they are incapable of such conduct. When a man denies himself he is reduced to nought. He will go hide in a cave and dream of merging in divinity. Men are energetic physical beings. Their arrogance forces them into believing they are manifestations of pure knowledge and they strive to merge into a godly existence, which is simply another way of celebrating ego. Women are tolerant and patient by nature. They are like the earth- full of gravity, forgiving and patient. When a man develops feminine qualities he becomes angelic, when a woman develops male qualities she turns into a runt. Men are attracted to women who are feminine to the core; Malti has never drawn me to her in that manner. I can't explain what a woman means to me. Perhaps she is the embodiment of all that is graceful and lovely in the world. I expect her not to retaliate with violence even if I try to kill her. I expect her not to be jealous if I love another woman right under her nose. If I can find such a woman I will fall at her feet, give myself up to her and surrender to her utterly."

Mirza nodded his head, "You will never find a single woman like this on earth."

Mehta slapped his palm on his thigh. "Not one but a hundred, Mirza! Had there not been such women, the world would be absolutely barren and destitute."

"Can you furnish any example of such a woman?"

"Mrs. Khanna, for instance."

"Mrs. Khanna!"

"Khanna is so unfortunate. He possesses a diamond but thinks he is saddled with fake glass beads. There is such an amazing level of love and sacrifice in her. Khanna's skin-deep love will never fathom the depths of her attachment but if any misfortune strikes him, she will give up anything to protect him. If he goes blind or turns into a leper, it will not alter her commitment towards him. Today, he might not realise her worth but one day he will worship the ground she walks on. I don't want a wife with whom I can discuss the principles of Einstein or who can proof read my texts. I want a woman who can illuminate my life and sanctify it with her love and sacrifice."

Mirza stroked his beard wisely in a gesture that implied he was reminded of some long forgotten postulate, "Your views are perfect Mr. Mehta. I will also marry such a woman if I come across her but I am fairly convinced she does not exist."

Mehta laughed and said, "Lets both lookout for one. You never know when you get lucky."

"But remember, Miss Malti is not letting you walk away that easily. I can give it to you in writing."

"I consider women like her as objects for entertainment; not for marriage by a yard! Marriage is surrender."

"If marriage is surrender, what do you have to say about love?"

"When love manifests as surrender, it takes the form of marriage; otherwise it is nothing but lust with another name."

Mehta put on his clothes, bid farewell and took leave. It was late evening. Mirza saw Gobar was still irrigating the plants. He was pleased at his diligence and told him to leave since he had done his job for the day. "Now you can go. Will you come again tomorrow?"

Gobar pleaded with all the humility he could gather, "I need a job, sir."

"If you are looking for a job I can give you one."

"How much will I get, sir?"

"Whatever you want."

"What can I say, sir? You pay me whatever you please."

"We will pay you fifteen rupees and work you to the bone."

Gobar was not afraid of hard labour. He was ready to work all day if he got paid for it and if he was paid fifteen per month, that was wonderful. He would slog hard; he could do anything for that amount of money.

He said, "If I get a small room I will stay here. It will be a great help, sir."

"Ok, done. I will organise something for you. You can stay right here in this hut."

Gobar thought the gates of paradise had finally opened to let him in.

❁❁❁

14

Hori's entire harvest went to the village council as penalty which he had to cough up for transgressing social mores. The month of April and May weren't so difficult but by June, the silos at his home were empty. With five mouths to feed and not a single grain at home; this was more than a difficult situation. If not two square meals, they needed at least one to keep body and soul together. No one survives on sheer hope but who dares to spare a loan for those, who have nothing to repay; even the first installment of interest. Hori's family avoided every money lender because they owed something to each one of them. There was so much work to be done in their own fields how could they slave at any other household for a fistful of food even if they tried? The sugarcane saplings were ready to be planted and irrigated but with a body weakened by hunger, attempting that was labour in itself.

It was one such evening. The little infant was crying. With hardly any food to go by, milk had dried and the baby clung listlessly to his mother's breasts. Sona realised the problem but Rupa insisted for food and clamoured for *rotis*. Today, she was wailing at the top of her voice. All day she was fobbed off with an unripe mango which she suckled to its core but as dusk descended, she stomped her feet, demanding something more solid. Hori had made a visit to Dulari Sahuain to loan a fistful of grain but she had closed shop and gone home. Mangru Sah not only refused to part with a loan but gave a piece of his mind instead.

Hurting from those scalding comments Hori was sitting in the courtyard when Puniya came in to light an ember to build a fire at her home. She paused at the kitchen door as the mud stove had nothing but cold ash. "*Bhabhiji*, why have you not lit the fire in the kitchen yet? It's so late already."

Since the day Gobar ran off, there was a thaw in the strained relations between Dhania and Puniya. Puniya was obliged by Hori's attitude of service and turned quite vocal in condemning Heera for his misdeeds. That murderer scampered off after killing the poor cow. How could he ever return now that he had fallen so low? And if he did, she won't allow him inside. How she wished the police had arrested him and forced him to hard labour.

As she stared at her quizzically with her foot halfway into the kitchen door, Dhania's options were severely limited. She had to tell the truth. "There is not a single grain in the house, how do you expect me to cook? Your law abiding brother-in-law has dutifully deposited everything we had with the community council. His children might starve but do you think the community is bothered?"

Puniya's fields produced a rich harvest and she unambiguously gave the credit for it to Hori. It was his hard work and sincerity that resulted in such abundance. Heera could never manage such a feat. She said, "Why didn't you send someone over to pick up some from my place? What I have is also the result of his labours. We can fight when the times are good but we have to stick together in times of stress. I am not blind that I don't realise I would be out on the streets if your husband had not come forward to bail me out."

She went back taking Sona with her only to return within minutes with two sackfuls of grains which she deposited in the centre of the courtyard. Dhania opened her mouth to speak but she was gone and came back instantly with another large basket of lentils and went straight into the kitchen to light firewood.

There was enough wheat flour in it to last them a fortnight. For the first time in her life she felt crushed, but with a warm glow of tender pain in her heart. Her eyes swam with tears of gratitude and affection as she said, "Did you leave anything at home or you have transferred everything to my kitchen?"

The baby was still crying in the wooden cradle in the courtyard. Puniya lifted him up in her arms and started fondling him as she spoke, "With your blessings, there is enough for all of us, sister. We harvested fifteen mounds of barley and ten mounds of wheat. There is no reason I should hide from you; we have another five mounds pea pods. It is enough for both households. In another two or three month, it will be time for corn. God willing, we will survive."

Jhuniya came out of the room into the courtyard and bent down to touch the feet of her other mother-in-law and Puniya blessed her. Sona busied herself in lighting the fire, Rupa picked up the pitcher of water and made her way to the kitchen. Puniya asked why Hori was in such a tearing hurry to pay the fine.

Dhania said sarcastically, "How else could he become the apple of their eye once again?"

"Sister, if you don't mind, may I say something?"

"Tell me, I will not mind."

"I think I shouldn't say it. You will definitely take it otherwise."

"I promise you. I won't say a word. Now tell me."

"You shouldn't have allowed Jhuniya into your house."

"What could I do? She was ready to go kill herself had I sent her away."

"You could have sent her to my house. Nobody would have objected to that."

"You are telling this to me now. If I had sent her to you then, you would chased her away with a broomstick."

"The amount of money you threw away was more than what was required for Gobar's wedding expenses."

"Who can control the wheels of fate, dear girl? Our troubles are not over yet. Bhola is demanding payment for the cow. When he gave it to us, the deal was that we help to fix up a partner for him. Now he tells us to forget all about fixing him up with some woman; he wants cash for his cow. His sons are itching for a fight and there is none on our side who can handle them. I must say that accursed cow ruined us bad."

After making some more small talk, Puniya left for her home with the smouldering ember of fire she had come to borrow in the first place. Hori heard everything they discussed. He came in and spoke approvingly of Puniya's kind intentions.

"Perhaps Heera had similar honourable intentions as well," Dhania said caustically.

She had accepted the help but felt insulted and ashamed, blaming fate for subjecting her to such humiliation.

"Your problem is you never accept kind gestures with grace," said Hori testily.

"Why should I feel obligated? It's my husband who has toiled ceaselessly to stock her larder. I have not taken alms from her; I will repay all she has loaned us."

But Puniya continued to repay her brother-in-law's kindness, knowing fully well how Dhania perceived her gestures. She quietly replenished the grain when she noticed the stock was dwindling. This carried on till the advent of the auspicious quarter of the year, late August, which was peculiarly dry and the spell of scanty rain worsened the situation further each passing day. The rainy season had arrived but not a cloud was visible in the sky. Wells ran dry and the sugarcane shrivelled in the fields. There was little water in the river and every other day scuffles broke out over sharing it for irrigating the fields. Soon there was little left to fight over. There were frequent pilferages from homes and a spate of serious robberies in the village. Very soon, this lawlessness spread its tentacles all over the state.

Thankfully with the onset of September, finally one day the rains arrived and sparked a new life in the dying spirit of the peasants. There was great jubilation that day! The parched earth soaked up every drop that fell from the skies as the farmers rejoiced ecstatically. For them it was as good as gold coins raining from the heavens. The fields which had cracked up, overflowed with gushing streams and the ploughs were out. Small bands of excited children trooped around in glee, visiting every pond, inspecting each body of water that formed in ditches and low lying areas. They discussed each gushing rivulet and scouted the village in a bid to be the first to sight any new watery puddle that appeared over night.

But the sugarcane crop was beyond redemption; it was gone. There was no way the saplings could grow taller than an arm's length. However, the harvest might not be enough to pay off taxes but surely there would be sufficient fodder for cattle and the corn would help peasants survive a few more months. That was some relief, nonetheless.

When the season drew to a close and Bhola didn't see any signs of recovering his money, his irritation got the better of him and one day he barged into Hori's house and thundered, "Is this how you keep your word? You had committed to return my money after crushing sugar cane. That was over months back. Where is my money? I want it right now."

When Bhola did not budge an inch from his stand, despite Hori's long drawn litany of excuses and narration of woes, he blurted out in sheer frustration, "Now get this straight- I don't have any money nor can I get a loan from any quarter. We have nothing and as things stand, we are hard pressed for our next meal. If you don't believe me come and search my house. If you find anything that will help you pay for your loan, you're welcome to take it away."

Bhola retorted with calculated indifference, "I have nothing to do with your financial situation. I am least concerned and have no interest in searching your house to find if you have money or not. You promised to pay me after you crushed sugarcane. You have crushed the sugarcane. Now hand over my money."

"You are aware of my situation. Tell me how should I comply with it?"

"I think I will take your bulls."

Hori stared at him in disbelief, taken aback by what he had just heard. What was Bhola aiming at? Did he want to reduce him to beggary? If he took away the pair of bulls, he could as well chop off both his hands.

His voice broke as he said, "If you take away my bulls I will be destroyed completely. If your conscience permits, go ahead and take them."

"Whether you are destroyed or not is none of my concern. I want my money back, that's all."

"What if I say I have already given it you?"

It was Bhola's turn to be taken aback. He couldn't believe his ears. Hori was not the one to cheat so blatantly.

He turned aggressive, "Will you hold the holy water of the Ganges in your palm and swear that you have already paid me the money? If you do that I won't say another word."

"I really feel like doing that; I am so pushed into a corner. But I won't."

"You can't. You dare not"

"Yes brother. I dare not. I was trying to be funny."

For a moment Hori swayed between indecision and dilemma. Finally, he looked straight at him and said, "Why do you nurse such hatred against me? You think I gained something because Jhuniya came to live with us? I lost my son and was forced to pay up two hundred rupees as damages. I am ruined. And now you come to hammer the last nail in my coffin. God is my witness, I had no inkling what my boy was up to. I assumed he was going to your place for the musical congregation that is held every evening. The first time I realised what was actually cooking, was the day Jhuniya knocked at my door in the middle of the night. Had I not sheltered her at that time, where would she have gone? What would have become of her?"

Jhuniya stood behind the veranda, keenly listening to the conversation. Her father was no longer one of her own; he was a demon, an enemy. She worried if Hori would hand over the bulls. She went up to Rupa and told her to hurry up and call her mother home. "Tell *amma* it's very important. She mustn't delay a moment."

Dhania was in the field tossing manure over the crops. She scurried home as soon as she got the message and said, "Why did you send for me like that, girl? I almost panicked!"

"You saw my father outside, didn't you?"

"I did. He's squatting outside the gate, looking every inch the butcher that he is. I didn't give him as much as a look."

"He is demanding both of our bulls from *dada*."

Dhania's stomach convulsed in a spasm of fear. "He's come for the bulls?" she repeated.

"Yes. He says either we pay up his money or he takes our bulls with him."

"What did Hori say?"

"He told him if his conscience was comfortable with it, he could take them."

"Let him take them," she grimaced, "but I will curse him that he becomes a beggar and comes to our door for alms. If our blood is what he wants, let him suck it dry."

Infuriated, she stomped out of the door where the two men sat and went straight at Hori, "If he insists on the bulls, why don't you let him take them? Let him celebrate it, God's with us. He won't cut off our hands, will he? So far we have worked for ourselves; now we will work for others. If God is merciful, we will earn enough to buy more heads of cattle and if we can't, there's nothing wrong living as labourers. At least we will be rid of worries of cold, heat, blight on the crops and taxation. Had I known this man is so full of hatred for us, I wouldn't have taken that cow. Our misfortunes began the day we brought that miserable animal to our house."

Bhola had a special weapon of assault in his armoury. He realised this was the most opportune moment to unleash it. He was convinced they had nothing to support them except the two bulls that were vital to their survival as peasants. He knew they would be ready to go to any length to retain the bulls. Like an expert marksman he unsheathed his final arrow and took aim, "If you assume you will be at peace after insulting me in the way you have, you have another thing coming. You assume you are unfortunate because you had to lose two hundred rupees? Here, I have lost a hundred thousand rupees worth reputation, prestige and name. You will be wise to throw Jhuniya out of your house just as easily as you took her in. Then I will neither take away your bulls nor press you to pay up for the cow. That girl humiliated me before the world; now I want her to be taught a lesson. Let her be kicked around a bit. Here she sits pretty comfortable in your home, whereas I am shamed and disturbed. That is something I just cannot tolerate. She is my daughter; I brought her up as a little baby but I can't bear such humiliation. I gave her as much love as I give my sons but now I want to see her beg door to door and scrounge for crumbs in a dump heap. I am her father; you can very well visualise how deeply I must be hurt that I contemplate such suffering for her. This ungrateful wretch has marred the reputation of seven generations in our family. Now if you offer her shelter in your home, will it not be a direct affront to me?"

Dhania stepped forward and hardened her stance to a point of no return. "In that case Bhola, get this very clear. You will never get what you aim for even in a hundred lives. Jhuniya will remain close to my heart. You take the bulls if you want. If you insist on taking them and think that it will somehow assuage the hurt caused to your ancestor's reputation and helps you salvage your pride- just go ahead and do it. Jhuniya did commit a mistake; she is at fault, I agree. The day she arrived at my door, I ran after her with a broom; but when her eyes welled with tears, I felt pity on her. You have grown old, Bhola, yet you are obsessed to marry again. She is still a young girl, isn't she?"

Bhola turned his eyes towards Hori, appealing to his mature judgement, "Hori, you hear this woman? Now you shouldn't blame me for anything. I am not leaving without your bulls."

Hori replied with grit in his voice, "Take them."

"Fine. But don't regret it later."

"I won't."

Bhola had barely untied the leash of one of the bulls from the tether when Jhuniya appeared in a chequered saree, her baby resting on her hip and spoke in a voice, quivering with emotion, "*Kaka*, hold for a moment! See, I hereby leave this house. I am going away and as you desire, I will go and beg on the streets for me and my baby and if we don't get any alms, we will go drown somewhere."

Bhola was irritated. "Get out of my sight. God forbid I see your face again, you sinful wretch! Yes, go ahead, it is only proper that you drown and end your disgusting life."

Jhuniya did not bother to look back at him. She was engulfed in an anger that wanted to consume her; a wrath that wasn't seething with violence but brimming with total surrender. Had the earth shook and cracked open to draw her into her bosom, she would have considered herself blessed. She moved towards the gate.

She had taken barely two steps when Dhania rushed forward and holding her by the arm, chided her affectionately, "Where are you off to, daughter-in-law? Get back home. This is your house for as long as we live and even after we are no more. Not you, but they should go jump in a well who have such hatred for their own children. This man does not bat an eyelid mouthing such abuses on his own child. He only knows how to throw his weight around, specially at me, this lowborn creep! Go, take the bulls and drink their blood..."

Jhuniya wept inconsolably, "*Amma,* when my own father turns me away with such bitter words, it's better that I die. I am so miserable; I have given you nothing but sorrow. You have suffered since the day I came to your doorstep. My own mother would not have given me the love you showered on me all these days. May I come from your womb if I am born again, that is the only blessing I can wish for myself."

Dhania hugged her and said, "He is not your father. He is your enemy, this murderer! Had your mother been alive, perhaps, he would have thought differently. Let him go and get married again; his woman will beat him with slippers, I know."

Jhuniya followed her mother-in-law back into the house. Bhola hurriedly opened the leash of the bulls and turned towards his home, panting and huffing, as if he had gone to an invite for a feast and instead of being served goodies, had been greeted by a rain of slippers. He cursed Hori under his breath. He kept muttering to himself, "Now let's see how he ploughs the field and lives happily ever after? They want to insult me; God knows what they have against me from previous lives that they vent it out in this lifetime. Why should any sane man want to protect such a girl and offer her shelter in his house? They have all gone mad and are completely shameless. That lout Gobar was not getting married; no one wanted him. And imagine the shamelessness of Jhuniya, she dared to come before me and look me in the eye! Any other girl wouldn't have dared to show her face after what she did; grace and chastity is dead in this age. Everyone is either cheap or stupid. They think Jhuniya belongs to them now. The fools don't realise such a girl won't be with them for long. These are bad times or I would have dragged the wretch Dhania through the streets, pulling her hair. How abusive she was towards me, so disgusting!"

He turned his attention to the bulls. Such sturdy, fine specimens- they made a good pair. He could easily sell them for a hundred rupees to recover the eighty rupees loan and yet have more left over.

He had not crossed the village limits when he saw Datadin, Sobha, Pateshwari and a dozen or so other men running up behind him. Bhola's blood froze in his veins. Now they would start meddling, they might snatch the bulls; who knows they could also attack him. He braced himself to face the situation. He would not give up without a fight.

Datadin was the first to speak as they came up to him. "What a terrible thing you have done, Bhola! Eh? You walked away with his bulls, emboldened, since he didn't raise a whimper? Everybody was busy in their affairs and knew nothing about it. Had Hori sent a word, you would have been thrashed soundly. Leave the bulls and go away if you want to remain in one piece. Don't you have any sense of humanity?"

Pateshwari said, "This is solely due to Hori's timidity. If he owes you money, go to the court, send him a notice, request for confiscation orders. What gives you the right to walk away with his bulls? If he files a case you've had it!"

Bhola felt outnumbered and hence spoke meekly, "Lala sahib, you think I walked away with his bulls perforce? He himself offered them to me."

Pateshwari told Bhola to return the bulls. "No farmer will happily give away his bulls. He would rather yoke them to his plough and tend to his work."

Bhola stepped forward and stood in front of the two bulls. "You get me my money. I will return the bulls. I don't need them."

"We are taking the bulls back and dare you stop us. If you want your money, lay a claim on him, file a case in the court, do whatever you want. You palmed off a godforsaken, blighted cow to him and now walk away with his nice, sturdy bulls! Very clever indeed!"

Bhola stayed put, unmoving, feet firmly planted in front of his new proud possessions. He was determined to fight to the finish; there was no way he could match wits with Pateshwari's logic and guile.

Datadin took a step forward and straightened his bent back as he challenged the assembled men, "Why do you just stand and gape? Can't you beat the daylights of this man and tell him to beat it? He dares to walk away with two bulls robbed from a fellow villager!"

Banshi was one of the athletic young men. He gave a massive shove to Bhola that sent him stumbling a few feet away before he fell to the ground. As he started to get up, Banshi dealt him another blow.

Bhola saw Hori come running towards the crowd from a distance. He hastily took a few steps towards him as he caught up and motioning towards his tormentors blurted out to him. "Swear on your heart, Hori; did I take your bulls away by force?"

Datadin reinterpreted the question, "He means you gave them away willingly and happily. He thinks we are fools to buy that!"

When Hori spoke he was quite hesitant and almost contrite. "Well, he told me that either I throw Jhuniya out of my house or give him back his money or else he takes away my bulls. I told him I was not ejecting my daughter-in-law from my house and I did not have money to pay him. I left it to his conscience. After that he untethered them and walked off."

Pateshwari's face fell. "If you left it to his conscience, then it implies nothing was done forcibly. His conscience allowed him, he took it," and turning to Bhola he added, "You can go, brother. The bulls are yours."

Datadin supported him, "Well, once it is a conscience thing what can others do about it?"

Feeling vanquished, the assembly of men gave Hori scathing looks of scorn and disrespect as they turned back in retreat while Bhola, cocky and confident in victory, pulled at the bull's leash and marched triumphantly towards home.

❁❁❁

15

Miss Malti's ebullience and chirpiness was neither because she considered life to be a merry picnic nor was her individuality so central to her life, that she focussed all activities on herself. Nothing like that! Her spirited and light-hearted nature helped her to relieve some of the tension that came with her professional and personal responsibilities. Her father was one of those people whose smooth talk unlocked vaults of the rich and doors of the influential. Helping wealthy *Zamindaars,* securing further loans, selling their estates or facilitate their affairs by setting up meetings between them and senior government functionaries and officials, was his vocation. In other words, he was a middleman.

This was a prolific, talented tribe. Its members would take on any job or responsibility where they sniffed money and accomplished the jobs fairly well. They would fix the marriage of some minor king with the princess of an estate and make a neat pile of twenty or thirty thousand for themselves, in the bargain. When smaller middlemen fixed small deals they were labelled as 'touts'. Once they started operating at higher levels, they were invited to go game hunting with the 'maharajahs' and have tea with Governors.

Malti's father, Mr. Kaul was one of those fortunate enough to be in that rarefied league. All three of his children were girls. He wanted to send them to England and give them the best education and settle them there. Like other great men of his times, he believed that education in England transformed people inside out. Perhaps, the English air and water had magical powers that created dramatic intelligence and exerted a positive effect on human beings. Unfortunately, only one third of his ambitions could be realised in his lifetime.

Malti was in England when he was paralysed and rendered out of service. It needed two assistants to make him sit up or lie down. His speech was severely hampered, almost entirely lost for all practical purposes. With loss of speech, there followed a tangible loss of income as everything he earned was because of his gift of the gab. He was not in the habit of saving for a rainy day. Unrestricted income had prompted uncontrolled spending, which resulted in a tight financial crisis within a few years. The entire burden now fell on Malti. His indulgent lifestyle could not hold together within the means of what Malti earned in her practice. Yet, somehow the other two sister's educational expenses were met and they had a reasonably comfortable lifestyle. Malti toiled day and night. She would have liked her father to lead a more austere life but he was so fond of good food and choicest drinks that it bordered on addiction. Whenever he didn't find any other recourse, he signed a pro-note against his bungalow and borrowed one or two thousand rupees from a certain moneyed gentleman. This particular person was an old acquaintance and friend who had made a fortune many times over and hence gave him whatever he demanded, without a murmur. The loans ran up to twenty five thousand rupees. He could have attached the bungalow and have them evicted any day but he remained bound by gratitude and old friendly ties that held him back from such a severe step.

The brazenness that creeps into the attitudes of self centred people was present in Kaul in full measure. He was least bothered about the debt and brushed aside gentle enquiries about repayment schedules. Malti's patience was strained to the edge but her mother, who was steeped in spirituality and believed that a woman's destiny was to serve her husband, would intervene and prevent any strife between the father and daughter.

Evening had crept up yet the breeze bore remnants of a blistering hot afternoon that day. There was a dull haze in the sky. Malti and her two sisters sat on the grass in front of their bungalow. There were bald patches in the lawn where the grass had dried for lack of proper watering.

Malti enquired, "Isn't the gardener spraying water over the lawn regularly?"

Saroj, the sister younger to Malti, said, "He is sleeping all the time; that good-for-nothing pig. He has a hundred excuses if you point out something to him."

Saroj was an undergraduate, studying for her BA; thin, tall, pale, quite dry and equally bitter. She had no appreciation for anyone outside herself. Doctors recommended that she should preferably stay up in the hills but the conditions at home did not allow such indulgence.

The youngest one, Varda despised Saroj because the household was so exercised about the elder one's condition. She felt such molly-coddling was unnecessary and resented the fact that the disease which prompted such fuss from the household did not visit her. She was fair, proud and healthy, with eyes that swam with mischievous energy and an intelligent aura surrounded her face at all times. She sympathised with the whole world except her elder sister Saroj.

She felt duty bound to oppose everything her sister said. "All day Papa keeps him on his toes, sending him on one errand or another; when does he have the time? He has no respite and she says he sleeps all the time!"

Saroj sneered at her, "When does Papa send him to the bazaar, you liar?"

"He sends him every now and then. Everyday! He sent him some time back today as well. You want me to call him and confirm?"

Malti was worried. If the two started squabbling, sitting there would become an ordeal. Switching the topic, she said, "Ok, that will be enough! Saroj, was there a lecture by Dr. Mehta at your college today?"

Saroj wrinkled her nose, "Yes there was a lecture but nobody appreciated it. He said women have a different place in society and their entering the domain of men is a curse of the present age. The girls hooted and clapped at inopportune moments just to annoy him. Poor guy, he was shamed and had to cut short his talk. He went on to say 'love is the creation of imaginative poets and there is nothing like love in real life'. Lady Hukkoo made great fun of him"

Malti cut in sarcastically, "Lady Hukkoo? So she had the guts to delve into such an issue? You should have listened to his lecture attentively. Imagine what an impression he will carry about the girls?"

“Who has the patience to sit through the entire speech? All he did was to be sarcastic about women.”

“Then what was the necessity to invite him? After all he is not a woman hater. Everybody talks about what they believe to be true. He is not one to speak only pleasant things which women love to hear and who knows if the path on which women want to progress is the right one? It is quite possible; we might have to alter our views with time.”

She narrated ideals of certain women from France, Italy and Germany and said, “Very soon, he will lecture at an event under the aegis of the ‘Women’s League.”

Saroj was curious.

“But you also agree that women should have equal rights as men.”

“I still maintain that. But it is important to listen to the other side. What if they are right and we are in the wrong?”

The name of the institution Malti dropped was a new one and had come into existence with considerable help and encouragement from Malti herself. All the educated women of the city were members of that league. Mehta’s first speech there had ruffled many feathers and the League had decided to give a fitting and hard hitting response to him. This onerous responsibility was given to Malti who spent quite a few days scouting for apt parables, arguments and examples to buttress her stand. Many other ladies were preparing their addresses.

When Mehta reached the hall in the evening on the appointed day, it was bursting at the seams. He was elated. Such enthusiasm and what a crowd that had assembled to hear him speak! And this enthusiasm was not confined to the flashy eyes and bright faces alone; all the ladies were decked in fine silks and gold as if they were invited to a wedding reception. All energy was garnered to defeat Mehta and who could object if glitter and glamour was utilised as yet more energy? Malti had selected a special saree that was the rage and had a new jumper stitched to the latest cut. She had spent time making herself up and wore flowers in her hair as well.

The last row was occupied by Mirza, Khanna and the editor. Rai sahib arrived just before the speech began and stood behind them.

Mirza requested him to join them, “How long will you keep standing? Come, take a seat.”

Rai sahib said, “No man, I will suffocate if I sit here for long.”

“Let me offer you my seat.”

Rai sahib pressed Mirza’s shoulders, forcing him back on his seat, “Please, no formalities. When I am tired, I will myself tell you to vacate the seat. Oh, I see Miss Malti is the Chairman, I mean Chairperson, of this event. Khannaji, she must be rewarded! What do you say?”

Khanna made a sad face, “Well her eyes are on Mr. Mehta. I am out of the scene tonight.”

Mr. Mehta began his address, "Worshipped Ladies....When I address you with this suffix why do you not feel peeved? Why do you consider this respectful address as your right? Have you ever heard a woman addressing a man as 'worshipful' or 'divine'? If you call a man 'worshipful', he will assume you are pulling his leg. You can be addressed like this as you have piety, sacrifice and mercy to offer to the world. What do men have to offer? Men are not givers, they are usurpers. They utilise violence to secure their rights, they fight and wage wars...

A round of applause sounded across the hall. Rai sahib smiled, "What a clever way to suck up to women."

The editor of 'Bijli' was none too pleased- "This is nothing new. I have expressed such sentiments umpteen number of times."

Mehta went on...."That is why when I find worshipful ladies with progressive attitudes scrambling towards a life of struggle, strife and violence, claiming disillusionment from a life of mercy, compassion and sacrifice; I find it extremely difficult to compliment them on their choice."

Mrs. Khanna stole a glance at Malti who was sitting quietly with her eyes fixed on the floor.

Khurshid whispered, "What do you say? Mehta is a bold man. He speaks the truth, right on their faces."

Evidently unimpressed, the editor of 'Bijli' wrinkled his nose and knotted his eyebrows, "The days are dead and buried when ladies would get carried away by empty verbosity. You keep treading on their rights and call them 'exalted mothers', 'worshipful deities', 'saints'!" and so on....

Mehta kept up the tempo..."I am pained to see women acting like men and endeavouring to step into their shoes as much as I am hurt by men trying to take on the role of women and encroaching into their domain. I am sure such men will never earn your trust and respect and let me assure you men also do not look at similar women with love or faith."

Khanna's broad smile seemed to emerge from some deep recess of his being.

Rai sahib took a dig at him. "You look very pleased, Khannaji."

Khanna said, "Just let me meet Miss Malti! I would like to know how she reacts to this?"

Mehta went on, "In the evolution of living beings, I consider the position of women on a higher evolutionary scale just as I consider love and sacrifice superior to strife and violence. If our ladies want to step down from their altar of universality and creativity and step into the demoniac morass of violence and strife, it will not help society in any way. I am absolutely convinced of this. In his egomania, man has always considered his glory above all else. He perceives victory in depriving his brother of his freedom and shedding his blood. The children whom women nurture with love and care are fodder for his huge cannons and innumerable guns. And when our mothers offer their blessings as shields and anoint his head as he sets out to battle, it is surprising how he perceives destruction as the sole path to the good of the world. His violent nature grows manifold by the day and today we are witness how brute power tramples humanity and the entire world under its feet as it marches on, scorching lush green fields and demolishing thriving civilisations. Worshipful ladies, I ask you - do you want to be a part of this violent unfolding and subscribe to its strength by co-operating with this monster in your misdirected bid to do good to the world? I appeal to you; let this monster wreak its havoc but you carry on with your divine responsibility and duty towards the world.

Khanna said, "Malti can barely lift her face."

Rai sahib gave his approval on another subject, "What Mehta says is solid facts."

The 'Bijli' editor protested, "But he has hardly said anything! The enemies of women's liberation take recourse to similar strange arguments. I don't accept the dictum that simply love and sacrifice is responsible for all progress in the world; I think it's due to valour, intelligence, industriousness and enterprise."

Khurshid looked back impatiently, 'Oh, come on! Will you let us listen to him or sing your own song?"

Mehta's speech was going strong. "I am not one of those who say women and men have the same energies, capabilities and aptitudes and are not different from each other. There is no other terrible myth than this. This is one fallacy that strives to smother centuries of accumulated experience, like a cloud that tries to hide the sun from our eyes. I caution you not to get entangled in this web. A woman is as superior to man as light is to darkness. Forgiveness, sacrifice and non violence are the superior qualities of humanity. Womanhood has achieved all of them. For ages, men have tried to attain that level through religion and spirituality but have failed consistently. I can go so far as to say that the forbearance and sacrifice of women far outweighs all spiritual achievement men can ever boast of."

The hall reverberated with applause. Rai sahib was overwhelmed, "Mehta speaks straight from the heart."

Onkarnath looked at it differently, "But all his ideas are stale and decadent."

"If an old idea is presented with passion, it is as good as new," retorted Rai sahib.

"Someone who makes a thousand rupees per month and blows it up in hedonistic pursuit can never have that kind of passion. This is just a ploy to win the admiration of old fashioned women and men with obscurantist ideas."

Khanna stared at Malti, "Why is she so delighted? She should be hanging her head in shame."

Khurshid said, "Khanna, now you must prepare a treatise too or Mehta will chase you out of the race very soon. He has already made a mark today."

Khanna was needled, "Don't worry about me. I have netted enough birds and have lost count of them."

Rai sahib winked at him and said, "Now-a-days, you are seen a lot at the Ladies' Club. I believe you have become one of their prominent donors, eh?"

Khanna's face flushed, "I don't visit clubs that indulge in nefarious activities on the pretext of promoting art and music."

Meanwhile, Mehta's address continued unabated. "Men say all inventors and discoverers were males. All great saints were men. All warriors, all sailors, all great leaders and all great politicians were men. But what did these great men achieve? The great preachers and religious convertors achieved little except generate more bloodshed and mayhem. They encouraged men to slash the throats of their brothers. The achievements of great world politicians is lost in architectural ruins or lost civilisations, while inventors have succeeded in making man a slave of machines. What problems have these greats solved? Where is peace in this civilisation built by men? Where is love and where is co-operation?

Onkarnath almost got up from his seat with an expression of finality as if he was about to leave, "Listening to lofty statements by playboys is too painful to bear."

Khurshid caught hold of his hand and pressed him to be seated, "Oh come on, Editorji, don't be a moron! There's a wide world out there everyone says what he or she feels like, even if it is nonsense. There'll always be people to applaud anything. There will be innumerable Mehtas who will cross your path time and again but the world will go on as usual. Why are you getting so worked up?"

"I can't tolerate falsehood and pretentiousness."

Rai sahib added his bit to spur the editor on, "Right, sir! Who will not balk at hearing harlots talk like nuns?"

Onkarnath took his seat again as Mehta continued with his speech. "Let me ask you a question. Is it worthy of a swan to give up its peaceful existence in a serene lake, and try to prey on little birds just because it sees the hawk do the same thing as a matter of course? And suppose it does become a bird of prey, will you approve of that and compliment it? The swan does not have sharp claws as the hawk. It neither has a sharp beak, nor keen eyes to track down prey. Actually, it doesn't possess an acute thirst for blood either! It will take centuries for it to develop those qualities and equipment and even if it does, it will never become a hawk but one thing is for sure- it will definitely not remain a swan, the beautiful bird that swoons in ecstasy.

Khurshid murmured under his breath but loud enough for those sitting nearby to hear, "These are poetic allusions; not tangible arguments. The she-hawk hunts prey as fiercely as the male."

Onkarnath grinned broadly, "And he calls himself a philosopher; based on those spurious arguments!"

Khanna let out his steam as well, "Philosopher? He isn't a shadow of one! A philosopher is one who..."

"...doesn't waver from the truth," Onkarnath completed the sentence for him.

Khanna was not impressed with the editor's effort to fill in the blanks for him. He said, "I don't know much about truth and stuff. I will consider someone a philosopher, if he actually is a philosopher."

Khurshid chuckled and complimented him, "Wow! Allah be praised! What a wonderful definition of a philosopher. 'A philosopher is someone who is actually a philosopher'. Sure, why not?"

Mehta was still at his speech. "I do not imply women do not need education- they do and possibly more urgently than men. I am not saying women don't need empowerment. They need both education and empowerment, but not in the way men have utilised it by turning the world into a stage of violent theatrics. If you imitate that education and empowerment, the entire world will turn into a graveyard. Your rights and your education lie not in violence and destruction but in nature and nurturing. Do you think votes will give you that right? Or do you think pushing pen in an office or using your wits in a courtroom will give you that right and status? Are you ready to forsake the rights gifted to you by nature in exchange of such artificial, unnatural and destructive rights as you seek today?"

Saroj had held herself back out of respect for her elder sister. She couldn't restrain herself any longer. She rose and shouted, "We want equality with men!" Her cry was echoed by chants of other girls in the hall.

Onkarnath stood up and said loudly, "Down with the enemies of women's liberation."

Malti banged her fist on the table and said, "Silence please. All those who want to speak for or against, will get their chance to be heard."

Mehta said, "Who says the scope of your life is limited and lacks opportunities of self expression? We are humans first and foremost; all other designations are merely outward covering. Our life is our home. That is where we are born and that is where we are nurtured. All of life's developments take place within the confines of the home. If a home is limited, where does infinity lie? Is it in the stressful struggle that is nothing but organised hijacking of human potential? Would you like to leave the crucible of humanity for the factories where humankind is enslaved?"

Mirza retorted, "Isn't their rebellion instigated by the oppression of men?"

Mehta said, "Undoubtedly, men have been unfair but this is not the correct response. I agree it is necessary to combat injustice but not at the cost of destroying one's own self."

Malti interjected, "Women want rights so that they can make good use of them and prevent men from misusing them."

Mehta responded, "The greatest rights in the world come with sacrifice and service and you already have them. I am sorry my sisters are building their ideals with ideas from the West, where women have lost the special status they commanded and have fallen from being the ruler of what they surveyed to a plaything of what they sought to destroy or equal. The Western woman wants to be free so that she can pleasure herself as much as she can. Our women never had pleasure as their sole goal. They have extracted their rights through service and commitment to the family at home. We must accept and learn from the great aspects of western civilisation. There is always a give and take and interflow of ideas between cultures but aping something blindly, is a symptom of weak intellect. The Western woman does not want to be the mistress of her home. The desire for enjoyment has made her bold and reckless. She is sacrificing her grace and dignity on the altar of promiscuity and sensual pleasure. When I see educated girls in those nations bare their bodies and strut around exhibiting their beauty, I can only pity them. They are so blinded by desire that they are unable to see how society is encouraging and luring them to lose their dignity and self respect."

Rai sahib applauded. The hall exploded into a deafening applause like a staccato of firecrackers.

The editor remarked indifferently, "This is the only sensible part of his entire speech."

"That means you have also turned into a Mehta fan!"

"No, please! We are not fans of anyone. You will read our comments in the next issue of Bijli."

"This means you are not interested in the fight for rights but are only worried about pushing your own agenda."

The editor was unmoved, "The advocate's job is to protect his client's interests. He is not concerned about uncovering the truth or letting sleeping dogs lie."

"In other words, do you imply you are an advocate for women?"

"I am an advocate for all those who are weak, helpless and oppressed."

"Goodness! You are so utterly shameless, man."

Mehta's speech wasn't over yet. "This is a male conspiracy. To bring down women from their high pedestal and draw them to their base level - the level of men who are cowards, who have no sense of responsibility towards their household, who run amok and revel in uninhibited sexual freedom like wild bulls, straying into other's fields to graze nonchalantly and satiate their unbridled urges. Their conspiracy has worked in the West where worshipful ladies have donned the firmament of fickle butterflies. I am sorry to say the same breeze is now blowing in our own country and it is especially afflicting our educated sisters who are increasingly falling under its spell. They are readily discarding domesticity to adorn the hues of butterflies."

Saroj was so riled and inflamed by these comments that she stood up from her seat. "We do not seek advice from men. If they are free to think about themselves, so are we. Young women of today are not ready to treat marriage and wifely duties as their holy profession. They want to marry for love and no other extraneous consideration."

There was a spirited burst of applause, especially from the first few benches which were occupied by young girls.

Mehta replied, "What you call love is a chimera; it's an illusion, a disfigured form of unquenchable lust just as spiritual mendicants are a sophisticated version of beggars. If 'love' is lacking in the confines of marriage, it is totally absent in unshackled abandon. True peace and true happiness can only be found in service and commitment. The desire to serve is the only cement that will keep couples together - bound for life in a voluntary and delightful companionship which cannot be torn asunder by the severest of storms. When there is an absence of the spirit of service and dedication, you will find mistrust, strained relations and divorce. Moreover, you have a greater responsibility as the commander of the ship of life in which men are your co-passengers. If you want, you can steer the boat to safety in the most difficult of squalls and typhoons. But if you are negligent and callous, the boat will sink, taking you with it."

He closed his arguments. The topic was riddled with controversy. A number of ladies wanted to respond and sought permission from the Chair to put their point across but it was quite late, hence Malti called the meeting off after thanking Mehta. It was announced that next Sunday other ladies will give their opinion on the same issue.

Rai sahib walked up to Mehta and congratulated him, "You spoke from the heart Mehta. I agree with every word you spoke."

Malti laughed softly, "Why not? You will definitely agree with him; crooks make good blood brothers! But what bothers me is why should women be expected to bear the entire burden of sacrifice, service and commitment?"

Mehta said, "Because only they can appreciate it."

Khanna looked at Malti with wide open eyes, as if by looking at her intently he could fathom what was going on in her mind, "I think his ideas are at least a century old."

"Which particular idea are you talking about?" she asked sharply.

"Well, the one about service and sacrifice..."

"If you think these thoughts are ancient, please educate me about the contemporary views on the subject. Do you have any new prescription to help couples live happily ever after?"

Khanna felt irritated. He thought his words would please Malti but they only brought a frown on her face. He said, "I am sure Mehta will come up with a remedy."

"He has said his piece; we know what he thinks and we also know that according to you, his ideas are a hundred years old. It is you who should come up with the new prescription. Don't you realise there are some issues that will never be out of date? These questions will be raised in every age as the issues involved remain the same."

Mrs. Khanna had moved to the veranda. Mehta went up and greeted her. "What did you think about my speech?" he asked.

Mrs. Khanna lowered her eyes and said, "It was nice. Quite good, in fact. But at present you are a bachelor; no wonder women are 'worshipful' ladies for you. You consider them exalted, great, nurturing angels. Once you are married, I will ask you to present your revised thoughts on women all over again. And I believe you will marry, for you have labelled all unattached flamboyant men as cowards."

Mehta grinned, "Exactly. I am preparing grounds for that already."

"Miss Malti and you will make a good couple."

"Only if she sits at your feet and learns about womanly duties before that."

"You are at it again! Just like any other selfish man! Have you learnt your duties as a husband?"

"I am wondering where I should learn those."

"Perhaps Mr. Khanna can be a good teacher."

Mehta burst into laughter- "No, I will learn a man's duties from you."

"Okay. You may take my advice on this. First lesson is that you must forget about women being superior creatures and every responsibility resting on their shoulders. It is men who are superior and the burden of the entire household rests on them. Only men can generate the emotions of service, sacrifice, discipline and commitment in women. If he is deficient in these emotions, his woman will also be lacking in similar sentiments. The revolt that you see amongst women is because men have completely abdicated their responsibility and are devoid of those essential qualities."

Mirza sahib ambled over and taking Mehta in a bear hug, lifted him high. "Congratulations!"

Mehta looked at him with questioning eyes. "Did you like my submission?"

"The merits of the submission could be debated but I must say it was a hit. You arrested the djinn in the bottle. Count yourself lucky that she, who doesn't let anyone come close, is now singing paeans in your glory."

Mrs. Khanna said in a barely audible voice, "Just wait for the euphoria to subside."

Mehta shrugged his shoulders indifferently, "Who will fall for a bookworm like me, ma'am? I am a committed idealist!"

Mrs. Khanna saw her husband moving towards the car so she followed him in that direction. Mirza also stepped out. Mehta picked up his staff from the table at the dais and was about to depart when Malti came and caught him by the wrist. Staring at him with pleading eyes she said, "You can't leave as yet. Come; let me introduce you to papa. You can eat with him tonight."

Mehta touched his ears in mock exasperation. "Oh no! Please excuse me. Saroj will have me for dinner if I go there. I am mortally scared of girls like her."

"Not at all! You don't worry about that. I take responsibility for it. She won't utter a word."

"Ok, you go ahead. I will see you later."

"This is not possible. Saroj has left with my car. You will have to drop me home."

They sat in Mehta's car to Malti's home. He asked Malti, "There are rumours that Khanna beats his wife. Ever since I came to know that I hate to see his face. Such a brute can't be human. And he wants to act as a well wisher of women! Haven't you ever tried to make him see reason?"

Malti squirmed, "It takes two to tango, Mehtaji."

"I can't imagine one reason why a man would want to hit his wife."

"Even if the wife is foul mouthed...?"

"Yes."

"That means you are a new species of man."

"If a man is foul mouthed; should he be lashed with a whip?"

"A woman can be more forgiving than a man. This is what you propound."

"Then, is that the reward for her tolerance? I think you encourage Khanna unnecessarily with your attention. The awe in which he holds you and the hold that you have over him, is enough to make him mend his ways; that is, if you insist. By speaking in his defence you become a party to his crime."

Malti was incensed. She retorted with passion, "You have raised this subject unnecessarily at this time. I don't want to criticise anyone but you have yet to recognise Mrs. Khanna for who she is. You see her coy, peaceful face and think she is one of your 'worshipful' ladies. I will not place her on such a high pedestal. If you knew the extent to which she has gone to malign me and the sort of calumny she has spread about me. If I tell you all about it you will be astounded. If you knew the real story, you will realise what treatment she deserves."

"If she has such venom for you; don't you think she could have a reason for that?"

"Why don't you ask her? I am no expert in reading people's minds."

"One doesn't have to read someone's mind to understand everything. If any man tries to come between me and my woman, I will shoot him and if I am unable to shoot him, I will shoot myself. In the same way, if I try to bring another woman between me and my wife, she has full right to do whatever she wants. There can be no compromise on this. This is a primal uncivilised instinct we have inherited from our forefathers. These days it will be rejected as barbaric and unsocial conduct but I have still to conquer this mentality and am certainly in no hurry to do so. I have no fear of the law, if it comes to it. My home is my jurisdiction."

Malti asked him with an edge to her voice, "But how did you come to the conclusion that in your words which you clearly imply, I have any intention of coming in between Mr. and Mrs. Khanna? You insult me by making that insinuation. Khanna is as good as the sole of my slippers- I hardly spare a thought for him! He means nothing to me."

Mehta was clearly sceptical, "You are yourself not convinced of what you say, Miss Malti. You think the world is foolish? If Mrs. Khanna thinks what everybody else is thinking, I don't blame her one bit."

Malti's irritation grew with every passing moment. "The world relishes concocting rumours about every other person. This is its nature; what can I do about it? But this is rotten gossip, a mischievous canard; though I must admit I am not so impassive that if I see Khanna warming up to me, I tick him off sternly. My profession is such that it requires me to be nice and polite with all whom I meet. If others read it differently, then they...then they..."

Her voice trailed off as it choked with tears. She turned her face away and wiped her moist eyes. She was quiet for a moment and spoke after almost a minute, "Just like others....you too... I am pained. I didn't expect this from you of all people."

In the next instant she regretted her moment of weakness. She snapped at him angrily and said, "You have no right to accuse me of anything. If you are also like other men who will raise their eyebrows if a man and woman as much as talk with each other, then you are welcome to your opinion. I am least concerned. If a woman would come to you on some pretext or the other every second day, look up to you for advice, sit at your feet, hang on very word you utter and claim to jump into a pit of fire at one word from you, I can say for sure, you will never remain indifferent to her. If you are able to reject her, you are not human. You may bring as many arguments and explanations against this but I will not believe you at all. I think indifference is a far cry; you will be swept off your feet and worship the ground she walks on and soon she will become the beloved worshipful queen of your heart. I request you with folded hands. Please don't mention Mr. Khanna to me ever again."

Mehta rubbed and warmed his cold hands over this simmering fire. "Only if I don't see you with Khanna ever again."

"I will not throttle the call of humanity. If he comes to me I am not going to ignore or cold shoulder him."

"You tell him to behave properly with his wife; as a gentleman should."

"I don't interfere in anyone's personal life. I don't think I have any right to do so."

"In that case, you have no right to be critical of wagging tongues."

They had reached Malti's bungalow. The car rolled to a stop. Malti stepped out of the car and went inside without shaking hands. She also forgot she had invited him over for dinner. She just wanted to go to a secluded corner of the house and cry her heart out.

❁❁❁

16

When the news of an incident in the village reached Rai sahib and he learnt that the village *panchayat* had penalised Hori, he summoned Nokhe Ram and gave him a severe dressing down. Why was he kept in the dark about the development? An irresponsible and unreliable subordinate like Nokhe Ram did not deserve to be his representative in the village council.

When Nokhe Ram could not take it anymore, he lost his cool and blurted out in exasperation, "I wasn't the lone person in the committee. There were others as well. What could I do?"

Rai sahib gazed at Nokhe's rotund belly and his voice cracked like a whip, "Stop that nonsense! You should have protested the very instant saying no decision should be taken until Rai sahib is informed. What right does the *panchayat* have to come between me and my constituency? Is there any other source of income in these parts other than fines, damages and taxes? Taxes go to government coffers, the middlemen make merry with the fines; where does that leave me? What should I survive on? It's a shame that two generations in your family have worked as my subordinates, yet I have to teach you to understand elementary things. How much did they receive from Hori?"

Nokhe Ram felt crushed and barely came up with a whisper, "Eighty rupees, sir."

"In cash?"

"He didn't have any cash, sir. Part payment was bartered in grains and for the remaining, he pledged his house."

For once, Rai sahib gave up his self interest and spoke for Hori, "Oh! So you and those cunning village elders connived to rip off one of my poor men? Will you explain who granted you the authority to collect without my permission? If I want I can send you, that measly *patwari* and that slimy *pundit* to jail for seven years for this insubordination. Perhaps, you thought you are the lords and masters? Let me warn you- if that amount does not reach me by this evening, I will turn the heat on you. Each one of you will have to serve hard labour. You may go now. But tell Hori and his son to come see me right away."

Nokhe Ram was almost apologetic when he opened his mouth to speak, "His son ran away from home, sir. He decamped the night before this happened."

Rai sahib bristled with anger. "Don't lie to me. You know very well how lies put me off. I have never heard of a lover who elopes with his girl, drops her home and makes a run for it! If he had to run away, why did he bring the girl in the first place? I am convinced you people have something to do with it. If you stand waist deep in the Ganges and swear on the holy waters, I will still not trust you. I know you would have threatened them with a social boycott. What could the poor chap do other than run away from it all?"

Nokhe Ram considered it better not to respond to whatever his master said. Everything the master says is unquestionable. He did not have the courage to ask him to conduct his own enquiry if he did not trust his version of what transpired that day. The wrath of the wealthy demands complete surrender. It is not accustomed to counter questions, much less ripostes.

When the village elders heard Rai sahib's orders, their euphoria turned tail. Hori's sacks of grain were still piled up in the granary but the cash had long gone. Hori's house was pledged to the village council but nobody wanted anything to do with it any more. Just as a Hindu woman is the lady of the house as long as she lives with her husband but is worth a nought no sooner either she leaves him or he abdicates her; Hori's house, in a similar manner, might have meant the world to him but for all practical purposes, it was hardly worth the mud with which it was built. To make matters worse, it was amply clear that Rai sahib was not willing to settle for anything less than full payment of the fine collected in cash. They blamed Hori, assuming he had ratted on them. Pateshwari was scared the most. He was certain he would lose his job. The elders wracked their brains but failed to find a solution to the problem. They blamed each other and eventually had a massive argument.

Pateshwari nodded his head in regret. "I was against it from the beginning. We should have clammed up on Hori's issue. In the cow's case, we had to cough up the bribe. There will be no bribe or comfort money in this case; we might end up losing our jobs. But you're so greedy, the whole bunch of you. You insisted on making money out of it. Now everybody must cough up twenty each. Things are still under control; if Rai sahib lodges a complaint, we're sunk."

Datadin threw up his hands in despair. "I don't have twenty *paise,* what to speak of twenty rupees. I had recently organised a feast for the Brahmins, held religious ceremonies and they were certainly not free, were they? I spent a lot over it. Moreover, does Rai sahib have the guts to throw me in jail? I am a Brahmin; I will reduce his house to ashes with my curses. He hasn't dealt with a Brahmin before; so let him learn the hard way."

Jhinguri Singh made similar noises. He said he was not Rai sahib's servant. He didn't beat Hori, he didn't exert any pressure on him. Hori wanted to repent so he offered him the way out. He had personally not committed any crime but it was Nokhe Ram who was neck deep in this mess. He savoured the benefits of kingship without wearing a crown. With a salary of ten rupees per month, he collected more than a thousand rupees annually by twisting arms and hedging bets. He lorded over a thousand men, quite a few of whom were ever ready to prostrate themselves at his service. At police stations, they vacated a chair for him when he sauntered in. Such latitude was not available to the moneyed gentry and though Nokhe Ram had never tasted it, his proverbial bread was buttered on both sides.

As for Pateshwari, he had turned into a loan merchant and had no escape. He was caught in a bind and had no place to hide. For a few days he remained at home, mulling over his future course of action. One day it came to him in a flash.

He had seen copies of a newspaper, Bijli, at the courts. If they sent an unsigned letter to its editor, informing him that Rai sahib unilaterally imposes fines and extracts money from his constituents, he will be hard put to explain. Nokhe Ram readily agreed to this plan. Both put their heads together, composed the letter and sent it by registered post.

Onkarnath, the editor of Bijli, was always on the lookout for such scandalous stuff. As soon as he received the letter, he sent a message to Rai sahib informing him that he was privy to certain scandalous information about him but the correspondent who sent it possessed such incriminating evidence that he could not ignore it easily. Was it a fact that Rai sahib has extracted a fine from one member of his constituency because that man's son had married a widow and brought her home? As an editor he was duty bound to verify the facts and if true, bring them to light in public interest. The editor sincerely wished the news was proved wrong but if it was verified, he would have to publish it as a matter of duty. The pulls of friendship would not keep him away from professional commitment.

Rai sahib felt like hitting his head on the wall when he read the message. At first, in a rush of anger, he wanted to go and crack fifty whips on the editor's back and tell him to go publish what he liked but when he thought about its repercussions, he mellowed down and decided to pay him a visit immediately. Any further delay might send a wrong message and if the news was published, his reputation would be blown to smithereens.

Onkarnath had come back from his daily walk and was sitting with his pen poised in mid air, sifting through several ideas, wondering what to write for that day's editorial. He could barely collect his thoughts as his mind fluttered restlessly like a caged bird. His wife had passed certain comments last evening which turned in his mind like a knife in a wound. If someone called him poor, unfortunate, stupid – he could take it in his stride, but to be called impotent was too much to bear. And more significantly, did a wife have any right to use that word for her husband? She was expected to repudiate such a charge and silence those who might throw such innuendoes with malicious intent. Was this the reward for his tolerance and concern? He was not rolling in money; he couldn't afford a silken *Banarasi saree* for his wife. She should be content wearing a *khadi saree*. Didn't he himself wear *khadi* clothes? After all, he was a freedom fighter and nationalist. The only wealth a nationalist possesses is the wealth of devotion for his nation's cause.

He paused for a moment. This sounded like a perfect heading for the day's editorial. But his thoughts strayed to the issue at hand. He was expecting a reaction from Rai sahib to the message he sent, some days ago. If he offered a satisfactory explanation, the matter would be closed but if he harboured thoughts the editor Onkarnath would be daunted by fear or prevented by old ties, he was mistaken. The only silver lining to his tribulations was his power to expose thieves amongst the high and mighty. He knew Rai sahib had connections in the right places. He was a member of the Council and was on first name terms with senior government officials. He could easily entrap him in false cases and slap concocted charges against him. What's more, he commanded an army of toughies and bouncers who could thrash him at will. But these fears didn't scare Onkarnath. As long as he lived, he would never let the struggle against evil cease for a moment.

He heard a motor car stopping outside his door. Shuffling the loose sheets in his hands, he started scribbling with his pen in right earnest. In a few seconds, Rai sahib entered his room.

Onkarnath did not rise to welcome him. He did not bother to greet or offer him a seat. He looked up from his papers as he would at a supplicant in a court of law and his voice carried a righteous and haughty tone as he spoke, "You got my message? I was not obliged to send it, my job is only to look into it but often one has to hedge principles in deference of old ties. Is there any substance to the report?"

Rai sahib could not deny the authenticity of the news. Though he had not received the money yet and he could have convincingly denied receiving it, he played on because he wanted to see what game this man had in his mind.

Onkarnath expressed regret saying since there was no denial, he was left with no other option but to publish the news. "I am pained to write against a very dear friend but in the line of duty, personal relations cease to exist. If an editor fails in his duty to inform about the truth, he relinquishes the right to be one."

Rai sahib drew a chair and settled down in it, popping a pinch of betel nuts into his mouth he said, "But that will not be in your interest. What happens to me is a conjecture for the future but your punishment will be swift, immediate and severe. If you are the one to spare no thought for your friends I am a bird of the same feather."

Onkarnath donned the expression of a martyr and said, "I am not afraid. The day I took up the vocation of journalism, I bid farewell to fear and attachment to life. For me, an editor's death is glorious if it comes as the price for commitment to truth and justice."

"That's okay with me. I accept your challenge. I considered you a friend but if you want to become an adversary, its fine with me. After all, why do I contribute such heavy donations to your paper? It is simply to keep it under my thumb. God has made me rich. I pay seventy five rupees just to seal your mouth. When you wail about losses and appeal for help--and mind you, it happens every three to four months--I am always at hand to bail you out. Why? Every Diwali, Dussehra and Holi I send substantial gifts and invite you to parties and feasts; to what end? You cannot carry bribes and commitment to duty in the same basket."

Onkarnath turned aggressive, "I never accept bribes."

Rai sahib lashed out curtly, "What is that exchange if it's not bribes? Do you assume everyone is an ass that they want to cover your losses selflessly? Just check your account and see how much you have received from my estate? It should run in thousands. If you have no qualms in printing advertisements of foreign medicines and goods in your paper, despite crying yourself hoarse in the name of *swadeshi,* why should I flinch in twisting it a bit to garner fines, taxes, damages and rents from my constituents? Have no illusions that you are the sole benefactor of the peasants; I live and die with them, my fortunes are linked with their well being. There is none more concerned about their welfare than I, but how am I supposed to survive? How will I throw parties for the officials? From where do I raise donations for the royal treasury, how can I feed the swarms of hangers-on and relatives who depend on me? You are well aware of the expenses of my household. Do you think money grows on trees in my orchard? It ultimately comes from the homes of my constituents. Probably, you labour under the illusion that *zamindaars* have it all going for them. What do you know about their actual condition? If they live like saints, they will not survive a single day. We are not crazy scorpions who sting out of habit. We don't enjoy fleecing the poor but there are things that cannot be helped. Just as you want to benefit from my opulence, there are scores of others who perceive us as the hen that lays golden eggs. Come to my home and see how I am targeted day in day out. There are hordes knocking at my door for one or the other favour or help. If I stop sending gift hampers to the higher-ups, they will consider me a rebel. None of your articles in the press will save me. I joined the Congress and am still suffering from the displeasure it caused to our rulers. I have been blacklisted. Will you ever know the debts that are piling on my head? If all lenders come at once to claim their loans, I will have to sell even the ring on my finger, if not clothes I am wearing. You might ask me why I have created such a mess for myself. That's because I am unable to extract myself from what we are accustomed to for seven generations. I can't go and hoe the fields like a commoner. You are not weighed down by land, properties and hassles of living it up even; you can afford to be fearless yet you are troubled and have your own problems. Are you aware of the amount of bribes that change hands in courts? How the poor, especially women, are exploited daily? Do you have the guts to write about it? I will provide all material with hard evidence."

Onkarnath softened a little and said, "Whenever I have been presented with an opportunity I have not been found wanting."

Rai sahib softened his tone in equal measure. "Yes, I accept that you have acted courageously a few times but your aim is more or less selfish and not completely dedicated to the good of people whose cause you espouse. Don't glare at me like that and please don't get mad at me. Whenever you have taken up a good cause it has resulted in your personal glorification and an increase in your personal income. If you are also playing the same game as I am, let me take good care of you. I will not give you money, for that could be construed as bribe. Should I get some ornaments designed for your wife? Will you agree to this? Now let me tell you the truth. The news that came to you is wrong. However, in the same breath let me admit that I do take fines and damages from my people like every other

Zamindaar and it adds up to five or ten thousand annually. If you snatch this away from me, you will also suffer for it. You want to lead a comfortable life and so do I. Where is the logic if you deprive me and yourself as well, in the name of justice and duty? Open your heart to me. Please, I am not an enemy; how many times have we sat at the same table and broken bread! I am aware your finances are going through a rough patch. It is abundantly clear to me that your position is more precarious than mine. However, I can do little if you want to be holier than thou. That will be your decision. I must go now."

As he finished the monologue, Rai sahib stood up from his chair. Onkarnath held his hand and spoke in a conciliatory tone, "No, no. You aren't going so fast. I must clarify my position. I am grateful to you for all the kindnesses you have extended to me but in this case, it has become an issue of principles and you will appreciate principles are so close to ones' heart."

Rai sahib took his seat and spoke rather sweetly, "As you say, brother. Go on, write whatever you want. I don't want to you to compromise on your principles. At worst, I will earn a bad name- what else? I can't expect to save my reputation all the time. But is there a head of any district who does not tweak the arms of his people to some extent? If a dog is expected to guard over a bone what is he expected to eat? The maximum I can do now is to assure you that there won't be a cause for complaint, if you pardon me this time. I would never apologise to any other editor, on the contrary I will have him whipped, but we share an old friendship, hence I will go the extra mile. This is the age of newspapers. The government itself runs scared of them. Who am I to challenge the supremacy of the press? You can make or break anyone. Any way, let's drop this for now. Tell me, how is your paper faring these days?"

Onkarnath spoke unwillingly, with apparent disinterest, "We try to manage somehow and in the present condition, I don't expect too much from it. I did not take up this profession for money or power and that is why I have no complaints. I came to serve the public and try to do it to the best of my capacity. My only desire is to do good to the country. An individual's joys or tribulations are of no consequence in the bigger picture."

Rai sahib turned still more humane and said, "That's fine, my dear brother, but to serve you must first stay alive! Economic woes will never allow you to serve with single minded devotion. Is the paper's subscription figure not growing at all?"

Onkarnath was now crestfallen. "The problem is I want to maintain high journalistic standards for my paper. Our subscribers will increase rapidly, if I devote columns to film stars and print their pictures but that is not my editorial policy. There are so many other ways through which newspapers make money but I don't subscribe to those tactics. I think they are improper."

"But that is exactly the reason why you are so respected today! I want to make a proposition, although I am not sure if you will appreciate or accept it. You kindly add a hundred free subscribers and allow me to pay for their subscriptions."

Onkarnath bowed his head in gratitude and said, "I accept your donation with humility. It is sad to see how indifferent the masses are to newspapers. There is no dearth of money for schools, colleges and temples but no one spares a thought for newspapers. There are hardly any donors who help newspapers, though they are a better and more economical vehicle of spreading awareness and education. Just as colleges and educational institutions are given grants, if journalists are also offered some sort of subsidy or assistance, then the time and newsprint they waste in advertisements can be better utilised. But I am really grateful to you."

After Rai sahib left, there was no trace of satisfaction or joy on Onkarnath's face. Rai sahib had not placed any conditions or bindings but Onkarnath had gone ahead and accepted the donation despite being subjected to such a bitter outburst from him. His circumstances forced him to swallow his pride as his workers were not paid wages for three months and the paper supplier was threatening to stop supply until his accounts were cleared. He was lucky he didn't have to spread his palms for alms.

His wife Gomti came in and protested "Isn't it time for lunch yet or is this a new regimen that unless it is past one, you will not leave your desk? How long can anybody sit before the stove warming your food?"

Onkarnath cast a sad eye towards his wife. Her anger dissipated in a flash. She realised his difficulties. She did feel jealous when she saw the fine *sarees* and ornaments of other woman and vented her frustration on him, often saying hurtful things, but her disappointment was not directed towards him but at her own misfortune. Onkarnath was merely caught in the crossfire between her emotions. She felt annoyed with his ascetic existence, yet sympathised with him. She did think he was slightly cynical, if not whimsical. Seeing his sad face, she enquired with genuine concern, "What happened? Is something wrong with your stomach?"

Onkarnath could not help but smile. "Who says I am unwell or sad. On the contrary, I am as happy as I was on my wedding day, perhaps more. I have made fifteen hundred rupees this morning. This is my lucky day."

Gomti didnt believe him. "You're lying. You aren't getting fifteen hundred from anywhere. Had you said, fifteen, I could believe you."

"No, my dear. I swear on you! Rai sahib was here minutes back. He has promised to pay for a hundred subscriptions."

Gomti's face fell, "Oh yes, he said it and you got it!"

"No, Rai sahib is a man of his word."

"I have yet to see a *Zamindaar* who is a man of his words. My grandfather worked with one. For years he wasn't paid full wages. He left him to work for another. He didn't give him a *paisa* for two years. When *dada* lost his temper one day, he was kicked out. Their promises don't mean a thing."

"I will send him a bill today."

"You send him ten bills. He will tell you to come the next day. The next day he will be travelling. Back after three months."

A nagging doubt arose in Onkarnath's mind. She was right. What would he do if Rai sahib went back on his word? Nevertheless, he steadied himself and said, "This is not possible. Rai sahib is not a cheat."

Gomti stuck to her stand, "That's why I say you are a simpleton. Somebody just has to act sympathetic and you're taken for a ride. He is a big fat rich man. He can afford to forget promises. If he fulfills every promise he makes, he will be driven to beggary. The chief of my village did not pay worker's bills for two, even three years. If they insisted, he threw them out. His servants worked for a year. When they asked for wages, out they went. Who's next? This Rai sahib of yours is of the same stock. Come, have lunch and get back to the grind, which is your destiny. Consider yourself fortunate if these rich people condescend to be your friends. If they give you one *paisa,* they will take four from their people. Today you are free to write whatever you want. Be thankful for it."

Onkarnath sat down for lunch but the morsels stuck in his gullet. It was becoming increasingly tough to eat in peace without unburdening the load off his mind.

He grimaced, "If he does not pay up, I will teach him a lesson he won't forget for a long time. I have him by the neck. The people from his village will not lie to me; their news is authentic. A report against Rai sahib has fallen in my hands. If I publish it, he will not know what hit him. This is no charity what he is doing for me. It took him some time to come round to it. At first, he tried to threaten me. When he saw threats won't work, he threw this dice. Well, I also thought about it; setting one man right would not change the system. Why shouldn't I accept his donation? I have diluted my principles, to be sure, but if Rai sahib cheats me, God in heaven, I will stoop still further! It will not be difficult to tell my conscience there is nothing wrong in looting those who loot the poor."

❁❁❁

17

Word spread like fire that Rai sahib had summoned the village elders and not only reproached but forced them to cough up the fine charged from Hori. The grapevine had it that he was ready to send them to jail but deft grovelling, coupled with appeals for mercy, saved them. Dhania felt personally vindicated. She went to town with it; lampooning the five committee members who had fined her. "They won't listen to cries of the poor but God isn't deaf. They wanted to rob and feast with her money but God brought down his stick so hard on them that they had to pay in double measure for whatever they stole;" she would tell anyone who listened.

But ploughing the fields without bulls was an onerous task. It was the seed sowing season. It is a saying in villages that if a peasant's bulls die in the month of October, it kills the farmer as well. Hori was similarly handicapped while seeding was in full swing elsewhere. In fields across the countryside, a stray song or chorus could be heard as women busied themselves in sowing the fields while Hori's lay unattended like a forsaken orphan. Puniya and Sobha had their own fields to manage and could not spare time or energy for anything else. Hori flitted from one field to another; helping sow seeds at one place or just sitting and keeping watch over others. This earned him a few fistfuls of grains. Dhania, Sona and Rupa busied themselves sowing seeds in other's fields. As long as sowing was in full swing, they continued to get something to eat every day. They weren't comfortable but did not starve, though fights between the couple became a daily ritual before they retired for the night. But soon the season was over and there was no work in the village. Now the future depended on sugarcane still standing in the fields.

It was a cold night. There was nothing to eat at Hori's house. In the morning, they had only roasted grams but the fire was not lit in the evening for want of anything to cook. Rupa sat on the courtyard fence, sobbing silently. She was learning not to protest loudly.

When hunger pangs became unbearable, she flopped down from her post and crossed over to Puniya's house and told her she had come for a coal to light fire.

Puniya asked if they had not lit a fire in their kitchen yet.

Rupa replied weakly, "There is nothing at home. It's no use lighting the fire."

"Then why do you want a fire?"

"*Dada* wants to light his *chillum*."

Puniya threw a smouldering piece of dung cake towards her but Rupa barely noticed it. She went closer to her and said, "Your *rotis* smell good, *kaki*. I love barley *rotis*."

Puniya smiled at her, "Would you like to eat one?"

"*Amma* will scold me."

"Who's telling her?"

Rupa ate to her fill and ran back without washing her face or hands.

Hori was sitting crestfallen inside the house when Datadin came to his door and called his name. Hori's heart skipped a beat; he wondered if this was another calamity knocking at his door. He came out and touched the old man's feet reverentially and placed a stool for him, requesting him to be comfortable.

Datadin rested his behind on the low stool and was quite sympathetic. "I see there is no activity in your field. You didn't send word to us or Bhola wouldn't have dared to walk away with your bulls. He would be dead before he touched them. I swear Hori, I was not a party to the fine imposed by the village elders. Dhania singles me out unnecessarily. This is Lala Pateshwari and Jhinguri Singh's mischief. I merely sat in the village Council when the meeting took place. These people were in favour of a sterner sentence but I had it mellowed down. Now they regret it. They probably forgot that it is someone else's writ that runs in the village, not theirs. Anyway, what are you doing about sowing seeds in your field?"

Hori was almost ready to burst into tears. "What can I say, *Maharaj?* It seems the field will remain barren this season."

"That will be so unfortunate!"

"How can we challenge the will of God?"

"Don't worry. Your labours will not be in vain. I am there for you. Tomorrow I will ensure that the seeds are sown. The earth is still moist and it might take about ten days for the seedlings to take root. That's no big deal. We will split the produce in half between us. That will be fair and square. I was very disturbed when I saw your well ploughed fields run dry for want of seeds."

Hori was confused. All through the last quarter he readied the soil; ploughed and prepared the earth with manure and now, he had to commit half his produce for nothing. Worse, he was supposed to feel grateful for it! He wondered if it was better to just give it up. But the next moment he realised that if he did not raise some money, attachment notices would surely be issued for his house.

He accepted the proposal.

Datadin was delighted. He said, "Let's go and I'll give you the seeds rightaway so you don't have any problems in the morning. You had your dinner, I presume?"

Hori was embarrassed but he told him the truth.

Datadin was all over him with sweet accusations, "What? You didn't have anything at home and you didn't care to inform me? I am no stranger; such lack of trust on your part hurts me so! My good man, why should you be embarrassed about this? We are all the same, Hori. What if I am a Brahmin and you a lower caste? Who knows a similar calamity may strike me tomorrow? Whom will I turn to other than you in that case? Come with me at once. I will give you a mound of grains along with the seeds to take care of your immediate needs."

Within half an hour Hori was back with a basket of wheat. Once again the grinding wheel came alive in their house and as Dhania turned it round and round, she wiped her tears and wondered what she did to deserve the life she had.

The next day they began sowing the seeds; Hori's entire family got into the act and Datadin was glad he had organised labour at throw away cost. As days passed his son, Matadin also started visiting him off and on. He was a flirtatious young man with a smooth tongue who squandered everything his father wrested from the peasants. He was entangled in an affair with a low caste woman, and hence was still unmarried. Religious purity seems to have such a strong link with food. If our food is untainted by impure substances nothing can dare threaten religious sanctity. Our round fluffy *rotis* are such a wonderful, not to mention convenient, shield against irreligion!

Since his father and Hori were sort of partners, Datadin's son had more opportunities to interact with Jhuniya. He contrived to visit Hori's house on one pretext or the other at times when none but Jhuniya was home. Jhuniya was no beauty, but she was young and a better prospect than a low caste girl. Having lived in the big city for a few years, she had gathered a certain sense of urban etiquette and sartorial intelligence. Besides, she was also prone to shyness which adds a mysterious element to a woman's personality. Matadin often lifted her baby in his arms and played with him, overwhelming her in the process.

One day he asked her, "Jhuniya, what did you see in Gobar that you became his child's mother?"

Jhuniya blushed, "Fate took me to him, *Maharaj*. What can I say?"

Matadin said, "But he's such an unfaithful chap; drifting-God knows where, leaving you alone at home. He is an unstable person; it raises serious doubts in my mind. I hope he is not involved in something we should worry about. Such fickle people should be shot. A man's duty is to be loyal to the one he loves. It is wrong to spoil someone's life and stray elsewhere."

The poor girl, pent up as she was, started sobbing. Matadin looked around in all directions. Seeing no one in the vicinity, he came closer, held her arm and began comforting her, "why do you worry about him, Jhuniya? What if he is gone? You have nothing to worry; you don't lack anything. Allow me to help if there is anything you need."

Jhuniya removed her hand from his grip and said, "You are merciful, *Maharaj*. I feel so lost. I feel such a drifter. I lost my home, my past, present everything. I don't know the ways of the world. His honeyed words entrapped me. I feel so helpless."

Matadin began counting everything that was wrong with Gobar. He was such a loafer; he shirked work at home and ran from responsibility outside it. If he ever came across money, he would immediately gamble it away. Drugs were his favourite pastime, other than loafing around with lazy louts. Once, the police almost hauled him off to jail. Had it not been for their help, Gobar would be rotting in prison to this day.

Suddenly Sona appeared and said, "*Bhabhi, amma* says we must take the grains out and show them the sun or else they will go bad."

Matadin said defensively, "Is it the first time it has rained over your house?

Everything gets damp in this weather---wood or grain." His voice trailed off, enumerating the normal effects of rain, he stepped out. Sona had thrown a spanner in his works.

Sona asked Jhuniya, "Why was he here?"

"He was asking for a spare leash. I told him we don't have one."

"That's just an excuse. He is a bad man."

"I think he's just fine. What do you find so bad about him?"

"Perhaps you don't know. He has a keep- that woman called Siliya."

"Does that make him bad?"

"What else makes a man bad?"

"Your brother has also kept me in your house. Does that make him a bad man too?"

Sona did not respond to this and said, "If he ever comes over again, I will tell him to get lost."

"What if you get married to him?"

Sona blushed, "*Bhabhi*! Now you are calling me names!"

"Why? Where's the name calling in this?"

"If he says that to me I will scald his face."

"What do you think? You will marry an angel from the skies? Is there any young man as charming as him in the village?"

"Why don't you go to him? You are a hundred times better than Siliya!"

"Why should I go to him? I have already come away with one man. For good or for bad."

"Then I will also go with the one I am married to. For good or for bad."

"And if you get married to an old man?"

Sona laughed, "Then I will bake nice soft *rotis* for him, prepare his medicines, make him sit up and lie down if he can't on his own and when he conks off, I will cover my face and bawl my eyes out."

"But what if your husband is a smart young man, then?"

"Then a load of rubbish! You're impossible."

"Ok, tell me? Would you prefer an old man or a younger man?"

"He who will love me is young, even if he is old."

"O God! Wish you get a doddering old husband, and then we'll see your unconditional love! Bet you'll pray every morning that he croaks, so you run off with the next young chap who comes your way!"

"Shut up"

"Actually, I will pity that old man."

Beyond the banter of these girls, across the fields, a new world was taking shape. Within a year a sugar mill had opened nearby. Middlemen and other workers from the mill scoured the adjoining villages, buying standing sugarcane crops off the fields. It was a mill set up by Mr. Khanna.

One day an employee dropped by this particular village. The farmers negotiated rates with him and concluded there was no profit in making jaggery from cane juice on their own. If crushing sugarcane at home brought the same amount of money as selling direct to the mill, what was the sense in labouring over cane stalks at home? The entire village was ready to sell off their standing crops. A few *paise* less didn't matter, as long as there was cash down payment. Everyone had one or the other pressing need. Someone wanted to buy a pair of bulls; someone had a loan to pay off while another was hard pressed to clear last year's dues. Hori wanted to buy his bulls back. This year he expected a low yield. However, the biggest fear was if sugar was available at the same price, who would like to buy jaggery, which was an unrefined sweetener? Everyone took an advance against their crops. Hori expected a payment of a hundred rupees for his; enough to buy one pair of bulls. But the sceptre of loan sharks loomed above him. Datadin, Mangru, Dulari and Jhinguri Singh waited patiently like hawks, biding their time till the peasants emerged from their holes with payments for their crops. If he paid the money lenders, all money would vanish immediately. There was no way he could sell the crops and keep it secret from them. Once he got his bulls back, they would not be able to do anything about it. But when the carts were loaded and the mill men paid them the money, the whole village would know. It was quite possible Mangru and Datadin stood next to him when the transaction took place. The money would just fly into their hands!

In the evening Girdhar asked him, "When is your turn to cut the crops and send to the mill?"

Hori bluffed saying he really had no idea when they'll arrive and asked him the same question.

Girdhar said the same thing. "I have no idea when they'll come, *kaka*."

Every peasant skirted the question and avoided committing anything definite. Everyone was deeply suspicious of everybody else. Each one owed something to Jhinguri Singh and they were quite worked up, worrying how to avoid losing all they earned.

Sobha said to Hori, cursing under his breath, "I pray he gets dysentery and dies."

Hori smiled and said, "Why do you wish that for him? Doesn't he have a wife and children?"

"Should we worry about his kids or our own? He can afford two women and we are worried about our next meal. He will take away everything; we'll have nothing to take home."

"My condition is terrible, brother. If I don't get my bulls back things will only get worse."

"There is still some time- it will take a few more days to transport the cartloads. We can coax the accountant to weigh the bundles fast and fob off the likes of Jhinguri Singh by saying we haven't got the money yet."

Hori pondered over this for some time and said, "He is smarter than you and me put together. He will go directly to the accountant and collect our payments from him. We will be left twiddling our thumbs. That man Khanna who owns the mill is also in the business of lending money. They are on the same side."

Sobha was disappointed, "When will God save us?"

"Not in this lifetime," said Hori and added, "we are not looking for silks and satins, we are content with coarse meals, we merely want to live in peace with dignity and even that is denied to us."

Sobha said with rude determination in his voice, "*Dada*, I will grease the accountant's palm to delay our payments and make us run many times for it. I don't think Jhinguri can keep pace and follow us every time."

Hori smiled broadly and said, "Nothing like this will happen. Your best bet is to fall at Jhinguri's feet. When you are caught, the more you flap your wings, the tighter the trap closes around you."

"Oh, *dada*! You speak like a defeated old man. It is cowardice to be content in prison. The noose be damned, I am going to strain very hard to break free. I have decided to pick up my payment only when Jhinguri isn't around."

Hori was so tense; he could not make up his mind about the right course of action.

"Whatever you say," was all he said.

"We'll get the crops weighed and collect payment later."

"Ok, that is what we'll do."

Next morning almost every farmer was in his field cutting sugarcane. Hori went to his field, a sickle propped on his shoulders, accompanied by Sobha who had volunteered to help. Puniya, Dhaniya, Jhuniya, Sona and Rupa- they were all there. They divided the work, cutting the stalks, gathering them, tying the stalks in separate bundles and moving them aside to one end of the field. When the creditors saw the rush of activity, they felt a stirring of anticipation. Mangru Sah came running, Dulari followed him and Jhinguri Singh scurried along with Datadin close at his heels. Jhinguri Singh's lackeys came with him but sat at a safe distance, merely emphasising their presence.

Dulari came up to Hori, all dolled up with large ear-rings, kohl-lined eyes and heavy bangles on her wrists. "Give me my money before you touch the crops, Hori. For two years, you haven't paid me a single paisa as interest. It seems you take my patience for granted."

Hori pleaded, "*Bhabhi*, allow me to cut the crop; I will pay you as much as possible. I won't run away from the village and I am also not dying tomorrow. I won't get money unless I cut the stalks."

Dulari snatched the sickle from his hands and said, "The problem is your intentions are mean. That is the reason for your misfortune."

Five years ago Hori had borrowed thirty rupees from her. It had become hundred rupees in three years. The interest on hundred for the last two years itself was fifty rupees.

"*Bhabhi*, my intentions are not bad. I promise to pay up. It's just that my days are bad. You may do as you like."

Not a minute after Dulari left, fuming and angry, Mangru Sah walked up to him. With his buck teeth and dark belly hanging below his waist, he was quite a sight. He propped himself on a *lathi* which he used as a crutch, thanks to a debilitating arthritis. "Hori, I had given you a loan, not a charity. You haven't paid anything yet. But don't think I will let you go easy. I will bring your corpse to life if I have to extract money from you."

Sobha had a sense of humour. "Why do you worry, *Sahuji*? You can only make his corpse pay up. And if you are patient, perhaps you will join him in the other world in a few years. Perhaps you should settle your accounts in heaven."

Mangru cursed Sobha with his prolific vocabulary. "When you come to ask for money, you are purring but when it's time to pay up, you start growling."

Sobha threw a barb yet again. "Tell me honestly, how much did you loan him that is three hundred rupees now?"

"When you don't pay interest every year, the amount is bound to grow."

"How much did you loan in the first year? Fifty, isn't it?"

"But do you know how many years ago?"

"Perhaps five...or six."

"It is ten years! This is the eleventh year running."

"Aren't you ashamed to demand three hundred for a loan of fifty rupees?"

"I am not asking for charity. I am asking for my money which was agreed upon."

Hori pleaded with him as well. Datadin was Hori's partner. He had given the seeds so it was against ethics to throw dust in his eyes.

As expected, Jhinguri Singh had already tied up with the manager, whose men transported bundles of sugarcane on their back to a waiting boat by the river which was half a mile from the village. A single trip could transport almost fifty cartloads of sugarcane bundles. In a single day the boat could easily make seven to eight trips. This arrangement was especially put together by Jhinguri Singh and it had earned him a back slapping camaraderie with the mill manager. It had also earned him easy access to the cashier's desk who happily kept him posted of the dealings of the day. Jhinguri Singh had soon wormed his way in and was now sitting at the mill gates, weighing the bundles, issuing receipts for the weights, collecting cash and paying the peasants after duly deducting what they owed him. Their pleas and cries for mercy fell on deaf ears as he worked like an unfeeling robot.

Hori got a hundred and twenty rupees. Jhinguri deducted his dues and thrust twenty-five rupees in Hori's outstretched palm.

Hori stared at the money in his hands and indifferently told him to keep the remaining amount as well. "I will earn enough to stay alive, carrying loads on my back."

Jhinguri threw the notes on the floor and said his job was done; Hori could take them or throw them in the river for all he cared. "I am sparing this for you. Because of your misdeeds I have to listen to Rai sahib's abuse. If he turns the screw on me perhaps you will not get even as much."

Hori picked up the fallen notes in slow motion. When he stepped out, Nokhe Ram called out his name. Hori walked up to him and handed him the money wordlessly and left. He was feeling dizzy. Sobha was at his side and was carrying a similar amount. As they stepped forward, there was Pateshwari waiting outside the gates. When Sobha saw him, he shouted before that man could open his mouth. "I don't have anything and I am not giving you anything."

Pateshwari reacted in the same vein, "You just sold your crops. Didn't you?"

"Yes, I did."

"Didn't you promise to pay up after selling it?"

Yes, I did."

"Then why don't you give it to me? You have paid the others, haven't you?"

"Yes, I have."

Then why don't you give me?"

"Whatever I have left with me is for my children."

Pateshwari challenged him, "You will pay willingly and you will pay right now. If you want to talk nonsense, go ahead and have your say for a moment. Just one complaint and you go to jail for six months. Not a day more, not a day less. Don't gamble with me. I am no servant of the *Zamindaar*. I work for the government-the white man, the one who rules the world and who is the boss of both your Rai sahib and every other authority which you fear."

Pateshwari moved on, confident and sure of his power. Hori walked quietly and Sobha didn't say a word as if the verbal assaults had emasculated them. Suddenly Hori broke the silence, "You must give him the money, Sobha. Tell yourself the crops caught fire. I am trying to convince myself in the same way."

The hurt showed in Sobha's voice. "I know I will. There's no way I can't,"

When Hori reached home, Rupa ran to get him a glass of water. Sona brought the *chillum,* Dhania put salted grams before him in a small bowl and the three stood in front of him, staring expectantly. Hori did not touch the water. The salted grams lay in the bowl, untouched as well. He felt ashamed, crestfallen, frightened and guilty, as if he had accidentally killed someone.

Finally Dhania spoke. "How much did it come to?"

"I got a hundred and twenty but everything was lost to them. Not a *paisa* was left."

Dhania's anger manifested in an unusual way. Her body trembled but she felt like gouging her nails into her own face. She said, "If I ever meet God I want to ask Him why he created a stupid man like you. I have wasted my life. Strange, why He doesn't give me death; at least it's a relief from this grind. How do we get our bulls back now? Will you yoke me to the plough or step in yourself? You have grown old- why didn't you bring at least some money so we could at least get the bulls back? Winter is at the door and none of us have proper clothes to cover our bodies. Take us to the river and dunk us in it. It's better to die in one stroke than perish every day. For how long will we snuggle into straw to spend the night and even if we do, will we eat it as well to survive? If you want to live on hay, you are welcome to it. Keep me and my girls out of it."

As she completed the last sentence, Dhania smiled. While she went berserk with frustration, the logical part of her mind was still working simultaneously. She knew if a farmer had money in his hands and creditors know about it, it was next to impossible to come unscathed with the money intact.

Hori's face was bent low and he was staring guiltily at the floor. He did not see her smile. He mumbled, "We will work as labourers. That is how we will survive."

Dhania asked where they will find work in the village. She joked about his reputation and dignity.

"There is no sin in working like a common labourer. If a labourer comes to good fortune, he becomes a farmer; if a farmer hits bad times, he turns a labourer. If it wasn't my destiny to turn a labourer, why would we suffer so much? Why did the cow die? Why did our son prove to be a nuisance?"

Dhania told her daughters and daughter- in- law to go inside. "Move on girls. Why do you stand here staring blankly? They are different men who bring something or the other when they return home from the bazaar. Here, he will be scared to bring anything home, not even half a *paisa* worth of stuff. No wonder, we starve all the while. When you are afraid to spend, fate contrives to keep you poor. Those who will not buy good stuff, don't want to wear good clothes, why should they be blessed with money - so that they bury it under the floor?"

Hori burst out laughing. "So where is the buried gold, tell me?"

"You'd know better. Don't ask me. Had you brought four *paisa* worth of anything for the children, heaven would not have fallen. Had you held back a rupee from Jhinguri Singh saying you wanted to buy something for your kids, he would have relented."

For the second time that evening, Hori turned regretful. It was a great mistake to hand over twenty-five to Nokhe Ram out of sheer frustration.

Jhuniya went inside and said to Sona, "I feel sorry for *dada*. He comes tired and exhausted and *amma* starts her lament right away. If the creditor was after his life how could he help it?"

"Then how do we get the bulls back?"

"The creditors want their money. They have no concern for what happens to you."

"If it was *amma* and not *dada*, she would never have given him the money."

Jhuniya teased Sona. "Well, if you want, you can get a lot of money. You simply have to smile coquettishly at the money lenders and they will write off all loans. Imagine, what a big relief it will be for your *dada*?"

Sona cupped her hands on Jhuniya's mouth and pressed it. "Not a word more! If I tell *amma* all about Matadin, you will cry."

"What will you tell *amma*?" Jhuniya asked. "There is nothing to report to her. If he drops over on one pretext or the other what do you expect me to do? Tell him to run away? He doesn't take anything from me. He will never get anything except sweet talk from Jhuniya. I know how to sell sweet words at a good price. I am not a fool to be misled by creeps like him. Yes, the day I come to know your brother has ditched me and taken another woman; I will not be bound by any ties. Today I trust and believe he is mine. It is due to me that he is searching his fortune in some strange land. I know that. Sharing a laugh and acting friendly is one thing, cheating is quite another. If you love one and flirt with another, you are soon left with neither."

Hori heard Sobha call him from outside. He gave him Pateshwari's money and said, "*Dada*, you give this to Pateshwari. I don't know what came over me; I should have handed him the money when he asked for it."

Hori pocketed the cash and as he entered his house again, he heard the sonorous sound of a conch shell. At one end of the village there lived a *thakur* called Dhyan Singh. He worked with the Imperial army and had retired after a decade of service. He had seen a number of foreign places like Burma, Singapore and Baghdad during his tenure of army service. Having settled in the village with his fortunes, he looked forward to a contented matrimonial life. He relied on regular oblations and offerings in the temple to placate divinity and facilitate the path to matrimony.

Hori said, "It seems the holy ceremony is complete. They are offering the final oblations."

Sobha thought so as well and asked if he would also like to go pay his obeisances and take the *aarti*.

Hori told him to go and that he will follow.

When Dhyan Singh had moved to the village, he had sent a seer of sweets to each house as a gesture of goodwill. Whenever he met anyone on the road he was very polite and courteous. Going to a ceremony organised by such a decent person and not offering anything for the *aarti* did not appear dignified to him. Actually, he thought it was downright insulting.

The *aarti*- plate will be in Dhyan singh's hands as he will pass it around for people to touch the holy flame reverentially. It would be outright petty, if not rude, not to leave any offering on it. It would be better not to go at all; he won't miss him in the crowds and wouldn't remember if he had attended the ceremony or not.

Silently, he lay down on the cot.

His heart pulled him like an obstinate child whom he tried to hush half heartedly. He did not have even one *paisa*; not even a bent, rotten dime to place in the *aarti*. It was not about the spiritual significance or beauty of the *aarti*; social etiquette and custom was what concerned him most. The issue here was about reciprocation. He could pass his hands over the *aarti* and accept the deity's blessings, in return of the humble offering of devotion in his heart, but his worry had nothing to do with spiritual but everything to do with temporal aspects. He didn't want to become an object of mockery for those who watched over offerings and not the sentiment.

On an impulse he sat up. Why should he be a slave to false prestige? Why should he forsake the blessings of the *aarti* for baser considerations? People will smirk and laugh- they can't do any better. He doesn't care. May God keep him away from falsehood and sin; he needs nothing else.

He got up and took steady steps towards the temple bells pealing in *Thakur's* house.

18

Khanna and his wife Govindi were never on the best of terms with each other. There was no one reason for this lack of cordiality in their relationship. Astrological charts did not reveal any adverse planetary influence. Before they were married, an intense scrutiny of their birth charts was conducted and approved by leading astrologers. There could be sexual or emotional incompatibilities but the jury was still out on that. What was certain was that they did not see eye to eye on a host of issues. Khanna was rich, good-looking, a romantic at heart and quite well educated as well. He figured prominently amongst the well known personalities of the city.

Govindi was no raving beauty but did have a charming presence. A dusky complexion, large shy eyes that fluttered tantalisingly and lips that weren't red, but quite attractive and full. Her body was proportionate and slim with sleek arms, her gait had a sensual touch and there was a distant look on her face which reflected indifference and probably traces of pride, as if the world and its routine were something less or inferior.

Khanna possessed all the superficial trappings of luxury--an excellent bungalow in the city's up market area, high class furniture, a superior car and enough money to last a lifetime. But none of this held much value for Govindi. She remained thirsty in an ocean of abundance. Bringing up children and other involvements of domesticity kept her mind from thinking about any other indulgence. She barely spared a thought on the merits or demerits of being attractive or good looking. She was not a plaything seeking male attention, so why should she make an effort to be more attractive? If her partner did not have time to appreciate her real beauty and ran after other seductresses, then it was his loss, not hers. She served her husband with the same attention and dedication that was expected from her, as though her heart was above jealousy and spite. In fact, the vast expanse of luxury suffocated her soul. Her mind sought to distance itself from the constricting space of social pretences. She dreamt of a world in which she could freely lead a natural existence, devoid of sham and hypocrisy. There would be no Malti in that world to poison her life. No dance clubs, wily women, doubt, pretence or unrest that would throw thorns in her path. As a small girl, during her school days, she was bitten by the poetry bug which taught her that pain and dilemma were intrinsic elements of creative life. It educated her that indulgence was something meant to be consumed in the bonfire of vanities. She composed verses but didn't know who to recite them to. Every word of her poems spoke of a longing to settle in a dreamland, away from lust and desire where she could live a Spartan life with simple creature comforts. Whenever Khanna chanced upon her poems, he laughed at the expressions and sometimes actually tore and threw away the pages.

The wall between the couple grew steadily and widened the chasm between them day by day. Khanna's grace and etiquette with his friends and business contacts was replaced by aggression and arrogance in his dealings with his wife. At times he openly rebuked her. For him, politeness and civility were merely tools to impress the world and not a state of grace for the mind. On such occasions Govindi remained at home, nursing her bruised heart while Khanna uncorked champagne at the bar and revelled amidst friends at the club. In spite of this, Khanna meant everything to her. Crushed and insulted, she was still his hand maiden. She would cry, fight, might protest but perhaps not as vehemently, but would remain with him forever. She could not imagine a life without him.

Today, Khanna awoke to a bad start. The first letter he opened informed him of the big fall in a couple of his stocks which ran up to a few thousand rupees. The workers in the new sugar mill had gone on strike and were getting violent as well. He had bought silver with an eye to profits but the metal's value had fallen below his buying rates. The deal which was to be finalised with Rai sahib was delayed endlessly. To make matters worse, yesterday's hangover was hitting him hard as his body was wracked by stiffness and pain.

A few minutes ago, the chauffer came up to tell him the engine of the car was giving starting trouble and someone had filed a civil suit on his bank in Lahore. As he sat wondering where to begin, Govindi came in and said- "Bhishm's fever shows no sign of abating. You must call for a doctor today."

Bhishm was their youngest child who suffered from ailments, ever since he was born – a weak underweight infant. One day he would have cough, the next day it was mild fever that would turn into an asthmatic attack or a running stomach, if nothing else. At ten months, he appeared as small as a newborn. Khanna was convinced at the back of his mind that the baby won't survive, which explained his indifference but for the same reason, Govindi devoted more attention to him than she did to the other children.

Khanna replied with the affectionate bearing of a father, "It's not healthy to make children dependent on medication but you are addicted to administering medicines for every minor disease. Watch him for another day; today is just the third day of his affliction- perhaps the fever might subside on its own."

Govindi was persistent, "Its three days already. I have tried every home remedy."

"Tell me who I should send for? You have any particular doctor in mind?" Khanna asked, giving up promptly.

"Call for Dr. Nag."

"I will if you insist. But I hope you realise a long list of degrees is no mark of a good doctor. Nag charges the sky but I have yet to see one person cured with his prescription. He is better known as the doctor who sends more patients to heaven than any other."

"Then call whoever you want. I insisted on his name because he has already visited us a few times and is familiar with the child."

"How about Miss Malti? She charges much less and besides, a lady doctor will understand kids better than a male doctor."

The mention of that name irked Govindi and she said, "I do not consider Miss Malti a doctor."

Khanna returned her pointed look with more aggression. "She is successfully treating thousands of patients; doesn't that mean anything to you? Do you suggest she didn't go to England for her medical degree and wasted her time vacationing there?"

"Maybe she did maybe she did not. She should only concentrate on curing the legions of wounded hearts she leaves behind her. That is her sole expertise."

That did it! Khanna roared in anger. Govindi also gave full vent to her frustration. The sheer mention of Malti's name in their conversation was an invitation to disaster.

Khanna threw all the papers in his hand on the floor and said, "You make life impossible."

Govindi spoke sharply, "Why don't you go ahead and marry her? It's not too late for that provided, she entertains your request."

"What do you think of me? Who do you think I am?"

"I think you are someone she will use as a convenient slave, not as a life partner."

"Am I so depraved in your eyes?"

Touched to the quick, he ran a list of evidences to the contrary. Malti has more respect for him than Govindi has ever had. She cold shouldered Rai sahib but complained if she didn't meet him every day.

Govindi punctured his defence in one breath, "...That's because she considers you dumb and is unable to make a fool of others with such ease."

Khanna boasted she would marry him the moment he gives an indication that he was willing.

Govindi was not impressed- "You may grovel for as many lifetimes as you want but she is not keen on you. You are her little pony; she will feed you, pet you, stroke your snout but only so that she can take you for a ride. She has idiots like you for breakfast every day."

Govindi went too far that day. She seemed itching for a fight; calling for the right doctor was merely a ruse to settle the issue once and for all. On his part, Khanna was equally livid. How could he take such a direct affront to his abilities, charm and manhood?

"If in your opinion I am a dumb fool, why do so many people hang on every word I say? Why is it that right from junior officials to kings and royalty – all prostrate before me daily? I take each one of them for a ride every day."

"This is exactly her speciality. She throws dust in the eyes of the craftiest of all crooks and has them wagging their tails within seconds."

Khanna's eyes were blood red with anger. "You can say what you like against her but you aren't worth the dust she flicks off her shoes."

"I think she is worse than a prostitute because she is never upfront like them about her intentions."

The knives were out, unsheathed and had hit their targets. Govindi might have forgiven Khanna for any other slight to her dignity but a comparison to her foe was intolerable for her wounded pride. Khanna could have also faced Govindi's barbs but by aiming a direct insult at Malti, she had crossed the Rubicon. Both were aware of each other's weak spots. Their shots had hit the mark and thoroughly infuriated both of them. Khanna's eyes and Govindi's face turned red with anger. Khanna rose from his seat, trembling with rage and caught hold of her ears and slapped her hard three times right across the cheek. Govindi ran inside the house, crying.

In some time, Doctor Nag, Surgeon Todd and faith healer Shastri trooped into the house one after another but Govindi did not venture out of the room with her child. She did not pay any attention to their advice or consultations. Her biggest fears had come true that day. Khanna had practically snapped off all ties with her; it was as though he had ejected her out of the house and bolted the door after her.

A woman who hawked her beauty, a woman whose shadow even was anathema to her, would lord over her obliquely? No, this won't happen. Khanna was her husband. Govindi had all the right to try to make him see reason; for once she could tolerate his assaults as well. However, to be lorded over by Malti? Never! But she couldn't move till the child's fever had subsided as self respect lost before the call of duty.

The next day when his fever broke, Govindi called for a *tonga* and left home. She would not stay at a place where she was subjected to such degradation. The wound was so deep, it deadened the pulls and attachment to her children. She had fulfilled her duties towards her husband. What remained now was his responsibility. However, she couldn't leave an infant to fend for himself; he was her responsibility so she would take him along. Nothing else belonged to her. If he thought he was the family maker and brought in the bread, she will show him survival was possible without his support. Her three elder kids were out at play when she left. At one moment, it struck her that she should give them a hug before she took this step but finally decided against it. She wasn't forsaking them; they could seek her out and come to her if they wanted. She would come and meet them when she pleased. It was just that she was rejecting Khanna's patronage.

It was evening and the park was alive with people, many of whom lay flat on the grass, enjoying its pleasant freshness. Govindi took a turn from Hazratganj towards the zoo when she saw Khanna drive past her with Malti at his side. She thought she saw Khanna point out at her and imagined Malti staring at her impassively. Khanna might not talk ill of her but Malti was such a shameless woman! She probably had a good medical practice but strangely chose to sell herself cheaply like this. Why didn't she get married? On second thoughts, who would marry her? Well, perhaps there could be someone who'd be willing. There must be many who'd feel elated to be chosen by her but she must select or pick one in the first place. Moreover, what was the charm in getting married? Today she was the queen of so many hearts; marriage would turn her into the possession of a single individual. Perhaps, her decision to not marry had its logic. Khanna worshipped the ground she stood on. But she had no need to marry him.

Govindi felt an unfamiliar surge of sympathy for Malti. Maybe she was wrong in accusing her. It was not that she was ignorant about her situation. When she was witness to the appalling miseries of marital life, it was no wonder she avoided it like the plague.

The zoo was very quiet and not a sound was heard. Govindi stopped the *tonga* and alighting from it, moved towards the grassy park. She had barely taken three steps on the grass, when her slippers splashed into ankle deep water. The park was watered some time back and a lot of water had collected, hidden from view in the grass. In her anxiety to step out of the puddle, she took a few quick steps forward and found her feet soiled in mud. She looked down at them. Where would she get water to wash them? Her stream of consciousness was rudely interrupted by more immediate concerns. It was not possible to think straight with soiled feet.

In a distance, she spied a snaking pipe in the grass. It was the same pipe that was disgorging a steady stream of water into the lawns. She washed her feet and slippers in its flow. She also washed her hands, face and even cupped her hands to drink from it and moved a considerable distance away on dry grass and settled herself on it.

Sorrow has a propensity of raking up morbid moods. She wondered what Khanna would do if she died right there as she sat on the grass? The *tonga* driver would carry the message to Khanna immediately. He would be overjoyed to hear it but would hold a handkerchief to his eyes for appearances sake. For the kids, toys and games were more important than a dead mother. There was not a soul to shed a tear for her! She was reminded of the days when her mother-in-law was alive and Khanna was yet to get into his wayward habits. Those days she hated her mother- -in-law's interfering ways and often got irritated with her. Today, she discovered a sweetness in her rebuke. When she was grumpy her mother-in-law would pamper and try to appease her in so many ways. Today she could spend a lifetime being grumpy; nobody would bother the least. Her thoughts travelled to that old woman. Her situation would have been different if she were still alive. At least, she offered a warm hug and petted her till she stopped crying. But Govindi decided not to think too much about her. She didn't want to bother a departed soul with her worries. The poor woman had done enough for her and she would allow her to rest in peace. Moreover, there was no reason for her to weep. She was free and not under subjugation anymore. Now she could make a living on her own to fend for herself.

She decided to go to Gandhi Ashram the next day and get odd items to sell on the streets, No shame in that. She didn't care if people pointed fingers and said, 'Hey, that's Khanna's wife!' While on that, what was the necessity to stay in the same city? She could go to another town where no one knew her and start life afresh. Her mind was working overtime with new ideas and thoughts- 'When I am financially independent no one will dare to run me down. The only reason he pushes me around is because I am living off him.' She was firm in her mind to break free and take her life in her own hands.

Suddenly she saw none other than Mehta coming towards her. She was discomfited to come across him at this moment as all she sought now was to be left alone. She was in no mood to chat with anybody and this man had appeared from nowhere to disturb her. As if on cue, to add to her woes, the baby started crying.

Mehta came up and asked her, "What are you doing here at this hour?"

Govindi tried to shush the baby as she replied, "I am here just as you are here, Mr. Mehta."

Mehta smiled and said, "Don't compare yourself with me. I am a rootless vagabond. Give me the baby; let me quieten him."

"Since when did you learn the art of comforting babies?"

"I want to practise it. Someday I will have to pass these tests."

"Oh! Is it because the exams are close?"

"It depends entirely on my preparedness. As soon as I am ready, I shall appear for the exam. We burn the midnight oil for minor exams; this is about a significant test of living life. I have to be prepared!"

"This I've got to see! I am quite interested to know what grades you get." As she spoke, she passed the bawling baby into his outstretched hands. Mehta played with the child, throwing him up in the air ever so gently, cooing to him, till he quieted. Elated like a child, he boasted, "See that? My magic charm worked perfectly! Now I am going to get a baby for myself."

Govindi joked with him, "Just a baby or a mother along with the baby as well?"

Mehta shook his head solemnly in mock disappointment, "Where do I get woman like that?"

"Why? What about Miss Malti? She is beautiful, educated, attractive and overflowing with good qualities. What more do you want?"

"Miss Malti has none of the qualities I look for in my life partner."

Govindi loved this comment but kept her obvious delight under wraps. "Will you let me know what's wrong with her? She is always surrounded by admirers. I assume these days men adore women like her."

The baby was intrigued by Mehta's moustaches and wanted to pull it with his tiny hands. He tried to move his face away from his reach and said, "My wife has to be a different sort of woman. She must be someone I would want to worship."

Govindi laughed, "That means you are looking for an idol, for I doubt such a woman exists."

"Not at all! On the contrary, such a woman exists and right here in this city."

"Really? I would like to meet her so I can try to become like her."

"You know her very well. She is the wife of a very rich man but doesn't care much for riches. She is unmoved and steady, despite a consistent onslaught of his indifference and disrespect. She has sacrificed herself on the altar of motherhood and considers self abnegation a significant right. She is well worthy of being worshipped."

A shiver of delight coursed through her body. She realised what he was hinting at but continued with her pretence of innocence. "You might praise such a woman; but I think she is to be pitied."

"You insult her by speaking of her like this," said Mehta, with frank surprise.

"The standards you speak of are not applicable to this age."

"Those standards are sacrosanct and eternal. By compromising on them mankind is paving the way for its destruction."

Govindi was bubbling over with excitement in the core of her being. Those paroxysms of delight were rare as she put Mehta above all the men she had come across and such effusive praise from him was making her delirious.

Reeling under quite a heady feeling, she requested him to introduce that woman to her.

Mehta stared at her with child like eyes, "She is sitting right here."

"Where? I don't see anyone."

"That goddess of whom I speak is the one who I am talking to."

Govindi burst out laughing, "So you've decided to amuse yourself at my expense?"

Mehta replied with serious reverence, "My dear lady, you do more injustice to yourself than to me. There are very few people in the world that I look up to. You are one of them. Your patience, sacrifice, goodness and gentility are admirable. You are the greatest example of the best in womanhood that I can imagine. The qualities which I consider the epitome of womanhood – they are all present in you in ample measure."

Govindi was overwhelmed. With those words like armour, she could ride fearlessly into a million battles. Every particle of her being seemed to resonate with music. Firmly reining in her girlish enthusiasm, she said, "Why do they call you a philosopher, Mehtaji? You should have been a poet."

Mehta's laughter was unaffected and childlike, "Do you think someone can be a poet without being a philosopher? Philosophy is what one encounters on the journey to poetry."

"So I understand you are on the way to poetry. I hope you are aware that life in general and the world in particular is not very kind to poets."

"What the world calls sorrow, is joy to the poet. Wealth and fame, beauty and power, erudition and intelligence all these qualities can mesmerise the world but they hold no attraction for the poet. His joy and delight lies in shattered dreams, misty memories and a pain in the heart. The day his heart loses affinity for these sentiments, he stops being a poet. Philosophers merely indulge in acrobatics with these sentiments, poets live with them. I have read a few of your poems and I can appreciate every sparkle, tremor and ache that pulsates within those words. Nature has been unfair to us by not making more like you."

Govindi's tone hid a lament, "No Mehtaji, this is simply your illusion. You will find such women in every town and village and I am the least of them. A woman who cannot create a space for herself in her husband's heart and who cannot make him happy isn't worthy of womanhood. Sometimes I wonder if I should go to Malti to understand this art. She succeeds where I fail miserably. I am unable to win the heart of those who are my own and she rules over the hearts of those who aren't hers. Doesn't she deserve kudos for this?"

Mehta made a face and said, "Alcohol gives a high which is unheard of with water. Should it therefore be considered better than water which quenches thirst, energises the body and is so life-giving?"

Govindi took the sails off his argument by making light of it. "You can say what you please but the bitter fact is that water is considered plebeian and flows unattended in municipal taps whereas alcohol flies off shelves in exclusive places and people are ready to sell hearth and home in its pursuit. The more sharp and heady it is, the better it is supposed to be. By the way, have I heard right that you are yourself a devotee of Bacchus?"

Govindi's disillusionment with life had reached the grey realms where human beings begin to doubt existence of truth and faith but Mehta hardly noticed the despondency in her voice. His attention was riveted to the last part of her sentence. The embarrassment and shame he underwent at this moment was far beyond any discomfiture he might have gone through when confronted by better arguments and scathing discourses against it. He was well equipped to counter arguments against liquor with sharp logic but he was rendered speechless by an unintentional wisecrack. He regretted using the example of liquor to drive his point home. It was his own comparison of Malti with liquor that boomeranged on him. Suitably chastened, he replied, "Ma'am, I admit to this attachment. I will not commit the heresy of quoting its creativity stimulating qualities to explain why it's necessary for me, for that will further compound my crime. But I take an oath, here and now, that this moment onwards I will not taste a drop of liquor for the rest of my life."

Govindi was stunned. "What is this Mehtaji? God forbid! That was never my intention. I am extremely sorry."

"No, on the contrary, you should be glad you have saved one person."

"Huh? I have saved you? But I was about to beseech you to save me."

"Me save you? I am flattered!"

Govindi spoke to him in a pained voice, "Yes. Other than you I am unable to think of anyone who will listen to my tale of woe. Please keep this to yourself though

I really don't need to tell that to you. My life has become unbearable. I have tolerated enough, as much as I possibly could, but now it's gone too far. Malti is bent on ruining my life. I am powerless before her and have no foil for her designs. You have a hold over her. She respects you more than she does anyone else. If you can somehow save me from her, I will be eternally indebted to you. She is bleeding me of whatever I can look forward to in my life. Please protect me from her if you can. Today I had left home never to return back. I tried hard to wrench myself away from all bonds of attachments but a woman's heart is weak, Mehtaji! Those bonds are her very life. It's impossible to break them as long as she is alive. I have kept my pain bottled up within me all this while but today I must beg you on my knees, please deliver me from Malti. That seductress will be the end of me. I am dying."

Her words were drowned in tearful sobs as she wept openly.

A few years ago, one of Mehta's literary creations had received encomiums from a French academy of letters that hailed it as an important work to emerge from this part of the world. The sense of pride and achievement he felt at that time was insignificant as compared to the emotions that rose in him at this moment. He was totally floored by the realisation that his idol whom he held in such high esteem and from whom he drew inspiration and courage to unravel life's many complications, was begging him for help. A strange surge of strength rushed through him; he could uproot mountains, fly over the seas giddy with the headiness of a little boy astride a wooden horse who imagines he is superman. Not for a moment did he worry about the impossibility of the task he was invited to accomplish. He wasn't bothered if he had to circumvent his own ideals and ambitions in the process. He spoke in a reassuring voice, "I had no idea you were so disturbed. It's my foggy mind to blame. Had I known, you wouldn't have to bear this suffering for so long."

Govindi did not think it was so pat. She had her doubts and said, "Do you know how difficult it is to coax a tigress to give up her prey? I hope you understand that."

Mehta was confident. He said, "A woman's heart is like the earth. It has all the elements of sweetness as well as bitterness. The fruit depends on the strength of the seed that is implanted in her mind."

"I am sure you'd be wondering what twist of fate brought you into this mess," said Govindi in distress.

Mehta folded his hands and said, "Will you believe me if I say I have found real joy of my life today?

"I have burdened you so much," said Govindi.

Mehta was almost apologetic and spoke words laden with admiration and devotion, "You're embarrassing me, lady. I am telling you, I am your servant. If I die in your service, I will consider it my good fortune. These are not words of a poet, spoken on the spur of the moment, nor are they an excessively sentimental response, but they are the truth of my life. I can't help but tell you about my life's mission. I worship nature and prefer to perceive humans as natural entities who laugh when happy, cry when sad and kill when angry. I don't want to have anything to do with those who don't differentiate between joys and sorrow and suppress both equally, for whom crying is a weakness and laughter, mere frivolousness. For me, life is a playful celebration of joy which is uninhibited, innocent and where jealousy, envy and hatred are conspicuous in their absence. I don't worry about the future and the past holds no meaning for me. The present is all that I know and experience. Concern for the future makes cowards of us and the burden of the past weighs us down. Our lust for life is weak as it is; but by spreading it thin over the past and future, we dilute it to abysmally low levels. We groan under the weight of traditions, rituals, beliefs and history; unable to rise-- having lost all ability to think for ourselves. The energy and life force which was better utilised fulfilling the destiny of mankind, is dissipated in nursing old grudges and repaying the debts of our forefathers. And as far as the merry-go-round of faith and liberation is concerned, it is of no significance to me. The desire for liberation and deliverance is the height of arrogance which is destroying the essence of humanity. Wherever there is life and playfulness, there will always be love and God. Our constant endeavour should be to bring joy to life. The knowledge seekers say one should be unshaken by pain and unmoved in joy. This is strange, if you can't laugh and cry to your heart's content you are not human, but a stone! The philosophy which yokes men to inanimate knowledge is a conveyor belt, not a human progression of life."

He was carried away by his own rhetoric but stopped abruptly. "I seek your pardon; I got into a long winded speech. It's quite late; allow me to drop you back. The baby has also fallen asleep."

Govindi said, "I have come in a *tonga*."

"Let me send it off."

Mehta went up and paid the *tonga* driver. When he returned Govindi said, "Where do you plan to drop me?"

Surprised, Mehta said, "Your home; where else?"

"That's not my home Mehtaji."

"Do you think it is Mr. Khanna's home?"

"Does one have to ask that? But it is not mine anymore. The place where I am ridiculed and insulted day in day out can never be a home for me."

Mehta spoke slowly, emphasising each word as it came from deep within his heart, "No, my lady, that is your home and that is how it shall remain- forever. You have created that home; you have created every person that resides in that home. A body thrives only if the soul breathes life in it. If the soul is gone, of what use is the carcass or the body? A mother's role is to bestow life. Someone with such a vital power in her hands should not be concerned about anyone scowling or frowning at her. Just as the body cannot survive without the soul; the body is also its appropriate shelter. I don't have to sermonise to you about faith, duty and sacrifice. You are a live example of living faith. I can only say..."

Govindi grew impatient and cut him short, "But I am not a mother alone. Am I not a woman as well?"

Mehta was silent for a while before he spoke. "Yes, you are a woman as well but in my opinion a woman is only a mother; every other designation beyond that is merely an interpolation of motherhood. Motherhood is the most sublime penance, the greatest worship and the most lasting victory. In one word, it is a lyrical motion of life, individuality and womanhood. Please realise, a man like Khanna has taken leave of his senses. Whatever he does comes from a mad delirium but don't you worry; this madness will not go on for long. I see him returning to his senses pretty soon and the day is not far, when he will realise you are the lady of his life."

Govindi did not react to his words. She took slow, gradual steps towards the parked car. Mehta reached out and opened the door for her. Without a word, Govindi sat in it and closed the door. The car started to move. Both were absolutely silent.

When Govindi reached her house and got out of the car, Mehta saw under the streetlamp, that her eyes were welling up with tears.

Her children came running out of the house, screaming '*amma*', *amma*' and hugged her. Her face lit up with a bright glow of maternal pride.

She turned to Mehta and said, "Thank you for all the trouble you took for me," and lowered her eyes. A lone tear drop fell on her lips and glistened in the streetlight.

Mehta was moved. He was sorry to see a woman's heart in pain amidst such opulence and plenty.

❁❁❁

19

Mirza Khurshid's compound had multiple utilities- it was a club, court and gymnasium- all three rolled into one. There were people milling around the compound all day. The localities nearby had no space for a gymnasium; Mirza constructed a shed and converted it into one where two score and more wrestlers could practice their skills routinely. Mirza would also hold neighbourhood courts in his premises where minor domestic squabbles were resolved by wise old men. Differences and petty arguments between husbands-wives, problems with in-laws and sibling tensions were resolved and settled regularly. Thus, Mirza's house had become the hub of social activity and had lately progressed into a platform for sharing and propagating political ideas. Every now and then they met to sort out political campaigns and plan future strategies. Political volunteers shacked up here; planned their movements and conducted the city's politics from these quarters.

Gobar had been around here for a year. He was no longer the simple village bumpkin that he was a year ago. He had seen quite a bit of the world outside his cocoon in the village and was now quite familiar with its ways. Deep inside, he remained a rustic for he was very stingy with money, neither letting his guard down when it came to his self interest nor shying away from hard labour but he had developed the urban proclivity that puts city dwellers apart from simpler rural folk. In the first month of his life in Lucknow, he toiled hard, starving himself despite having enough to afford good food and saved a reasonable sum of money.

Soon he left Mirza Khurshid's employment and set up a makeshift kiosk for selling potato and pea savouries when he found it to be more profitable than working as a labourer. In the summer, he added ice lemonade and *sherbet* to the menu. He was honest and squeaky clean with his dealings and therefore built up a somewhat enviable reputation.

When winters set in, he wound up the ice business and started selling hot tea. His daily income shot up to no less than two to three rupees per day. His hairstyle changed, it had a side parting - a very English style, so popular amongst the city's youth. His sartorial preferences also came in for a transformation. He wore pump shoes and a fine muslin *dhoti*. He bought a red woolen shawl and occasionally, indulged in the luxuries of chewing *paan* and a casual puff of English cigarettes. He attended a few political meetings held in the compound and began to understand the political thoughts of the day. He was now able to comprehend the meaning of nation and class. He had overcome fear of social approbation and understood the limits and pitfalls of certain restrictive social customs and ways of life. Daily discussions, talks and seminars which he attended whenever they were held in Mirza's premises, boosted his confidence. He realised that the sort of incidents like the one due to which he had to flee his village were a common occurrence in the city- actually far worse things happenned here as a matter of course and no one felt pressured to run for cover. He realised there was no need to fear and he should not run scared.

All these days he hadn't sent a single *paisa* home. He didn't trust his folks to be careful with money. They would start splurging no sooner they came into some fortune. *Dada* would immediately want to invest in a cattle and the only thing his mother would want to do was buy new ornaments. He had no money to spare for these senseless expenses and pursuits. He disbursed small loans on interest to drivers of horse carriages like *Tongas* and *Ekkas* besides, sundry washermen and other petty workers. In the last eleven months, given his single minded devotion to work, and his sound economics helped him carve a niche for himself amongst his peers in Mirza's compound. At times, he contemplated bringing Jhuniya from the village to join him in his newfound habitat.

It was three in the afternoon. He had just come back after taking a shower at the community tap by the roadside and was boiling potatoes for the evening when Mirza Khurshid came to his door and paused outside. Gobar was not his employee anymore but displayed the same respectful attitude that got him the gardener's job barely a year ago. He walked up to the door and said, "Yes sir? Is there something you'd like me to do for you?"

Mirza didn't move from where he stood and said, "If you have some money spare me a few rupees. For the last three days, the supply has gone dry. I don't have any liquor left. I have a great urge to drink."

Gobar had loaned him money on earlier occasions too but it was never returned. He was reluctant to part with money as he was afraid to ask him to pay up and Mirza was not the one to remember. He was very irresponsible with cash. He lost money within minutes he got it. Gobar could not summon the courage to refuse pointblank so he started highlighting the ill effects of drinking alcohol. "Sir, why don't you give up drinking? What do you gain by it?"

Mirza made himself comfortable on the cot in the room and said, "Do you think I am addicted to it and don't want to give it up? My problem is I can't live without it. You don't worry about your money. I will return every *paisa*."

Gobar was unmoved, "Trust me, master. I wouldn't have refused if I had some in my pocket"

"You mean you can't spare even two rupees at the moment?"

"Not at this moment. No."

"Then keep my ring. Let me hock it to you."

Gobar was keen to take it but now it was difficult for him to change his stance so he spoke weakly, "Come on sir. You shouldn't talk like this. Don't mention the ring. I will not refuse you money if I had it."

Mirza demeaned himself further, "I will never ask you for money again, Gobar. I can't stand straight, right now I need liquor. I've ruined my status and burnt all my fortune for liquor and am reduced to beggary. I have decided to take it to the very end. I am not giving up the bottle, even if I am driven to the very bitter end of misfortune."

When Gobar still did not relent, he went away, rather disappointed and broken. Mirza had scores of acquaintances in the city who could help him. A majority of them had made their fortunes with his assistance. There were quite a few whom he had bailed out when they were up against adverse times but now he wasn't willing to meet them. He knew the tricks of the trade; making money was something he had never forgotten but he wanted nothing to do with those people. He despised money and sought to spend it as soon as it came into his hands. He would constantly hunt for an excuse to blow up his money and sure enough many opportunities came his way, sealing his fate surely and steadily with each.

Gobar began peeling potatoes. His low cunning and street smart ways surprised him more than others. The shack where he lived was given to him by Mirza himself. The rent for that space was easily no less than five rupees a month. Gobar was living in it for almost a year; not once did Mirza ask him for rent and not once did Gobar volunteer to give it. In all probability, Mirza did not have the foggiest idea he could make money from it.

In a few minutes an *Ekka* driver came up to him. Bald-headed and one eyed, this man with a salt and pepper beard was called Aladdin. He was sending his daughter off to her in-laws and was in dire need of five rupees. Gobar gave him the amount at an *anna* per rupee.

Aladdin thanked him and asked when he would bring his wife from the village. "How many more days will you cook for yourself, man? It's time you got your wife and child to stay with you."

"How will I make both ends meet with added responsibilities?"

Aladdin scornfully turned down Gobar's plea that survival for a family was difficult in his meagre income.

"Allah will provide for the expenses, brother," he said, lighting a *bidi*, "Why don't you look at the positive side? It will be so convenient for you. Believe me, you will run your household within the same means in which you survive as a single man in the city. A woman can work magic in the home. Allah be praised, when I lived alone in the city, I wouldn't save a *paisa*. I spent every little bit I earned. To make matters worse, I had to feed the horse and take it for a walk everyday and when I returned exhausted after a day's work, I didn't feel like cooking and had to make a beeline to Nanbai's shop for my meals. It was so disgusting! Ever since my wife came in, I am able to provide for her in the same income while the sense of peace and rest that she provides to the home is another thing altogether. A man toils so he can live in peace. Take it from me, your earnings will increase once you have a woman to manage your house. You can sell a few more cups of tea in the time you fritter away cooking food for yourself; tea sells throughout the year now. In the evenings, your wife will even massage your feet. You'll be thoroughly refreshed."

The logic behind his ideas struck roots in Gobar's mind and he brooded over those words. The potatoes continued to boil in the pot on the fire even as he made up his mind to go home. Suddenly he remembered Holi was round the corner. It was important to buy stuff for everyone as the festival was close. The propensity of the miserly to splurge only on special occasions sprang to life in his consciousness. He was saving for such a day after all, wasn't he? He would buy a *saree* for his mother. For Hori, it would be a *dhoti* and a large shawl. Sona would get a bottle of perfumed oil and a pair of slippers. For Rupa, he decided to buy Japanese bangles that had flooded the market those days and for Jhuniya, he selected a little box which contained a comb, oil, vermilion and a small handheld looking glass. Readymade frocks and bonnets were sold at a number of garment shops for babies and children; he bought a pair for the baby.

Tying the money he had saved in a secure knot in his clothes, he went and bought everything he wanted. By afternoon all shopping was done; his sleeping stuff was wrapped and tied in a bundle and the buzz had gone round the neighborhood that Gobar was off to his village. Quite a few men and women turned up to see him off. Gobar entrusted the safety of his house to them and bid farewell. "I am leaving everything in your care as I go. If all goes well, God willing, I will be back two days after Holi."

A young girl stepped forward and smiled at him, "Dare you come back without your wife! We will send you back as you come!"

Another older one gave him a piece of advice, "She's right! You've spent enough days doing a woman's job in your kitchen. Let the right person handle it when you return."

Gobar folded his hands and bid farewell to all. The crowd was mixed; there were as many Hindus as there were Muslims, all co-farers and partners in joy and pain. Those who observed the *Rozas* during *Ramzan* fasted for forty days and those who observed *Ekadasi* fasted on their earmarked pious occasions on different dates in the same calendar. Often in jest, they poked fun at each other's beliefs but it was always under the umbrella of playful good humour. Gobar would laugh at Aladdin's *Namaz* postures when he would sit down to pray, terming it as a push up exercise that didn't do much to improve his physique. On his part, Aladdin labelled the consecrated stone *Shivlingam* below the *peepul* trees as a large bird dropping. Neither comment ever drew anything other than a smile. Gobar was going home. The entire neighborhood had come together to give him a pleasant farewell.

Bhurey came with his *Ekka* and pulled to a stop right in front of Gobar's house. He had just returned from his daily round of the city since morning. As soon as he heard Gobar was off to his village, he changed course and rode the carriage to his house. The horse resented the sudden change in routine and refused to budge. A few sharp cracks of the whip and he fell in line. Gobar loaded his bags and bundles on the carriage. The *Ekka* moved forward; the see-off party walked some distance behind the carriage till it hit the main road.

The *Ekka* rolled swiftly on the road. Gobar was elated with the heady feeling of going home at last and after so many days. Bhurey was happy to be of help in transporting him to the railway station. The horse was determined to prove a point as it galloped swiftly through the traffic. Within minutes they were at the station.

Taking a rupee coin from his pocket, Gobar stretched his hand toward Bhurey and said- "Here! Take some sweets for your folks when you go home."

Bhurey stared at him gratefully but his look was of scorn and tone of polite admonishment, "Don't you take me as one of your own? If you take a ride on my *Ekka* one evening should I accept payment for it? I'd give my life for you, brother; you mean so much to me. I am not such a shallow man and even if I do take it, my family will clobber me for stooping so low."

Gobar didn't say anything. Embarrassed, he unloaded his luggage and went towards the ticket window to buy his ticket.

20

Spring arrived, spreading its zesty exuberance and heralding a rebirth in nature. Flowering mango trees spread a delicious fragrance in the atmosphere and the *koel* hopped on the branches, regaling the earth with its soulful cries.

The season for planting sugarcane saplings was near and villages were buzzing with feverish activity. The sun was not up yet but Hori was already at work in the sugarcane fields. Dhania, Sona and Rupa lifted bundles of sugarcane stumps, damp from lying in the pond as Hori busied himself with the sickle, chopping the stumps into smaller pieces.

They had resigned themselves to their new status as labourers in Datadin's fields without any fuss. From farmers to farmhands; their relationship with Datadin had morphed into that of master and worker.

Datadin wobbled over and shouted at him. "Move your ass, Hori, speed up a little. At this rate, you will not chop them till nightfall."

Hori straightened up with whatever dignity and hurt pride he could muster and said, "*Maharaj,* I am not loitering, I am working as fast as I can." Datadin was a slave driver. Hori was aware of it but he also knew he could not do anything about it. Due to his bullying nature, no labourer stayed more than a month with him.

The *pundit* planted himself right in front of Hori and snapped at him, "'Going-as-fast-as-I-can means nothing. It could mean not completing the job till sundown."

Hori swallowed his pride and increased his tempo. The last few months he was not getting enough to eat. At least once in the day, he was forced to substitute meals with a fistful of grams or any other chewy stuff; sometimes not even that. He wanted to move his hands faster but his strength gave way. Datadin was never far away; always at hand to pull him up for actual or perceived slackness. He wanted to take a break to recharge his dwindling strength but fears of a tongue lashing kept him from it. Dhania and her two daughters trooped in with wet bundles of sugarcane stumps on their head. Clad in mud spattered, wet sarees with bundles of stumps on their heads, they dumped the load on the ground and paused for a moment to catch their breath. Datadin growled at Dhania, "Why do you stand there gaping at the sky, Dhania? Get on with your work. Half the day is past and you have not brought one cartload of stumps. It will take the whole day to shift them here at this speed."

Dhania turned towards him and retorted, "Won't you let us catch our breath, *Maharaj*? We are human beings, aren't we? We have not turned into bulls just because we are yoked to your fields. Try carrying a bundle on your head and you'll understand what I mean."

Datadin was furious, "You are paid to work, not catch your breath. If you are so fond of taking a break, why don't you go home?"

Before Dhania could say what she felt about it, Hori chided her, "Why don't you move on, Dhania? Is it necessary to make an issue of everything?"

"Fine! I am on my way but why should anyone hit a weary mule with a stick?"

Datadin glared at her. "Seems your misfortune has not chastened your temperament. No wonder you suffer."

There was no stopping Dhania. "Well, I don't come to beg at your door."

Datadin was merciless. "With an attitude like this, you soon will."

Dhania was ready with another rejoinder but Sona pulled her away to the pool otherwise, there was a real chance of the verbal duel spiralling out of control. However, once when they were out of hearing distance, she vent her bile loudly, if only to the winds, "It is you who will beg, the begging class that you are! We are labourers, we will find our four-*anna* worth work since we are willing to toil."

Sona pulled her up. "Come on *amma,* let it be. You will always pick up an argument, unmindful of time, place or circumstance."

Back in the field, Hori was in a chopping frenzy as he attacked the stumps fanatically. He was on fire, consumed by an unearthly emotion. The primal notions of self respect which he had inherited through generations of humility fuelled his suppressed anger like an engine strained beyond its limit, filling him with a blind energy. A darkness gathered before his eyes though his hands moved like clockwork- without a break, ceaselessly and tirelessly. His head was spinning like a top. Rivers of sweat flowed over his body, his mouth was open in a half snarl and there was a hammer knocking away in his head but at the moment, he was a man possessed.

All of a sudden he blacked out. He felt he was sinking in the earth. Instinctively, he threw his hands out in a bid to claw at whatever he could clasp for support and fell unconscious on the ground. The sickle dropped from his hands and he lay prone, face down on the earth.

Dhania arrived on the scene almost at the same time as Hori lost consciousness. She saw a crowd of men standing around a worker who had fallen or probably lost his foothold at work. One of the men was complaining to Datadin. "You shouldn't have spoken to him the way you did, sir. It takes time for one to face up to reality."

Instinctively she charged up to them, throwing her bundle of stumps by the side and put his head on her thighs and wailed loudly. "What's happened to you? Rupa, Sona, run and get a glass of water. Tell Sobha his brother is in a bad shape. Oh God! What should I do?"

Lala Pateshwari hurried to the spot. His demeanour was of an outwardly strict person who held nothing but concern and affection in his heart. He pulled Dhania up for losing control over herself. "Come on, pull yourself together, Dhania! Nothing's wrong with Hori. He's got a touch of the sun, that's all. He will be okay in a minute. It won't do any good if you panic like this."

Dhania fell at his feet, "What should I do? I can't help but worry. God has taken away everything from me yet I bore it patiently. I can't bear it any longer. Oh Hori! What's become of him?"

Sona brought water. Pateshwari sprinkled a few drops on Hori's face. Some men were fanning Hori with whatever they could lay their hands on. His body was turning cold. Pateshwari was concerned but he didn't let his worry show and kept telling Dhania to cheer up and that things were under control.

Dhania's nerves were on edge. "Nothing like this has happened before. It's the first time he has fainted in this manner."

Pateshwari enquired if he had something to eat last night.

Dhania told him he had two *rotis* last evening. "I had made *rotis* for him but you know our plight, you know what we are going through. We don't get a full meal a day. How many times I have told him to not strain himself, work within his capacity, but he won't listen to me."

Hori opened his eyes listlessly and stared at the commotion around him.

A new breath of life swept over Dhania. She hugged him and said, "How do you feel now? I must have died a hundred times these last few minutes."

Weakly, Hori managed to say- "I am feeling fine. I don't know what came over me."

Love and anger makes a curious cocktail when the two comes together. She chided him, "You go to such lengths to do justice to work; does your body also keep up with you? Our kids are lucky; it's their good fortune that saw you through today."

Pateshwari said, laughing. Dhania was crying herself hoarse, beating her chest."

Hori asked her eagerly if it was true.

Dhania gave a mild shove to Pateshwari, pushing him away and said, "You never mind what he says. Don't believe him. Why not ask him why he hurried here from home, leaving all his important papers and accounting work?"

Pateshwari was in a playful mood. "She held you in her arms and called your name every time she rocked you to and fro! Now she's blushing; then she was beating her chest."

Hori softened his gaze at her, "You're crazy. What use am I to you Dhania?"

Two men placed Hori on a string cot and carried him home. Datadin was frowning, he was obviously distressed about the delay in his work but Matadin was not as heartless. He ran to get hot milk from home and also brought a small phial of rose water. Hori's condition improved visibly once he had a glass of nourishing milk.

It was at this moment that they noticed Gobar coming down the road with a labourer carrying a load on his head.

Stray dogs from the village ran up to him, yapping excitedly. Rupa exclaimed, "*Bhaiya* is here, *bhaiya* is here" and ran inside the house, clapping her hands in glee. Sona took a few steps forward but contained her excitement. In the last one year she had become conscious of her feminity. Jhuniya drew a veil across her face and came to stand by the door.

Gobar bent down to touch the feet of his parents and affectionately lifted Rupa up in his hands. Dhania blessed him and felt her motherhood rewarded simply because she held him close to her. She was overjoyed and her heart was bursting with pride. Today she was the queen of whatever she surveyed. She was an empress, even in her tatters. Her eyes, her face, her gait-all reflected a royal status! Real time queens would pale in comparison. Gobar had grown taller, and was well dressed! Dhania never felt unnerved in his absence she wasn't one to worry unduly. All through his absence a small voice told her he was well and happy. Seeing him standing before her, she felt relieved to find the precious gem she had misplaced in her grubby life, but Hori was unimpressed. He stood alone, looking the other way.

Gobar asked his mother what was wrong with him.

Dhania did not want to spoil his homecoming with sad tales of all that had transpired nor burden him right away with the difficulties they were up against. She said it was nothing; probably he was having a headache. She told Gobar to come in and wash himself. And once inside, she began bombarding him with questions....Where was he all these days and why did he not bother to enquire about their welfare for over a year? They had worried themselves to death, hoping against hope that he would come back one day. There were strange rumours going around; some said he had gone to Egypt, others said he was on a secret island.. "Where were you all these days?" she asked him finally. Gobar squirmed and said he wasn't gone far; just a few miles away in Lucknow. "You were so close and yet didn't send a letter to inform us of your welfare." Meanwhile Sona and Rupa had opened his box and were busy sifting through its contents.

Jhuniya stood at a distance, removed from the vigorous unpacking, divisions and allocations of the stuff the girls fished out from the box with loud exclamations. She wanted Gobar to get a taste of what she went through when he deserted her and ran off, leaving her to fend for herself. Now was the time to get even. When creditors come across those who owe them money after a very long time, they are quite keen to recover even those amounts which they might have written off earlier. Her baby was twisting and turning, intrigued by the sudden excitement in the house. He grabbed at whatever he could reach for with the sole intention of putting it into his mouth but Jhuniya held him back firmly in her arms.

Sona said, *"Bhaiya* has brought a comb and mirror set for you, *bhabhi!"*

Jhuniya spoke with exaggerated indifference, "I don't want combs and mirrors. He can keep them with himself."

Rupa had taken out the brightly coloured bonnet of the baby- "Aha! This is

Chunnu's cap," she said, placing it on the infant's head.

Jhuniya took the bonnet and threw it away. She saw Gobar enter the room and turned back into the inner recess of the house. Gobar saw the entire contents of his box strewn around the room. He wantsed to rush inside and apologise to Jhuniya profusely but was unable to gather the courage to do so. He planted himself right there and started giving away the stuff to those for whom they were meant for, but Rupa was unhappy because her share did not include the slippers he brought for Sona. To make matters worse, Sona was already teasing her about it. "What will you do with fancy slippers? Get lost and play with your dolls. I am not jealous that you have a doll and I don't have one. Why do you grudge my slippers?"

Dhania took up the task of distributing sweets to everyone. She planned to send a sweet to every household as her son has come back safe and sound. It was a joyous moment indeed and meant to be shared with everyone. Rupa grabbed the entire sweet box for herself so she could eat as and when she liked at leisure.

Next to be opened was the trunk which had the *sarees*-all of which had embroidery on the sides, just like those worn by women in *Patwari's* household. But they were so fine and delicate! How long would they last in the tough conditions at home? The rich can afford as fine and as delicate *sarees* as they want; their women have little else to do except sleep and rest. How will this stuff look on women working in the fields? She spied a shawl along with Hori's *dhoti*. "That is very thoughtful of you, son. Your father's shawl is gone completely torn and tattered."

By that time Gobar had got a fair idea of the condition at home. Dhania's *saree* was patched heavily, Sona's was torn and wasted at the part that covered her head and her dark hair was clearly visible through the tear. Rupa's dress was so worn out that its edges appeared like a frayed design. Their faces and hands were dry. Everything about them mirrored poverty and an overbearing aura of deprivation.

The girls were busy admiring the sarees. Dhania was worried about what to cook for her prodigal son. There was a small portion of flour she had kneaded for the evening. They could scrape through with their meal but this was not the Gobar she knew. She wondered if he would be able to swallow the coarse food they ate routinely. She was convinced he had the best of things to eat and drink while he was away. She decided to visit Dulari Sahuain once again. This time she was not subjected to the usual questioning on when she planned to pay up the debt. Instead, she was readily offered flour, rice and ghee. Dulari was also quite curious.

"Gobar has done well for himself. Hasn't he?"

Dhania said, "Don't know as yet, sister. He hasn't revealed anything so far and I don't think it is appropriate to rake up that question so early. But yes, he has brought *sarees* for all of us with embroidered borders. Your blessings have brought him back that's good enough for me."

Dulari was genuinely happy and blessed him, "May God be merciful and give him happiness and joy. Its true, parents don't want much else besides that. The boy is intelligent and understanding unlike other boys of his generation who know little except how to squander money. By the way, Dhania, I will appreciate it if you will pay back the interest, if not the loan you had taken from me. The load is increasing unnecessarily every day. Isn't it?"

Back home, Sona was pulling the frock and cap on Chunnu, dressing him up like a little prince but he was more interested in eating his new shoes and clothes than wearing them. Meanwhile, Gobar and Jhuniya were playing the blame game in another room inside.

Jhuniya put forward her case, "You brought all this on me and took the easy way out, decamping to a distant city. After that you had no time or inclination to know what's become of me and now you wake up after one year. You're so wicked. Here I am thinking you are following right behind me and you take off, only to return after one full year! Who can trust men? Who knows you might have linked up with some other woman when you were in the city. I am sure you would have thought that you had already bagged one for the home, why not have a spare one for outside it?

Gobar tried to explain, "Jhuniya, God be my witness, I swear on Him, I have never as much as noticed another girl. I did run away from home, scared and ashamed, but you were always in my thoughts. Not for a moment did I stop thinking about you. I have decided to take you back with me; that is why I am here. Did your folks get really mad at you?"

"My father was so angry, he could have killed me."

"Oh my God! Really?"

"Yes, the three of them were here but *amma* gave them such an earful they didn't look back after that day. But unfortunately, they took away our bulls."

"That's too much! And *dada* didn't say a word?"

"How could he handle everyone all alone? He can't fight the world single-handedly. The villagers did put their foot down and tried to tick them off but you know *dada,* he's so simple. He didn't object; how could anybody help in that case?"

"So how do we manage the fields?"

"It's all gone. There's some farming left but that too is under patronage of Datadin. We haven't sowed sugarcane this season."

Tied to his waist, within the folds of his garment was a bundle of two hundred rupees that Gobar had saved and brought from Lucknow. It provided him with an aggressive confidence; this news pushed that cockiness to the verge of recklessness.

He said, "I think I must first go and settle these issues with them. How dare they walk away with our bulls from my doorstep? This is robbery, sheer plunder! They'll be sent away for three years, all three of them. If they don't return my bulls they'll do so under orders from the court. I will pound their snootiness to pulp."

He got up to leave simmering in anger, but Jhuniya caught hold of him and said, "What's the hurry? You go at a time you choose; don't rush things. Take rest and eat. You have the whole day tomorrow. Do you know, there was a major village council meeting and they fined us eighty rupees and over and above that, we had to pay with three mounds of grains. That is why we are in such a pathetic situation."

Sona had finally dressed up the baby in his new clothes and brought him in regally. Gobar took the baby in his arms but he didn't find much delight in petting and playing with the child. His blood was boiling and the little purse around his waist was pushing the temperature still further. He would pick on each one of them separately, one by one. What right does the *panchayat* have to charge his family? Who gave them the right to dictate his private affairs? If he filed a case against them they would be handcuffed and sent to prison. They had virtually ruined his household. The child in his arms smiled for a moment and then let out a wail as if he had seen something scary.

Jhuniya picked the child from his lap and told him to go freshen up. "What are you thinking? If you pick up fights with everyone, there will be little else in your life. Only those with deep pockets are supposed to be good and great. If you are poor everyone lords over you."

"I was such an ass to run away from home. Otherwise, no one would have dared to come within an arm's length."

"You say this because you've now got the airs of the city or else why did you run away in the first place?"

"I am in half a mind to pick up a *lathi,* go across to Datadin, Jhinguri Singh and Pateshwari and beat the hell out of them."

"It seems money has gone to your head as well. Let me see how much you have brought from the city?"

She came forward and put her hand on his waist. Gobar sprang up and said, "What could I earn in such a short time? When you go back with me, perhaps, I will be able to earn and save better. The first few months were spent in getting to know the ropes and familiarising myself with the ways of city life."

"Will *amma* let me go?" she was clearly sceptical.

"Why won't she let you go? What has it got to do with her?"

"Nah! I am not going anywhere without her permission. You are the one who walked away; had she not let me in where do you think I would have gone? I will sing her glories to my dying day and moreover, I don't think you'll be abroad forever?"

"What's in it for me here? Slog and perish! What else can one do here? A little bit of intelligence and willingness to work hard is all you need to survive in the city. Here intelligence is stunted. By the way what's the matter with *dada* for instance? Why does he appear so angry with me?"

"Bless your stars that he appears merely angry. The stage you set for us and the scene you created was such that if he laid his hands on you when it was happening, he would have thrashed you black and blue."

"In that case, he must be cursing you as well?"

"Never! Not even by mistake. At first *amma* was slightly annoyed but *dada* never said a word. Whenever he talks to me, he is very polite and loving. If I get a headache he worries his heart out. When I think of my father I consider *dada* as good as divine. He always tells *amma* not to say anything to me, though he does get mad at you, blaming you for putting me in a fix. They are facing lots of financial problems. Earnings from the sugarcane harvest didn't reach home; it was all gone in settling old dues. They are reduced to working as labourers in the fields. Poor *dada*! He fainted in the field today. It was a panicky situation and he's all quiet since then."

Gobar had a wash and spent considerable time combing his hair after which he set out to the village on a mission. He went to the residences of both uncles and visited the homes of a couple of his friends. Not much had changed in the village. Pateshwari had built a new extension to his house and shifted the living room into that space while Jhinguri Singh had a new well dug right outside his home. Gobar's rebellion grew as he digested this information. All those whom he met were very respectful and nice to him. Young boys and men especially took him as their hero and most were ready to go to Lucknow with him. What a change in just a single year!

He came across Jhinguri Singh, bathing at his well. He ignored and passed him by without as much as a perfunctory greeting or salutation. He wanted to rub it in that he cared two hoots for that man.

It was Jhinguri Singh who made the first move. He called after him, "When did you come back, Gobar? I hope you are good; did you take up a job with someone in Lucknow?"

Gobar replied haughtily, "I didn't go to become a slave in Lucknow. All said and done, a job is another name for slavery. I have gone into business."

Jhinguri looked up and down at him, staring open mouthed. "How much did you make in a day?

Gobar turned his knife into a spear and aimed for Jhinguri's heart that was turning green by the minute. He said, "Well, about two and a half to three rupees per day. If I was lucky I got up to four but never less than two in any case."

After much haggling and scraping Jhinguri made not more than twenty five rupees a month and this unlettered, rustic lad was already pocketing around a hundred rupees per month! His pride took a beating; how could he order him about in the changed circumstances? This was no time to compete with him. Prudence demanded that he be nice to him and try to extract whatever he could from his newfound affluence. He said, "It's a good amount, son and you should utilise it well. One can't even earn three *annas* a day in the village. If you can help find some work for Bhavania (his eldest son) I'll send him to you. He's such a lout - hardly interested in studies, just loves to idle all day. If there's an opening for any accounting job, do let me know. You could take him with you, if you deem it proper. He's your friend, isn't he? Wage is not so important, just see that there is scope to make some more on the side you know what I mean."

Gobar smirked and said, "It is this desire of making easy money on the side that is our undoing, but we are so addicted to it that we aren't satisfied unless we make money through dishonest means. There are openings for clerks with many businessmen in Lucknow but they look for honest people. I can fix up Bhavani with someone but if he tries his tricks with them, it will harm my reputation. In the city they respect you more for honesty than your expertise."

After handing him a stinging slap with these words, he moved on to his next destination. Jhinguri Singh felt slighted but there was little he could do about it. He cursed Gobar for acting so holier-than-thou. He thought the boy had grown too big for his boots.

Gobar rubbed it into Datadin whom he met next. Datadin was about to sit down for lunch. When he saw Gobar he smiled pleasantly. "How are you, Gobar? I hear you've managed to do good for yourself in Lucknow. Why don't you get Mata din involved in something there? He does nothing except laze around the village and is always high on drugs."

"You don't lack anything! You simply have to pay a visit to one of your religious constituents and walk away with something or the other. They'll gift you on a birth; they'll have something to offer you on a death, on weddings, winter, summer--any occasion is good enough for some sort of a donation for your holiness! You liaise for others, give loans to them and if they err, you clamp heavy fines and squeeze their last drop of blood. Isn't that enough to satiate your hunger for more? To what end are you hoarding so much wealth? Who knows, you might have found some wily way to carry it across to the other world?"

Datadin noted Gobar's irreverent attitude. What an uncouth lad, he thought to himself. He seems to have forgotten his father works like a slave for him. How true it is! Shallow rivers overflow their banks in the first shower of rain. He sensed intense haughtiness in the boy but didn't let irritation show on his face. When infants play with their moustaches, older men simply laugh it off; Datadin did the same and jested with him, "Lucknow has done things to you, Gobar! How much have you earned in the city? Honestly, I missed you a lot. I hope you will be here for some time?"

"Yes, I am here for a few more days. I have to settle some scores with the village elders who robbed me of a hundred and fifty rupees by imposing a stupid fine. Let me see who dares ex-communicate me or boycott me socially?"

His open challenge to authority deeply impressed the band of young boys following him on his victory march.

One of them piped up, "Oh yeah! File a suit against them, Gobar *bhaiya*. That oldie is a real viper- his bite will kill a stone. You gave him something to chew on for some time. Now teach a lesson to patwari as well; he's a real bad one, that swine. He can incite fights between father and son. He's hand in glove with his henchmen; together they rob us every day. We've got to irrigate his fields before we turn to our own. When we go to plough the fields, we are expected to plough his field first."

Gobar patted his moustaches. "You're telling me? It's merely a year that I have been away. I am not the one to forget so soon. I don't want to live here or I would have rubbed their noses in dirt. This time round you must celebrate Holi with great fervour. Let's have a great masquerade and present caricatures of these old fogies. Let's give it to them, boys!"

They started working on their programme for Holi in right earnest. Sweet and sour *bhang* was ground on the pestle to brew a heady concoction for the revelry. Special colours were prepared along with black paint that was specially set aside for the faces of the village elders. They knew Holi gave everybody a licence to indulge in any prank with the assurance of no reproach as the joyful festival was meant to let your hair down. They could create theatrical performances mimicking those in authority and poking fun at them, all under the umbrella of good humour, howsoever raucous it may be. Raising money for the festivities was no issue. Gobar was back from the city with pots of money!

Gobar ate his lunch and left immediately that same afternoon for Bhola's residence. He did not want to rest till he got the bulls secure and tethered in his yard. He was in a mood to fight to the finish.

Hori tried to stop Gobar- "Don't' stretch it too far, Gobar. He took away our bulls, God be merciful to him but we did owe him something, didn't we?"

Gobar flared up and said, "*Dada;* you keep out of this. Their cow was for fifty rupees. Our bulls cost us a hundred and fifty. We yoked them to the plough for three years but they are still worth a hundred at the going rate this day. They could have filed a case against us, sent us a notice. Who gave them the right to walk away with our pair? And what should I say about you? On the one hand you lose your bulls and on the other you meekly submit to the elders and pay up a fine of a hundred and fifty! This is what you get for being meek and gentle. I bet they wouldn't have dared to walk away like this if I was around. I would have buried them in our courtyard. I would have never responded to summons from the village council. Nobody could have dared to ex-communicate me but you simply sat and fiddled your thumbs doing nothing!"

Hori lowered his head like an accused but Dhania was not one to let it pass unchallenged. "Son, I think you are going too far. If they had boycotted us, could you imagine how difficult it would have been for us? We have young girls, don't we have to settle them somewhere within the community? The community is a part of..."

Gobar cut her short, "We weren't ex-communicated, the community was not mad at us so why couldn't I get married? Tell me? Was it not because we didn't have money? If you have money there's no ex-communication and no boycott. The world recognises wealth and nothing except wealth."

Dhania heard the baby wailing so she went in to find out what was wrong. Gobar turned to leave at the same time. Hori sat alone, wondering at the dramatic change in his son's attitude. It was amazing the way he talked. His pragmatic intelligence had vanquished Hori's arguments of ethics and faith.

Hori tried yet again, "Should I come with you?"

"I am not spoiling for a fight, *dada*. Don't worry for me. The law is on our side. I have no reason to get violent."

"Do you have a problem if I accompany you there?"

"Yes. I have a huge problem. You will mess everything up." That shut him up and Gobar went on his way.

When Dhania emerged from the room and saw Hori sitting all alone she panicked and lashed out at him, "Has Gobar gone all by himself? Oh God, when will you pass on some intelligence to this man? Bhola will not hand the bulls on a platter. The three of them will pounce on him like vultures. God be merciful! Who should I turn to now? You are just no good. I give up!"

Hori picked up his *lathi* from a corner and ran after Gobar. At the village outskirts, he ran his eye across the expanse of wide open land. He saw a small dot moving on the horizon. Gobar had travelled so far in such a short time! He was mad at himself. He should have spoken sternly to him and commanded him to sit down and desist from going to Bhola's. He was confident Gobar would have listened to him had he been more firm. He was out of breath and unable to walk fast. Defeated, he sat down and looked skywards- "Merciful God, protect my son."

As Gobar approached Bhola's village, he came across a group of men sitting under a tree playing a game of dice. They must have been gambling for they wrapped up the board and scattered in different directions in a hurry. They thought it was a cop. One of the gamblers was Jangi, the elder of Jhuniya's brothers. He exclaimed, "Hey look! It's Gobar!"

Gobar saw him lurking behind a tree. He said, "Don't be afraid, brother. It's just me. I arrived this morning and thought of dropping by for I don't know when I will be back again. I am doing well and by your grace, the nobleman for whom I work advised me to bring a few able and willing men from our village. He needs watchmen for his premises. I told him 'sir, I wiil get you such fine men they'd rather die than compromise on the tasks assigned to them'. If you are up to it you may come with me. It's a good life out there."

Jangi was impressed more by what he saw than what he heard. He didn't have proper slippers to wear and here was Gobar in his shiny boots. The rustic Gobar he had seen last year was a different person; in a clean striped shirt and well combed hair, he was every inch a city lad. The grudge he held against him dissipated over time and its last vestiges vapourised as he beheld the new incarnation before him. He was a gambler with an addiction to drugs. His money situation was bad. The proposal seemed too attractive to refuse. He said, "Of course, I will come with you. As it is, I do little except swat flies in this godforsaken place. How much will they pay me?"

Gobar replied confidently- "Don't worry about that. Everything is under my control. I can get you whatever you want. I say when I have my own man why should I help rank strangers?"

Jangi was curious- "What is the job like?"

"It could be anything. You might have to watch over the house at night or go on a collection spree in the day time. The latter is a job after my heart. You go to a debtor, strike a deal, and report to your boss that the debtor was not at home.

You can easily make an extra eight *annas* to a rupee this way, everyday!"

"How about accommodation? Will they provide a place to stay?"

"There's plenty of space to stay there. It's a palace, brother! Flowing water in taps, there's electricity as well – there's nothing more to ask for. Is your brother Kamta home or he has he gone out?"

"He's gone out to sell milk. Nobody allows me to go to the market. They don't trust me and say I will blow up the money in drugs. I don't' drink so much, brother but I do need a few *paise* every day. You don't let Kamta into this. I will come with you."

"Sure! Definitely."

"So I am coming. It's done."

Both reached Bhola's residence, chatting amiably on the way. Bhola was sitting outside the door making jute ropes, spinning them into slender threads. Gobar bent down and touched his feet. As he did so, suddenly Gobar was overwhelmed with genuine emotion and his voice choked when he said- "*Kaka,* forgive me for my mistakes. Pardon me for all the wrongs I have done."

Bhola put down the strings he was weaving and replied stonily, "What you did was unacceptable, Gobar. Had I cut your head off there would be no sin in it; but you have come to my door what can I say to you? I leave it to God to pass judgement. When did you arrive?"

Gobar spiced up the story of his success and embellished it with exaggerated details of his good fortune. He also asked for his permission to take Jangi with him and help him build a career in the city. For Bhola it was a dream come true. Jangi was a nuisance at home. If he went to Lucknow, he just might turn a new leaf. He didn't expect him to make a fortune but if he could fend for himself that would be a major achievement in itself.

Gobar said, "No *kaka,* God willing he will do well and in a year or so he will go places."

"He might, if he persists."

"I will go back after Holi. Let me get things back on the rails. I want to go back convinced that everything is fine here."

"Tell Hori to retire and devote himself to spiritual stuff. It's high time he moved on."

"I do tell him that but will he ever listen?"

"Do you know any doctor in the city? My cough is killing me. If you find some medicine do send it for me."

"There's one famous *vaid* who lives very close to where I am. I will tell him about your condition and send the potion he prepares for your cough. Does your cough worsen at night or it's the same in the day?"

"No son, it's worse at night. I can barely sleep. Actually, if there is any scope I will not mind moving there. There's no future here."

"There are opportunities galore in Lucknow, *kaka*. No one will pay one rupee for a seer of milk here; perforce you have to sell it cheap to sweet shops. Out there, you can sell it at three times the price and it goes within seconds."

Jangi had left to make *sherbet* with milk for Gobar. Finding him alone, Bhola leaı ed forward and said, "I am bored and sick of this mess. I don't have to tell you anything about Jangi; you know better. Kamta goes out to the market all day. Moving the cattle, mixing their feed- I am saddled with every responsibility around the house. Now I feel like doing nothing but live a retired life in peace. There's a limit to what I can do. Everyday affairs and constant bickering is killing me - I can't play peacemaker every time. My cough is so bad that it keeps me awake at night but nobody enquires about my health. The cattle shed is falling apart but no one is bothered. If I don't repair it, it will go from bad to worse."

Gobar was all attention. He chose his words with care and spoke affectionately, "You come with me, *kaka*. Come to Lucknow where you can sell milk at good rates and in hard cash. I know so many rich clients. I guarantee sales for at least 10 seers. I have a tea shop and consume as much in my shop. You will have no problems."

Jangi came with the milk *sherbet*. Gobar downed a glass and said, "If you do nothing but mind the tea shop morning and evening, a rupee per day is the least you get."

Bhola hesitated for a moment before he spoke. "When a man loses his temper he says things he doesn't mean. He turns blind. I took away the pair of your bulls. You take them back today. It's not that I yoke them in the fields."

"But I have already paid the advance for a new pair!"

"No, No! Why do you want a new pair? Take the old ones back."

"Ok. Then I will send your money."

"That money is not with outsiders, son. It's at our home. The community- caste thing is a big sham. How are we any different from you? Honestly, I should be relieved that Jhuniya is at a decent place and she is happy. What a fool I was to bay for her blood."

Late in the evening when Gobar left for home, he held the leash of the pair of bulls that trotted beside him and bringing up the rear was Jangi with two large pots of yoghurt on his head.

❁❁❁

21

For no less than six months a year rural India resonates with the sound of cymbals, drums and horns as one or the other festival is celebrated in all parts of the country. A month before Holi and yet another after it, the festival's joyful reverie lingers in the air in every town and village, especially in the northern plains. As spring draws to a close in these parts, the season of ballads begins, closely followed by the monsoons when the sonorous music of *Kajri* fills the air. Once this singing is over, it's time for 'Ramayana recitations' which continues for the better part of late autumn.

The village of Semri was no exception to the rule. The fear of moneylenders and bullying henchmen failed to dim the magic of these festivities. There was no money in the pocket, no grains in the silos, no clothes to cover emaciated bodies–but who cared? The lust for life was irrepressible. Nothing could smother laughter of the soul or crush a spirited celebration of the human spirit.

Nokhe Ram's courtyard was the main venue for the centre of all musical celebrations during Holi. From brewing the heady *'bhang'* to boisterous dancing and smearing of colour on all and sundry; Nokhe ram's courtyard was the place where all the action was. It meant an expense of five to ten rupees and the gentleman was only too willing to incur this annual indulgence, for who else could dare to support an event of such magnitude?

However, this year silence reigned in Nokhe Ram's venue. All the young men of the village are drawn to Gobar's house where they ground *'bhang',* wrapped bundles of betel leaves to chew at leisure and mixed a rainbow of colours in huge pots. The stage was set, carpets were laid out and music was at a crescendo. Such a contrast from Nokhe Ram's courtyard where he had laid out the *'bhang'* but there was nobody at hand to grind it? Drums and cymbals were lying on the table but who would play on them for everyone was gravitating towards Gobar's doorstep.

The heady drink served here was laced with cardamoms and had a distinct flavour of saffron to it. Yes! Gobar bought a sack of cardamom himself. The concoction was so tasty and its effect so inspiring that with just a few swigs every pore of one's existence came alive and eyes seemed to pop out of their sockets. He also got first grade tobacco, specially packed for the occasion. The phials of coloured water had drops of rose essence; if he knew how to earn well he was equally adept in spending it right. There was no fun in hoarding wealth or keeping it under lock and key. The beauty of good fortune lay in utilising it well and it was not about *bhang* alone.

Everyone was invited- the revellers, musicians, singers- no one was excluded. They were welcome to stay back for the feast. There was no dearth of good singers or mimics in the village. Sobha alone could bring the house down with his caricature of a cripple. His expert mimicry of animal sounds was a sure scene stealer. He could also mimic voices of other individuals. Girdhar had a talent for theatrics. He could play the role of a lawyer, a policeman, an orderly, a rich gent or a village headman- you name it, and he would do it. Unfortunately, the poor guy did not have the means to organise make up and props, but this year Gobar had sent for that stuff hence his performance would be something to look forward to.

The news of Gobar's feast spread so fast that by evening a huge crowd had collected at the grounds in front of his residence. Groups of spectators arrived from nearby villages and by ten o'clock there were almost three thousand men jostling for space in a good humoured anticipation of a jolly good time. When Girdhar stood up on stage to mimic Jhinguri Singh, the fervour reached a peak and the enthusiasm was a hair's breadth from chaos. It was the same bald head, those familiar dark moustaches and protruding belly! He was sitting down, having dinner and his first lady was gently fanning his corpulent body.

They looked at each other coyly and he said, "My darling, you are so captivating even at this age that young men sigh deeply when they see your beauty."

The senior lady of the house blushed but feigned annoyance "Is that why you brought another woman into the house?"

"She's here to serve you, sweetheart! She is nothing compared to you."

The junior lady of the house, sitting nearby, overheard it and walked away in a huff. In the following scene, Jhinguri was resting on the cot and the second wife was scowling in a corner. He turned her face to him but she brushed him aside. When this cajoling failed to register every time he approached her, he squeaked at her- "Oh come on my love, why are you mad at me?"

"You go wherever your love is! I am merely your plaything! I am here merely to delight you?"

"No, no, my dear. You are the queen of my heart. That old hag is here only to take care of you."

The first wife overheard this conversation and rushed in with a broom and spanked him as he ran all over the stage in exaggerated panic.

After this it was the turn of another skit. In this episode a moneylender- whose identity was not left to imagination prepared a document of ten rupees but handed only five as loan to a poor peasant after deducting charges. The peasant was flummoxed and said, "But this is only five rupee sir!"

"No, they are ten. Count them carefully."

"No sir, they are five."

"One rupee is for application. Isn't it?"

"Yes sir."

"One rupee for consideration expenses."

"Yes sir."

"One rupee for the paper."

"Yes sir."

"One rupee for the processing fee."

"Yes sir."

"One rupee for interest."

"Yes sir."

"I gave you five in cash. Doesn't that make it ten?"

"Yes sir, it does. And now you keep those five with you."

"Are you mad?"

"No sir, one rupee is a gift for the junior lady, one rupee as a mark of respect for the senior one. A rupee to buy betel leaves for the junior lady and another rupee for the senior one for the same thing. The one rupee left is for your coffin."

Jhinguri Singh was not the only moneylender who was the butt of jokes but even Nokhe Ram, Pateshwari and Datadin were the target of pungent humour which had the audience in splits. The insults were tame and the mimicry old and repetitive but the manner in which Girdhari presented the act tickled the simple hearted audience that laughed readily, even at moments when the script didn't demand it. The performances went way into the night as oppressed souls delighted in giving it back to their tormentors, albeit in make-believe. When it finally wound up and the last of the scripts were played out, the birds were already twittering in the trees.

Next day, every villager greeted one another with the same dialogues, one-liners and songs of last night instead of the usual greetings. The village elders became the butt of their jokes. Little boys followed them wherever they went, passing the same comments. Jhinguri Singh had a sense of humour, so he took it in his stride but Pateshwari took the insults to heart and Datadin was furious. He was used to subservience and respect. Not just the villagers but Rai sahib also regarded him with awe and bowed his head whenever he passed him by on the street. It was difficult for him to bear such humiliation on his own turf.

If he had the powers vested in his caste in mythological times, he would have struck those wicked people down with an angry look but the magic of that golden era had dwindled in the modern age. For this reason he took recourse to weapons appropriate to this age. He came up to Hori's doorstep and snapped at him, "Won't you come for work today, Hori? Do you know how my work suffers in your absence?"

Gobar was rubbing his eyes and was about to rise from bed when Datadin's angry words assailed his ears. Not only he didn't greet him nor bend down to touch his feet but also spoke in a very challenging tone, "He won't work for you now. We have to sow our own sugarcane."

"That's not for you to decide. You can't opt out in the middle of the season."

Gobar yawned and said, "He is not your slave. He worked till he was comfortable with it. Now he doesn't feel like it so he won't. You can't force him into anything."

"In other words, do I understand Hori is not coming for work today?"

"No."

"In that case, please return my loan with interest immediately. Three years interest adds up to a hundred rupees; with the principal amount of a hundred the total comes to two hundred. I had offered to deduct three rupees as interest every month but if you don't want it that way it's entirely your lookout. Give me back my money. If you want to pose as a big man better start acting as one."

Hori looked at Datadin pleadingly and said, *'Maharaj,* when did I say I am unwilling to remain in your service? It's just that I have to attend to my fields; that's the problem."

Gobar scolded his father, "What service? Whose service are you talking about? Nobody is serving anybody here. We are all equal. This is such a joke! You give a hundred rupees loan to someone and extract lifelong labour from him by way of interest and the principal remains as it is! This is not a loan, it is loot."

"No issues, brother! Simply pay back my money. I charge six *paisa* per rupee; since I considered you family, I levied merely three *paisa* interest. Return my money and do as you please."

"We will pay interest at the rate of a rupee per hundred. Not a *paisa* more; if you want more, let the courts make us pay for it. One rupee per hundred is not a mean amount."

"I think your money has gone to your head."

"Only those who charge ridiculous rates have a swollen head. We are poor peasants. We can't afford to have airs. I remember distinctly you loaned us thirty rupees to buy bulls. According to you thirty rupees grew into hundred and now it's two hundred. This is exactly how farmers have been reduced to poverty and people like you have annexed their land, turning them into paupers. You want two hundred rupees for a loan of thirty rupees? How many years is it, *dada*?"

Hori was confused. He said, "About nine or ten years."

Gobar appeared shocked. "Two hundred for thirty in nine years! What kind of robbery is that?"

He drew a rough calculation on the ground with a stray pebble. "In ten years, it should be thirty six rupees. If we add the basic loan, it should be sixty six. Ok, we can give you seventy in rounded figures. That's all you get from us."

Datadin drew Hori into the discussion. "You hear that, Hori?" he said, "Gobar wants me to accept seventy in place of my two hundred and suggests I file a case if I refuse it. The world will come to an end if this is the way people will keep their word. You have the temerity to sit and listen quietly? Oh fine! I forsake these seventy rupees and won't go to the courts either, but remember I am a Brahmin and I will get my two hundred rupees. You will come with folded hands and request me to take the money due to me."

Datadin gnashed his teeth and withdrew from the scene. Gobar didn't move an inch. But a forbidding sceptre of religion and faith flashed before Hori's eyes, menacingly. If the money belonged to any of the other castes like the merchant community or *thakurs,* he would probably have taken the side of his son but a Brahmin's money was not to be trifled with. A Brahmin's wrath was to be feared. A Brahmin's curse could wipe out generations. Hori's fears of religious transgression drove him to the edge. He sprang up and ran to Datadin, almost falling at his feet. "*Maharaj,* as long as I live, I will try to pay back every single paisa I owe you. Don't pay any heed to that boy. The deal was between you and me. Who is he to speak for me?"

Datadin softened his stance. "Did you notice his haughtiness? He wants me to accept seventy instead of two hundred rupees and threatens me that I should go to court to make him pay what is rightfully mine. He has no idea what litigation and law is all about. A single day in jail will pull him down from his high horse. A few days in the city and the boy turns into a dictator!"

"I am telling you *Maharaj;* it my job to return your amount."

When Datadin had gone, Gobar gave a dirty look to his father and said, "I hope you succeeded in appeasing his holiness? It is people like you who are responsible for their arrogance."

Hori tried to introduce an element of ethics and honesty in his argument. He said, "It is important to be fair and square and ethical in one's dealings, son. When we took the loan we agreed on a certain rate of interest. It's wrong to change the rules midstream. We will never prosper on wealth saved by dishonourable means."

"I am not for resorting to dishonourable means. Did I ever mention we should deprive a Brahmin of his dues? My only contention is that we will not pay an exorbitant rate of interest. The men at the bank charge 12 *annas* per hundred; I am offering to pay him a rupee per hundred. If this is not reasonable, what is?"

"Won't it hurt his feelings?"

"How does that matter to us? I will not cut off my hand if it pains him to see it attached to my body?"

"Son, allow me to live the life I have led as long as I am alive. When I am gone you do as you please."

"Then you repay the loan. I was stupid to interfere on your behalf. You brought this on yourself; now you resolve it. Why should I get involved in this?"

Grumbling, Gobar got up and went inside the house. Jhuniya asked him why he was arguing with his father so early in the morning.

He narrated the whole story and added in the end, "His debts will keep on mounting day by day. How long can I keep repaying it? He has toiled for others foolishly; I see no reason to fall in the same hole he has dug for himself. He did not consult me when he took the loan; therefore I am not responsible for it."

Meanwhile, the village headmen were hatching a conspiracy to settle Gobar. If this brat was not tamed he would create a great upheaval in the village. From a knave he had turned into a knight; no wonder he was flying at a tangent. Where did he pick up those legal terms? Just imagine he wanted to pay seventy rupees instead of two hundred! Last night he created such a nuisance with his loud music and feasting along with other boys from the village.

There was a lot of jealousy amongst the headmen as well. Each was tickled and a bit flattered at the lampooning they were subject to last night. Pateshwari and Nokhe Ram were discussing this privately as an aside, "Give the devils their due; these boys do know the inside story around here. They had such fun at Jhinguri Singh's expense! That bit about his two wives was so funny."

Nokhe Ram chortled gleefully- "I must say the mimicry and caricature was quite close to the truth. I have often noticed his younger wife gossiping and flirting with young men."

"I also hear the older hag wears a lot of kohl in her eyes and paints her hands and feet to appear younger."

Yes, the two are at each other's throats day and night. Jhinguri is so thick skinned; any sane person would have given up by now."

"I hear they lampooned you real bad as well."

"Just you wait. I am going to push them to pay up field taxes right away. He will not know what hit him."

"But Hori has already paid that tax, I think."

"But I haven't issued him a receipt yet. He has no proof to claim he has. I will send a man over to summon him here."

Elsewhere Hori and Gobar were busy irrigating their field. There was no way they could get a regular sugarcane crop. Due to their poverty their fields lay unattended and had gone dry. With the bulls back at home, they now wanted to take a chance and try their luck once again.

But the father and son were like different poles today. They were avoiding each other despite working at close quarters. Hori was guiding the bulls and Gobar was tending to the land. Sona and Rupa were regulating the flow of water into the field and while they were at it, they had yet another of their usual spats. This time the topic of debate was whether Jhinguri Singh's wife ate before her husband had his meals or later on when he had finished. Sona was of the opinion that she served him food first but Rupa was convinced she ate later.

Rupa put her point across, "If she eats before he does, why is she not as fat as him? He is so fat if he falls on her she will be crushed."

Sona countered her argument, "Do you think eating well makes someone fat? Those who eat well become strong, not fat. People grow fat if they eat junk food."

"So you say she is strong and healthy?"

"Of course she is. Just the other day they had a fight and she shoved him so hard he fell and injured his knee."

"This means you too will eat before you offer food to your husband."

"For sure, I will."

"But *amma* gives food to *dada* first and eats later."

"Exactly! That's why *dada* gets mad at *amma* on every little thing. I will become strong and healthy and keep my man under my thumb. Your husband will thrash you and break your bones, just wait and see."

Rupa pouted her lips, ready to burst into tears, "Why will he beat me? I won't do anything bad."

"He won't listen to what you say. He will kick you for nothing."

This infuriated Rupa and she tried to tear Sona's saree with her teeth. Sona held her back, therefore in a sheer frustration, she started pinching her wildly.

Sona held her at an arms distance as she struggled to wrestle with her and baited her further, "He will cut off your nose as well."

These ominous forecasts were too much to bear and Rupa dug her teeth into Sona's arm. Blood oozed out of the cut she made with her sharp teeth. Sona gave a massive push to Rupa who was thrown off and landed at some distance. She got up and wailed loudly. Sona looked at the teeth marks on her arms and started crying as well.

Gobar heard their cries and came hurrying toward them in a fit of rage and gave a resounding slap on their cheeks. Both girls ran from the fields, crying loudly. Work came to a standstill as father and son argued over this incident.

Hori said, "Now who will run the water? You have driven them away now you call them back.'

"It's you who has spoilt them."

"If you beat them like this they'll turn absolutely shameless."

"Don't give them anything to eat for a day and they'll fall in line."

"I am their father, not a butcher."

Often it so happens that a foot hurt in a minor stumble is hurt again repeatedly the same day. It soon turns sore and hurts for a long time. The father and son had a brush up twice earlier in the day and a third disagreement made matters still worse.

Gobar went home and told Jhuniya to come with him and run the water in the field. Dhania watched in silence as he took Jhuniya away to the field. Dhania did not appreciate Gobar's action at all. If he had walloped Rupa it was understandable, but hitting a grown up girl was totally improper.

That very night Gobar decided to go back to Lucknow. It was becoming impossible to stay on in Semri. Why should he stay at home if they won't listen to him? He can't have an opinion on money matters; he tries to discipline spoilt sisters and his folks don't look at it kindly. It's as if an outsider who had slapped them and not their brother. If that's the case, he was not interested in extending his stay in the village.

Later that evening, a messenger sent by Nokhe Ram came up to Hori as soon as he emerged from his house after dinner. "Sir wants to see you," he said.

Hori told him with a hint of pride in his voice, "Why does he want to see me so late in the evening? I have paid my dues already."

The messenger said, "My brief was to give you the message. You say whatever you want to him."

Hori was not in a mood to go but eventually he did as Gobar sat indifferently in another corner of the house. Half an hour later he returned and started puffing at his *chillum* at another end of the house. Gobar couldn't contain his curiosity any longer. "Why did he call for you?" he asked.

Hori's voice cracked as he spoke, "I have paid every single *paisa*. Now he says there are dues pending against me for the last two years in my account. The other day I sold sugarcane and handed him twenty-five rupees and today he says there's still some dues remaining. I told him I won't pay a *pie*."

Gobar wanted to know if he had a receipt.

"When do they ever give a receipt?"

"You mean you make payments without taking a receipt for it?"

"How was I to know they will cheat me? This is entirely your fault; we are punished for your actions. Last night you made fun of them. If you pick on a lion in his den then you are surely inviting death. He says I owe him seventy rupees inclusive of interest. Now where do I get that from?"

Gobar clarified his position, "Had you taken a receipt you would be safe today. I fail to understand how you can be so irresponsible and callous? If they don't give you a receipt you could have sent the amount by post. At worst, it would have meant a few rupees as postal surcharge but you would have been covered and spared such maliciousness."

"If you hadn't stirred the hornet's nest nothing would have gone wrong. You annoyed every village elder and now they are threatening to attach our property and evict us. God knows how I will get out of this one."

"I will go and talk to them."

"Don't do that you will just add fuel to fire."

"If it is required I will do just that. They want to start proceedings against me let them go ahead with it. I will make them swear with holy water in their hands; you keep sitting in a corner with your tail between your legs. I will fight to the last. I don't want to deprive someone of his money but I will not let anyone push me around."

He got up immediately and headed straight to Nokhe Ram's house. When he reached there he saw a meeting of the elders was in progress. They became cautious on seeing Gobar in their midst. A musty air of conspiracy hung in the air.

Gobar asked aggressively- "What is all this about pending dues? *Dada* paid his taxes recently; where did these dues come up all of a sudden? What's the meaning of this hocus pocus?"

Nokhe Ram was resting, half inclined on a soft bolster. He spoke airily, "Unless Hori is around, I don't want to discuss anything with you."

Gobar asked with an air of injured innocence- "Am I a nobody in our house?"

"You might be everything in your house but here you don't mean anything to us."

"Very well, if you insist – go ahead and file proceedings against us. I will pay you after making you swear in court on your honour and in front of witnesses. I will produce many who will vouch for it that you never issue receipts for payments. Since these peasants are dumb and simple, you assume everybody is a fool and you can get away with it. Judge sahib stays very close to where I stay in the city. Perhaps you in the village think he is unapproachable; I don't. I will put him on to the story and see how you succeed in milking us twice in a row."

His words carried the courage of conviction. For timid minds, even truth is a weakling. The same cement which turns rock hard on bricks comes crumbling down if it is coated on mounds of mud. Gobar's fearless demeanour ripped through the armour of deceit behind which Nokhe Ram's weak spirit thrived under its illusion of invincibility.

He tried to act as if he was recollecting something- "Why do you have to lose your temper? Is there any reason for you to get so heated up over this? If, as you say, Hori has actually paid up, it will be entered in the accounts somewhere. I will re-check the papers once again. I do recollect vaguely he did come to me with a payment; don't know when it was, but he did. You can be rest assured if Hori has paid up his money it will definitely be accounted for. I am sure he will not lie for a small amount like that, nor will I grow rich misleading you about it."

When he was back Gobar came down so heavily on Hori that the old man was one breath away from bursting into tears. He said, "You are worse than a small child who is terrified by the mewing of a cat. How long can I go on protecting you? I will give you seventy rupees. If Datadin accepts it; clear his dues and get on with it. I am not struggling abroad so that you allow yourself to be looted and I compensate every time you are ripped off. I go back tomorrow but please remember not to borrow from anybody and not be so eager to give away everything."

Dhania had eaten her dinner so she came out and joined them. She said, "Why are you going back so early, son? Stay back for a few more days. You should be around till the crops ripen and go once all the accounts are settled properly."

Gobar replied vainly, "I am losing two to three rupees on an average in my business if I stay here. I hope you understand that? I don't get one tenth of what I can make there. I will take Jhuniya with me because I am up against a huge problem of managing my meals."

Dhania replied hesitantly- "Well, you know best but won't she have a problem managing the entire household single-handedly? How will she look after the baby and the house at the same time in a foreign place?"

"Do you want me to attend to my work or worry about the baby and waste hours in the kitchen over a smoky stove?"

"I don't mind if she goes with you but living in a new environment, for the first time, with a small baby and no one at hand to help or assist her – won't it be a problem for her?"

"One can always find company amongst neighbours anywhere, mother, even in foreign lands. And it's a selfish world out there. If you have money, there are enough who suck up to you as near and dear ones. If you are penniless even parents do not have time for you."

The sarcasm was not lost on Dhania. A bolt of rage wracked through her body. She said, "So you put parents in the same bracket as fair weather friends?"

"It's quite evident, isn't it?"

"No, you are mistaken. Parents are not as stone hearted as you think. On the contrary, it is sons who look the other way once they start making money for themselves. I can give you not one but dozens of examples of ungrateful boys in this village. Parents take loans but for whom? Is it for the future of their children or their own personal luxuries?"

"Who knows for what you took all those loans? I never benefited from them even once."

"Did you grow up on air? We didn't have any role in it?"

"What role did you have other than feeding me milk when I was a baby? After that you let me on my own. I ate what everybody else ate. You never gave milk or butter or set aside anything specifically for me. You and *dada* both want me to clear all your loans, pay all your taxes and marry off your girls. As if my life is meant to be wasted in your service. I have a life too; don't I have my family and kid to worry about?"

Dhania was stunned. In one instant, the great dream of a happy home came crashing down. Up till now she believed she had seen the last of her miserable days. Since Gobar returned home, her moods improved and she had a pleasant expression on her face at all times. Her tone was softer and there was perceptible generosity in her attitude. If God was kind to her she mustn't let it go to her head - she ought to remain humble. Her inner equanimity reflected in a co-operative attitude on the outside. But Gobar's words fell like hot coals on her heart and singed her tender aspirations in one cruel stroke. Her pride took a severe hit. What was there to look for after listening to such rhetoric from her own son? The life jacket she clung to in the raging sea of life, was punctured; what was the point in hanging on to hope any longer?

But wait, just a moment! This was not like Gobar. He was not so selfish. He had never talked back rudely; he never threw a tantrum, never asked for a thing! He ate whatever was offered to him. Why was that affectionate, simple hearted boy mouthing such scorching words? Nobody had gone against his wishes; his parents hung on every word when he opened his mouth to speak. It was Gobar who raised the issue of loan repayment no one asked him to contribute towards clearing debts. His parents are content if he did well for himself and led a secure, happy life. If he was able and willing to assist his family, he was welcome to it and his help would be appreciated but if he could not his parents would never pressurise or shame him into it. If he desired to take Jhuniya along, he may gladly do so. She was only concerned if the problems of settling with her in a different place did not outweigh the benefits of her joining him there.

There was nothing in her suggestion to infuriate him so much. Perhaps, it was Jhuniya who was behind his outburst. She was probably the one who was working on him behind the scenes. She was unable to either live up or dress up as she pleased while she was here. On top of that, she had to lend a helping hand around the house. In the city she would have free access to his earnings, eat better, dress better and relax to her heart's content. Cooking food for two was no big deal. Money would take care of many things. Certainly she was the cause of this outburst. She had lived in a city earlier and now longed for its bright lights. At her father's house nobody cared a fig for her; she found this dumb boy and led him into her honey trap. When she landed at her home all hassled, disturbed and five months pregnant, she mewed like a wet cat. Had she not got shelter she would be begging on the streets now. And this is what she gave in return for the compassion.

Dhania's thought process was fast and furious. 'We lost face in society. We lost our son for a year; we paid heavy fines all for her. Now this wretch dares to bite the hand that feeds her. The whiff of new money has revealed her true colours. When he dumped her and ran away; she had time to sit beside me and serve me well; now she wants him all for herself.'

Pained, she turned to her son and said, "Who is feeding you with these notions, son? This is so unlike you. Your parents belong to you. Your sisters belong to you. This house is all yours. No one is an outsider. We won't be around for long. If our household retains its dignity, it is in your own interest. Man earns for his family otherwise you know even pigs can fend for themselves. I didn't know Jhuniya will turn against us and poison our lives this way."

Gobar was incensed at this new twist. He said irritably, "*Amma,* I am not a child who will be led astray. You shouldn't be mad at her. I can't take up all responsibilities of your household. I will certainly try to help as much as I can but I can't fetter myself to your door forever."

Jhuniya also came out from her room and said, "*Amma,* don't blame the tools for the workman's faults. He is not an innocent baby who doesn't know what he is doing. He knows what's good for him. No one wants to suffer all his life and shrivel away joylessly. Everybody wants happiness; everyone wants to have some money to call his own."

Dhania gritted her teeth in anger. "Don't lecture me, Jhuniya. It appears you have turned very knowledgeable of late. Where was your knowledge and sound advice when you were falling at my feet, pleading for mercy and shelter? Had we put our needs and safety first, imagine what that would have meant for you?"

This signalled a virtual free for all. Sarcasm, caustic remarks and abuses flew with explosive ferocity as old wounds and grudges were brought to the open and scattered in full public view. Gobar would add a stinging comment now and then which made the situation very ugly indeed. Hori sat quietly in the veranda, listening to the turmoil inside his house. Sona and Rupa stood in the courtyard, their heads hanging low and eyes downcast as Dulari, Puniya and half a dozen other women, drawn by the commotion, tried to intervene without much success.

Both women were bent on proving each other wrong while simultaneously claiming their innocence. Jhuniya was raising ghosts from the past. She expressed great empathy and sorrow for both Hori and his long lost brother Heera, who she felt were victims of her mother-in-law's infamous temper and irrational behaviour. According to her, Dhania could not get along with anyone in the village. Dhania also tried to put her point across and speak in her defence but public opinion tilted towards Jhuniya that day. One reason could be Jhuniya's restrained and coldly reasoned missives presented a picture of a suffering underdog while Dhania's aggression underlined her unreasonableness. Another reason could be the fact that Jhuniya was the wife of a well earning young man and it's always good to keep a rising star in good humour.

Hori walked into the centre of the courtyard and said, "Dhania, do you want me to fall at your feet? Just shut up. Don't disgrace me so. Haven't you heard enough?"

Dhania turned to him angrily, "So you will also speak for the milch cow? Am I the only one at fault?"

The battle opened on a new front.

"It doesn't behove you to speak like this about children."

Dhania was not willing to consider Jhuniya as a child.

"By what flight of imagination will you call her a child?"

"Ok. I agree she is not a child, she is an adult. If an adult doesn't want to stay with you how do you intend to keep her back? It's the parent's responsibility to bring up children; once they are old enough they go their way. What do you expect; it's their turn to feed you in the nest? Parents are duty bound to bring up children; children cannot be expected to look after their parents. If they want to go; send them off with your blessings. God is with us. He will take care of us. We will accept what fate has in store for us. We have already spent four to five decades doing little except suffer; the rest will not be any different. There aren't many years left, I assure you."

Meanwhile Gobar had begun packing up his things. He was determined not to delay a minute. If a mother could be so bitter towards a son would he like to see her face again. Jhuniya put on her new saree. Chunnu looked cute in his new clothes.

Hori's voice choked as he said, "Son, I don't know how to say it but I can't help it. Won't you take her blessings and touch the feet of the woman who bore you as a child? Is it too much to ask of you? It won't make you any smaller if you do."

Gobar turned his face away- "I don't consider her my mother."

Hori winced in pain, as though struck across the face. He said, "Well, do as you please. I will pray for your happiness wherever you are."

Jhuniya did come up to her mother-in-law and touched her feet reverently. Dhania stood still; not a word of blessing escaped her lips. She barely turned to look at her. Gobar walked ahead with the boy astride his hip. Jhuniya followed him with the bedding tucked under her arm. A *chamar's* son carried their trunk case. A number of men and women from the village went to see them off at the village limits.

Back at home, Dhania was sitting on the floor, crying inconsolably. It was as if someone was sawing her heart in two. Her motherhood was like a house on fire in which everything was reduced to ashes. There was nothing left standing--not even a crumbling wall on which she could go and hit her head.

❁❁❁

22

Negotiations for the marriage of Rai sahib's daughter had been going on for some time. Elections were also round the corner; yet above all those pressing issues was a civil case which he had to file for which the court fee itself was fifty thousand rupees plus other additional expenses. Rai sahib's brother-in-law died at a young age in a car accident, leaving his estate without an heir. His cousins had taken control of the estate and were not willing to part with any share in Rai sahib's favour. Rai sahib wanted to stake claim to his brother-in-law's estate on behalf of his son and wanted to file a civil suit for it. He wanted to settle the matter through negotiations and was willing to forego his claim on half of the income from the estate in favour of his deceased relative's cousins. But the greedy cousins were not ready for a negotiated settlement and had already started collecting revenue from the estate by force. Thus pushed to the edge, legal recourse was the only option left for Rai sahib.

A civil suit meant expenses running into lakhs, but it was worth the risk as the estate was worth no less than 20 lakhs. Lawyers had assured Rai sahib that he would definitely get a decree in his favour. No one, least of all Rai sahib, could afford to let go of an opportunity like this. However, the problem was that all three issues – daughter's marriage, election and the civil suit – had risen at the same time and none of them could be postponed or delayed.

Rai sahib's daughter had turned eighteen and he was still not able to fix her marriage due to lack of the right amount of money. The estimated expenditure on the marriage was one lakh. Wherever Rai sahib went, looking for a groom for his daughter, unreasonable demands of dowry were thrown at him. Recently a good opportunity had come his way. Kunwar Digvijay Singh's wife died of consumption and Kunwar sahib was keen to marry again as soon as possible. Rai sahib managed to fix his daughter's marriage with Kunwar sahib quickly, but he had to marry off his daughter in the designated period lest the groom look for greener pastures after coming out of the mourning period.

This Kunwar sahib had a colourful past of indulgence in almost every vice under the sun. He was fond of all substances that took him on a high---wine, marijuana and opium. Indulgence in an assortment of vices is a matter of pride for an aristocrat. An aristocrat sans a couple of vices was no aristocrat at all. After all, how else could they spend their ill-gotten money? Yet despite all these bad habits, he was such a brilliant person that even eminent scholars respected him for his abilities. He had few equals in music, drama, palmistry, astrology, yoga, wrestling, shooting, and other arts. At the same time, he was a very brave and equally dominating person. He contributed liberally to the freedom movement, albeit secretly -- a fact not unknown to government officials. But still he was a much respected person. Even the Governor turned up at his parties as a guest once or twice a year. He was in his early thirties- not a day older than thirty-two but had such a voracious appetite that he could eat a full grown goat all by himself.

For Rai sahib, he was a God send opportunity. Kunwar sahib had still not completed the sixteen days of mourning for his wife when Rai sahib sent feelers for his re-marriage. For Kunwar sahib, this marriage was a wonderful way to increase his power and influence. Rai sahib was not only a member of the Council but also an equally influential person. The sacrifices he made for the freedom struggle had paid good dividends and his stock was high in the social circuit. It suited both parties so there was no hurdle to this matrimonial alliance and the marriage was finally fixed.

But the impending election was stuck like a golden hook in the throat which Rai sahib could neither swallow nor spit out. He had been already elected twice to the Council; he had to spend a hundred thousand during each election. But this time, Raja Suryapratap Singh had stood for election from the same area and declared openly that even if he had to pay one thousand to each voter, or sell off his estate worth fifty lakhs, he will not allow Rai sahib to be elected to the Council for the third term. Friendly government officials had also assured him of their help and support.

Rai sahib was a rational and intelligent person who had a knack of understanding which way the wind was blowing. But he was also a *Rajput* and an aristocrat; he couldn't run away from a challenge. Rai sahib would have welcomed him, had Raja Suryapratap Singh come to him and said: "Brother, you have already been elected to the Council twice, let me have a go at it this time." But now, he had no option but to take him up on his challenge.

There was one more problem. Mr. Tankha had advised him to stand for the election but at a well timed moment, give up the fight after accepting one lakh rupees from his opponent. Mr. Tankha informed him that Raja sahib did not want to let go the chance to unseat him and the main reason for this was the matrimonial alliance between Rai sahib's daughter and Kunwar sahib. Raja sahib considered an alliance between these two influential families harmful to his interests. Rai sahib, on the other hand, nursed fond hopes of sinking his teeth into his brother-in-law's property. This was yet another thorn in Raja sahib's flesh. If Rai sahib got the property—the law weighed heavily in Rai sahib's favour in any case—then Raja sahib was up against a new competitor.

Hence, it was imperative for Raja sahib to crush Rai sahib and destroy his public stature.

Poor Rai sahib was in deep trouble. He smelt a rat and suspected Mr. Tankha had taken him for a ride for his own benefit. Rai sahib had also found out, much to his chagrin that Mr. Tankha had turned into a Raja sahib supporter. For Rai sahib, this was like adding insult to injury.

He tried to call Mr. Tankha many times, but he was either not at home or when he got the message, conveniently forgot to keep his promise of meeting Rai sahib or calling him back.

One day Rai sahib decided to go to Mr. Tankha's house to meet him. Luckily he found him at home, but he had to cool his heels for an hour before he met him. This was the same Mr. Tankha who came daily to Rai sahib's house. This insolence infuriated Rai sahib no end. The moment he entered the room with a cigar dangling from his mouth, Rai sahib lobbed a verbal grenade at him. "So at last you find time to see me after making me wait for almost an hour. I think this is a deliberate insult."

Settling himself comfortably on a sofa as he smoked his cigar, Mr. Tankha said, "I am sorry if you choose to take it that way. But you see I was up all night doing some important work. You should have called me up and taken an appointment."

This further stoked his ire, but Rai sahib held his temper in check. He had not come spoiling for a fight. Instead, he said, "Oh yes! Of course, it was a mistake. Perhaps you are very busy these days."

"Oh yes! Very busy indeed, otherwise I would have certainly come to your house."

"I had come to see you about that vexed issue I mentioned earlier. I don't see any signs of a compromise. On the contrary, I see they are readying for a fight."

"You know Raja sahib is very obstinate, almost mad. If he fancies something or fixes his ideas on a particular issue, he will not listen to anyone, no matter how much it might cost him. This time he is bent on humiliating you. Despite a debt of forty lakhs on his head, he is still undeterred and continues to splurge. His servants have not been paid salaries for six months but there is no lull in the construction of his new mansion. It has marble floors and such brilliant eye-catching carvings. He sends gifts to senior officers every day. I have even heard that he is going to hire a British manager."

"Then why were you so confident you could help formulate a compromise formula?"

"I did what I could; in fact more than what I could possibly do. If someone is hell-bent on squandering four lakh rupees, there's no way I can control hold him back."

Rai sahib lost his patience and blew his fuse.

"Sure! Especially when you are also likely to get twenty thousand from those four lakhs."

Now why would Mr. Tankha take that sitting down? He said, "Rai sahib, don't push me into saying things that are better left unsaid. Neither you nor I are saints here. We are all here to make money. I am also on the lookout for people with more money and less wisdom as much as you are. I advised you to stand for the election and you took it in the hope of pocketing a hundred thousand rupees. Had it worked out, you would have made one lakh and got your daughter married without taking loan of a single penny and filed the suit as well. But hard luck, it did not materialise. If you have not made anything, neither have I benefited from it. That is why I switched to his camp. One does need a boat to cross the river- and the bigger the better."

Rai sahib's anger boiled over and threatened to spill out into the open. His fingers itched to coil around that devil's neck and strangulate it in a slow painful death. The rascal had tricked him into this unpleasant situation and was trying to explain his position when cornered. But he had no option but to control his mounting anger under his present circumstances.

"So I understand you can't do anything now."

"Yes."

"I am willing to arrive at a compromise for fifty thousand rupees. Do you think Raja sahib will accept it? Will he agree on twenty-five thousand?"

"No chance! He made himself very clear on the issue."

"He said anything specifically or this is your version of what he thinks?"

"You don't trust me, do you? You think I am lying."

Rai sahib softened his one, "I don't mean to say you are a liar, but I do know that if you want, it can be done."

"So are you now implying that I thwarted a compromise?"

"No, I don't imply that either. What I mean to say is that if you wanted it enough, this compromise might be possible and I would not have to get into unnecessary wrangling."

Mr. Tankha glanced at his watch and said, "Rai sahib, if you want me to be upfront with you and tell you the truth, then listen to this. Had you signed me a cheque for ten thousand rupees, you would have definitely got your one lakh rupees today. Do I make myself clear? Perhaps you thought you'll throw a couple of thousand at me after you got the money from Raja sahib. I am no fool, Rai sahib. You would have taken the money from him and locked it in your safe. What could I have done in that case? Tell me? Do you think I could have gone to court to file a claim?"

Rai sahib felt hurt. "So you think I am dishonest?"

Tankha got up from the chair and said- "Who says this is dishonesty? Now-a-days it is called 'pragmatism' and 'being smart'. How to make a fool of others is the mantra of being successful, and you, Rai sahib, are a master of this art."

Rai sahib clenched his fist in anger. "You are talking of me?" he said, in shocked surprise.

"Yes, you! I worked for you whole-heartedly in your first election. You gave me five hundred rupees and took your time giving it. In the second election, you fobbed me off with an old rickety car. I was fooled once; I won't be taken for a ride again."

Tankha stood up, got out of the room and called for his car.

Rai sahib's anger knew no bounds. There was a limit to insolence. Tankha made him wait for an hour and now he was telling him to leave so callously. Had he been confident of knocking Tankha down, he would have done so. But he had a stronger build than him. So when Tankha started his car, he too left for Mr. Khanna's residence.

It was nine o' clock, but Khanna was still enjoying his sleep. He never went to bed before two o' clock and habitually slept till nine every day. Here too Rai sahib had to wait for half an hour. When he came around nine thirty, smiling broadly, Rai sahib pulled him up, albeit mildly- "Well! So now you wake up at nine thirty! You have become really rich; no wonder you are so carefree."

Mr. Khanna offered him a cigarette and said cheerily- "I retired late last night. Where are you coming from so early in the day?"

Rai sahib narrated his problems in as few words as he could. In his heart of hearts, he never liked Khanna. He thought Khanna was ever ready to cheat him despite being an old friend and classmate while remaining sugary sweet in person.

Khanna pretended to look worried and said, "Listen to me. I suggest you forget about the election and file a suit against your brother-in-law. As far as the wedding is concerned, it's only a three-day opera. It is not wise to go bankrupt for it. Kunwar sahib is my friend, so there is no question of any demand from his side."

Rai sahib said sarcastically- "Mr. Khanna, you conveniently forget that I am not a banker, but an ordinary person. Kunwar sahib will not insist on dowry—God has given him everything—but you forget this is about my only daughter. If her mother were alive today, she would have spent a fortune on the wedding and yet felt it was not enough. Maybe I would have told her to hold her hand and spend in a controlled manner. But now I am both mother and father to my daughter. I will go to any length to do good for her. I spent my life as a widower only for the love of my two kids. I can suppress my heart's desire, but I can't ignore my wife's wish which I consider my bounden duty. It's also not possible for me to run away from the electoral battle. I know I will lose. I am no match for Raja sahib, but I want to show him, I am no pushover."

"And there is no way you will not file the suit?"

"Everything hinges on it. Now tell me, what help can you offer me?"

"You know our director's orders regarding this. And Raja sahib is also one of our directors. They are leaning on me to get past dues cleared. Probably, in the circumstances, issuing a new loan might not be possible."

Rai sahib was crestfallen- "You will rock my boat very badly if you don't give me a loan, Khanna."

"On a personal level, you have my full support. But as far as the bank is concerned, I have to obey my directors' orders."

"If I get the property I am looking at—which I am convinced I will—I will return every *paisa*."

"Will you tell me what the total amount of your debt is?"

Rai sahib hesitated for a moment and said, "Five to six lakhs. It could be less..."

"Either you are forgetting or you are hiding something."

Rai sahib was emphatic. He said - "Neither I am forgetting, nor am I hiding. My present property is worth fifty lakhs. My in-laws' property is worth as much."

"But how can you say there is no debt pending against your in-laws' property?"

"As far as I know, that property is free of any encumbrances."

"But my information says there is a debt of no less than ten lakhs on it and as things stand at the moment, no loan can be given against that property. Also, there is already a debt of almost ten lakhs on your property. So it's not worth more than twenty-five lakhs. Under these conditions, no bank will offer you a loan. You are standing on the mouth of a volcano, Rai sahib. A slight push can land you in a deeper mess. You should tread carefully at this juncture."

Rai sahib held Khanna's hands and said, "I understand this very well, my friend. But such is life; you have to do things your soul doesn't want you to do. You will have to arrange at least two lakhs for me"

Khanna took a deep breath and said, "My God! Two lakhs! Impossible! Absolutely impossible!"

"I will kill myself at your door, please understand. I am really desperate. I depend on you for all my plans. If you disappoint me, I will go home and swallow poison. I cannot bow out of this fight against Raja Suryapratap Singh. My daughter's marriage can be postponed for another two or four months. There is enough time for it; but elections are very close and that's my biggest worry."

Khanna was quite surprised, "So you will spend two lakhs on elections?"

"This is not just about an election, it's about prestige. Do you think my honour is not worth a mere two lakhs? Even if I am forced to sell the entire estate, I don't give a damn. But I won't let Raja sahib walk over me."

Khanna contemplated on it as he blew whorls of smoke, "I have explained the bank's position to you. The bank has stopped issuing loans. I will try my best so your case gets special treatment, but you know business is business. And what will be my commission? I will have to push your case against all odds. You know the immense influence Raja sahib has on other directors. I will have to organise a coterie against him. I hope you understand the entire game now depends on me and has to be played out with utmost caution."

Rai sahib was crestfallen. Khanna was one of his closest friends. They had studied together, they partied together; yet he was expecting a commission. How mercenary could he be? After all, he had lavished so many favours on Khanna. Was it not for a day like this? He always sent the first crop of fresh fruits and vegetables from his garden to Khanna. It was Khanna who was the first to receive invitations for any festival or party at his home. And this is what he got in return for his kindness?

Rai sahib shook his head sadly and said, "Whatever you say, but do remember I consider you a brother."

Khanna said gratefully, "You are very kind, friend. I too have always treated you like an elder brother and still do so. I don't hold any secrets from you, however business is a different ballgame altogether. In business, no one is a friend or a brother. Just as I can't insist for a higher commission using the liberty of our long association, you should also not ask for any concession in my commission. I assure you I will try to manage the maximum discount that I can. You come to office tomorrow and initiate the paperwork. By the way, did you hear this one? It's the latest! Mehta sahib has fallen madly in love with Malti. All his philosophy has flown out of the window. He visits her more than twice every day and they go together for their evening walk. I am the only person who has never gone to her house. Perhaps she is trying to get back at me this way. There was a time when it was Mr. Khanna who was everything for her. Whenever she needed money, she would send me a note. But now she looks the other way. I got a watch from France, especially for her. I went to give it to her but she declined to accept it. I sent her grapes from Kashmir. She returned them as well. I am really surprised how people change."

This news about her insolent behavior warmed the cockles of his heart but Rai sahib kept up a façade of polite concern and expressed his sympathy- "Even if she was in love with Mehta, there was no reason to be discourteous with friends."

"That is my main grouse, brother! I knew right from the beginning I won't be able to woo her. Honestly, I was never under the illusion that Malti was in love with me. I never expected anything remotely like love from her. I merely admired her beauty. We know a snake is a poisonous creature yet we offer it milk. There is no bird more uncaring than a parrot, but people still keep it as a pet in a golden cage- only for its beauty and sweet squawk. For me, Malti was like a parrot. I should have realised what was coming. I spent thousands of rupees on her. Whenever her note arrived requesting me for money, I dispatched it without delay. By the way, the car she drives is mine. I ruined my personal life for her. I neglected my wife for her. For years, I have not spoken a kind word to Govindi. Like an ill man who develops distaste for good food, I rejected Govindi's love and attachment for me. Malti made me dance to her tune like a puppet on a string and I did it gladly. She would insult me and I would laugh thinking she was cute. She ordered me around and I bowed to her. She never listened to me and I accepted her unquestioningly. I must admit she never led me on but I followed her like a poodle. And now I see such discourteous behavior! But brother, take it from me, Khanna is not one to take it lying down. I have preserved all her notes asking for money. I will recover every *paisa* from her and see to it that Mr. Mehta leaves Lucknow for good. I will make it impossible for him to live here."

At that moment, they heard the horn of a car. Craning their necks they saw it was none other than Mr. Mehta. A fair-complexioned guy in the pink of health, dressed in *achkan* and pajama, wearing gold-rimmed spectacles, he appeared a very affable and courteous man as usual.

Khanna walked up to his car to shake hands with him. "Come in Mr. Mehta, we were just talking about you."

Mehta shook hands with both men and said, "Bless my stars! I am lucky indeed to see you both at the same place. I am sure you must have read in the papers about a plan to build a gym for women in the city. Miss Malti is the President of the committee in charge of constructing it. It is estimated to cost about two lakh rupees. You know very well how essential it is to have a facility like that for women of this town. I want your names at the top of the donors' list. Miss Malti wanted to come down herself but her father was not too well so she couldn't make it."

He shuffled his papers and passed the list of contributors to Rai sahib. The first name on the list was of Raja Suryapratap Singh and the amount entered before it was rupees five thousand. Kunwar Digvijaya's name figured next with three thousand rupees. They were followed by many other names with varying figures. Malti had donated rupees five hundred and Mehta had given a thousand.

Rai sahib said gloomily- "I see you have already mopped up forty thousand rupees."

Visibly elated, Mehta said, "The credit goes to well wishers like you. And by the way, this is a result of a mere three hour campaign. Raja Surypratap Singh seldom participates in any social work, but he wrote a cheque for it today without being asked. There is a growing awareness in the country and people are willing to contribute for any good work. A major comfort factor is the trust that their money would be spent properly. I look forward to a good contribution from you, Mr. Khanna."

Khanna wasn't impressed, "Count me out. I am not interested in such useless enterprises. I am amazed how far you people can go in kowtowing to western ideas. As it is, women are losing interest in household chores. If they get into this physical exercise thing, they will forget their homes. Women who attend to their homes do not need any physical exercise. And I don't want to help those who want to avoid household work and indulge in frivolous worldly pleasures."

Mehta was not discouraged and continued with his pitch, though with a slight change in strategy. He said, "In that case, I will not ask you for anything. If we don't believe in a cause, there's no point in shelling out money to promote it. Rai sahib, you don't agree with Mr. Khanna, or do you?"

"If I am involved with and committed to a certain mission, I don't care if it's sinful or not."

"I want you to think about it, and contribute only if you consider this work useful for society. I like Mr. Khanna's policy of being upfront about his ideas."

As amatter of fact, Khanna said, "Just because I speak my mind I am singled out for blame. I don't beat around the bush."

Smiling feebly, Rai sahib muttered under his breath- "I can't decide for myself therefore I simply copy what other gentlemen are doing."

"Then sign a good amount for the cause."

"I will write whatever you say."

"Then you shouldn't sign a cheque for less than two thousand."

Rai sahib said in a hurt voice, "Is that all you think I am worthy of?"

However he quickly picked up a pen, wrote his name on the list and scribbled 'five thousand' against it.

Mehta took the paper from him, feeling quite embarrassed. He was so confused he forgot to thank Rai sahib for his gesture.

Khanna flashed a look at Rai sahib that conveyed both surprise and sarcasm, as though he wanted to tell him he was an ass to be duped in this manner.

All of a sudden Mehta gave a bear hug to Rai sahib and exclaimed loudly: "Three cheers for Rai sahib, Hip Hip Hurrah!"

Khanna was sufficiently riled and could not hide his irritation any more. "Well! After all, men like him are kings. If they won't donate left, right and centre, who will?"

Mehta switched his charms on Khanna, "I consider you the king of all kings. You rule over them. All their fancy mansions are mortgaged to you."

Rai sahib was tickled. He chortled in delight - "Rightly said, Mehtaji. We are kings only in name. The real king maker is our banker."

Mehta went full throttle with his charm, "I don't hold anything against you, Khannaji. If you don't want to be involved with this project right now, it's no problem; but I am sure one day you will. All big institutions and projects run on the support of wealthy people; they have financed the nationalist movement for two to three years. Who pays for these proliferating schools and *dharamshalas*? Today bankers have the whole world in their pocket. "

He was unstoppable and continued with his monologue- "The government is under the control of bankers. I am not giving up on you yet. Spending two to four thousand rupees is nothing for a person who can boldly go to jail for the cause of the nation. We have decided that Govindi Devi will lay the foundation stone for this Gym. Very soon we will meet the governor and I am sure he will help us. You know how keen Lady Wilson is about women's empowerment? Raja sahib and some other gentlemen wanted Lady Wilson to lay the foundation stone, but we decided otherwise and insisted the honor should go to one of our own sisters. I hope you will at least drop by on the occasion, won't you?"

"Yes, of course! When Lord Wilson is coming, it is almost obligatory for me to be present. This way you will manage to rope in quite a few others as well. I can now see your game plan. Rich aristocrats deserve this for they are fooled easily. When people have more wealth than is required by them, wealth finds it own exit routes. If it is not spent otherwise, it will be spent on gambling, racing or indulging in other vices."

It was eleven o'clock and time for Khanna to leave for his office. Mehta took leave and Rai sahib also got up to go but Khanna waved at him to remain seated.

"Don't go yet, Rai sahib. You can see for yourself what a pickle Mehta has landed me into. He has cleverly manoeuvred it so the foundation stone will be placed by Govindi. How can I stay indifferent to it all? I fail to understand how he got her to accept this and what puzzles me most is how he got Malti to toe his line on this. Do you think there is more than what meets the eye here?"

Rai sahib spoke what Khanna wanted to hear. He said, "In my opinion, a woman should consult her husband before deciding on such issues."

Khanna warmed up to Rai sahib as expected, "Govindi gets my goat for exactly these reasons and they blame me for being short tempered. Don't you think I should stay away from this hassle? It is meant for those who have spare money, spare time and a huge craving for attention. I know where all this is headed. A few gentlemen will step in as general secretaries, treasurers and other office bearers; they will find reason to invite senior officials and party with them besides flirting with young college girls under the guise of the club. Physical fitness is a camouflage since such clubs are started with entirely different goals in mind. The end losers will be people like me and my friends who are wealthy. Unfortunately, Govindi will be the cause of all this."

He got up from his chair impatiently and sat down again. His irritation at Govindi was mounting by the minute. He caught his head in both hands and said- "I don't know what it's coming to?"

"Don't you worry," said Rai sahib, in a bid to assure his friend, " It's simple- you tell Govindi to send a letter expressing thanks and regrets and that will be the end of it. I walked into this trap; how come you landed in this mess?"

Khanna paused to consider what he suggested and said, "It's not as simple as you think. The news must have reached Lady Wilson by now and the whole city must be aware of what's up. Who knows? It might be in the newspapers in a day or so. I suspect this is Malti's mischief. It's her way of getting back at me."

"I agree. It sounds quite probable."

"She wants to humiliate me."

"You can go out of town suddenly a day before the foundation stone laying ceremony."

"Oh no, Rai sahib! That alone will blow up into a big issue. I have to attend the programme even if I am down with cholera."

As soon as Rai sahib took leave, Khanna promptly went to Govindi and accosted her rudely, "Why did you accept the offer to lay the foundation stone for this health club?"

Govindi wanted to tell him how delighted she was to receive that honour and with what dedication she was penning her speech for that day other than the marvelous verses she had composed to recite to the august audience. Actually, she had assumed Khanna would be pleased about it. After all, any honour accorded to her was indirectly an honour for her husband. She didn't have the faintest idea that Khanna could have an objection to what she had accepted to do. Lately, she had perceived warmth in her husband's attitude towards her and felt quite upbeat about it. As a result of those pleasant vibes she was enthused with a positive energy to charm the audience that day.

When she saw Khanna's sour face and heard what he said, her heart skipped several beats. Guiltily, she said, "Doctor Mehta was insistent; that's why I accepted it."

"If Doctor Mehta requests you to leap into a well, I guess you will be equally obedient and obliging."

Govindi was at a loss for words. She simply stood tongue tied, looking searchingly at him.

"If God has not blessed you with intelligence, why don't you consult me before opening your mouth? Mehta and Malti are tricking me into coughing up at least two thousand for their club and are using you as their pawn towards this end. But I have decided not to allow them to succeed and won't give them a single *paisa*. Now you sit down and write a letter to Mehta expressing your regrets and inability to honour that commitment."

Govindi thought for a moment and said, "Why don't you write that letter?"

"Why should I write that letter? You discussed everything with him. It's you who should put it in writing and refuse him"

"If he asks me for a reason what should I say to that?"

"Go take a flying leap! That's what you should tell him! I simply am not interested in contributing anything for his house of sleaze."

"But who is pushing you to contribute?"

Khanna bit his lip in exasperation.

"How silly can you be? Will you lay the foundation stone and not announce a donation towards the cause? Do you have the faintest idea how these things are done?"

Govindi felt cornered and crushed. In sheer frustration she said, "Ok, that's fine. I will send him a note today."

"Do it right now."

Khanna went out and started checking the mail which had just arrived that day. The servants always brought the letters to his residence if he was delayed in reaching the office. He opened the first envelope.

Sugar stocks were up. He brightened visibly and opened the second letter. The committee appointed to fix a ceiling on the rate of sugarcane had decided against passing an order to that effect. He had heard of the proposal but Agnihotri raised such a hue and cry and insisted on forming a committee to go into the issue. He had got a fitting reply from the committee and justifiably had egg on his face. The question of right pricing was an issue between peasants and sugar mill owners. What did the government have to do with it?

He heard a car in the porch and saw Miss Malti step out of it. She was pleasant and fresh like a lotus, the very epitome of energy and enthusiasm. She appeared like a little doll without a care, unhurried and relaxed – as if supremely confident the world would always roll out the red carpet for her. Khanna went out into the veranda to greet her.

"Was Mehtaji here?" she quizzed.

"Yes, he did drop by briefly."

"Did he say anything? Do you know where he was going?"

"No. He didn't mention anything like that."

"God knows where he is hibernating! I looked for him everywhere. How much did you give for the health club?"

Khanna had guilt written all over his face.

"I have not given any thought to it as yet."

"What is in it that you need to exercise your mind about so much? All that can wait; what's needed now is a donation for the project. I pushed Mehta to talk to you about it. He was hesitant and unwilling to discuss anything with you. He was scared he didn't know how you would react to his request. Are you aware what your miserliness will cost us? No one from the business community will come forward with anything if you hold on to your wallet. I have a feeling you have made up your mind to make me cut a sorry figure. Everybody wanted Lady Wilson to lay the foundation stone. I opposed them and proposed Govindi's name, yet you say you have not thought anything about it? You handle intricate banking riddles with ease but turn absolutely dense when it comes to basic life issues. I can only conclude that you somehow want to humiliate me. If that is the way you want it, so be it."

Malti's face had turned red. Khanna was quite flustered himself. With his bluster gone, he realised that though he was caught in a cleft that pinned down his wallet, poor Malti was caught in a worse quicksand as her reputation was at stake and she was gradually being sucked into it- a deep morass of social embarrassment. Loss of reputation and social credibility was a much more disturbing predicament than being robbed of money. Gleefully, he decided to let her stew in her own juice for a while. He had landed her in a soup and despite having no courage to annoy her, he found vicarious pleasure in discovering an opportunity to give her a piece of his mind. He also wanted to impress on her that he was no cakewalk; he wasn't dumb and knew exactly what was happening.

He pulled himself straight in front of her and said, "Your sudden benevolence surprises me, Malti."

Malti knitted her eyebrows and said, "I didn't get you."

"Is your attitude towards me the same as it was a few days earlier?"

"I don't see any difference. Why do you ask?"

"But I see a world of difference."

"Okay, fine. If for a moment we agree your reading is correct, what of it? I am here to ask a favour of you for a good cause. I have come to test the strength of my credibility in the world and in your opinion as well. But if you think by making a small donation you can extract anything more from me, other than the fame and gratitude that will come to you following your contribution, you are living in a fool's paradise."

Khanna was devastated. He was caught in a bind; there was no space to manoeuvre or squeeze out of the tight corner she had pushed him into. He dare not complain about her caustic remark, despite the thousands of rupees he had spent on her. He felt small and shrunken, cowering in shame. Embarrassed, he sputtered at her, "You got me wrong, Malti. I didn't imply anything like that."

Malti's tone was mocking- "Wish to God I am mistaken and have got it all wrong, for otherwise, I will put miles between you and me. I am attractive and I have scores of others who angle for me. I have been graceful enough to accept your gifts and even take money from you, at times, when I needed it for I have turned down presents and gifts from everybody else. If you developed different ideas because of your presumptuous and haughty nature, you can still be forgiven for it as it is a common error of male vanity. But I want you to understand very clearly that no man has ever won a woman's heart by flaunting his wealth. It has never happened in the past and shall never happen in the future."

Khanna heard her in shocked silence. Each word sounded like a thunderclap on his reddening ears. With each word he sunk lower into the ground. At last, he could take it no longer and pleaded with her- "I beg of you, Malti, don't humiliate me any further. If nothing, you should at least retain friendly feelings for me."

Even as he spoke those words, he reached into the drawer of his desk and took out his cheque book, signed one for a thousand rupees and handed it over to her with some trepidation.

Malti plucked the cheque from his hand with a caustic comment, "Is this the fees of my friendship or a donation for the health club?"

Khanna eyes misted as he said "Stop it, Malti. Spare me, please. Why do you insist on rubbing it in?"

Malti burst into peals of laughter, "Now look at this! I give you a chiding and walk away with your thousand rupees as well. I hope you will not be a naughty boy again?"

"Not for the life of me. No."

"Now pull your ears, if you are really sorry."

"I'll pull my ears but please have mercy and let go of me. Leave me alone to chew on this and cry in solitude. Today you have snuffed all joy..."

Malti's laughter rang out like bells, more strident than before.

"Now watch out, Khanna – you have insulted me enough. You know very well beauty will not be slighted. I have done you a good deed and you blame me for it?"

Khanna stared at her perplexed, confused and slightly angry- "You have done me a good deed or struck me below the belt?"

"Of course, it's a good deed. I was pinching your hard earned money and building a fortune for myself. Now you have wisened up."

"Why are you rubbing salt in my wounds? Why insist on turning the knife? I am human and vulnerable, am I not?"

She looked at him curiously, as if sizing him up, wondering if she really doubted he was human.

"So far I do not see any evidence to support your contention."

“I always thought you were an absolute riddle. Today it’s proven beyond doubt.”

“For you I was always a riddle and shall remain one forever.”

With those parting words, she turned around and breezed away like a free bird, leaving Khanna holding his head with both hands and wondering how much of that woman was fact and how much of her was fiction.

❁❁❁

23

Hori's home wore a forlorn deserted look since the day Gobar walked off in a huff with his wife and child. Dhania missed little Chunnu. Though, Jhuniya was Chunnu's mother but it was Dhania who actually nursed the child since he was an infant. She would bathe him, massage his body and clean it with a paste of flour, oil and turmeric powder every morning and whenever she had time to spare from her daily chores, she'd sit down and play with him. Her affection and love for the child was an antidote to the miseries of her existence. When he smiled at her, she would admire his glowing baby face and drift into a different world, far removed from worries and tribulations. That source of reprieve was now gone. When she saw his vacant cradle, she felt pained beyond measure.

She failed to understand why Jhuniya had turned against her. Gobar had not once talked back at her; but this wretch made him dance to her tune. She barely bothered to nurse the child; what she would do once she was freed of constraints of the larger family, worried Dhania no end. She would doll herself up and be more concerned about her styling her braids and wondering whether they were well oiled or not, rather than look after the baby. The poor child would cry, all alone, unattended on the floor. As it is, he was always under the weather--cough cold, loose motions; she felt more irritated as she thought about it. But Gobar retained the same soft spot in her mind. She laid the blame squarely on Jhuniya, the temptress who had cast a spell on her gullible son. Rebuffed and isolated by her own family, she chanced upon a dumb boy like Gobar and wormed her way into his heart.

Hori often ticked her off on this. "You only blame Jhuniya for whatever happened," he said, "why don't you blame our son who is a different man today? Do you think she could have left without his willful consent? The city has done things to him, he is not the old boy you knew."

Dhania turned on him. "You keep your mouth shut," she snarled, "You are the one responsible for her ill behaviour. I would have sent her packing the day she arrived; it was you who pushed me into keeping her or I would have sent her away."

Bales of corn had piled up in his home. Hori was all set to leave for the village mart to thresh the corn. He looked back over his shoulder and said, "If for a moment, we assume she has actually turned Gobar against us; why should you tie yourself into knots over it? This is what's happening in every home all over the world. Gobar is not any different. He has his own family to worry about. Why should he bother about us?"

"I think you are the root cause of all problems."

"Then throw me out as well. You take the bulls and thresh corn. I'll sit back and smoke my *chillum*."

"You mind the kitchen; I will look after the fields."

Irritation was swamped by light hearted banter which is its instant remedy. Both laughed as Dhania sat down to comb Rupa's unruly hair and Hori went on his way to thresh corn.

Spring was in full bloom, extending an amorous invitation to life through the pleasant aroma wafting in the bracing breeze. *Koels* hopped from branch to branch in the mango trees, stirring tired hearts awake in renewed joy with their sweet and soulful cries. A crowd of *mynahs* sat on *mahua* trees. The fresh tangy aroma of neem and eucalyptus made the atmosphere heady and light. When Hori reached the mango grove, he saw sunlight create starry patterns on the ground as it filtered through the dense foliage. His morose and disappointed mood perked up and a song burst forth his lips.

Decked in a resplendent pink *saree*, Dulari Sahuain was approaching from the other end. She wore large silver anklets on her feet and a thick chain of gold around her neck. Unlike her face which was dry and shrivelled, her mood was fresh and feisty. There was a time when on his way back from the fields, Hori flirted with her casually. She was like a sister-in-law and a continual banter was the usual custom between the two as a part of the relationship. Ever since her husband died, Dulari hardly ventured out of the house alone. From the ramparts of her shop, where she spent all day, Dulari kept herself abreast of the latest gossip and rumour. She was ever present to resolve disputes between people but had no hesitation in charging hefty interest from them if they bought anything for credit. Unfortunately, she rarely got her loans back as creditors took it easy with her while the poor woman kept calculating the rates of interest and money due to her. Since filing cases or approaching the police to recover dues was beyond her; she utilised her sharp tongue in place of legalese and corporal authority. Unfortunately, as she advanced in age, the sharpness of her tongue blunted simultaneously. Of late, people laughed when she threw shrill insults at them and took her protests in their stride. They would tell her it was high time she gave amnesty to all her debtors. They said their blessings would help her in the afterlife. But Dulari hated the mention of an afterlife.

Hori teased her, "*Bhabhi*, you are looking so young today."

Sahuain dimpled and said, "It's Tuesday, the day of the evil eye. When I dress people stare at me unnecessarily as if they have never seen a woman. Pateshwari has still not got over his old ways."

Hori paused in his tracks. This was too interesting a conversation to let pass. He turned towards her as his bulls lumbered ahead.

"Don't say it! He is a reformed man, my lady, he's almost a saint. Haven't you noticed, every fortnight on the full moon day, he attends spiritual discourses and goes to the temple for prayers twice every day?" said Hori.

"All scoundrels turn saintly as they advance in years. They have to atone for their sins, don't they? I am an old woman; why would they flirt with me?"

"You are not an old woman, *bhabhi*. I think you..."

"Not another word! Hold your tongue unless you are hungry for an earful. You have a grown son who's started earning abroad, yet you never offered me a treat for his achievements."

"Trust me, *bhabhi;* I haven't touched a *paisa* of what he earns. I have no idea what he saved, what he brought and where he spent it. I merely got a pair of *dhotis* and a *pagri*. That's all."

"Count your stars that he's started earning! One day he will take over and manage all your affairs. God bless him. Now you should also consider paying back some part of your loan."

"I will return every *paisa* I took from you, *bhabhi*. Just let that money come to me. And if it takes time, please remember, we are no outsiders or strangers. We are family."

Sahuain was disarmed by his words. She smiled and went her way. Hori went to the market and settled the bulls in a corner. There was a huge crowd at the mart where people were threshing corn and drying hay. Right from blacksmiths, woodcutters and priests and beggars, everyone was making an effort to make their presence felt. There was a carnival-like atmosphere. A poor woman sat hawking berries and cashew nuts, a straggler was selling *pakodas* and some sweetmeats. Pandit Datadin arrived to check out Hori's crops. Jhinguri Singh strolled in and took a seat close to him.

Datadin took out a pouch of tobacco and began rubbing it on his palm before he offered it to Jhinguri Singh. He said- "Did you hear the latest about what the government is coming up with? They are cautioning moneylenders to reduce interest rates or face arrest."

Jhinguri Singh took a pinch of the snuff, popped it in his mouth and replied, "Well, one thing is for certain. If you are needy, you will always come to me- whatever be the interest that I charge. This announcement doesn't bother us- unless the government itself makes arrangements to deliver loans to these guys at their doorstep. We will write lower rates in the books but deduct the relevant amount before releasing the loan. What can the government do about it?"

"That's' well said, but they are also wise to it; rest assured, they will think up some way to get around those tactics."

"They can't do anything."

"What if they rule that unless we sign on a stamp paper, countersigned by the village headman, the loan papers will not be held valid?"

"If someone needs a loan real bad, he will see to it the headman vouches and signs it. We will deduct our twenty-five percent, come what may."

"Fine ! But what if you are caught forging papers? In you go for fourteen years!"

Jhinguri Singh guffawed loudly. "What do you think, *pundit*?" he said, "You assume the world will change if they add a few lines to the law book? Law and justice will always rest with him who has money power. Aren't there laws that prohibit force and intimidation of these people? How many of us are scared of that law? Those peasants who wise up to it are co-opted by us. We use them to subjugate others. This is how the writ runs. We have nothing to fear. Nothing is going to change. Trust me."

He stood up and took a round of the mart and came back within no time and sat down, pulling the stool closer to him. He said "Whatever happened to Matadin's marriage plans? You are a father and I suggest you should get him married soon. He's getting a bad name unnecessarily."

Datadin knew the implied insult behind this remark. He flared up and said, "Anyone can talk behind my back. They can say whatever they please but let me see who dares talk about this in my presence. Before pointing fingers people should emulate, at least, half the austerity we practice. I know dozens of people who rarely go to the temple, nor practice basic tenets of religion. They have nothing to do with scriptures but have no qualms in calling themselves Brahmins. How dare anyone smirk at us? We haven't missed a single holy day of fasting, we've never tasted a drop of water--what to say, food--without proper ablutions. It's no joke, no mean feat adhering to the regulations. Is there anyone who can accuse us of eating anything cooked outside our house or tasting anything in the marketplace? If anyone can prove that I have sipped water from a vessel provided by anyone outside our caste, I will eat the dust below his feet. I am not saying Matadin is covering himself in glory by his actions but if he has made a mistake once, it's now his duty to make amends and stay away from her. I can say boldly- no shame in it; womankind is purity incarnate."

In his heydays, Datadin was himself quite a romantic but was obstinately steadfast in following the regulations of his calling. Matadin tread the path blazed by his illustrious father where the essence of religion lay in rituals of worship, tenets and principles that were secured within the strict adherence of dietary restrictions. When father and son clung so tenaciously to the rigid codes of that essence, how dare anybody question their sanctity?

Datadin rattled off a long list of exemplary Brahmins, mentioned in the Mahabharata and the Puranas, who by their expansive act of accepting women from other castes, actually elevated their social standing. He explained that the progeny of those women were considered Brahmins and most Brahmins of the present age were their direct descendents. Since this co-option of women was coming down the ages, there was nothing to be ashamed of having a low caste in one's backyard.

Enamoured by his eloquence, Jhinguri Singh said, "In that case, why do some Brahmins hide behind their caste names?"

"Down the ages our great name has lost its potency. It is smothered under the gibberish of a modern age. Now we have to perforce live within the community and observe social compromises. I did ask many--you included--to suggest something but if no one comes forward to offer their daughters hand in marriage there is a limit to what I can do about it. I can't conjure up a bride for my son magically."

Jhinguri Singh pulled him up on this and said, "Don't you say that! I herded fathers of two girls before you but you acted pricey and scared them off. On what basis do you demand a dowry of five hundred or a thousand rupees from them? What can you boast of other than ten measures of land and a propensity to beg?"

Datadin was touched to the quick. Stroking his beard sagely, he said, "Maybe I am a beggar and don't own more than ten measures of land but I gave away no less than five hundred rupees each in the weddings of my two daughters. Why shouldn't I demand a similar amount for my son? And as far as social status is concerned; you might consider a clergy man seeking donations as a beggar but for me it's like an investment, it's like a bank. *Zamindaars* and banks may come and go - but the clergy's relationship with its constituents is forever. As long as the Hindu caste system survives, Brahmins and their patronage will be relevant forever. I make a neat packet without stepping out of home. If I am lucky I get three to four hundred in one go, besides clothes, utensils and other stuff. If nothing, the least I get is a few brass plates and three or four *annas* as donations. A *zamindaar* or moneylender's job is no patch on this. Moreover, Siliya the girl, who works for us, is of more use than any Brahmin girl who will do little except sit at home like a nice high caste bride, at best cooking a few *rotis*. On the contrary, Siliya is equal to three girls working day and night. I don't give her anything except basic meals; a new *saree* once a year, nothing more than that."

In the shade of the adjoining tree was Datadin's private threshing space. Four bulls went round in circles, threshing the grain. A *chamar* called Dhanna handled the bulls as Siliya carried the threshed grain to separate it from the chaff. At another end of the shade sat Matadin, rubbing oil on his *lathi*.

Dusky complexioned and slight of build, much of what Siliya lacked in beauty was compensated by her charm. Her laughter, her eyes and the suppleness of her limbs emanated a sprightly exuberance, which shone through her frame, sweaty with husk and dust-laden grime and tousled hair. She ran up and down, tossing the grain in the air to blow away the chaff as if it was a game that she loved and played intensely.

Matadin said, "We must chaff the grain by evening, Siliya. If you are tired, I can take over."

Siliya replied brightly, "You don't have to chip in, *pundit*. I will finish the job before evening."

"Ok, then I will take the bags to the granary. How can you handle everything alone?"

"Don't worry. I will chaff the grain and transfer the bags much before nightfall."

Meanwhile Dulari Sahuain was on her rounds, recovering all petty dues pending with the villagers. Siliya had borrowed two *paisa* worth of colouring powder on Holi from her shop and hadn't paid up yet. She came up to Siliya and said, "It's over a month now but whenever I ask for the payment, you strut away making one excuse or the other. I insist on taking the payment today."

Matadin slid away quietly. He had no intention of bailing Siliya out of her debts despite his exploitation of her innocence and youth. He used Siliya as a machine and did not consider her more than an automated farming implement. He knew how to use her attachment to him for his benefit. When she raised her eyes to look for him, he was nowhere to be found. She said, "Please, Sahuain, don't scream your lungs out. Here, take this grain worth four *paisa* instead of the two I took from you. I wasn't going anywhere, so don't get so worked up."

She scooped about a seer of grains from the mound on the ground and poured it in Sahuain's open apron. At that moment, a visibly irritated Matadin appeared from behind the tree where he was hiding and caught hold of Dulari's apron and said- "Drop everything, Sahuain; this is no loot."

Turning blood shot angry eyes at Siliya, he barked - "How dare you give her these grains without permission? Did you ask anyone? Who are you to give away my grains for free?"

Sahuain threw back the grains on the heap as Siliya stared at him, astounded and dumbstruck. She felt helpless as if the branch on which she had settled down in comfort was axed in one binding flash. Embarrassed and blushing wildly, she turned to her tearfully and said, "I will pay up later, Sahuain. Please excuse me today."

Dulari looked at her in pity and threw a look of disgust at Matadin before she turned back and walked away.

Siliya continued with the chaffing and asked him with hurt pride- "Don't I have any right over your things?"

Matadin glared at her. "No! Certainly not. You have no right over my possessions. You work, therefore you eat. If you think you can eat and trash my things as well, you need to think again. If you aren't happy here, go work someplace else. I can get more people to work for me. We don't make you work for free; you get food and clothes, don't you?"

Siliya looked at him like a pet bird whose owner suddenly releases it from its cage after clipping its wings. It wasn't clear whether her eyes bore signs of pain or disgust. Unable to bear the weight of her incapacitated wings,. Siliya wondered if she had any other refuge to turn to. She was a married woman; her husband could beat and thrash her but she had no choice, no alternative. She remembered it was not over two years when he followed her in the groves and river banks, blinded by desire. One day, he took his *Janeyu* in his hands and swore on the holy thread that he would treat her like his wife for the rest of his life. Today, he trashed all that for a handful of grains; her confused mind couldn't fathom this dichotomy in his behaviour.

She didn't utter a word. Her throat felt parched, her hands were numb as she went about her job in a daze.

Suddenly her father, two brothers and a few other *chamars* appeared on the scene and surrounded Matadin. Her mother was also there in the gaggle of people following them. She came up to her and snatched the basket from her hands and muttered choicest expletives. "You idiot! If you had to labour like this, why did you leave home and come here? If you had to remain a low caste *chamarin* what was the need to humiliate your community? You should be dead, disgraceful wretch!"

Jhinguri Singh and Datadin scampered up to them and sensing their aggressive stance tried to cool their frayed tempers. Jhinguri Singh asked Siliya's father if everything was all right. "What is it, *chawdhary*? Why are you so mad?"

Siliya's father, Harkhu was sixty years old, dark, emaciated and wrinkled like a dry chilly pod and equally bitter. He said, "We have not gone crazy, *thakur*. Today we will either convert Matadin into a *chamar* like us or bloody this field with blood- his or ours. Siliya is a woman; she has to go to someone's house. We have nothing to say on that but whoever keeps her with him should become one of us. You cannot make us a Brahmin; we can make you a *chamar*. You convert us into Brahmins - our entire community is willing and waiting. If you can't, then you become one of us. Eat and drink with us, stay with us. If you want to trample and walk over our honour; allow us to at least, walk into your religiosity."

Datadin stomped his *lathi* on the ground. "Mind your words, Harkhu! Your daughter is right there in front of you. Take her and go away. We have not tied her to our doorstep. She works for us; she is paid for it. We have many who will replace her."

Siliya's mother gestured with her finger and said sarcastically, "That's wonderful, *pundit*! I love your fairness! I wonder if you would be as sane and composed if your daughter had run away with a *chamar*. We are *chamars,* therefore we are not supposed to feel bad about anything. We will not leave this place with Siliya alone; Matadin will come with us. He's the one who has trifled with our honour. You are so sanctimonious; you'll sleep with her but won't drink water if she offers it to you! It's this stupid woman who wags her tail despite such humiliation. I would poison the man who did this to me."

Harkhu called out to his men- "Did you hear what they said? Why do you stand like fools doing nothing about it?"

This was the cue for two men from the crowd accompanying Harkhu to pounce on Matadin and grab his arms. One tore off the *Janeyu* around his neck before Datadin or Jhinguri Singh could reach for their *lathis*. Two *chamars* came up and shoved a large bone into Matadin's mouth. Matadin gritted his teeth but the horrible thing had already touched his lips. He felt nauseated and his mouth opened in revulsion. The bone fell deeper into it. By then almost everybody in the market had gathered there, hearing the commotion, but strangely, not one made an effort to hold back the desecrators of faith. No one really liked Matadin. His dishonourable intentions towards their mothers and sisters raised the hackles of almost everyone in the village. In their heart of hearts they were relishing his predicament but outwardly they tried to admonish the *chamars*.

Hori said, "OK, that will be enough, Harkhu! Watch out; I suggest you leave immediately."

Harkhu replied unfazed, "You have daughters as well, Hori Mahato. You should know better. If things go on like this, no one's honour will remain intact in this village."

After making their point so vehemently to the enemy, the attackers thought it wise to leave. Popular opinion could swing any way. It's better to be cautious, prudent and know when to retreat.

Matadin was throwing up violently. Datadin rubbed his back and said, "I'll have them sent to jail for five years at the very least. They'll suffer for their sins."

Harkhu replied arrogantly, "Who cares? We don't have a comfortable life like yours. We'll earn our bread or half of it; wherever we toil and sweat. Jail is fine with us."

Exhausted after throwing up his lunch, Matadin lay listless on the ground. The notions of superiority which prompted his philandering, pride and masochism were blown apart. That piece of bone had sullied not only his body but his soul as well. His faith hinged on ideas of sacredness in food and caste distinctions. He doubted if all his piety, remorse and regret could restore his sense of self-worth. Had this happened in private, he could have papered over it but this was a real-time incident, witnessed by a large number of people. He was demeaned utterly. He feared he would be considered an outcaste from his community for having violated the tenets, even if accidentally and by force. It was so shameful that none from the crowd of onlookers stepped in to prevent this attack on religion. He was sure his mother would hate him along with the multitudes of others who bowed reverentially before him in the past. Now they wouldn't mention it but look the other way when they crossed him on the street. He couldn't go to a temple nor touch the utensils in his family kitchen.

Siliya stood with her eyes transfixed to the ground, halted in her chaffing by this sudden development. She felt devastated; the humiliation heaped on Matadin seemed a direct attack on her. Her mother strode up to her angrily. "Why are you looking so shocked? Why are you standing here like this? You've ruined the name of your ancestors; what else do you want to wreck beyond this? Come home or I will break every bone in your body."

Siliya didn't move an inch. She felt angry with her father, mother and brothers. Why didn't they just leave her alone? Why did they meddle in her affairs? She would lead the life she wanted. Matadin's behaviour had hurt her deeply but her people had no business to interfere in her life like this. They had wanted to convince her she was humiliated in Matadin's house. Seconds ago, she was very disturbed by his comments and behaviour but now her anger was diverted to her parents and other members of her community. Their unpardonable acts of sacrilege had turned her mounting indifference to a two-timing cheat into a guilty attachment for her wronged husband.

"I won't go," she said, "won't you let me survive in peace?"

The old woman snapped at her, "So you won't come with us? Eh?"

"No!"

Her brothers caught her by her wrists and began to drag her away. Siliya prostrated herself on the ground. Her brothers held her by the hair and dragged her. Her saree ripped at the edges; the skin around her waist was blue with all the pulling and dragging but she stood her ground firm.

Harkhu turned around to his boys and said- "Let her be. We'll assume she is dead. But if she dares to come to our door I will skin her alive."

Siliya risked an immediate reaction by retorting defiantly, "Ok, skin me alive if I do. Who's coming anyway?"

The old woman delivered a few kicks to her before her husband pulled her away.

Siliya cried out, "Is this why you raised me from a baby? You should have killed me in your womb. You defiled my man's faith in your hatred for me; what did you gain by this sacrilege? Now he will be mad at me as well. But I don't care. I will remain with him, even if he rejects me. I cannot leave him after the humiliation you've heaped on him for my sake. I'd rather die than leave him. He held my hand once; I will be his forever."

Datadin poured his irritation and frustration on her. "Why didn't you go away with them, Siliya? What more do you want? You've ruined us; isn't that enough for you?"

Siliya looked up at him. Her eyes shone with the light of conviction. "Why should I go with them? I will stay with the one who held my hand and called me her own."

The old brahmin threatened her, "You dare step into my house! I will beat the daylights out of you."

Siliya replied with equal audacity, "I will stay wherever he takes me--in a palace or under a tree by the roadside."

Matadin sat still throughout. The afternoon sun was shining through the trees. The sunlight created patterns on his face as beads of sweat formed on his brow but he had remained impassive, shocked into numbness. But now he broke his silence and said, "What now, father?"

Datadin put a loving hand on his head and said, "What can I say, son? Go take a bath and get dressed. We will do whatever other *pundits* advise us to do. However, one thing is for certain, you will have to forsake Siliya."

For the first time after her people left, Matadin looked at her angrily, "I won't ever see her again but will I be fine after due repentance?"

"There is no stigma after you repent."

"Then go seek their advice right away."

"I will, son. Yes, I will"

"But if they say repentance isn't enough?"

"Then that's their decision; what can I say?"

"You won't tell me to go away?"

Datadin was overwhelmed, "That will never happen. I can give up my faith, forego all prestige and recognition in the community but I will never forsake you, son."

Matadin stood up and started walking slowly behind his father. When Siliya got up and limped after them, he turned around and spoke harshly, "Don't follow me. I have nothing to do with you. Haven't your people done enough to me?"

Siliya held his hand and said, "Of course you have everything to do with me! There are many in the village more handsome, rich and honourable than you; but I know no one but you. You have walked me into a one way street. You cannot wish it away and I am also not going anywhere. I will beg and slave but won't leave you ever."

She let go of his hand and went back to her job, chaffing the grain. Hori was still around, threshing his bales of wheat. Dhaniya had come to call him for meals. Hori pulled the bulls out of the threshing zone and tied their leash to a tree. He said, "You too should go and eat, Siliya. Dhaniya is here; she will mind your stuff while you are gone. Oh! Your *saree* is torn and there's blood on it! Your folks are so cruel."

Siliya looked at him with a pinched face, "Who isn't cruel, *dada*? There's no mercy in the world."

"Why? What did he say?"

"He says he's got nothing to do with me."

"Oh, really? So that's what he said?"

"They think they will save face by dumping me but how can they brush aside what's obvious to the world? How does it make a difference to me? If they don't want to bother about feeding me; I am ok with that. I will continue to labour as I do today. As for a place to rest my head, if I ask someone to provide me a little space where I could sleep at night, nobody will refuse. Would you?"

Dhania was touched and said, "Of course, my girl, there's plenty of space for everyone in God's world. You come and stay at my place."

However, Hori was circumspect and cautious, "I hope you know what you are doing. How will the *pundit* take it?"

"We are not obliged by them in any way. They took away her self respect, forcing her community to excommunicate her and now they say she doesn't mean anything to them. They are worse than butchers."

But Hori was not convinced. He maintained it was not a very bright idea to invite Siliya into his home. He did not like the attitude of Siliya's folks. She was their daughter; they could have taken her back, lovingly or forcibly but they had no business destroying Matadin's faith.

Dhania poured scorn on him. She said, "Well, your ideas of justice are so skewed. All men think alike. Such issues were not raised when Matadin played with her sentiments and wronged her. Now that he has got a taste of his own medicine, why does it hurt everybody? I think Harkhu and his men did a great job. Siliya, you come with me. I am amazed at the nerve of your parents to attack you in the manner they did."

Turning to Hori she said, "You go and tell Sona to hurry here immediately. I will be home shortly."

When Hori turned to go, Siliya fell at Dhania's feet, crying bitterly.

❁❁❁

24

Sona was in her seventeenth year and it was high time she was married. Hori was thinking about it for the past two years but there was not much he could do about it, given his bad financial state. But this year the wedding had to happen, whether he had to borrow or sell off the fields. If Hori had his way, he would have got her married two years ago. He wanted the ceremony to be a simple one. But Dhania said that no matter how austere the arrangement, at least two hundred and fifty rupees would be required after cutting all corners.

After the Jhuniya episode, their image had taken a beating and it was not possible to find a suitable match without spending that amount. Last season they had not made much money. The pact with Datadin stood at fifty percent but the wily old man interpreted the calculations of seed costs and labour charges so craftily that ultimately their share came down to twenty-five percent in real terms despite having to pay full taxes. The other crops were destroyed because of heavy rains and termites. However, this year the yield had been good and additional crops too had flowered well. Grains for the marriage were already in store and if they could somehow manage an extra two hundred rupees, the problem was not insurmountable.

If Gobar would give one hundred, Hori could manage the remaining hundred on his own. Jhinguri Singh and Mangru Sah had softened their stance after Gobar's visit and had turned more forthcoming with help. With Gobar earning well in the city, repayments would not be a big issue.

One day Hori floated the idea of going to meet Gobar for a few days.

But Dhania had not forgotten Gobar's harsh parting words. She refused to take any money from him, not even a *paisa*.

Sufficiently irritated, Hori said, "But how are we going to manage without him. Do you have any suggestions?"

Dhania shook her head and said, "What if Gobar had not gone to the city, what would you have done then in that case? Do that now."

Hori had no answer to that. A moment later he asked Dhania, "I give up. What do you think we should do?"

Dhania had a ready answer to this- "Thinking is a man's job."

Not to be put down, Hori had his rejoinder ready as well, "What if I wasn't alive today? What would you have done? You tell me; we will do that."

Dhania looked at him with scorn, "I would have married her off without spending anything and nobody would have jeered at me."

Hori agreed that would have been the best way out, but what about family prestige? When his sisters were married, hundreds of guests had attended the festivities. The dowry was also a pretty heavy amount. Shows, dances, music, horses, elephants- there was quite a bit of pageantry to boast of. Even today his family enjoyed a good reputation despite the recent incidents. He had enough contacts spread over a dozen villages around his. How would he face them after an insipid wedding ceremony? It was better if he were dead. If he sold off one part of his land, he would get a hundred rupees. But a farmer's fields are dearer to him than his life and he had only three decent measures of land. If he sold one, how would he grow crops?

Days passed as they debated the right course of action. No decision could be reached and soon the Dussehra festival was round the corner.

Jhinguri, Pateshwari and Nokhe Ram's sons had come home for their Dussehra vacations. All of them studied English in a local school in the adjoining town. Though they had all crossed the age of twenty they were still struggling to reach the university. They were content spending two to three years in every class in school. All the three were married. In fact, Pateshwari's heir had already sired a child. All day they would play cards, drink *'bhang'* and loaf around like dandies. During the day they would saunter past Hori's house; ogling and staring, several times a day. They timed it so that Sona would be standing at the door for some or the other work. These days she wore the same sari that Gobar had brought for her. Hori's blood seethed at it all. He didn't like it one bit.

One day, they went to bathe at the same well at which Hori was drawing water to irrigate the crops. Sona was standing by his side. When Hori saw those boys his blood began to boil.

The same evening he went to Dulari Sahuain. He thought women being tender-hearted; perhaps Dulari will pity him and give him a loan at a low rate of interest. But Dulari had her own sob story ready. There was nobody in the village who did not owe her some money, even Jhinguri Singh owed her twenty rupees; but no one was prepared to return the amount. How could she spare money for Hori?

Hori pleaded, "*Bhabhi,* it would be an act of mercy. It is not money that you will lend me; you will loosen the noose around my neck. Jhinguri and Pateshwari are eyeing my fields greedily. It is the only inheritance left for me by my forefathers; it will be shameful to lose it. Sons are expected to add to the family property, how can I be the one to squander away this ancestor's property?'

Dulari swore on the name of God that she had no money with her at that time. Those who borrowed from her had not returned the money, what could she do? Hori was not a stranger to her Sona was like her own daughter, but she was helpless. But the truth was that nobody had any money with them, so how were they to pay it back? "I can see the situation they are facing that is why I hold myself back. Everybody is struggling to make both ends meet. I wouldn't advise you to sell off the land. At least retain your self-respect, if nothing else."

Bending forward in a conspiratorial way, she said, "Pateshwari's son and his friends keep loitering around your home. All three are the same. Be cautious. They have become city boys; they don't understand the village norms. We have young boys in the village too, but they have some consideration, respect and decency in them. These mutts are rascals. My daughter was here for a few days from her in-law's place. When I saw the attitude of these boys, I called her father-in-law and sent her packing. Who has the time to play guard?"

Dulari noticed the faint mischievous smile playing on Hori's lips. She feigned annoyance, and said that if he didn't mend his flirtatious ways, she too would give it back to him. She reminded him that he was the same as he was in his youth. He would come to her shop twenty-five times a day on some pretext or the other, but she never encouraged him and barely glanced in his direction.

Hori was in a playful mood. He reminded her that no one walks in without a bait. Birds return to peck in the courtyard for the second time only if they have not been shooed off the first time.

"Goodness! You have no shame, liar!"

"Maybe you avoided looking me in the eye, but your heart always waited for me. It called me, in fact. I could always hear it!"

"Forget it. You are no mind reader. I merely felt sorry watching you demean yourself at my doorstep. You were no prince charming and you knew that."

A new customer entered her shop. It was Husaini come to buy a *paisa* worth of salt hence the leg-pulling and banter had to be cut short. After she left, in a more serious tone Dulari asked why Hori didn't approach Gobar. He could merely go and look him up and see if it was possible to get some money from him.

Disheartened, Hori replied that he had no such hopes from his son. "When boys start making money, they refuse to recognise their own folks". Hori said that he was still willing to kill his self respect and go but Dhania did not want him to go. If he went against her wishes, she would make life hell for him.

Dulari said sarcastically, "You're her slave. You let her ride over you."

"What can I do if you refuse to even glance at me?"

"Had you promised to be my slave, I'd have married you."

"It's not very late yet. I'm ready to sign and pledge my soul for just two hundred rupees. It's not too much to ask of a man."

"You won't tell Dhania about it?"

"No, I won't. I swear I will not."

"But what if you tell her?"

"You cut off my tongue if I do."

"Then off you go! Get started with the wedding plans. I'll give you the money."

Tears in his eyes, Hori bent forward to touch her feet. He couldn't utter a word.

Sahuain pulled back her legs, saying, "Now this is what I don't like. I am not doing you a favour. I'll take my money back with interest within a year. I don't trust you but I have faith in Dhania. I've heard the old Brahmin is very annoyed with you. He says he'll have you thrown out of the village if that's the last thing he does. Why have you sheltered Siliya in your house? Don't you have enough problems already? You've invited more pain for nothing."

"It is Dhania's decision to bring in that girl. What can I do?"

"I've heard that Datadin went to Kasi. A famous pundit who lives there has demanded five hundred rupees for the atonement rituals for his son. How dumb is it! When you've lost all credibility what can a thousand atonements do to wash away the stigma?"

Hori's heart leapfrogged ahead of him on his way back home. On the way he stopped by at Sobha's house and invited him to the engagement ceremony. Then they went to Datadin's house to ask him for an auspicious date for the wedding. When they reached home they stood at the door discussing the arrangements that were to be made for the wedding.

Dhania came out and said "It's so late now. Don't you want to have your food? Eat it. You have the entire night to gossip." Hori asked her to join the discussion- "The engagement ceremony will take place as we decided, right on the auspicious time as scheduled. Tell me, what needs to be organised. I know nothing about it."

"What are you discussing if you know nothing about it? Has any arrangement been made for the money or you're chewing imaginary candy?"

Proudly, Hori replied, "What is it to you? You simply give me the list of things that have to be bought."

"But I don't chew imaginary sweets."

"Okay, just tell me what purchases were made for my sister's marriage?"

"First you come clean with me; have you got the money?"

"Yes, I've got the money. Do you think I'm crazy?"

"Alright, then have your meal first; we'll talk about it later."

But when she heard that he had talked to Dulari about the money, she wrinkled her nose as much in distaste, as in disbelief.

"Taking a loan from her is a trap. Has anyone come out of that bottomless pit? The witch takes such a high interest on the loan."

"I had no other option left. Who else would have lent me the money?"

"Why don't you say that money was just an excuse to go sweet talking with her? Even at this age you won't give up your crafty ways."

"Dhania, sometimes you act so childish. Will that hag smile at a person like me? She is so uncouth she barely speaks in a civil manner."

"Who else but people like you will go to her?"

"You know nothing, Dhania. The best of people go and rub their noses at her doorstep. She has loads of money."

"Hmm? I think she must have simply nodded her head and here you go running around as if the money is already in your pocket."

"She has not merely said 'yes'. She has given me her word. A solemn promise."

After Hori went to eat his meal and Sobha returned to his house, Sona came out with Siliya. She had overheard the conversation at the door. The fact that two hundred rupees was being borrowed from Dulari for her wedding was twisting like a knot in her stomach.

An earthen lamp burnt in an alcove by the door and the wall above it had turned black with soot. The two bulls were chewing from their tubs and a stray dog sat on the floor, tongue out, waiting for food leftovers. The two girls stood near the cow shed. Sona spoke first, "Did you hear that? *Dada* is going to borrow two hundred from Sahuain for my marriage".

Siliya knew everything in fine detail. She replied, "When there is no money in the house, what else can he do?"

Staring pensively at the dark trees before her, Sona said, "I do not want my mother and father to borrow money. How will they ever return it? They are already neck-deep in debt. If they borrow two hundred more, they will be finished."

"Is it possible to marry into a good family without paying dowry? Silly girl, if you don't pay dowry, you'll land up with an old or sickly man. Will you go for an oldie?"

"Why should I go with an oldie? Was my brother old when he married Jhuniya? Did he get any dowry?"

"Family prestige is compromised in dowry-less marriages".

"I'll refuse to marry if my would-be husband or his family demands even one *paisa* in dowry."

"And suppose he says, 'your father is the one who is giving, my father is the one accepting it; what can I do about it'?"

Sona thought her decision was a formidable missive but it fizzled out like a damp squib. Disappointed, she said, "But I will definitely speak to him at least once about this. If he says he can't do anything about it, then I can always go and drown myself in the river; it's not too far from our house, in any case. My parents burnt their guts out bringing me up. Is it fair to return their kindness by burdening them with more debt as I go? If God had blessed my parents with plenty, I would have no objection if they willingly gave whatever they liked to their daughter. But not when they are so hard up. If the moneylenders lodge a case against them and auction all their belongings, they will perforce become labourers. It's better for a daughter to drown herself and die than bring such suffering to her parents. If I die, at least the family land and other properties will be saved; at least there would be a source of livelihood for them. They will weep for a few days and then accept their fate. At least, they won't have to weep for their entire life after I am married. In three to four years two hundred will double as interest will pile up. From where will my father get all that money?"

For the first time Siliya looked at the problem from an entirely different perspective. Filled with emotion, she took Sona in her embrace and said, "From where did you get so much wisdom, my sweet sister? You don't appear so wise."

"This is not about wisdom, stupid girl. Am I blind to facts or do you think I am crazy? Two hundred for my marriage, which doubles in three or four years; then two hundred more for Rupiya's wedding. Will this ever end? They will be forced to auction the cloth on their backs and my parents will be reduced to beggary.

What else? It is better I give up my life instead of ruining their lives forever. You go to Sonari early tomorrow morning and call him here. But no, wait. Calling him won't help; I wouldn't know how to put it across to him. I'll feel shy. You just convey my message to him. See what reply he gives you. Sonari is not very far- it's just across the river. Sometimes he brings his cattle over to this side. Once when his buffalo wandered into my fields, I really gave him a mouthful. Poor man! He begged me with folded hands. But tell me, did you meet Matadin recently? It is said that the Brahmins are not accepting him back into their fold?"

"Why won't they accept him? They will for sure, but his old man doesn't want to spend any money, the miser that he is. His son is living in a shed outside the house."

"Why don't you forget him? Go with someone of your own caste and live in peace. At least he won't insult you."

"Don't say that. The poor man went through such an ordeal and I let go of him? Now whether he remains a *pundit,* turns an outcaste or becomes god; for me he is just my Matadin who followed me like a lovelorn puppy from day one. Even if he becomes a Brahmin and marries in his own caste, will any Brahmin girl serve him the way I have cared for him? If he leaves me now for the sake of his name and prestige, I know in my heart of hearts that ultimately he will come back to me in the end. Just you wait you'll see."

"High hopes! He'll chew you alive if you as much as cross his path."

"Do you think I am going to call him? We all have our own ethics and principles for life. If he forgets his vows should I also forget mine?"

In the morning Siliya prepared to leave for Sonari, but Hori stopped her. Dhania had a headache. Somebody had to take her place to water the fields. Siliya could not refuse him. It was late in the afternoon by the time she got free. She left for Sonari immediately.

Late that afternoon Hori went to the well again and found Siliya missing. Angrily, he quizzed Sona about her. "Where is that girl? She is here one moment, off in another. She can't concentrate on the job at hand. Sona, do you have any idea where she is?"

Sona thought fast and came up with an excuse, "I don't know. I heard her mention there were clothes to be collected from the washerman's house; may be she's gone there."

Dhania heard the conversation and got up from her cot saying- "I'll go and do the watering. Why are you getting so angry, do you pay her for what she does?

"Doesn't she stay with us? Aren't we defamed in the entire village because of her?"

"Ok, keep quiet now. Just because she's living in one corner of the house, are we going to make her pay for it?"

"She's not living in one small corner; she's occupied one full room."

"You are talking as if the rent for that room is fifty rupees a month?"

A few hours later the watering was done. Hori did not allow Dhania to exert herself. Rupa and Sona took turns and finished the job. After they were through with it, Rupa sat down to attend to the kitchen while Sona kept glancing towards the road that led to Sonari.

There was doubt in her heart, mixed with a sense of foreboding and some hope as well. More doubt than hope. She wondered if anyone will refuse easy money if it comes in dowry. The lust for money is never sated and her would-be father-in-law Gauri Ram was one greedy man. Unlike his father, her would-be husband Mathura did have a kind heart and certain goodness too, but he would have to obey his father. Sona decided she would not rest till she gave him a piece of her mind if he did anything of that sort. She'd tell him to go and get married to a rich man's daughter, because it was impossible for her to live with such a coward. However if Gauri Ram accepted her terms, Sona would worship the ground he stood on. She'd serve him obediently, with devotion and with such reverence the likes of which she hadn't accorded to her own father. And she would also stuff Siliya's mouth with sweets and buy her things she wouldn't have dreamt of. Sona had saved the money Gobar had given to her. Her eyes lit up with a bright glow and a blush appeared on her cheeks even as she rejoiced in the thought of happy tidings.

But why wasn't Siliya back till now? Sonari wasn't very far. May be they didn't let her go back so soon. And then she saw her walking slowly. Sona's heart sank. Probably the morons didn't agree or Siliya would have come running. If they showed attitude, Sona was not going to marry into that family. They could forget about it.

Siliya did come in but instead of coming to the well, she changed track and went towards the fields. Oh! She must be scared of Hori; he would ask where she was all this while, and what would the poor girl say? Sona ran to her, hurriedly finishing the job at hand.

"What happened to you? Did you die for some time? I almost turned blind staring in that direction."

Siliya was offended. She felt very cross with Sona.

"You think I went off to sleep? You don't talk about these things on the roadside. One has to wait for the right time. Mathura had gone to the river bank with the cattle. I looked around for him for a long time and when I met him I gave him your message. I can't tell you how worried he looked when I told him about your feelings. He fell on my feet and said, 'Siliya I've not slept a wink out of sheer joy since the day I heard Sona will soon come to my house. But what can I do about my father? He doesn't listen to anyone."

Sona interrupted, "Let him not listen to anyone; Sona is equally stubborn. She'll do what she's decided. They may sit back and chew on it."

Siliya continued, "That very moment he left the cattle and took me to his father, Gauri Ram who has four large fields and the well is his own private property. He has ten measures of grasslands too. Actually he looks very comical. I could barely hide my amusement. He looks every inch a grass-cutter; though, of course, a very fortunate and rich grass cutter. There was a big argument between the two. Gauri Ram told his son point blank that it was none of his business whether he accepted any money for his marriage. Mathura was equally upfront. He said that if there was a question of money, he should forget about it for he'll marry the way he wanted to. The argument took an ugly turn as Gauri Ram began beating up his son in a sudden fit of rage. Any other son would have retaliated at the insult.

Had Mathura landed a single punch on him, Gauri Ram would not have been able to stand up again but the poor boy remained silent even after being hit fifty times with a shoe. When his father was tired of raining blows on him, he rose and walked away quietly. He went away, looking at me silently, with tears in his eyes. Then he began scolding me. He said a hundred things to me, but I wasn't the one to listen silently. Why should I fear him? I told him frankly, without mincing words, that two hundred rupees is not such a big amount and Hori won't be put on sale for this sum. Neither will it make a big difference to Gauri Ram himself; he won't turn rich with two hundred rupees. That amount will be blown up in dance and celebrations in just one night but, he'll never find such a daughter-in-law like you."

With tears in her eyes, Sona asked her, "Mahato hit his son over such a minor issue?" Siliya had meant to keep this a secret. She didn't want to tell Sona about the humiliating words that were spoken. But hearing her question, she could not control herself. She said, "It is all about Gobar *bhaiya*. Mahato said, 'A man will eat leftovers only if they are delicious. The only way to hide a dark spot is to cover it with silver'. At this, Mathura retorted, "Which household is free from blemish? There are skeletons in every cupboard. Yes, it is a different matter that one secret is public, the other is hidden from public view.' Gauri Ram was involved with a *chamarin* like me long back. He even has two sons from her. But the moment Mathura said this; the old man lost all patience. He seemed like a man possessed. That man is as ill-tempered as he is greedy; I doubt, he will ever agree for the liaison without the money."

Both the girls took the dirt track back home. Sona carried a bag full of ropes and other stuff on her head. But at the moment the burden seemed lighter than a flower. It was as if a spring of happiness and energy had burst forth within her. The valiant image of Mathura rose before her eyes and she enthroned it in her heart, washing it with her tears. It was as if the heavenly goddess had picked her up in her arms and she was floating in the crimson evening sky.

The same night, Sona was down with high fever.

The following day Gauri Ram sent a letter through a messenger.

'Respectful obeisance and greetings to the honoured Sri Hori Mahato from Gauri Ram. We have thought with a cool mind about our earlier discussion regarding the subject of dowry. We have understood that exchange of money and gifts is a burden to the families of both the bride and the groom. When we decide on a marriage, then our behaviour should be such that it doesn't affect anyone adversely. You should have no worry on account of dowry; this is our solemn promise to you. You may provide whatever feast to the guests which you can easily afford. We will not demand even that from you. We have arranged for our own cook and meals. Of course, we will accept with joy and humility whatever you will offer to welcome us with.'

Hori read the letter and ran inside the house to read it out to Dhania. He was almost ecstatic with joy, but as she listened to the letter, Dhania seemed to be lost in deep thought. A moment later, she said, "This is so decent of Gauri Ram. But we have to fulfill our duty. What will the world say? We will not be found wanting in our duties. Money will come and go but one can't forgo family-prestige for the sake of saving money. We will offer the best we can and Gauri Ram will have to accept it. You mention this in your reply to him. Don't girls have a right over their parent's earnings? No, wait. There's no use writing it. Come on, I'll send a message through the messenger."

Hori stood dumbfounded in the courtyard as Dhania gave her message to the bearer, in response to the generosity that Gauri Ram's gesture had awakened in her. Then she offered the man fruit juice and sent him away with another basket as a token gift.

After the man left, Hori said, "What is this that you've done, Dhania? I fail to understand your moods; they shift and swing very other second. Earlier you were quarrelling with me and asking me not to borrow even a *paisa* from anyone. It was you who was saying there is no question of offering or giving any money or material in marriage. And now when God himself has inspired Gauri to write this letter, you are harping on family prestige. Only God can fathom your mind."

Dhania said, "A man is accorded respect and welcome according to his behaviour. Don't you know that? In the past Gauri was arrogant and proud. Now he is showing a gentlemanly spirit. A brick may be a fitting reply to a pebble, but an abuse is no reply to a greeting."

Hori made a face and said, "Then go ahead; show off your greatness. Let's see from where you get the money."

"Arranging money is not my worry. It's yours."

"I can get it only from Dulari."

"Then take it from her. Everybody charges interest. If one has to drown, it makes no difference whether one drowns in a puddle or in the mighty Ganges."

Irritated, Hori walked out to puff on his *chillum*. They had got off easy, but Dhania was not one to let anything proceed smoothly. She had the ability to turn everything upside down. She seemed to revel in upsetting the apple cart. She knew the difficult situation they were in; but would she ever listen?

❁❁❁

25

Bhola was engaged for the second time in his life. His life had turned quite bland without a woman. When Jhuniya was around she remembered to serve him his meals and organise his smoke and other little necessities. With her gone, he had none to attend to him. His daughters-in-law had their hands full with things to do around the house. An engagement appeared to be the only pragmatic solution to his problems. As luck would have it, he came to know of a young widow, Nohri, whose husband had died barely three months ago. The woman was also the mother of a small boy. She appeared as the perfect quarry and Bhola snapped her up real fast. He didn't flag in his efforts till he tied the knot with her.

Till he got married again, everything in the house was the fiefdom of the daughters-in-law. They ran the house as per their wishes and fancies. During the six months after his son Jangi and his wife left for Lucknow, it was his other son Kamta's wife who had a free run of the house. She presided over the place like a queen and in the last two or three months, had succeeded in stashing twenty to thirty rupees in her secret account by selling a seer or two of milk on the sly. The control now passed into the hands of Nohri, her step mother-in-law. She detested it and their bickering started from day one. Their rivalry took an ugly turn as gradually Bhola and his son were also sucked into the battle.

The daily fighting came to such a head that a partition and division of property seemed the only way out for peace. The unfortunate fact was that in such circumstances, right from times immemorial, a division does not come before a violent showdown. The tradition was followed dutifully in this instance as well. Kamta was a young man. Bhola's clout over him arose from his position as his father and head of family. However, with the entry of a new woman as his wife the respect he commanded from his son was severely dented. Kamta could not bring himself around to accept the reality of a new and younger wife of his father. The ensuing fight saw Kamta raining a number of blows on his father after throwing him down on the floor in a wrestling tackle. Thus declaring his victory, he forbade him from touching anything in the house. The neighbours were with Kamta on this as Bhola's remarriage had made him some sort of a pariah in their eyes.

Thus banished, Bhola spent the remaining part of the night under a tree but went to Nokhe Ram with his appeal for a hearing the first thing in the morning. Bhola's hamlet was within the jurisdiction of Nokhe Ram and he was the right person to listen to his complaint as the headman or man-in-authority in those parts. Nokhe Ram never had any sympathy for Bhola but since he was accompanied by a vivacious woman, he quickly agreed to offer him shelter in a small outhouse near the cattle shed. In any case, he was on the lookout for an experienced hand to tend to his cows. Bhola was appointed for three rupees a month and a seer of milk daily.

Nokhe Ram was a squat, long nosed and big eyed dark man. He wore a large turban and a flowing tunic over which he wrapped a loose quilt whenever he stepped out of his house in the winter months. He loved oil massages therefore his clothes bore a sticky oiliness which was dirty as well. He had a huge family. His seven brothers and their children were dependent on him. His own son was a student of class nine and studied English; his fancy lifestyle was a drain on his expenses. Rai sahib gave him a salary of twelve rupees a month but his expenses exceeded a hundred rupees. That was the reason why once a villager landed in his trap, he didn't let go easy and extracted the maximum he could from him. When his salary was six rupees, he wasn't as slimy as he was now that it had been doubled to twelve. The increase in salary bolstered his desire for a better life and his expenses shot through the roof as a result of which his exploitive nature became still more aggressive. This boomeranged on him because seeing his attitude, Rai sahib froze any further hike in his salary.

Almost everyone recognised his clout one way or the other; even Jhinguri Singh and Datadin accepted his superior position. The only one who stood up to him was Pateshwari. If Nokhe Ram had airs of being a Brahmin who could manipulate a *Kayastha* like a puppet, Pateshwari was of the view that as a *Kayastha,* he could afford to throw his weight around with his expertise in the field of letters. Who could challenge him on his turf as he wasn't an employee, however glorified, of the *zamnidaar* but an employee of a government in whose kingdom the sun never set? There was a subtle competition between the two. If Nokhe Ram kept a fast every fortnight on the full moon and fed five Brahmins that day, Pateshwari also held during the *Satyanarayan* ceremony every full moon and fed ten Brahmins.

When Nokhe Ram's son was well into his adolescence, he craved for the day when he would somehow scrape through the tenth class so that he could fix him up as a clerk somewhere. For this, he had already started making rounds of the district officials to deliver gifts as a token of his respect which he could reap at an appropriate time.

But Pateshwari was one over Nokhe Ram in another respect. There were strong rumours that the widow of one of his servants who he had sheltered in his house was actually his concubine. When Bhola came knocking at his door that morning, he smelt an opportunity to catch up with Pateshwari in that field as well.

He went out of the way to be kind to Bhola and assured him of his support. "You stay in my outhouse near the catteleshed, Bhola. Don't worry; if you need anything just let me know. You have a young wife; let me see if I can find some engagement for her as well. Sifting the corn, cleaning the granary, there is a lot of work. I am sure she can be of help."

Bhola persisted with his appeal- "Sir, please talk to Kamta at least once. You can ask him if he was right in behaving with me the way he did. I built the house, I purchased the cows and now he pockets everything and shows the road to me. If this not injustice, what is? Sir, you are the big chief. Shouldn't this issue be decided in your presence?"

"Bhola, you can't win in a war of words with him. He will get his just desserts; leave that to God. No one prospers on ill gotten gains. They call the world hell only because there's so much sinning going around here. No one cares for ethics and justice. But remember God knows everything. He is watching over everything. He knows your deepest desires. Nothing is hidden from Him; that's why he is called omnipotent. Nobody can escape His wrath. God willing, you will be better off here than there."

After some time, Bhola left Nokhe Ram and went to Hori fishing for sympathy but Hori came up with a long list of his own woes.

"Every relationship is changing, brother. You sweat it out for your kids but that doesn't mean anything to them. As soon as they grow up they turn against you. Take my own Gobar for example, it's been ages since he fought with his mother and left home. There's not a squeak from him. No letter, message, nothing! For all you know, we are as good as dead for him. My daughter's wedding is on us but does he care? I have mortgaged my land for a loan of two hundred rupees; what's got to be done has to be done. What one has to go through for children?"

Soon after he turned his father away from home, Kamta realised what a big help the old man was. Getting up early in the morning to prepare the feed for cows, milking them and later transporting the milk to the market place, attending to the cows once again immediately after returning from the market and milking them again in the evening; a fortnight was sufficient to bring his belligerence face to face with cold reality. The husband and wife had a blistering argument. She told him squarely that she didn't marry him to serve as a cook in his house. "If I am a burden to you, I can still go back to my father's place," she said. Kamta developed cold feet; he didn't want to add the task of managing the kitchen to his overflowing responsibilities. A servant was appointed to attend to odd jobs around the house but the arrangement was short lived as he was caught trying to sell off small portions of the hay and cattle feed from their store. He was given the marching orders. The husband and wife had yet another blistering showdown and a few days later the lady stomped out of the house, straight to her father's home. Kamta panicked and came running to Bhola, pulling every trick in the book to appease him. He said, "*Dada,* please forgive me for all the foolish things I have done. Please come back and take over your house. I promise to go your way."

Bhola resented living in Nokhe Ram's house as a menial servant. The cordial hospitality extended to him petered out after the first few months. Nokhe Ram would often order him to fill up his *chillum* or tidy up his room which Bhola found demeaning. He realised that disagreements or fights in one's own home didn't lead to subservience to another. He felt he could still maintain his dignity despite disturbances if he went back to his own home.

His wife Nohri blew her top when she learnt of his intentions.

"So you are ready to eat humble pie to return to those who kicked you out? Have you no sense of shame or self respect?"

"I am not living a life of luxury here either."

"Well, if that's how you look at it, you go ahead and humiliate yourself. I am not going anywhere. I stay put."

Bhola anticipated her opposition to this idea; he had a fair inkling of the cause for her resistence. In fact that had a major bearing on his decision to go back home. Here he was ignored and sidelined, whereas Nohri had a free run of the house. Even the servants and odd hands around the house recognised her special status. Her reply fuelled his simmering anger but he felt completely powerless. She might have followed him back if he had shown enough spine and walked away without her as Nokhe Ram didn't have the courage to shelter her so brazenly. He always needed a smokescreen to manoeuvre and snare his victim but Nohri knew Bhola only too well.

Bhola begged her- "Nohri, please try to understand; don't be so obstinate. You don't have any daughter-in-law problems anymore; all authority rests in your hand now. Don't you realise, we are cutting such a sorry figure before our community by working as menials in someone else's house?"

She cocked a snook at him and said, "You go if you haven't had enough as yet. Who am I to stop you? Perhaps, you find your son's abuse amusing; well, I don't. I am quite content as a menial."

Bhola was forced to stay back, much against his wishes. Kamta went to his wife and cajoled her into coming back. Meanwhile the buzz about Nohri went unabated. She wore nice *sarees*! Well, why not? These were mere fringe benefits of staying in Nokhe Ram's house!

Sobha was the village jester, the local know-all. He had the knack of commenting without stating the obvious. One day he came across Nohri and made a wisecrack which she promptly reported to Nokhe Ram. Sobha was summoned by the village elders and given a severe reprimand, the likes of which he couldn't forget for a long time.

Similarly Lala Pateshwari had a brush-in with her at a later date. It happened in the early days of summer. Pateshwari was in his mango orchard, supervising plucking of the fruit. He saw Nohri pass by, all decked up in her finery and couldn't resist calling out to her. "Nohri, sweetheart; come take a bite of these mangoes. They are real sweet, I promise you."

Nohri was confused. She couldn't understand if it was an innocuous invitation or a snide taunt. She thought he was making fun of her. She wanted people to recognise her eminent status and respect her accordingly. Haughtiness is a hair's breadth away from a nagging doubt of other's intentions. When people who walk with their head in the clouds have something to hide, they are easily touched to the quick. She wondered why he smiled at her. She wondered why everyone was so jealous of her; she didn't look for favours from people who claimed to be pristine pure? Would they dare to accost her directly?

Nohri had gathered enough knowledge of the dirt floating around in the village and knew its soft underbelly rather well. She knew Pateshwari had the widow of one of his servants living in his backyard yet nobody ever talked disparagingly about it. Just because she was poor and not of a higher caste, people took her for granted and passed frivolous comments at her. As for Pateshwari, it was like father like son. His younger son, Ramesri had eagle eyes for Siliya. These men! They lusted after the poor girls but were proud of their high caste.

She stopped dead in her tracks and snapped at Pateshwari- "Since when did you turn so charitable, *Lala*? You're the sort who'd make off with the morsel in another's hands; your generosity with mangoes is surprising. Don't trifle with me; I am warning you."

Oh! The milkmaid had acquired airs? Just because she had Nokhe Ram under her thumb did she think she could get away with anything? Pateshwari returned her jibe with a volley of his own. "I see that you are getting too big for your boots, Nohri. Mind your tongue; don't forget who you are, woman."

"What's your problem? Did I ever come to your door to beg?"

"If it wasn't for Nokhe Ram, you might have done just that."

Nohri was hit where it hurt most. She shouted at him, calling him whatever names she remembered at that moment. In the heat of the moment, she left the spot and barged straight into her hut and started gathering her stuff with an air of finality.

When Nokhe Ram got wind of it, he panicked and hurried to meet her.

"What are you doing, Nohri? Why are you removing your stuff from your room?

Did anyone say something to you?"

Nohri was an expert in the art of taming men. It was talent she had acquired over time. Nokhe Ram was an educated man and had a sound knowledge of the law; he had studied scriptures as well and worked under eminent lawyers but was reduced to putty in the hands of an unlettered Nohri.

She furrowed her eyebrows with a resigned look and said, "Not really, these are not the best of times for me. That's what brought me to your doorstep but I will not let go of my self-respect."

The old Brahmin came alive with righteous indignation. He twirled his moustaches and said, "If anyone raises a finger at you, I will teach him a lesson he won't forget for a long time.

Nohri realised it was the right time to strike. "Lala Pateshwari passes unnecessary comments at me. I am not for sale that I will tolerate anyone who come dangling cash before me. There are so many women in the village. No one takes liberties with them; why should they single me out for their attention? Just about everyone wants to take pot shots at me."

Nokhe Ram was livid. He picked up his *lathi* and stormed into the orchard and threw a challenge loud enough for everyone to hear, including the target of his ire.

"Come on, you coward! I will tear the moustaches off your face and bury you alive, right here. Come out and talk to me if you are man enough. One more word against Nohri and I will squeeze every drop of blood from your body. You'll never be the village *patwari* anymore. Do you think everybody is like you? What do you think of yourself?"

Lala Pateshwari stood transfixed, holding his breath. He knew it was suicidal to speak one word of protest as it would stir the hornet's nest. He never felt more humiliated in his life. Once he was beaten up for a similar indiscretion by some people at the village pond at night but that news wasn't public. Nobody had any proof that he was given a thrashing but today, his humiliation was complete and in full view of the village folk. The woman who had come seeking shelter now held all the aces in her hand. No one had the temerity to act fresh with her anymore. If Pateshwari couldn't utter a word, her victory was complete and final.

Nohri became the undisputed queen of the village. Peasants would give her the right of way when they came across her on the streets. It was an open secret that the easiest way to extract favours from Nokhe Ram was to get on the right side of Nohri. If somebody wanted a fair division of his property or an extension of the grace period for paying his dues or whether he wanted land to construct his house; without appeasing Nohri, nothing could be accomplished easily. Sometimes, she would pull up even well-to-do families in the village and soon started exercising her clout on senior functionaries of the administration.

Bhola disliked staying with her as a dependent. For him, nothing could be as low as living off a woman's earnings. He was paid three rupees a month but Nohri used all of it and left him with barely enough to meet his *chillum* expenses whereas she lived it up real well. Everybody was patronising at best but their usual attitude was scornful. Things came to such a pass that even servants told him to do odd jobs assigned to them. He would return home, exhausted and tired and lay himself on the loose string cot. There was no one to as much as offer him a glass of water. His evening meal consisted of leftovers of the day and at times even that was hard to come by and he was forced to settle for a few *rotis* sprinkled with common salt.

Pushed to the brink, he finally succumbed to his frailties and decided to pack and up and go back to his son.

Nohri put her foot down saying she was not interested in slaving it for his irresponsible and uncouth son.

Bhola hardened his stance and swallowed a bitter pill at the same time. "I am not telling you to come with me. It is my decision to go back and I am going alone."

"You will go away without me? Don't you feel ashamed saying that?"

"I have swallowed my pride. I have crushed it."

"But I haven't. You can't leave me. You can't walk away like this."

"You are so independent and free willed; why should I be subservient to you?"

"I will go to the *panchayat,* summon the village elders and embarrass you. Don't you dare me?"

"You have already embarrassed me enough. Do you still want to beat around the bush and throw dust in my eyes?"

"Oh my God! Your attitude suggests you buy me ornaments every month! Nohri will not tolerate airs from anyone."

Thoroughly harassed, Bhola got up, picked his stick at the bedside in a bid to leave right then and there but Nohri grabbed his wrist, making it tough for him to move out. He sat down like a cowering convict who's caught trying to escape. There was a time when he played around with many women but today he was sitting helplessly, cut to size by one woman, unable to escape to freedom or dignity. He realised his limits and made no effort to prise his hands free of her strong grip.

Why couldn't he boldly tell her that she was of no use to him and that he was going to break free of her? The *panchayat* and village elders did not intimidate him; if she wasn't scared of dragging the issue in the public domain, why should he spare a thought over it?

But this sentiment wasn't strong enough to enthuse the right amount of conviction and courage in his mind so that he could express it in words. Nohri had cast a sinister spell over him.

❁❁❁

26

Lala Pateshwari was the very embodiment of all the virtues inherent in his community. He did not take kindly to anyone extorting money or property from another. In the same vein, he was not pleased if any villager dilly dallied in paying back loans to the money lenders. His sense of fair play extended to every living being in the village. He disliked compromises and conciliations which he considered sure signs of lifelessness. He was an ardent devotee of aggression and strife which, in his view, were indications of being alive. Ever so often, he would try to infuse a new energy into his life on the same lines. He loved to ignite a new fire every day.

Lately, he had singled out Mangru Sah for his benevolent attention. Mangru was the wealthiest man in the village but he was totally disinterested in its petty politics. He had no lust for power or authority. He had built his house on the outskirts of the village where he had constructed a small temple and a well. A small orchard surrounded both the well and the temple. He had no children to take care of, therefore he spent major part of his time in spiritual activities. The numbers of those who had reneged on his payments of dues were in dozens but he had not once filed a case against anyone or initiated legal proceedings against any defaulter.

Hori owed him a hundred and fifty rupees but he did not lose sleep over it. He did pull up Hori a few times, threatened him and gave him a mouthful but seeing his pitiable condition, he didn't pursue the matter too seriously. However, this time Hori's sugarcane yield was the largest in the entire village. It was estimated by busybodies to fetch around two hundred and fifty rupees. Pateshwari impressed upon Mangru Sah that it was the best opportunity to recover all dues from Hori by filing a case against him. Mangru's reluctance to do so stemmed more from lethargy than kindness. He didn't want to exert himself over legal hassles but agreed grudgingly when Pateshwari offered to do the dirty work for him.

Pateshwari took upon himself the responsibility of handling the courts and gave an assurance that he would recover all dues from Hori. Mangru would not have to stir from home and yet he would get back the money. Mangru not only gave Pateswari permission to go ahead but also gave him an advance to meet sundry court expenses.

Hori was blissfully unaware of what was in store for him. He had no idea when the case was filed or when the sentence was passed. He got a rude shock only when the court officials arrived, armed with legal sanction, to attach and auction his crops to pay up the dues. Hori went running to Mangru while Dhania started mouthing expletives against Pateshwari. Her logical mind told her that it was Pateshwari's doing and Mangru was merely an instrument of his vendetta. Mangru Sah was busy with his prayers when Hori went to him. He waited but could not meet him. Dhania's abuses were ineffective and Pateshwari was least concerned. The crops were auctioned for a hundred and fifty rupees, ironically in favour of Mangru Sah himself. No one else had the deep pockets to match his call.

Dhania was livid and told Hori to go and confront Pateshwari. "Why are you sitting here doing nothing? Why don't you go and ask him if this is the way to treat a fellow villager?"

"He must have heard the words you used for him. What face do I have to show him after that?"

"If someone acts low, he should be ready to hear all this."

"So you want to have your say and expect him to react as a kind fellow villager?"

"Let me see who dares to touch my crops."

"The mill people will come and cut the crops; neither you nor I will be able to do a thing. You can satisfy yourself by showering abuses but that's not going to make any difference."

"You think anyone can cut my crops before my eyes; even as I am alive?"

"Yes. Even as you live. Even as I live. The entire village cannot protect us even if they wanted to. Now the yield belongs to him, not to you or me."

"Did Mangru Sah sweat and toil in the blistering June sun to grow it?"

"I agree it was you who worked hard for it but now it belongs to him. Didn't we owe him money?"

The crops were gone but a new problem raised its head. Dulari had agreed to loan them an amount against the crops. Now they had nothing against which to pledge the loan. She had presumed that after clearing her backlog of dues with the cash from their harvest, Hori could start afresh and she would loan him another two hundred for his daughter's wedding. That was what she had promised but the new development had changed everything.

The auspicious wedding season was close. The date was fixed and Gauri Mahto had finalised all preparations. It was next to impossible to go back on the plans. Hori felt so angry that he could have strangulated Dulari. He pleaded with her and tried to make her see reason but that woman was in no mood to listen. As a last resort he folded his hands and said, "Dulari, I won't run away with your money. I won't die so soon. I have my fields, a house and a young strapping son. Your money is safe with me; my prestige is at stake, help me, please."

However, Dulari did not want to mix social concerns with business. If she could be charitable as a part of her business, she had no problems at all but she was extremely uncomfortable doing business in a mood of charity.

Hori trudged back home. He looked up at Dhania and said- "Now what?"

Dhania vent her spleen at him. "This is what you always wanted."

Hurt, Hori stared at her sorrowfully, "You think it's all my fault?"

"It could be anyone's fault; but whatever is happening had to happen."

"Do you want me to pledge my land as well?"

"If you pledge away your land, what will be left for you to do?"

"Become a land labourer."

But their land was equally dear to both of them. Their sense of self worth, honour and esteem dwelt in its possession. Without their fields, they were bereft of any respect in society. Without the tag of owning land and fields, they were not householders but ordinary farm hands.

They were silent as neither had an answer. After some time, Hori said – "So what do you say?"

Dhania's voice carried the pain of defeat as she said, "What can I say? Gauri will come for the wedding with his guests; we will host one dinner for them and send off our daughter early next morning. If the world laughs at us, we can't help it. If God wants us to be humiliated and lose face in society, so be it."

Suddenly they saw Nohri coming their way, resplendent in a fancy *saree*. She drew a veil over her face when she saw Hori. He was her step- daughter's father-in- law, so she played the part of a respectful mother who avoids looking straight at a man. She had met Dhania and was on nodding terms with her. Dhania called out to her, "Where are you off to ? Come, join us."

Nohri had vanquished all opposition to her in the village; now she was on a goodwill hunting spree. She came up to them. Dhania gave her a critical look and said- "What brings you here?"

Nohri was all sweetness personified- "Just dropped by to look you up. When is your little girl's marriage?"

Dhania wondered what she was arriving at. "It depends on God's will. It will be done when he wishes it."

"I've heard it's sometime during the current auspicious season."

"Well, yes, we have come up with a date."

"You must not forget to invite me."

"She's like your daughter; you don't need an invitation."

"I am sure you have organised all the gifts for her dowry. Why don't you show them to me?"

Dhania was caught in a bind. She didn't know how to respond to that. Hori stepped in to save the blushes.

"We have not bought anything yet. Moreover we actually don't need much stuff. It will be a very simple and austere wedding."

Nohri stared at him with wide, disbelieving eyes. "Why will it be a simple and austere marriage? You are marrying off your first daughter; you should give her a load of stuff."

Hori laughed. It was a mirthless sound which conveyed the sorrow of his penury and surprise that she couldn't perceive the obvious.

"We are hard up on cash; how can we fulfill her desires even if we tried? There's no point hiding things from you."

"Your son is doing well for himself. You are working day and night. How come you have money problems? Who'll believe this?"

"Had my son been a dutiful and devoted boy, we would not be pushed into a corner as we are now. He hasn't looked back ever since he went away with his wife and child. There's not a word from him. It's two years and we haven't received a single letter from him."

In the meanwhile, Sona appeared in the doorway with a bundle of grass on her head for the bulls. Seeing a stranger she turned shy and bashful, like a young girl, trying to hide the signs of her awkward youth with her saree. She dumped the bundle of grass before them and hurried inside.

"Your daughter has grown into a little lady!" Nohri said, appreciatively.

"A daughter grows like a wild flower," said Dhania philosophically, "How long can one let her bloom unattended. She's here today, she will be gone tomorrow."

"You have fixed a groom for her, haven't you?"

"Yes, that part is taken care of. If we are able to organise some money, we'll marry her off within this month."

Nohri had a street smart mind that was as sharp as it was shallow. She had saved some money in the last few months and she was on top of the world. She thought if she helped them with money to get their daughter married, it would earn her a good name in society. Everyone in the village would praise her for her kind and noble gesture. They'd be completely surprised and taken aback that Nohri volunteered to help so generously. They would look at her in awe and admiration. Hori and Dhania would become her greatest public relations ambassadors as they would go to town singing her glories. Her prestige would get such a boost. With one kind gesture, she would seal the gossiping mouths and quieten all wagging tongues. Who would dare pass snide comments at her or speak lightly about her after that? Today the whole village was against her; then it would be on her side. Her face lit up as these thoughts crossed her mind.

"If it's just a small shortfall, you can take some money from me. There's no hurry to return it, take your time."

Dhania and Hori looked at her face intently, searching for a sign of malice and to see if she was joking. No, she didn't appear to be taking them for a ride. She looked serious. The husband and wife stared at her in disbelief, gratefulness and doubt. Nohri wasn't all that bad as people made her out to be.

"See, your prestige is also linked to mine. If the world will scorn at you, I will also be shamed. There is no point in talking about how it happened but the fact is our families are related and bound in a close relationship. You are my step daughter's in-laws."

Hori smiled hesitantly. "Yes, of course, you are family. We can always take any help from you. Those who are close to us will always be a big support but if we can manage from outside, why should we dip into the family reserves?"

"Yes, why should we?" Dhania seconded Hori.

But Nohri was riding the empathy wave. "When we have enough funds in the family, why do we need to beg from other people for help? We will have to pay interest, stamp duties, bring in witnesses to sign a loan agreement and worst of all, suck up to strangers and molly-coddle them. But if you have a problem accepting help from me; there's not much I can do about it."

Hori hurried to save the situation and said, "Not at all, Nohri, we understand that. If we can manage within the family, it'll be perfect. The only reason I wanted to avoid it was that since we are not doing too well these days- if you suddenly need the money back for an emergency we might not be able to return it in time and create difficulties for you not to mention, embarrassment for us. That was my only concern otherwise my daughter is as good as your own."

"I don't need this money back in a hurry."

"Okay. We will take it from you. If someone is to benefit from the piety of helping a poor girl to get married, why shouldn't it be someone from the immediate family?"

"How much money do you need?"

"How much can you spare?"

"Will a hundred rupees suffice?"

Hori felt greedy. If luck had come knocking at the door, why not ask for more.

A hundred will do and five hundred will do as well. Just see what you can spare conveniently."

"I have two hundred rupees in all. You can take them."

"We will manage quite well with two hundred. We have enough grains and other food materials in the house, the rest can be organised within that amount. By the way, I must confess I did not expect such grace from you, Nohri. Whoever volunteers to help anyone else these days? You have saved me from great humiliation."

There was a sudden nip in the air as evening drew to a close and it was time to light the evening lamp. The earth was blanketed in a hazy blue mist. Dhania went inside and brought out a trough of burning coals. They started warming their hands in the smouldering fire. In its golden glow, the excitable, vivacious and crafty Nohri appeared as an apparition of divine benevolence to them. There was a special glow of warmth and kindness in her eyes, an amazing expression of humility on her face and her mouth seemed to be the very fount of grace.

After indulging in small talk Nohri stood up and made to leave, saying it was getting late and that they could come to collect the amount first thing next morning.

"Let us walk you home."

"Oh! No, I can go by myself. Please don't worry."

"Worry? I feel like carrying you back to your home on my shoulders!"

Nokhe Ram's mansion was on the extreme end of the village. They took the circuitous road that went all along the outskirts as it was better and free of potholes.

On the way Nohri casually mentioned to Hori to make Bhola see reason.

"Why don't you give some sane advice to him? Why should he be rattling his swords at all the right and wrong causes? If one has to survive in society he should try to go the extra mile to make friends with people, not rub them the wrong way for perceived insults. He gets into arguments with every other person ever so often. He cannot keep me under a veil, I have to go out and work; how does he expect others not to talk, share a joke or generally exchange pleasantries with me? People will look at me; I will have to talk to them, they will also talk to me. How can I avoid it unless I live in *purdah*? Just imagine! What am I expected to do if anyone stares or ogles at me? Should I gouge his eyes out? By being nice and pleasant to others one can get so many things done with comparative ease. It is important to alter one's behaviour and attitudes with time and circumstance. If he was rolling in wealth in earlier days how does it help our present which is not so good? Now he is an ordinary labourer earning three rupees a month. My parents had many heads of cattle but I, their daughter, am just a petty labourer. Does my past or lineage matter any more? But will he understand? At one time he says he will go back to his sons and at another he plans to go settle in Lucknow. He's made life hell for me."

Hori nodded his head in agreement.

"Bhola is being very naïve. He is a mature man; he should understand all these things. I will try my best to make him see reason."

"Come tomorrow morning; make it as early as you can. I will give you the money."

"Err, what about any formal papers? Do I have to sign..?"

"Relax! I am confident you won't run away with my money."

They had reached her house. She went inside and Hori made a quick about turn, back towards his home.

❁❁❁

27

Gobar was in for a rude shock when he returned to the city. He discovered to his utter surprise that the street corner which he occupied for his make shift kiosk had been taken by another vendor. His regular clients had shifted loyalties to the new competitor. In the new unfamiliar surroundings, Jhuniya felt lonely and wept most of the time. Chunnu was used to playing in wide open spaces. Here he had to remain cooped up in the house. An unbearable stink lingered forever in the narrow street outside their door making it impossible for her to keep him in open any time in the day. There was hardly any elbow room in its cramped confines. The child missed his companions at the village and the innumerable kids from the neighbourhood, besides Sona and Rupa, who played with him all day. Left with no one to play with, the child clung to his mother for companionship.

On the other hand, Gobar was on a constant high with the headiness of youth; his long repressed desires itched to drown themselves in a never ending lust for more and yet more pleasure. He could not concentrate on his business and wasted his time in idle pursuit. When he went out with his cart selling stuff, he would hasten back as soon as he could. The labourers and *tonga* drivers of the neighbourhood played cards and gambled late into the night as a matter of routine. Earlier, Gobar would join them without fail; now Jhuniya was his sole entertainment. It did not take her long to get sick of the life of bleak drudgery she was exposed to all of a sudden. She yearned for solitude; so she could sleep and laze around at will but city life left her with no such opportunity, her irritation with Gobar grew each passing day. The romantic vision of city life which he had painted, appeared to her as a fake illusion even as her baby too got on her nerves. In sheer anger and frustration, she often pushed him out of the house where he cried his lungs out till frustrated even further, she let him in again. There was no milk in her dry shrivelled breasts. The baby would howl to be fed and when no milk came out of it he vent his anger by biting the nipples with his teeth. He was a two year old baby now and the sharpness of his teeth was accentuated by his irritability. At that moment she hated both her husband and the child he had thrust on her.

There was no one to assist her with her chores as a result of which she grew weak, lost weight and retreated into a shell. Every day she lay in a corner of the room with frequent headaches and lost all interest in eating or drinking. She wanted to be left alone but Gobar's relentless passion wracked her body so much that the mere suggestion of intimacy became more of an ordeal for her.

When, in that summer, the baby was down with diarrhoea and stopped pestering her for milk, she was almost thankful for it. With no energy left in her body to push him away, she welcomed the illness in a warped sense of relief. For her both husband and baby were leeches, sucking the life blood out of her. Her sense of relief was cut short within a week as he succumbed to the diarrhoea that left him a weakened shell. His death tortured her with pain and guilt and his laughing happy face, in better times, returned to haunt her waking hours every day.

The last straw broke when barely a week after they cremated the child, Gobar crept up to her and made demands of her body once again. "You are worse than an animal!" she cried in disgust, pushing him away.

The child's memory became dearer to her than what she ever felt for him when he was alive. When he was around she felt pestered but in his death, he cast a mist of remorse laced with a sweet remembrance over her. His memory created a new Chunnu in her heart, it was a new child shorn of the nagging and wailing. The image she nursed in her heart became more powerful than the real child she had held in her arms. The baby in her memory grew into a more pleasant, smiling and stable image. There was sweetness in the pain of missing the vision she had created of him in her mind. The external flesh and blood of her child was only a projection of the illusion she created in her heart. The reflection was absent but the original form was the one which struck roots in her mind. Her inner life seemed to be enriched with the mythical baby living in her imagination that she nursed with love and affection.

Now she was not bothered about the dark, dingy room and the foul, all pervasive odour that hung in it. She didn't care about the acrid smoke which filled the room when she cooked meals. She rose above the trauma of drudgery as if nothing like that ever existed in her life. The memory of the child imbued her with a new strength to carry on. What was once such an ordeal to bear, in death had turned into a fierce desire to live.

She hardly cared if Gobar came early or late, whether he liked the food or not, whether he was happy or sad. She did not once ask him how much he earned and how he spent the money. Her withdrawal into herself was total and complete; she was an automaton that worked without feeling for the present, comfortable and content with the visions in her mind. Her compassion was insulated from her surroundings to which she turned indifferent and passive.

Gobar could have come closer to her by sharing her grief and probing into her afflicted heart but an innate insensitivity kept him from wading into the recesses of her mind. He was a spectator, never coming close enough to discover, much less share, the concerns of her heart.

One day he asked her rather dryly, "How long will you lament for him? He's gone for five months yet you still cry for him."

You will never fathom my pain," she sighed. "Don't bother about me; you get on with your business."

"Will your constant crying bring him back to us?"

She had no answer to this. She didn't know he was so stony hearted. Ignoring him, she went away to peel potatoes and put the kettle on the fire. Gobar's lack of sensitivity further strengthened her attachment to the image of the baby in her mind. Now the vision was hers and hers alone. Earlier she saw a spark of that attachment in her husband's eyes; now the baby was all hers and no one had any right over him.

Gobar's business had all but collapsed in the face of new competition so he took up a job in a sugar mill. Buoyed by the success of his first venture, Mr. Khanna had set up another mill. Gobar had to report for duty in that mill early in the morning, therefore when he returned home, at dusk, he was totally exhausted. Back home in the village he put in equally hard work but never felt so broken.

Despite the day's back breaking work in his village, his mind felt light as a feather when he returned home. In the open fields and under a spreading blue sky, his tiredness would vanish in no time. The stress in the city was more in the mind and not as much in physical strain. The noise and deafening roar of machines bore down on him like lead. The constant fear of being upbraided by his bosses further strained his jangled nerves. All workers suffered from this depression, hence every evening, after work, they drowned their fatigue and emotional trauma in the popular local brew. Gobar started drinking, first casually, then as a habit and soon almost as an addiction. He would return home late in the night, sozzled and stoned out of his mind. He found any reason good enough to abuse Jhuniya and vent his frustration on her. On quite a few times, he beat her.

The way he ill treated her, Jhuniya began to suspect Gobar regarded her no better than a kept woman. Had she been his legally wedded wife, he would not have dared to abuse her in this manner. If they had a socially approved relationship, community pressures would have forced him to behave. She had blundered by eloping with him. Society scorned her and she hadn't gained anything in the bargain. The man for whom she faced such approbation turned out to be such a lout. She now looked upon him as an enemy. She was pregnant again and as the months flew past her anxiety grew in leaps and bounds. She wondered who would look after her in the aftermath of her delivery. She was afraid she might actually die if Gobar continued to beat her, during the days of confinement, after the birth of the second child.

One day while she was waiting to fill her vessel at the community water tap, a woman from the neighbourhood came up and asked her, "How many months to go yet?"

"I don't know, sister," Jhuniya said shyly. "I didn't keep count of the days."

The woman, her neighbour was obese, ugly, and heavy-bosomed. Her husband was a *tonga* driver and she ran a small shop selling firewood. Jhuniya often bought firewood from her and had nothing more than a casual nodding acquaintance with her.

The woman smiled kindly. "I would say it's any time now. Not more than a day or two. Have you arranged for a midwife?"

"I don't know anyone here," said Jhuniya, apprehensively.

"Is your man such a dummy? Is he not worried about you?"

"Yes. He doesn't care."

"Well, that is quite obvious. How about your mother-in-law and other relatives, sisters-in-law? During confinement you'll need someone by your side, won't you? Don't you have any relatives you could write to and who could come to look after you?"

"I have a few relatives but they are as good as dead for me."

As she sat down to clean the utensils, her heart beat faster in fear and foreboding. She was scared what would happen when she actually has to deliver the child. She thought, at worst, she would die and consoled herself cynically that perhaps that would be the best for her.

The labour pains commenced in the evening. She feared the worst. Soaked in sweat and with one hand pressed against her stomach, she lit the stove, put rice and *dal* to boil in a pan and, unable to stand the searing pain any more, fell on the ground, writhing in agony.

Gobar returned at about ten in the night, reeking of country liquor, mumbling under his breath like a man who has taken leave of his senses.

"I couldn't care less," he muttered, "whoever wants to stay, may stay or go away for all I care. I don't take any shit from no one--not even my folks; I won't stand any shit from her. The supervisor glares at me that good-for-nothing chap! I won't stand it. I have had enough of it, man. I won't stand it anymore! I will kill him; finish him off! I'm not afraid of dying. I'll show him how the brave go to the gallows laughing, defiant, with head held high. That's how it should be! Now, just look at this faithless woman. How she sleeps sprawled on the kitchen floor while the food burns; not bothered whether I eat or not. She will cook nice fluffy *rotis* for herself but see she plans to serve me lousy *khichri*! Come on you useless woman. Do it your way if you want to. God is watching. He'll set you right."

He didn't wake her up and skirted her as she lay on the floor and served himself two ladles of *khichri* on a plate and gulped down a few mouthfuls before he staggered to the veranda, plonked on the cot and promptly fell asleep. In the wee hours of the morning he woke up because he felt cold. When he went inside to get a blanket, he heard Jhuniya groaning in pain. The effect of the brew had subsided and he was a sober man now.

"How are you, Jhuniya? He asked. "Are you in a lot of pain?"

"Yes, it hurts real bad."

"Why didn't you tell me earlier? How can I get help at this odd hour?"

"Whom should I have told?"

"Me. Who else? I wasn't dead."

"You don't care whether I live or die."

By that time Gobar was in a state of mild panic. Where could he get a midwife and if anyone would visit them at this unearthly hour of the night? There was no money as well. If only this wretched woman had cautioned him about it much earlier; he'd have borrowed a few rupees from someone. Time was when he always had money to spare. Ever since this woman set foot in his house, the Goddess of fortune had abandoned him for good.

Suddenly he heard someone call outside his door. "Hey, there! Is that your wife crying? Is she in pain?"

It was the same fat woman who Jhuniya had met in the morning. She had woken up to feed the horse and had heard groaning sounds coming from their house.

"Yes," said Gobar, stepping out into the veranda. "Where can I get a midwife?"

"I knew the moment I saw her this morning that the time for delivery is close. A midwife lives nearby. Go fetch her and tell her to hurry. I'll watch over your wife till you return."

"I don't know the way to her house."

"All right, you sit with her while I go and fetch her. Trust fools like you to mess up things! The wife is ready to deliver any moment and he doesn't know where to locate a midwife!"

She got up and went on her way to call the midwife. Her real name was Chuhiya but behind her back neighbours called her 'fatso', a name which drove her mad. She was not away for more than ten minutes when she was back, grumbling and complaining loudly, "Nobody has any concern for the poor in this world. That woman wants five rupees in cash, paid in advance, before she condescends to come. She demands eight *annas* per day and one *saree* on the twelfth day as well. I told her to go take a walk; we will manage without her. I'm not the mother of twelve brats for nothing. I gave a piece of my mind to that horrible wretch. You let me handle this my way, Gobardhan. When it comes to the crunch, we must stand by each other. I will take care of Jhuniya. Just because she has handled a couple of deliveries in the neighbourhood, she thinks she's a midwife!"

She went inside to where Jhuniya lay moaning in pain and placing her head on her lap she gently caressed her swollen abdomen. "I knew your time was near the moment I saw you this morning. I couldn't sleep a wink; I was so worried for you. I knew you are all alone."

Jhuniya gritted her teeth in pain. "I won't survive . I know it I won't. If I die, please take care of my child. God will bless you for it."

Chuhiya touched her hair gently and said, "Come on, my child. It'll all be over in a minute. You had no reason to hide things from me. Had you told me earlier, I'd have got you a talisman from the *maulvi*."

At that moment Jhuniya lost consciousness and fainted. When she came out of it at about nine in the morning, she saw Chuhiya sitting with the new-born chortling in her arms and herself dressed in a fresh, clean *saree*. She felt weak, drained of all blood and energy.

After that day, Chuhiya would come every morning, prepare nutritious things for Jhuniya to eat and return a few times in the day to bathe the baby and clean him up. Whenever she found the chance she would snatch a few moments to feed milk to the infant. Even on the fourth day of delivery, Jhuniya's breasts were dry and there was no milk in them to nourish the baby which cried continuously as it would not take any other milk. Chuhiya tried to feed him by putting her breast to his mouth. That quietened him for a moment but when no milk came as he suckled her, the baby wailed loudly as ever. On the fourth day when Jhuniya did not lactate till the evening, Chuhiya got really very worried. She called a retired physician who lived in the neighbourhood, who after examining Jhuniya made a sagely comment- "How can she expect milk when she is so anaemic? She would have to take a long treatment with tonics and proper diet before she can hope to have milk in her breasts. It's going to be tough for the baby. How will the little thing survive without breast milk from its mother?"

That night Gobar lay in the veranda, drunk and reeking of country brew. Chuhiya sat with the child, a nipple pushed into his wailing mouth when suddenly she felt her breasts become heavy with milk. "O my God! Jhuniya. Your baby will survive! I have milk at last!" she shouted.

Jhuniya couldn't believe what she heard.

"Trust me, girl. It's true!"

"I don't believe this."

"Look," Chuhiya pressed her breast and a steady trickle of milk flowed out of her nipple.

Totally surprised and still incredulous, Jhuniya reminded her that her youngest daughter was almost eight years old and despite evidence to the contrary, she was surprised how a woman could lactate at that age. In the last couple of years, she had not conceived another child either.

"Yes darling, my daughter is eight and is my last child. It's true that my breasts had completely dried up. But strange are the ways of God. What else can explain this?"

After that day, Chuhiya turned up at least four or five times a day to suckle the baby. The child was weak at birth but fed on Chuhiya's milk, he turned into a bonny baby. One day Chuhiya was caught up in some work and was delayed, unable to make it in time during the daytime. When she arrived in the evening, the baby had tired itself out, crying hoarse as Jhuniya tried every trick she knew to try to soothe him. When Chuhiya held out her arms to pick it up, Jhuniya brushed her aside roughly and said she wished he died so she wouldn't have to depend on others.

Chuhiya was contrite and begged her to hand over the child. Jhuniya was quiet irritated but gave her the child after much molly coddling and expressions of regret.

Lately, the relations between husband and wife had fallen to abysmally low levels. Jhuniya was now certain that Gobar was utterly selfish and heartless and that she meant nothing more to him than an object for physical gratification. She thought he was least bothered if she lived or died. He would go and marry again if she died but she wasn't going to let him off easy. Moreover, he won't be lucky twice. She was a trusting fool who fell for him; no other woman would be so naïve. Earlier he would look up to her, hanging on every word she uttered and now he had turned so indifferent. His drinking was becoming a problem as he squandered so much of his earnings on liquor; leaving them short of cash all the time. They had only one worn-out quilt, in which they were forced to snuggle together. So close to each other, yet it seemed they were a hundred miles apart.

Gobar's heart warmed for the baby and he wanted to pick him up in his arms and play with him but kept himself in check. Often at night he looked at his sleeping peaceful face but his distaste for Jhuniya grew each passing day. On her part, Jhuniya did nothing to cement or remedy the cracks in their relationship and allowed the chasm to grow. The narrow differences grew into wide valleys of indifference and struck deep roots, growing strong and making them both more opinionated by the day. They almost made it a point to misunderstand each other so they could feed their petty grudges. They often dwelt on stray comments made by the other and let them fester in their hearts till they came out with vicious vehemence on the slightest pretext.

To make matters worse, some trouble or the other was always brewing at Gobar's workplace. The current year's budget had imposed an excise duty on sugar, making it a handy excuse for mill-owners to announce a cut in worker's wages. They had their own warped logic. If normal wages were paid to the workers, it meant a loss in profits for the mill owners; a wage reduction meant a definite increase. For many months, a tussle was on in the local mill with the labour union spoiling for a showdown. A cut in wages had the potential of becoming an incendiary topic for them to go on strike. When the mill-owners did not increase wages in the boom period, what right had they to levy a wage cut when the going was tough? The union was deeply suspicious and as it is they had to rely only on their word for it.

Mirza Khurshid was the president of the labour union and Pandit Onkarnath, the editor of 'Bijli', was its Secretary. They wanted a strike of such magnitude as would bring the mill to a grinding halt. They were powered by their own agenda and did not spare much thought over the difficulties the workers might face once they struck work in the factory. As a self styled leader of the workers and reckless to the point of stupidity, Gobar was ready to rush in head first at the slightest provocation. Once he was enraged, he lost all sense of proportion not caring about his own good or safety.

One day Jhuniya tried to reason with him. She thought he required some advice and needed to understand that as a family man he had more responsibilities than a maverick unionist. She thought it was not advisable for him to stick his neck out as far as he did. "Why should you take the lead in everything?" she asked him.

"I don't need your advice," was his terse reply to her entreaties. He said- "I don't need your dumb advice. Who are you to poke your nose in my affairs?"

This blew into a massive argument which concluded with Gobar thrashing Jhuniya. When Chuhiya got news of it she rebuked Gobar soundly.

"You keep out of this!" he screamed. "You have no business coming to my house to sermonise me."

Chuhiya replied sarcastically, "You think I come to your house to make two ends meet? You think I come here to steal stuff from your kitchen? My dear man, had it not been for me this woman wouldn't be alive for you to kick around when you please?"

Gobar swung a fist at her in the air, threateningly. "You keep away from her, woman. You are the one instigating her."

Chuhiya held her ground, refusing to be cowed by his threats. "Just shut up, Gobar. By thrashing a feeble woman with a baby in her lap you have not covered yourself in glory. Count yourself lucky for you've got a docile wife. Any other woman would have hit you back with a broomstick and left you for good."

Hearing the commotion, the neighbours collected and rebuked Gobar self righteously. The same men, who beat their wives almost every day, expressed indignation at Gobar's indiscretion. Fed up, Gobar left for work almost immediately.

Storm clouds were gathering at the mill and a distinct uneasiness hung in the air. The workers carried copies of Bijli, the revolutionary tabloid, in their pockets. Whenever they had a break, whether for a smoke or otherwise, they pored over it in small groups. The paper's circulation had skyrocketed as it flew off the racks. The union leaders sat up late in the office of the newspaper finalising strategies and when in the morning the headlines appeared, the public pounced on the paper hungrily with copies selling at many times the regular price. The mill owners and other senior staff cautiously watched it all; a strike at that juncture was very much to their advantage. There was a surfeit of cheap labour; unemployment was on the increase and they could easily have new hands at half the wages. This simple step of laying off workers following a strike could result in a considerable reduction in the cost of production. Agreed, the production would stop for a couple of days, but that was beside the point. The positives of a strike far outweighed the negatives of fall in production for a few days. At last the management arrived at a decision. A cut in the wages of the workers was decided upon. A time was fixed for its formal announcement and the police was duly notified. The workers had no idea what was in store for them. They had their own plans and were waiting to strike when the situation was opportune for them. That would come about when the present stocks were sold and demand was at a high. A strike at that time would squeeze the mill owners right and proper.

One day as the evening shift came to a close and the workers were filing out of the mill, they were read out the decision of the directors announcing a cut in their wages. Even as the announcement was being made, a posse of policemen arrived to see that nothing went out of hand. Grudgingly, the workers were pushed to go on strike right then and there. They did not want to strike work when the godowns were flush with stocks. Despite the heavy demand, the stocks were sufficient to last at least six months.

When Mirza Khurshid heard about it, he could not hide a smile. It was the smile of a seasoned warrior appreciating a clever move by the enemy. He closed his eyes and seemed to mediate on the remarkable strategy of his adversary and said- "If that is how they want it, so be it. The situation is no doubt favourable to the mill owners but we have truth, justice and right on our side. They will try to employ new workers and we have to thwart their designs. It's the only way to succeed in this battle of wits."

An emergency meeting was called at the office of the newspaper. Office bearers were elected and a long procession of workers was taken out at eight in the evening. The line of action for the following day was decided at ten and a clear warning was sent to the workers that there would be no violence as that would mean playing into the hands of the management.

But that was not to be. Incensed by the sight of a long queue of job-seekers outside the mill gate, the strikers lost their cool. They had not calculated that such a large number of workers would turn up. A smaller number could be influenced to leave but such a big crowd was difficult to handle, much less convince. If all those people were taken into employment, the chances of a compromise would be slim indeed. A hurried decision was taken to prevent the new employees from entering the mill premises. There was no way this could be done peacefully; some sort of force became absolutely necessary.

The new hopeful recruits were also in no mood to take it lying down. They were half starved men who were not willing to let go a chance to find a job. They gritted their teeth and prepared themselves for battle. The lines were drawn on both sides and all that was needed was a minor spark to light the fire of combat. The editor of 'Bijli' was the first to beat a hasty retreat and ran for dear life. The brunt of the attack fell on Mirza. Gobar, who presented himself as his Man Friday, took the full frontal attack in a desperate bid to save him. Gobar's arm was fractured and he collapsed bleeding on the ground. Mirza was a wrestler and an athlete of sorts, and was quite adept at dodging blows. Gobar was a dumb rustic; he knew how to wield the *lathi* but didn't know how best to prevent others from hitting him back. His aggression didn't know that defence was an integral part of an attacking game. When the strikers saw their front line fall, they lost nerve and scattered in a hundred directions. A few trusted and committed workers remained, forming a cordon round Mirza. The job seekers entered the gates, in triumph, as the workers licked their wounds of battle and transferred their casualties to hospital. There was hardly enough space for such a huge contingent of emergency patents and many had to be turned back. Mirza Khurshid was admitted to the hospital with injuries but Gobar was given first aid and sent home.

When Jhuniya saw Gobar's bruised and battered state, the feminine virtues of care and concern were aroused in her heart. Gobar had treated her badly, he constantly abused and beat her; but when she saw his sorry state, she forgot his tyranny and came out to look after him. Today he was a cripple, helpless and in a pitiable condition. She peered at his face through her tears. She felt a strange anger that was laced with sorrow. Gobar was well aware they were in dire straits; there was no money in the house yet despite her advice, to the contrary, he had rushed headlong into trouble. He did not spare a thought what his stupidity would cost them. She had warned him time and again that taking up lost causes was an exercise in futility. She had implored him not to expose himself to risk. As she had foretold and expected, the well-to-do instigators had escaped unscathed while the poor workers were left with nothing. But he wouldn't listen. Those whom he counted as friends were still roaming free while he lay bruised and defeated all alone in his shack. She felt a malicious vindication in her anger that was akin to what parents feel when a child stumbles and falls despite the repeatedly cautioning not to jump on chairs. Though the parents are concerned but they feel vindicated.

She gazed at him continuously, searching for signs that he was well and that he would live. But every passing minute, her hopes sank and a foreboding darkness enveloped her fearful heart.

Suddenly, Chuhiya burst into the room. "What happened to Gobar? I just heard about it."

Jhuniya was unable to utter a word. Her pent up emotions flowed unabated when she saw the concern writ large on Chuhiya's face. She looked critically at Gobar and felt for his heartbeat.

"He'll be all right," she declared. "Don't you worry. Many people died in that riot. Your love and good fortune saved your husband. Have you any money?"

Jhuniya shook her head.

"Never mind. I'll give you some. Go and get some hot milk for him."

Jhuniya fell at Chuhiya's feet- "*Didi*, you are like a mother to me," she said overwhelmed with emotion. "I have no one else but you to look up to."

The sullen winter evening darkened further into a sad night. A few hours later, Chuhiya was rocking the baby in her arms in the veranda and Jhuniya went to the kitchen to warm a glass of milk.

"I'm very unfortunate, *Didi,*" she said. "Somehow I can't help but blame myself for all this suffering. I say harsh things to him and I seem to hate him so much. It must be my evil tongue that has brought this misery upon him."

She broke down, unable to speak any further.

"That is such a dumb thing to say!" said Chuhiya, wiping Jhuniya's tears with the edge of her saree. "Your wifely devotion to your husband saved him. At the same time, you must remember that unpleasantness in relationships has a propensity to cause more unpleasantness in a more physical sense."

"Then what should I do, sister?"

"You must pray sincerely in your heart. God will help you. He has all the answers."

Gobar opened his eyes and seeing Jhuniya before him, he spoke in a feeble voice- "I am hurt real bad, Jhuniya. I didn't start anything. They came for me unprovoked. Please forgive me my sins. I have always been cruel to you; I think this is nature's way to get even. I don't think I will last long. I wil: die soon. My body hurts, I won't live for long."

"Nobody is going to die. You keep quiet and rest."

A faint light of hope crossed Gobar's face.

"There's nothing wrong with you. It's a minor wound on the head, and a broken arm. No one dies of a fractured arm." It was Chuhiya who had come up, hearing him speak.

"I won't hit Jhuniya again."

"I am sure you say that because you are scared she will hit back next time."

"She can do so. I won't mind."

"When you recover, you will forget all these promises."

"No, I won't."

Gobar talked like a child all through the days he was recuperating in his room. He had long bouts of silence, almost as if he were unconscious. Sometimes, he felt he was drowning and Jhuniya was trying to rescue him. Sometimes, he imagined a demon sitting astride his chest and a Goddess who resembled Jhuniya trying to shield him from the monster. He would often wake up with a start and ask a startled Jhuniya if she was sure he wasn't dying in his sleep.

For days, he lived in delirium. Jhuniya kept a vigil all night, wide awake, as if expecting death to come stalking. One morning, she hired a *tonga* and they took him to hospital. When he was discharged from the hospital, a few days later, he realised that he had escaped death by a hair's breadth. He was broken and repentant.

"Forgive me Jhuniya," was all he said.

During this period, Chuhiya had spent a couple of rupees from her own pocket. Jhuniya was embarrassed and reluctant to strain her meagre resources still further. Therefore, she decided to look for a job and find some work for herself. Gobar would take months to get back to work and they needed some support. They needed money for food and medicines.

Ever since she was a little girl, Jhuniya was adept at rearing cows and looking after them. She also knew how to cut grass and bring it home as cattle feed. Quite a few men and women in their neighbourhood used to go daily to the outskirts of the city to cut grass and earned about eight *annas* per day for their effort. She took up the same job. Entrusting the child to Gobar's care, she would leave home early in the morning and cut grass till late afternoon. From there she proceeded to the market; only to return home late at night. Despite such hard work, she managed to remain pleasant and reasonably cheerful.

At night her sleep was inextricably linked to Gobar's. She woke up when he did and rested only when he slept peacefully. She did not feel burdened; she went through it with a song on her lips, completely happy, composed and determined. Each morning on her way to the city limits, she joked and smiled with the other women who went with her. Even as they toiled, she always had a kind word to say and an amusing anecdote to regale them with. She didn't complain, bemoan her bad luck or generally curse life for not being fair to her. The sparkle of a positive outlook and the joy inherent in working voluntarily and willingly for one's loved ones shone through at all times. Her joy was that of a little infant who chortles in glee on discovering the delight of plodding two steps unaided on its own feet. A spring of happiness burst forth in her heart and it swept away all her sorrows. Inner happiness has such an amazing way of reflecting in physical health. Her limbs turned supple, the pale yellow on her face gave way to a rosy glow as her youth, locked up in a dingy corner of her life so far, stepped out into bright sunshine glowing and content with the world. She didn't snap at little things and brushed aside minor irritants with a laugh. When her baby cried not many weeks ago, she would lose her cool within seconds but now the fount of her patience never seemed to cease flowing.

In direct contrast to her uplifted mood, Gobar remained glum and withdrawn despite his steady recovery. If we are unkind to those whom we love, we can only feel their pain if we suddenly fall into adverse times. Good sense comes to prevail on us and we want to repent as fast as we can. Gobar was now desperate to make up to her. He was impatient to prove to her that, henceforth, his life would turn a new leaf. Now there would be pleasantness instead of bitterness and humility in place of false pride. He was discovering in his heart- the joys of giving. He had begun to realise that service to others was more joyful than extracting it from them for one's own enjoyment. He was firm in his belief that he was not going to let this opportunity pass him by.

❁❁❁

28

Mr. Khanna was of the firm opinion that the ongoing strike by mill workers was totally unwarranted. He had always tried his best to go along with their interest as he considered himself a man close to the masses. Recently, during the latest agitation against the British government, he was one of those few rich men who led from the front. He was the head of the local committee for freedom and everybody was witness to the great enthusiasm he was capable of generating amongst the protesting freedom fighters. He had gone to jail twice and suffered losses for his bravado which meant a setback of thousands of rupees in financial terms. He was not averse to addressing worker's grievances but it was only fair that he should not ignore the sugar-mill owners either. He could put his interest on the back burner if his feelings of compassion and benevolence were sufficiently propitiated, but trampling on shareholders interest was nothing less than sacrilege.

This was business; not an open-house of charity where all profit could be distributed equally amongst petty workers. The shareholders had invested money on the promise and assurance that their investment would fetch them no less than a fifteen to twenty percent profit. If they did not get a minimum of ten percent return on their investment, their opinion of the directors would take a beating and Mr. Khanna's credibility would not be spared as well. The investors would label them cheats and moreover, why should he reduce his salary voluntarily to appease popular socialist sentiments? He was not a profiteering leech and had already kept his salary way below the industry average. It was low as a piddling one thousand per month. Well, he did retain a certain commission from his dealings but then did he not manage the entire mill single-handedly?

Workers contributed with physical labour but a director chipped in with his intelligence, knowledge, education and talent to ensure that the factory produced better. There was a distinct difference between the two inputs and they were just not the same. Why couldn't the workers realise that due to the depression in the economy, labour was coming cheap. They should count themselves blessed and be content if they got a quarter percent of the profits. In fact, they were actually a contented lot and it was not their fault entirely. They were innocent but stupid like cattle. The real villains in the plot were Mirza Khurshid and editor Onkarnath, who were manipulating them like puppets for personal fame and perhaps some pecuniary advantages as well. They didn't care a damn if their abrasive attitude resulted in ruin for many poor families. Should it concern Khanna if Onkarnath's paper wasn't doing too well? Imagine, if he suddenly got a hundred thousand subscribers for his newspaper and made five hundred thousand rupees from it, would he merely retain a subsistence amount and distribute the major chunk of that amount amongst his workers? Won't that be silly? And that Mirza Khurshid the one who had suddenly discovered a newfound love for the working class was a complete turncoat. He was a millionaire himself before he lost everything due to his own blunders. The mill workers whose interest he tried to espouse were the very same men who lost their jobs in his business and found shelter here. Did he ever distribute profits as generously to his workers as he wanted Khanna to give? Never! He blew up his fortune romancing girls in European capitals. When he was doing well, he partied with government officials and sozzled himself up with liquor worth thousands of rupees. Every year he holidayed in France and Switzerland and today, so conveniently, his heart began bleeding for the poor workers!

Khanna had no love lost for these two self-styled leaders. Their intentions were transparent to him. He wasn't too convinced of Rai sahib's sincerity, despite his profuse and vocal support. Amongst all his acquaintances, there was only person who stood out as someone whom he trusted for his sound judgement and that was Professor Mehta. But ever since Mehta seemed to grow intimate with Malti, his regard for him fell a few notches. Malti held a very prominent position in Khanna's heart but she was never more than a plaything to him, howsoever prized. He dreaded losing her and moped for days when he thought she left him but despite his attachment to her she was never more than a toy. He did not trust her. She never penetrated the core of his soul. Had she proposed to him herself, he would not have accepted it and would have found an excuse to fob her off.

Like many others of his ilk, Khanna's attitude was ambivalent and confused. One part of him was warm, considerate of social responsibility and caring while the other was selfish and fond of indulgence with a keen desire to always be in control. The better part of his subconscious mind was full of a desire to serve with compassion while the remaining part revelled in luxurious living and cold selfishness. There was a constant friction between these opposing facets of his nature. Unfortunately, the lower part of his consciousness subjugated his superior nature with its aggressive and defiant posturing.

He failed to appreciate what made an intellectual and refined person like Mehta fall for a frivolous twit like Malti. Despite his best efforts, he knew he could not rein in Mehta's lust for Malti though he often doubted if there was some hidden aspect of that woman which was unknown to him and which was working its magic on Mehta.

After examining all pros and cons and giving the issue deep thought, he finally decided the only person who could set his doubts at rest was none other than Mehta himself.

Mehta was a workaholic. He slept at midnight and woke up before daybreak. He somehow managed to find time to do things despite seeming to be under pressure of work. Whether it was playing hockey or a debate in the university, rural development projects or attending a friend's wedding, he had both time and inclination for everything. He wrote for newspapers and was working on a book which was now close to completion. That day when Khanna approached him he was at one of his new hobbies. He was sitting in his garden, studying the effect of electric current in plants. He had presented a paper in a scientific journal that sought to propose a hypothesis that electricity could be used to induce growth in plants, albeit for a limited period of time. It could help in generating a higher yield and also grow crops out of season. Lately, he spent two to three hours every morning on this study.

Mehta heard Khanna's story and assumed a grave form as he spoke to him in all seriousness. "Was it really necessary to reduce workers wages just because the government increased duties on raw materials? You should take it up with the relevant authorities instead of taking it out on the workers. If the government refused to pay heed to your pleas that would also not be reason enough to tax poor workers. Do you think you pay such high wages to them that by deducting almost one quarter, it will not make any difference to their lives? Your workers live in smelly dark burrows; the sort of places where you'd throw up in an instant if you had to stand there for a mere second. You will not wipe your shoes with the sort of clothes they wear. Your dog will refuse to touch the food they eat every day. I have seen their lives at close quarters. You are only trying to squeeze them further to please your shareholders..."

Khanna shook his head impatiently and said, "Not all our shareholders are rich people. So many of them have given up all they had and invested it in the mill. They are totally dependent on it for their survival."

Mehta's stance conveyed that the argument cut no ice with him. "When someone decides to buy shares in a company he implies he is not dumb. He should know that such an investment cannot become the sole source of his income. He understands he might have to cut down on the number of servants if profits aren't good or he might be forced reduce the bills of imported butter or fruits in the kitchen. He knows that poor profits in investments will not make him a pauper on the streets. Those who sweat it out in the factory have more rights on the profits than those who throw some money in as an investment."

Onkarnath and Mirza Khurshid had forwarded the same argument on many occasions. Govindi had also said things to the same effect but Khanna had brushed aside their ideas. However, today, hearing it from Mehta's mouth, created an entirely different impression on his mind. He considered editor Onkarnath an utterly selfish man, Mirza Khurshid was irresponsible and his wife was not fit to comment on the subject. But Mehta's words carried character; they came from deep experience and conveyed the strength of sincere compassion.

Suddenly Mehta asked him if he had elicited his wife's views on the subject.

Rather hesitantly, Khanna said that he had.

"What is her opinion?"

"The same as yours."

"I always suspected that you consider that intelligent lady unqualified to have a correct view on the issue."

At that instant Malti sailed in and seeing Khanna with Mehta, expressed surprise and spoke cheerily. "Oh! I see you are here as well! I have invited Mehta for dinner. I will cook the meal myself. Let me invite you as well. Don't worry; I will request Govindi to forgive you for accepting my invitation."

Khanna was curious. So now Malti has started cooking food herself? The same Malti who could not put on her hunting boots without seeking assistance, the one who wanted someone else to switch on the electric lights for her in her own home was now preparing a full meal! He smiled softly and said, "If you are cooking, I will surely want to taste it. I didn't have the foggiest idea you had any cooking talent."

Malti responded without batting an eyelid. "Well, Mehta insisted and pushed me into becoming a chef of sorts. How can I refuse his orders? He is the dominant male, isn't he?"

Khanna savoured the statement and winked at Mehta as he spoke to Malti, "Since when did the dominant male species start meaning so much to you?"

Malti realised the import of what he said and blushed. However she gathered herself instantly and said, "It's true I am not enamoured of the male ego but lately, I have revised my opinion. The image of men that I had was built from certain acquaintances in my immediate circle but now I discover that that the male is much more beautiful and has a more tender heart than I imagined."

Mehta's expression was pained as he said, "Come on Malti. Spare me, please. Or do you want me to just walk away from here?"

Those days Malti was floating on cloud nine. She was full of Mr. Mehta and praised him to the skies with the zeal and enthusiasm of a neo-convert whenever she found a receptive audience. So obsessed was she with her pet passion that she discarded all sense of proportion in speech, much to Mehta's discomfiture. He relished hearing criticism but praise knocked him off his composed self. It made him feel foolish and embarrassed as if he were being ridiculed. But Malti was one woman who could never be contained. It was not in her nature to be subdued, subtle or quiet. She could be nothing but an extrovert both in her actions and thoughts. It was tough for her to keep things to herself. Just as she would not rest till she let the whole world see when she bought a new saree, she felt suffocated till she did not express to all and sundry, any interesting idea or thought that came to her mind.

Malti sidled close to Mehta and put her arm on his back in an apparently protective gesture.

"Okay. Please don't run away. I promise not to reveal anything positive. I think you adore being criticised. And if that is so, here goes, 'Khanna, this cunning gentleman is trying to snare me in his love..."

From where they stood they could clearly see the chimney of the sugar mill. Khanna turned his face away to look in its direction. The chimney stood stark against the sky like a proud sentinel – a visible pinnacle of the heights of his success. His eyes shone with a proud, complacent satisfaction. It was time for him to go to his office at the mill. He had to call an urgent meeting of the directors to decide on the future course of action. In the face of challenging circumstances it was incumbent on him to present to them his ideas on how to solve the present impasse.

But what was that? He thought he saw a thin column of smoke rising from outside the chimney and not from inside it as usual. Within a few seconds, the sky was overcast by dense dark smoke. The trio stared at the rising smoke apprehensively. Was that a fire? Indeed, it was.

They saw hundreds of people on the road, hurrying excitedly towards the mill. Khanna ran out and stood in the middle of the road and barked at them, "Where are you going?"

One man stopped for a moment and said breathlessly, "Can't you see, mister? The sugar mill is on fire."

Khanna stared at Mehta and Mehta stared at Malti. There was not a moment for expressing regrets or making sympathetic noises. None of them spoke a word. In the face of fear, our consciousness becomes keen and sharply focused to prepare for flight or fight. Khanna's car was parked nearby. The three of them scrambled into it, fear writ large on their faces. When they drove up to the main crossing, they discovered that probably the entire city was charging towards the mill. A fire attracts spectators like a magnet. Their car could hardly move an inch in the milling crowds.

Mehta said, "I hope you had the mill well ensured?"

Khanna drew in his breath and said, "No man, not yet. We were still discussing about it. How was I to know calamity would strike unannounced like this?"

They abandoned the car in the middle of the road and started running on foot, pushing and shoving through the frantic crowd and reached the mill. A sea of flames swayed majestically before their eyes. Large greedy flames of fire flashed menacingly, as if they would devour the entire sky. Black smoke billowed below the rising flames like dark clouds of thunder. Above the thick smoke rose a towering mountain of fire that shook and trembled as if it had a life of its own. A crowd of almost a thousand men stood in the courtyard before the mill. The police had arrived, so had the fire brigade. The water sprayed through hoses seemed puny and ineffective. The bricks were burning along with the steel girders and large streams of molten sugar flowed out in all directions from the building. The fire leapt out from the earth as well, as it incinerated the liquid.

Mehta and Khanna watched from a distance wondering why no one was venturing to do anything to fight the fire. They soon realised that given the intensity of the fire there was precious little anyone could do except wait and watch. In the circumstances it was outright dangerous to come within fifty yards of the fire. Large parts of walls and bricks cracked and fell to the earth as cinders flew in all directions. At times when the direction of wind changed, it created a stampede amongst the onlookers.

The three of them stood helplessly with the crowds. They didn't know what to speak, wondering what caused such a terrible catastrophe. They failed to understand how it spread so fast. Did anyone notice it in the initial stages? And if they did, whether they made any effort to control it? All sorts of doubts and questions rose in their mind but there was nobody who they could turn to and ask. Not a single person in the sea of faces around them appeared familiar.

Suddenly a quirky gust of breeze sent the flames flashing right onto their faces. The crowd moved back like a tidal wave. People fell over each other, scrambling and stepping over those who had fallen down, as if a lion had attacked a peaceful group of onlookers. Mighty flames leapt from all sides like a hydra headed dragon gone crazy, spouting fire through its mouth and myriad heads. Innumerable people were crushed in the stampede. Khanna fell on his face as Mehta held on to Malti lest she was swept under the feet of the panicking masses. They struggled to reach the safety of a wall and stood in a tight bunch under the solitary tree in the mill's courtyard. Khanna stared at the chimney of the burning mill in a daze. His eyes held a distant, unconscious indifference to the scene that was enfolding before him.

Mehta asked him if he was hurt bad. Khanna didn't reply. He just looked back at him with a blank expression. Mehta caught his hand and shook it vigorously. "I think we are standing here unnecessarily. I am worried you have hurt yourself badly. Come, let's get out of here."

Khanna kept staring at him and spoke cynically, "I know those who orchestrated this. If this is what they want, may God be merciful to them. I care a damn. I am least bothered about it. If I want, I can open a new mill even as I stand here. Who do they think they are? This mill did not make me, I made this mill. And I can build it all over again. But I won't spare those who did this to me. I know them all; I know everything."

On seeing his delirious state, Mehta was truly worried to the extent of panic. "Let's go. Let me take you home. You don't look good at all."

A cynical cackle of laughter escaped Khanna's lips. "What's wrong with me? You think I am falling into pieces because my mill has burnt down to ashes? I can open such mills whenever I like. My name is Khanna. Chandra Prakash Khanna! I ploughed everything I had into it. We made twenty percent profits in the first one. That is why I started this second mill. Half of the money invested in it is mine. I poured two lakh rupees from the bank into it. What do you think? Just an hour ago, no, only half an hour ago, I was worth ten lakhs. Yes sir! Ten lakhs. But now I am not just bankrupt, I am ruined! I have to return two lakhs to the bank. The house where I live isn't mine any more. Not even the plate I eat from; that's not mine either. They will throw me out of the bank. The Khanna who was envied by everyone is finished. He is gone. I have no standing in society any longer. My friends will not trust me; they'll only pity me. My enemies won't envy me; they'll laugh at me. You don't know me Mehta; I have trampled on every principle I held dear. I have taken bribes on umpteen occasions and given bribes on as many. The sort of men I employed to weigh the peasants' sugarcane, the fudged weights I used to weigh their crops- oh come on- what will you gain knowing these sordid details? But one thing is for sure Khanna will not live to see his life dashed into pieces. The world may say what it wants, friends may cluck their tongues in sympathy for all I care, and people may spit at my name but I just don't care. I will not wait to see his reputation paraded in the streets for all to scorn. He will die before anything like that happens. He is not a shameless wimp." Khanna's voice trailed off hysterically as he howled like a wild animal and wept openly.

Mehta hugged him close and whispered in his ears, "Khanna, please, please be patient. You are an intelligent man; it doesn't behove you to crack up like this. The respect a man earns because of his wealth is not due to his greatness but to the lure of his fortune. Your true friends will trust you even if you are a poor man. Even your enemies will respect you. Actually, you will cease to be a threat to them now and you won't have any enemies any more. Come, let's go home. Take rest for a while, you'll feel better after that."

Khanna didn't say a word. The three of them walked up to the main road. Their car was still where they had left it. In ten minutes they were at Khanna's mansion.

When he got down from the car he was much more composed. "You can take the car with you," he said, "I will not need it tonight."

Malti and Mehta were already out of the car. Malti said, "You go and take rest in your room. We will lounge outside in your living room and generally chit chat over things. We are in no tearing hurry to go home."

Khanna turned a grateful eye at her and said, "Malti, please forgive me if I have hurt you in any way. Other than you and Mehta, I don't have any good friend in the whole world. I hope you will not have a low opinion of me. Most probably, I will have to give up this house within a week or ten days. What hard luck! I have been pushed into nothingness."

Mehta said, "Trust me, Khanna. The deep respect that I feel for you today is exceptional. I have never felt more concerned and warm towards you before this."

They entered the living room. On hearing the sound of the main door opening, Govindi came into the room and said, "Are you coming from there? The cook gave me the bad news sometime back."

An enormous rush of pain and sympathy coursed through him when he saw Govindi. Khanna wanted to rush into her arms and cry but he merely said in a voice quivering with emotion, "Yes dear. You heard right. We are finished."

His listless, lost soul was starved for words of consolation. He needed assurance, much like a terminally ill patient who stares piteously at the doctor, expecting him to say something that will kindle hope in his dying heart. Before him stood the very woman whom he despised, ridiculed, insulted and made fun of at the drop of a hat. He wasn't faithful to her; he had abused her consistently, considering her a dispensable burden on his life. The same woman, whose death he had prayed for, stood before him completely forgiving and so concerned about his welfare. Her bearing was that of someone keen to somehow give his flagging spirit a fillip, a boost and assure him all was well. Her arms seemed to ache to hug him close; she was almost close to panic as if she didn't want to lose a moment to help him pick up his scattered life all over again. The rocks we avoid while boating in a lake and which we wish would disappear are the ones we hold on to for dear life if our boat capsizes.

Govindi led him to a sofa and settled him on it. Her tone was soft and full of concern as she spoke to him. "Why are you so worried? Is it money that bothers you, the same thing that is at the root of all evil? What happiness did your wealth give us? All day and night it was one big obsession that corrupted your soul. You had no time for your kids and your relatives never received a single letter from you asking after their welfare. Did it add to your prestige? Probably yes, and only because the world worships at the altar of wealth. It had nothing to do with you personally. They will wag their tails before you as long as you own a lot of wealth. No one will spare another look at you if you fall on bad days. The really good people do not put a rider of wealth when they build their relations. They are only concerned about what you do and what sort of person you are. If you are honest, industrious, are willing to sacrifice for others, then they will hail you as a great man. They will praise you for what you are and not for what you own or possess. It is their friendship and praise that you should seek and worry about. Isn't it right Mehta? I hope I didn't say anything wrong."

Mehta was mesmerised by her words and when he saw she was talking to him, he snapped out of his reverie with a jolt. "You are perfectly right.. What you say is what great men have said after decades and years of experiencing life's truths. What you say is the real essence of life."

Govindi looked Mehta in the eyes when she spoke next. "No one really bothers to find out how the rich ones really become rich. It is only by making fools of others. By using all their talents in throwing dust in other's eyes, people make money and earn the respect of even those they have fooled."

Khanna interrupted her. "No Govindi, one needs to be civilised and dignified to earn money. Mere talent and expertise isn't enough. Making money involves sacrifice and dedication as well. The amount of devotion put into producing wealth might bring a man to the level of spiritual enlightenment if he turns those energies in another direction. Wealth and fortune are the sum total of all our intellectual, physical and emotional energies."

Govindi's response did not have the sharpness of someone against that supposition but it had a more dispassionate feel to it. "I agree with you that making money does involve quite a bit of dedication and commitment but it does not deserve the importance we accord to it. I think I am quite relieved that now my husband is free of the burden of immense wealth. Now our sons will grow up into socially useful men, not stuffed mannequins of greed and puerile ambition. The joy of life is in giving, not in usurping it from others. Till now our entire life was centred on our own selfishness, enjoyment and pleasure. The Lord has opened new vistas of hope and joy for us by depriving us of our so called great fortune. If the road to that discovery is littered with a few trials and tribulations, one shouldn't mind it but welcome it. I think it is better to be victimised than be a victimiser. If we are able to claim our souls by losing all the wealth we possess, it's not a bad bargain at all. How can you not feel the happiness and contentment that comes in fighting as soldiers for justice?"

There was a strange glow of an inexplicable energy on Govindi's cheeks. Her dry face was suffused with a rare brightness as if her silent prayers were answered and everything that she had ever wished for had dropped into her lap, all at once.

Mehta stood in silence, staring at her with admiring, appreciative eyes. Khanna's eyes were downcast and he was still fumbling to understand what this little Goddess was trying to tell him. Malti was feeling terribly repentant – she did not know Govindi's heart was so noble and elevated. She marvelled at the woman whose sheer grace had touched her life so amazingly in the last few minutes.

❁❁❁

29

Not one to forget after doing a favour, Nohri loved to extract the maximum mileage she could derive from any good deed she did for others. It was embedded deep in her nature to go to great lengths to ensure that everyone heard about her charitable act. In fact, she wanted more credit than was due to her. Unfortunately, more often than not, that inevitably became her undoing. Not doing a good deed does not discredit anyone but making a kind gesture or act and bragging about it, most certainly sullies the image of any Good Samaritan. Instead of earning us friends, it makes enemies of those whom we tried to help in the first place. Charity loses its sheen once it is proclaimed from rooftops.

Nohri went to town talking about the sorry state of Hori's finances and how pushed to the wall he was and how he was so unable to make both ends meet and how he could not marry off his daughter. She narrated in exaggerated detail, how she felt bad for him, how her heart bled on learning that he had mortgaged his land for the wedding expenses and how she ventured to help him out as a matter of duty. She told everyone what a low opinion she had of Dhania who had her head in the clouds while her poor husband slogged day and night to keep body and spirit together. She explained that since it is the bounden duty of a fellow being to help others in distress, she went out of her way to ease the situation for them. Like it or not, they were related to each other and it was incumbent on her to come to their help. She gave them the money so that the hapless girl could be married off. If she had not done that she would remain an unmarried maiden waiting endlessly for a suitor.

But Dhania was not one to listen to such trash. The money was no charity, it was a loan. Nohri was talking utter rubbish, the slimy woman! The moneylender would charge an interest, so would Nohri, what was the difference?

It was one of those dark nights of the season and the village lay enveloped under a pitch dark, overcast sky. Hori was preparing to light his last puff of *chillum* before he retired to bed after a late dinner when he saw Bhola come and pause for a moment at his door.

"What's up, brother?" Hori was curious, "why don't you move to a new home away from where you live now? I am sure you are aware of the sort of stuff being spoken about you. Do you think it's proper? Don't mind my saying so, but you are related to me now that's why I am telling you as I feel concerned. I can't bear to see you insulted like this."

Dhania came over to leave a pitcher of water at Hori's bedstead. She heard the conversation and added her bit to it. "Had it been any other man, he would have chopped off his woman's head for what she had done."

Hori snapped at her in irritation for unnecessarily speaking out of turn. "What rubbish are you talking? Just leave the water and go to sleep. If you go down the wrong path do you think I will chop off your head for that?"

Dhania dipped her fingers in the pitcher and threw a few drops at him playfully, "May your sisters go down the wrong path! Why should it be me? I merely mentioned it in passing and you start cursing me. Do you feel better; now that we have both said hurtful things to each other? I for one do not consider a man to be a real man if he chooses to do nothing if his woman goes astray."

Hori was quite mad by now. Bhola must have come to unburden his heart to him and here she was going hammer and tongs at him. He spoke rather heatedly, "All day you go around doing what you fancy. Do I ever complain? You don't lose a moment to make sarcastic remarks if I as much as comment on your activities."

Dhania held no brief for subtleties. She piped up right away- "If a woman spills a pot of *ghee* or burns down the house, her husband might forgive her but God help her if he finds her straying."

Bhola agreed with her, sounding still more crestfallen. "I agree with you, Dhania. I should have cut her head off but perhaps now, I am not man enough for that. You try to drill some sense into her. She might listen to you."

Dhania had her tirade ready. "When you didn't have the guts to keep your woman in check, why did you rush into marriage once again? Did you expect- that she would be a dumb cow tied to your door? The woman who would tend to you in your illness and stand by you when you hit low times is the one who has lived the good life with you for a major part of her life. I wonder what great beauty or talent you saw in her. Shouldn't you have made some discreet enquiries before committing yourself? But you were a hungry, starved hyena and that is how you walked into the trap. If you go to jail for chopping her head off, perhaps it will be a small price to pay for the shame you bear every day.

The blood running in Bhola's veins coursed faster with a newfound energy. "So this is what you recommend, eh?"

"Exactly. You won't live very long as it is. What is the harm in retrieving lost prestige before you march into the sunset?"

This time Hori rebuked her sharply. She was going over the top. "Shut up, foolish woman! Don't act so pious and holier than thou. One can't hold a bird against her wishes in a cage, what to talk of a woman. Bhola, the best course open to you is to leave her and go back to your sons. Better a life with your own kin than with a woman who has gone astray. Your days of youth are long gone; it's time to make preparations for the afterlife. Move on, man."

It was impossible for Bhola to forget Nohri or get her out of his system. Even at that moment he could see her eyes glaring at him, weakening his resolve. But no, now he was determined to take his life in his own hands. He would leave her. Whatever life had to offer him, he would accept meekly. He must reap what he sowed.

"Brother Hori, only I know the pain of being saddled to this woman. I fought with my sons for her and at this late stage of my life; I have to cut such a sorry figure in society. Every day she taunts me that my daughter eloped from home. What if my daughter eloped? At least, she is safe and secure with her man- she is with him through thick and thin. I have never seen a woman as low as Nohri who sweet-talks other men and frowns when she is with her husband. I am a poor man- at best I earn a few *annas* a day. How does she expect me to provide her with milk, sweets, fish and meat?"

When Bhola left Hori's house a while later, a steely resolve seemed to grip his mind and gave him a breezy confidence in himself. Now he was determined to stay with his sons. But the next morning Hori saw Bhola walking towards Dulari's shop to buy a packet of snuff. When he got back home Hori told Dhania that he suspected Bhola had done nothing and was still with Nohri.

Dhania grimaced sarcastically- "Both of them are as shameless as each other. A man like him should drown himself in shame. I am surprised where all his bravado and machismo has gone? When Jhuniya came to our door, he went around the village with a stick to beat her with. At that time, his reputation was under attack. What happened now?"

Hori felt sorry for Bhola. The poor guy was ruining himself over that miserable wretch. But did he have any option? It wasn't easy to dump a woman. And Nohri was that type of woman who would not let him be at peace even if he walked out on her. She would summon the village elders and stake her claim on his property. Till now the story was under wraps and was discussed as rumour and gossip but if he walked out, it could be publicly discussed threadbare everywhere. Then Bhola would get all the blame. People would sympathise with Nohri and defend all her actions saying she had no option but to sue if her husband deserted her. A bad man would kill his wife; a bad woman would ruin a man's reputation.

Two months later, the village was abuzz with the rumour that Nohri gave a sound thrashing to her husband, beating him black and blue with her slippers.

The rainy season was long gone and they were readying for the next crop. Hori's sugarcane was auctioned but he didn't get enough money to pay for the seeds. One of his bulls was getting old and a new one was needed urgently. To make matters worse one of Puniya's bulls fell in a ditch and died. Now he had to alternate the field work with just one animal and look after Puniya's and his own fields as well. As a result, neither was well ploughed.

Hori took his bulls to the fields but Bhola was always on his mind. He felt concerned about him. Never in his life had he heard of an incident where a woman had slapped her husband with slippers. Today, it seems Nohri beat him with shoes and everyone just stood there and watched the spectacle. How should he help him escape her clutches? She was driving poor Bhola to suicide. It was so shameful. His life was one long story of insults and misery. No one would cry for him, he was so utterly lonely. His sons would attend to his cremation rites but only because it was the socially done and expected thing, not for any love for their father.

On the one side there was a woman like Nohri and on the other a low caste *chamaran* like Siliya and the contrast between them was amazing. She was ten times better looking than Nohri – if she wanted, she would charm the village with her coquettishness and lead an easy life but no, that girl worked like a common labourer for a good-for-nothing husband like Matadin who would have nothing to do with her. Who knows, had Dhaniya died, Hori himself would have been in a similar situation as Siliya.

Simply imagining Dhaniya dead made Hori's blood run cold. Her image came alive in his eyes, a goddess of service and devotion, sharp of tongue but with a heart like molten butter. A woman who refused to part with a single *paisa* but was ready to give up all she had for a just and good cause. She was also quite a looker when she was young. People would stare at her open mouthed at her charming bearing. Both Pateshwari and Jhinguri Singh were young men when she came into his life. They did stare at her secretly. Hori kept a hawk's eye on their intentions but they were only leering louts. He was quite hard up those days. Working far from home and had to often leave for full days. Dhania would be alone at home but not once did anyone see her making eyes at the dandy men in the village. Once Pateshwari made a pass at her but she gave him such a tongue lashing that he remembers it to the day.

Suddenly he spied Matadin striding up to him. What a heartless man and cheeky too, he wore a long caste mark on his forehead, heralding his exalted Brahmin status, as if he was the chosen one. The slimy fox! Hori was in no mood to bow in reverence to a Brahmin like him.

Matadin walked right up to Hori and remarked- "The bull on the left side of your plough is not doing too well. I don't think it will be good enough for the next season. He is five years old, isn't he?"

Hori patted the bull affectionately and said, "Five? He's going on eight, brother! If I had my way, I would retire him on a pension but a peasant and his bulls are parted only by death, neither can retire the other. My heart aches when I put the yoke on his head. Poor chap, he must be cursing me for pushing him so hard but I can't help it, can I?" said Hori patting the bull again. He then looked at Matadin and asked, "Where are you off to? I hope you are feeling better."

Matadin was down with malaria for the last few weeks. Just last week as he lay silently on his bed, the local quack couldn't locate his heartbeat and feared he was dead. People around him covered his face when he stirred. Even as his relatives thanked God for bringing him back to life, Matadin made a firm decision in his mind that he would go and make up with Siliya. His suffering appeared to him like a providential punishment for the way he had treated her. She was pregnant when he remorselessly pushed her out of his house. She continued to work in the fields all through the pregnancy. Had Dhania not taken pity on her, the poor girl would be dead by now. Chastened by a close brush with death himself, her travails now cut into his heart and turned like a knife of guilt. Shamed and moved, he had now come to Hori to pass on two rupees to her as atonement or an expression of regret. He wanted Hori to give her the money for which he would be very grateful to him.

"Why don't you do that yourself?" said Hori.

Matadin sounded hurt- "Please don't tell me to go to her. I can't face her. I am scared she will get turn me away. Please have mercy on me. I am unable to walk properly but I went quite a distance to one house for this donation. I have suffered enough for my sins. I can't bear the weight of my holy caste any longer. Anyone can sin in secret and no one will bat an eyelid but out in the open, it is another matter. The family name gets besmirched. Please make her understand. Plead my case for me. Tell her to forgive my sins. The chains of religiosity and social bindings are so hard to break. Any other person can survive breaking the codes but not a Brahmin. It's tough for him. His faith is little more than the sum total of the piety of his ancestors. He survives on the tradition of piety. We blew up three hundred rupees, wasted them in a bid to atone for my sins. So if I have to live like an outcaste from the fold, I'd rather do everything openly. Man has to follow some rules to humour society but as a human being, doesn't he have to follow the rules of humanity as well? Society will respect you if you adhere to its regulations but by following the rules of humanity God Himself will be pleased."

That evening when Hori handed the money to Siliya he was very hesitant and sceptical how she would receive it but was surprised to see that she took it as a great gift--as if it was a blessing. Siliya could bear the weight of her pain all alone but it was difficult for her to live alone and disconnected with others in her moment of joy. She simply had to share it with someone. Siliya wondered whom she could invite to communicate her happiness. She couldn't open her heart to Dhania and there was not a single person in the village who she could talk to as she wasn't that close to anyone. The excitement of this development gurgled like a spring, bursting to come out from her heart, through her words, to someone who would hear and be delighted about it. Hori's elder daughter Sona was her first real friend but now she was married to Mathura. Siliya was impatient to meet her. It became impossible for her to wait the night out before she told her the great news.

A whirlwind of delight raged in Siliya's heart. She wasn't all alone any more. Matadin had held her hand once again. She was no longer looking at the arid desert of loneliness and misery, now she was seeing green fields, swaying in their lush abundance. She almost heard the music of waterfalls and the calls of prancing deer in the forest. The love lying shrivelled and angry within her heart, suddenly unloosened its knots and rose to play and rejoice in newfound hope. She had cursed Matadin day in day out; now she must ask for his forgiveness. It was a huge mistake on her part to become the instrument of insult and the stick with which everyone beat her man all these days. She was a low caste, it didn't matter to her much if they rebuked her. Her man was a high caste Brahmin and because of her, his reputation was tarnished forever. She was so blind that in her anger she had trumpeted her love for him. His reputation was shattered so his irritation was justified. Why did she have to raise hell over it? She could have gone back to her home quietly. Everyone respected Matadin because he followed the regulations and social mores dutifully. Because of her he had suffered; she regretted not understanding his angst and dwelling only on her hurt.

A few minutes ago, she laid all blame at Matadin's door and now she gathered it up and dumped it on herself. His small gesture of regret and remorse had given rise to compassion and forgiveness in her heart. She took her baby in her arms and kissed the surprised infant repeatedly. He wasn't an unwanted lovechild any more- now he deserved all her love, respect and pride.

The silver moonlight of an October night enveloped the village and fell on it softly like a lullaby as it slumbered snug and drowsy. Siliya left her home quietly. She must go to Sona and tell her about the wonderful new development in her life. She couldn't keep it to herself any longer. There would be a boat on the river, it was not very late into the night. But when she reached the river, she saw that the boat was moored on the other bank and there was no sign of the boatman whom she could hail with her cries.

The milky moonbeam shone on the river with an uncanny light. She stood on the shore, staring mesmerised at the rippling waters. Certainly the river wouldn't be terribly deep this time of the year. She entered it tentatively; the sea of happiness inside dwarfed the petty river before her. The water reached her ankles as she strode in but rose to her waist steadily and soon it was bobbing around her neck. For a moment she panicked- she didn't want to drown. No, not now, please! But she carried on. Now she was midstream. Death touched her ears with wet cold fingers but she was unafraid. She knew how to swim and had swum across this river innumerable times as a small girl yet her heart beat fast. Suddenly she felt the water level go down. No fear now! She stroked harder and reached the shore, wet and dripping. Squeezing as much water as she could from her wet *saree,* she walked on, shivering in the sudden cold. There was total silence all around. Not a dog barked but the excitement of meeting and talking to her old friend had shorn the silent night of any foreboding.

But the moment she entered Sona's village limits, she started feeling hesitant. Whatever would people say? What would her folks say? Sona would also not be very pleased with her for coming at such an unearthly hour. In villages tired peasants retired to bed early. The entire village was in deep sleep as Siliya made her way to her friend's place. The house wore a desolate look- the doors were closed. Suddenly Siliya didn't have the guts to knock at that hour. If they see her all wet and shivering she wondered how they would react. There was a dying fire in a dug up corner outside the door. She sat down next to it, trying to warm her hands and dry her clothes. Abruptly someone opened the door and she heard Sona's husband Mathura's voice, "Hey! Who's at the door near the fire?"

Hurriedly Siliya pulled her *saree* around her and whispered- "It's me, Siliya!"

"Siliya!" Mathura was quite surprised, "What are you doing here at this hour? All's well I hope?"

"Oh yes, all's well back home. I was getting restless, thought of just dropping by and meeting all of you. I don't have a moments respite in the day."

"Did you swim across the river?"

"How else could I come? Moreover, it wasn't very deep."

Mathura took her inside. It was dark in the veranda. Mathura caught her hand and tried to pull her close. She sprang out of his grip and admonished him, "Now listen, Mathura. You are like a younger brother-in-law. Don't act fresh or I will tell Sona about it. It seems you are not content with one woman."

Mathura slipped an arm around her waist. "You are such a spoilsport, Sillo. Nobody is watching us."

"Am I any better looking than Sona? Why don't you count yourself lucky that you have such a pretty wife? Why do you want to act the philanderer? If I tell her, she won't ever look at you again."

Mathura was no cheap lout. He actually loved Sona very much. The starkness, solitude and a wet Siliya was a mix he just couldn't resist. Hearing her harsh words, he checked himself sharply. He loosened his grip around her at once and said, "I am sorry, Sillo. I beg of you. Don't tell Sona about it. Punish me in whatever way you want but please keep this to yourself."

Sillo felt sorry for him. She delivered a playful slap lightly on his face and said, "Your punishment is that you promise not to repeat this foolishness again. Not with me, not with anyone else, lest you lose Sona forever."

"I swear to God, Siliya, I won't. This will never happen again."

She felt the deep regret in his voice. She still felt sorrier for him. Her concern for him had softened with a strange edge of intimate compassion.

"But what if it does?"

"Then you do whatever you want."

Sillo's face was very close to his. Their breath was short and there was a tremor in their voice and bodies as well. Suddenly they heard a voice in the dark, "Who are you talking to there?"

Sillo stepped back and Mathura came out on the courtyard. "It is Sillo from your village. She's here."

Sillo stepped into the courtyard. She looked around and saw the comfortable surroundings in which her friend lived. On a string cot in the veranda she could see the dim outline of a comfortable looking mattress. A bolster and a pillow lay on one side of the bed. The bedspread was soft and clean, just like the ones on Matadin's bed. A tumbler of water, covered with a small plate was placed under the bed. In the courtyard, the moonlight spread a soft glow on everything it fell upon. A *tulsi* plant, in its planter and piles of bundles of hay were stacked at the other end of the courtyard. A small heap of pounded husk was scattered close to a pounding stone, next to a creeper that grew all over the tiled roof above it. Siliya heard the soft bells around a cow's neck that was hidden from view in a shed close by. It was a picture of languorous domesticity. This was the section that was Mathura and Sona's private space. Other members of the family must be in another portion of the house. Siliya thought to herself how happy and peaceful Sona must be in her new house.

Sona had also come into the courtyard but she wasn't making an effort to come close to Siliya or hug her. Sillo thought perhaps her lack of warmth was due to a hesitation caused by Mathura's presence. In another moment, she thought it was possible Sona had turned haughty and proud therefore she was acting so cold. Suddenly she felt nervous; the bubbling enthusiasm that had brought her there vapourised in an instant as thoughts of doubt raced through her mind. She observed Sona's complexion had cleared, her body looked radiant and glowing, she even sensed suppleness in those limbs as she watched, fascinated, the glow of womanhood on her friend whom she always knew as a girl.

For a few seconds Sillo stood transfixed, taking in the scene before her. She was the same Sona who ran around the house, back at the village, in her tousled uncombed hair, wearing grubby, tattered clothes, now she was the queen of her own dominion. Golden earrings adorned her ears and silver bangles clinked softly on her wrist, a heavy necklace hung from her neck and her eyes were lined with dark kohl. The parting of her hair was red with vermilion, underlining her married status. Perhaps Sona had turned too proud of her fortune. There was a time when she went to cut grass with Siliya, laughing and giggling and today she stood, curt and distant. How things change with time! Siliya had expected her to be surprised, moved to tears and thought she would give her a big hug, take her inside the house, offer her good things to eat and eagerly want to know everything about the village and the people they knew. She assumed Sona would be beside herself with joy and talk to her girly stuff confiding to her the secrets of her nuptial night but it was not to be. Sona stood stiff and silent. Siliya suddenly started regretting coming to her house at all.

When Sona finally spoke, her tone was none too soft or welcoming. "How come you are here so late in the night, Sillo?"

Siliya tried to hold back her tears. "It was ages since I met you. I was missing you- so I came."

The undercurrent of harshness in Sona's voice was much more evident now. "But does one make social visits in the day or so late in the night?"

Actually, Sona was not comfortable with the time of Siliya's visit. It was the time of the day she and Mathura spent in easy conversation, laughter and love making. Sillo's sudden arrival had put a brake to the routine and robbed her of intimate moments with her husband.

Sillo stared guiltily at the floor, she wanted the earth to split open so she could slide into it unnoticed, away from the embarrassing torture of discovering she was an unwelcome guest. Insult and ridicule was nothing new to her but what she felt at that moment had shattered something deep inside her heart, dislodging her composure and carefree attitude. She had expected welcome showers but a burning drought stared her in the face. The joy flowing in her veins dried up instantly and turned into a corrosive poison, hurting her bad. It is one thing to be denied an invitation to a feast but quite another to be evicted from the table. Siliya wanted to run away from the scene, her throat felt parched and suffocated at the same time. Desperately, she tried to figure out what was going on in Sona's mind. Siliya wanted to run away before the snake whose hiss she had heard in Sona's silence, escaped the pit and emerged in the open. But how could she simply bolt from the scene? She just wanted to evaporate in thin air?

Mathura had picked up the keys of the pantry to get something for Siliya but he stood transfixed beside her.

For Sona, the biggest sin for a man was to have lustful designs on another woman other than his own. There was no pardon for that sin. It was worse than robbery, murder, forgery. It was not that she was against casual flirtatious behaviour but only if it was indulged openly in public and light-heartedly at that. Her ideas of proper conduct were ingrained ever since as a child she watched how her mother refused to speak to her father if he dawdled and lingered for a little while longer at Dulari Sahuain's shop, even if it was to buy a pouch of tobacco. For some, it might be petty flirting and easily forgiven but Dhania took such things to heart and once had packed her bags and left for her parent's home solely on this issue. Sona's stance was stricter than her mother's on what could be assumed to be a non issue.

After her marriage, Sona's views on the subject had hardened into almost fanatic proportions. For her, even a suggestion of adultery was a heinous sin and those who indulged in it deserved to be flogged. She refused to accept that love existed beyond the duties and responsibilities of a marital relationship. Sillo was almost like a sister to her. She loved and trusted her. That she could have anything to do with her husband was her worst nightmare. Mathura and Sillo must have met earlier as well. Mathura must be meeting her clandestinely at the fields and beside the river. She should have guessed something was cooking between the two after she swam across the river so late in the night. Mathura must have informed her that it was the opportune time for their love tryst. Her curiosity to get to the bottom of it all was killing her. She wanted to know everything so that she could brace herself and secure her future. Why was Mathura still standing here? His presence was preventing her from broaching the subject. She turned to him and her impatience cracked in her voice.

"Why don't you go away? Will you stand here on guard all night?"

Mathura slunk away without a word. He was mortified and scared wondering whether Siliya would spill the beans.

Siliya dreaded the prospect of confronting Sona. She could see the sword swinging on her head.

Sona came up to her and spoke in a grave voice, "Listen, Sillo- you come clean with me. Tell me the truth or I will use a scythe on my neck right before your eyes. Then you can easily become the perfect 'other' woman for my husband. Mark my words. Look here! The scythe is here just next to the pestle in the courtyard. Two cannot share what must be for only one of them."

Saying this, she leapt towards the scythe and picked it up menacingly in her hands.

"Don't for a moment think I am bluffing. I mean it. I am serious. You don't know what I will do when I am angry. Tell me the truth."

A shiver of dread passed through Siliya's body. Words came out of her mouth as if from a gramophone. She couldn't hide anything. She watched in awe, the steely look of determination on Sona's face.

Sona fixed her spear-like gaze on her as Siliya squirmed under its intensity.

"Are you speaking the truth? You sure you are not holding back anything?"

"I have told you everything. I swear on my baby, I am not hiding anything."

"Then why didn't you kick that sinful man? Why didn't you bare your teeth and bite off his flesh? Why didn't you scream?"

Sillo had no reply to that.

"Speak up. Why didn't you gouge his eyeballs out? Had you hit him, I would have worshipped you. But because you kept quiet, in my opinion you are equally to blame. If this is what you had to stoop to, why did you make life hell for poor Matadin? Why don't you just mate anyone and settle down with him? Isn't that what your folks wanted you to do? You could have toiled day and night and your father would have blown all your earnings at the toddy shop, why did you have to malign that Brahmin? Why did you pound his reputation to dust? Why did you act the chaste woman who had been wronged? Why don't you go and drown in the river? Why do you want to poison other's lives? Listen to me, if I ever hear a repeat of anything remotely close to this I warn you, none of us will live to see another day. Now get out of here. From this day onwards you don't mean anything to me."

Sillo collected herself and stood very straight but quivering and afraid. Her legs felt weak and it took her quite some time to get to her bearings. She tried to say something in her defence but words would not form in her mouth. Her tongue was dry and a dizzying spell seemed to come and go every second as if her life was being sucked out from the pores of her body. She took every step as if she was avoiding deep pits and trenches in the dark. Somehow she clambered out and made her way to the river.

Mathura was standing outside near the door. He said, "Where will you go at this time of the night, Sillo?"

Sillo made no reply. Mathura didn't ask another question.

Outside, everything was bathed in the same silvery moonlight. It danced on the rippling waves of the river. Almost in a trance, broken and crumbling, Sillo entered the water like a shadow from a dream.

30

Though almost the entire mill of Mr. Khanna was reduced to ashes but he soon began making a determined effort to rebuild it all over again. He invested all his energies towards this cause. The worker's strike was still on but the sting had gone out of its tail. New employees had signed up at half the salaries paid to the striking workers and they were sparing no efforts to work hard and prove to the mill owners they are as good, if not better than their earlier counterparts. A majority of them had gone through bad times and were extremely careful to see they did nothing to upset their new employers. Mr. Khanna could make them work as hard as he wanted to and they would not murmur a protest. Even if he gave them no leave from duty, they would not complain. With lowered heads, they would work like trained oxen. You could snap at them and throw choicest abuses at them what's more, if you felt like swinging a club at them, they did not mind.

The striking workers- poor fellows! They were left with no recourse but to return to work for half of what they earned before they blundered into their strike. They lost all faith in Pandit Onkarnath and wanted to give him a good hiding for instigating them. Even Onkarnath cut a sorry figure- hiding from sight like a whipped dog. After dusk, he didn't venture out of his office for security reasons and in the day time, made it a point to suck up to the government officials who he despised earlier. However, Mirza retained the spirit of bravado and couldn't-care-less attitude. Since he found himself powerless to do anything to salvage their situation, he sincerely wanted them to be re-instated, somehow or the other. At the same time, his heart also went out to the new workers. He didn't want their interests to be harmed in any way therefore, he smiled apologetically at the old workers when they approach him and told them to do as they pleased.

When Khanna came to know that the old workers were willing to return to work, he hardened his stance further despite secretly wanting them to return as he soon realised the old lot was much better than the new recruits. These men could not match half the efficiency of the earlier lot even after stretching themselves to their limits. The old workers had put in almost a lifetime in the mill having worked there since they were barely out of their teens. The new workers consisted of mostly peasants displaced from their fields who sorely missed the open atmosphere of the outdoors and the bracing breeze of their fields. They felt suffocated in the cloistered space of the mill and were scared of fast moving machine parts.

When the old workers ultimately resigned themselves to their fate, Khanna agreed to take them in but fearful of their future, the new appointees announced they would opt for further cuts in wages if they were allowed to stay on. This created a schism within the management, some wanted to retain the new workers for their low costs while some rooted for efficiency of the old ones.

Khanna was the soul of the company- his word was treated as law and the other directors were like puppets in his hands. The final call was his and his alone but Khanna insisted on knowing the opinion of each one of them. Not only his directors, he was taking the advice of those outside the company as well that included his wife Govindi. Ever since he fell out with Malti and came to know the great esteem Mehta held for Govindi the couple had come closer and were discovering newer and more positive things about each other. Perhaps, it was not really affection but it could comfortable be labelled as conviviality. The anger and jealousy which characterised their relationship was replaced by some sort of mutual respect. The insurmountable wall between them was finally broken.

Elsewhere, Malti's attitude was also undergoing a subtle change. Mehta, who had spent his entire life in the pursuit of contemplation and study of metaphysical subjects, was also arriving at the conclusion that the median path between attachment and indifference to materialism essentially went through the high road of selfless service. The spiritualists called it the path of selfless karma but not one to quibble over nomenclature; he considered that path to be the right one. He did not believe in an all-knowing God. He often expressed his views on this subject very colourfully more so because he was never sure of any finality in them but he was quite convinced deep down in his heart that joy and sorrow, birth and death and good and evil did not have any relevance or connection to the idea called God. In his view, it was man's giant ego which made him believe that God made him in his own image.

If God's ways were so abstruse and cryptic and it was difficult to fathom them what was the point in trying to apportion reason and sense into something so confounding? How could such farfetched theories provide solace to the human race? According to him, the only raison for the idea of God was the ease with which his name could be used to build a concept of one-ness and unity amongst humanity. His approach to non-violence and universality was based on a practical utilitarian model and not any spiritual mumbo jumbo. However, he did accept that despite never having significantly influenced or inspired history down the ages, the idea of God certainly had a major impact on the cultural development of the human race.

He subscribed to the unity of man but did not find it necessary to include the idea of a metaphysical concept to give it a backbone. His love for mankind was not based on the presence of the same spirit dwelling in every living being. Various spiritual doctrines and philosophies were merely tools to bring humankind together in peaceful co-existence with itself and nature. They were merely just some of the ways to encourage hope and peace amongst people. The feeling of unity of man and the one-ness of people had struck such deep roots in his psyche that he did not need a spiritual reason to sustain that spirit. Having felt it in his bones, he was not one to let the feeling lie dormant in his heart. It had become essential for him to devote as much time as he could to selfless work. It had become vital for his inner peace. Fame, money or a sense of obligation was not the driving force since he openly scoffed at those sentiments. He considered them petty and totally abominable. Selfless service was his mantra and he loved it.

His ideas cast a spell on Malti, quietly, unobtrusively. All the men she had met all through her life were solely attracted to her beauty; nudged on by hope that one day she might encourage them further. On their part, they fanned her desire for luxury, comfort and attachment to the good things of life. On the contrary, Mehta's company drew her away from those frivolous pursuits and instilled in her a desire to channelise her energy to serve the poor. Every thinking person nurses a dormant desire for philanthropy in his heart. The right connection and climate spark it to life. However, if a person continues to run after name and fame, it can be safely understood that he has not yet 'arrived'.

Malti had started seeing poor patients as well, often in their own homes. Her attitude and behaviour towards them underwent a dramatic change though she still paid great attention to her makeup and cosmetics. Giving up the attachment to preserving a gorgeous outer appearance was proving to be a much more tough exercise than managing the diverse pulls within her.

Lately, both Mehta and Malti had started visiting nearby villages and spent hours with the peasants, chatting with them in their hamlets, sometimes staying back for the night and eating food cooked by them in their own surroundings. They considered themselves blessed to partake of the humble offering of the peasants and loved the time spent in their company.

On one of these visits, they went to Bellary and stopped by at the village Semri. Hori, as usual, was squatting outside his door, smoking his *chillum* when Mehta and Malti walked across to him. His face looked familiar and Mehta recognised him instantly. "This is your village, isn't it? I remember you from the Dussehra ceremony, we had come to Rai sahib's residence and you played the part of the gardener in the theatrical performance."

The memory of that day returned to Hori in a flash. He remembered Mehta as the man in the elaborate masquerade incident and instantly got up to rush to Pateshwari's to borrow chairs for his guests.

"We don't need chairs. We will sit on your cot. We are not here to sit on chairs- we have come to learn a few things from you."

Hori watched them confused, perplexed, wondering what he should do to appear hospitable. Finally he managed to say a few words- "Should I get you water to drink?"

"Yes, we sure are thirsty," said Mehta

"Should I also bring some sweets along with water?"

"Yes, please, but only if they are there at your house. You don't have to buy anything for us."

When Hori went inside to get water and sweets, a gaggle of kids from the neighbourhood gathered in sheer curiosity and was staring at the newcomers with the same interest as they would ogle at an animal in the zoo.

Sillo was passing by with her baby straddled on her lap and she also stopped by to watch the strangers.

Malti went up to her and took the baby into her arms, cooing and making baby talk to the surprised infant.

"How old is he?" she asked her.

Sillo did not know his exact age. Another woman standing close by volunteered to reply to her query.

"He must be a year old. What do you say?" she said, looking at Malti and turning to Sillo at the same time. Sillo nodded in agreement.

Malti was in a pleasant mood and inclined to jest. "That's one cute baby! Will you give him to me?"

Sillo's bosom swelled with pride. "He is as good as yours already, ma'am."

"Then may I take him with me?"

"Sure, please! He will get a good life and probably grow into a gentleman."

A few other women had gathered around them and they took Malti inside Hori's house. Standing outside in front of other men, they could not talk as freely as they wanted. Malti noticed a cot was pulled into the room and a clean sheet was spread over it- the one that was borrowed from Pateshwari's house minutes back. Malti settled herself on it and soon they were chatting about child health and womanly tips on bringing up children. The women listened to her quietly, in rapt attention.

Malti was telling them that cleanliness wasn't an expensive exercise but its benefits far outweighed the effort needed to bring it about.

Dhania piped in with, 'How can we go ahead with the levels of cleanliness and hygiene you talk about, ma'am. We can barely make both ends meet. How are we to maintain special cleanliness?"

Malti explained that it was just intelligent handling of things around the house. One didn't need money; it only called for wise housekeeping efforts.

Dulari Sahuain was quite curious. "How did you learn all this stuff, my lady? You aren't married- where did you learn this?"

Malti was amused. "How do you assume I am not married?"

The women looked at each other and smiled knowingly. "Come on, Miss sahib, this is nothing that can be hidden. It is written all across a woman's face."

Malti was surprised to find herself blushing. "Well, I didn't marry so that I could come and serve you."

A chorus of 'amazing! You are blessed! 'Great!' rose all around the room.

Siliya started pressing her feet, massaging them gently. "Ma'am, you have come from so far away. You must be tired."

Malti drew her legs away hurriedly. "No! Not at all! I am not tired. I drove here in a car. I would like all of you to go home and come back with your children right away. I will give you some tips on how to keep them healthy."

Within minutes, there was a crowd of at least twenty-five laughing, bawling children scurrying all over the room. Malti began examining each one separately. Many children had muddy eyes and Malti cleaned them, adding eye drops to disinfect them. A majority of them were weak and malnourished. Malti was taken aback to hear that hardly any household bought milk for their children. Butter was a rarity, seen once in a year, if at all.

Malti explained to them the importance of proper nutrition, just as she did in every village she visited. She often felt irritated that these people paid scant attention to eating proper food. She felt angry at them. Why weren't they more careful about their health? If they could manage to feed their cattle, surely they could buy some nutritious food for themselves. Why did they toil all their lives and not eat some of the abundant food they grew themselves? Her mind was perplexed and she wondered why they considered food only as a necessity for survival and not as a basic component of life. Why didn't they ask the government for loans at nominal interest and save themselves from the clutches of money lenders?

Whomsoever she spoke to had the same story to narrate. They were all caught up in a vicious web of loans and interest. A major chunk of their earnings went in paying off the interest of loans. Another bane of their existence was splits and separations in their joint families. The animosity was so much that there was hardly a person who wanted to stay with his brother. Everyone wanted a separate existence; even if it meant spending twice as much had they lived together. Their selfishness and narrow mindedness was to blame for their miserable lives. Malti dwelt at length on these issues with the women. Their frank eagerness, trusting nature and willingness to learn spurred her enthusiasm and the desire to serve them rose steadily in her heart. This simplicity of selfless service seemed so much greater and fulfilling than the emptiness of her glamorous lifestyle. Her silken garments with *zari* embroidery, the perfume sprays on her body, her carefully coiffured hair and face, delicately touched up with rouge made her embarrassed and almost apologetic. The slim golden watch on her wrist stared at her accusingly and the pearl necklace seemed to silently tighten around her neck.

The women crowding around her were real angels, despite their grubby clothing, living invisible lives, in penury yet hopeful, innocent, even joyous. She felt small before their graceful presence. She knew so much more than these women. She had a wealth of information, intelligence and abilities but the stubborn strength with which these women grappled with their tough lives was something she couldn't face for a day, much less a lifetime. They were totally devoid of a sense of self importance or ego, they toiled day and night, skipping meals as a matter of course to feed their families, at times crying in desperation yet smiling through it all even joking about it off and on. Their lives were so absorbed in love and care of others that they hardly had time to bother about their personal egos and interest. Their success and achievement was focussed on their children, their husbands and other relatives. By preserving the essence of this sentiment and expanding it further, perhaps the future ideal of womanhood could be built on this foundation. Their somnolent and probably unawakened state was far better when compared to the sheer crudity and selfishness of the enlightened women in her society who never thought beyond what was good for them and them alone.

The women were showing no signs of having had enough of Malti's company even as evening fell. Her words held them in awe. A few insisted that she stay back and Malti, moved and delighted by their open invitation, accepted to stay on. The women promised to regale her with their songs at night as Malti decided to go to every house in the village to acquaint her with their special needs. For the women of the village, her unaffected empathy and sincerity was as good as a boon from heaven.

At the same time, outside the room, Mehta sprawled on another cot as he watched a wrestling match which the peasants had set up on the spur of the moment for his entertainment. He rued the fact that Mirza was not with him on this trip. He would have found him a sparring partner as well. He was quite surprised how so called educated people turn into monsters while dealing with people like these peasants who shared such a child like enthusiasm for life.

Sitting in the midst of poor country folk, Mehta was wrestling with the whys and wherefores of their piteous condition. He was unable to realise that the nobility assigned to their simplicity was squarely responsible for their poor condition. Had they been more of human beings and less of gods they would not have been pushed around with such impunity. The state of the nation and the changes sweeping the country held no meaning for them. The meekness with which they greeted anyone who came to them with the trappings of power was their undoing. Only a violent and cruel mishap could shake them out of their silent indifference. Their soul had become so weak that it had clobbered its own feet and was stumbling for crutches to stand up to the emerging realities. They seemed to have lost awareness of their human existence.

It was late in the evening and many of those working in the fields came hurrying to see the spectacle of the couple from the city. Mehta observed Malti, deeply engrossed in an animated discussion with the women from the village with a child in her arms, talking to them as if she was one of their kinds. It warmed the cockles of his heart to see her like that. Malti had unconsciously moulded herself into the woman Mehta always respected and admired - yet he was surprised to observe that his heart did not resonate with the affection that could make him believe he felt something more than admiration for her. Unless he had those feelings, it was outright silly to propose any serious turn in their relationship. She had arrived at his door, unannounced and Mehta had welcomed her in. His welcome had more to do with chivalry than love. If Malti felt he was worthy of her affection, he was obliged to honour her sentiments. The other factor that influenced his attitude towards her was that he wanted her to step out of Govindi's path. He knew quite well that unless Malti found another secure foothold, she would not let go of the doorway in which she had planted her other foot rather firmly. He felt guilty that by leading her on, he was doing Malti an injustice for which his conscience pricked him every now and then.

However, a strange development was also taking place on the sidelines. As he observed her closely, he discovered that she was indeed a very attractive woman. Obviously, for Mehta physical beauty was not the mainstay for attractiveness. The inner qualities which he stumbled upon as a consequence of being thrown together with her for long hours both surprised and delighted him. In his mind, true love could only be something that leads to commitment; anything otherwise would be based on attachment and infatuation with physical beauty which could be fleeting. However, he was concerned whether the stone selected by the sculptor for his creation was worth the effort, for not every stone from the same block could be shaped into an enchanting sculpture. Within a short time, Malti had lit up hitherto dull corners of his mind with a new light but the collective brightness of her influence had not evolved so strongly so as to dazzle his eyes and sweep him off his feet. But today, by reaching out to the women of the village, unaffected, sincere and happy, she had brought all the bright spots in focus- concentrated, recognisable and familiar. For the first time he felt one with her. As soon as she returned from her trip around the village, he left for the riverside inviting her along. He had decided to spend the night in the village. For some reason, Malti's heart seemed to skip a beat when she heard his decision to stay back. She saw a glow and eagerness on his face and in his eyes which was totally alien to her.

A glowing carpet of silver seemed to cover the sandy bank as the river hummed softly, singing the song of its gently lapping waves, glittering with its milky jewels, in a quiet dance with the silent audience of the moon, stars and trees with bent branches swaying and nodding in fitful slumber. Mehta was mesmerised with this sight of nature. His childhood seemed to return to him with its careless abandon. With a whoop of delight, he rolled on the sand and raced towards the river, wading ankle deep into it.

"Don't catch a cold the water; is quite cold," said Malti genuinely concerned about his health

Mehta scooped water in his palms and splashed at her. "I want to swim across the other side. I really do!"

"No, no! Nothing like that! I will not let you attempt anything like that. Come out of the water at once."

"Why? Don't you want to come with me to that deserted land where dreams reign supreme?"

"I don't know how to swim."

"OK, come here let's make a boat and go across on it."

He stepped out of the water. There was a small forest of *jhau* trees close by. He went into the thicket and slashed a large number of branches with his pocket knife. There was a large net of jute strung on the shore. He cut the net and started stringing branches with a rope which he fashioned from the net. He was so pleased with what he was doing. It was almost as if he was preparing to conquer Everest. His fingers bled a few times as the rope cut into them or the knife hit the wrong spot. Malti grumbled a few times, urging him to be sane and return to the village and quit his games but he wasn't bothered. His school boyish enthusiasm and obstinacy rode supreme and roughshod over all his science, philosophy and intellect.

Finally, the rope was ready. The branches were strung together, tied at both ends with small twigs stuffed and netted in within the spaces and entwined with rope so that water should not rise above the flat raft. The boat was ready. The night turned still more dream-like.

Mehta threw the raft on the water and took Malti's hand in his. "Come, sit."

She touched the raft doubtfully. "Will it hold the weight of two people?"

Mehta smiled at her philosophically- "The postulates on which we base our lives are much more doubtful and uncertain than this. Why are you afraid?"

"I am not. You are here to take care of me."

"You really think so?"

"So far I have covered all hurdles on my own. Now I have you. Why should I fear?"

They climbed on the raft and Mehta used a branch as an oar to steer them into the water. The raft bobbed and shook perilously but held together as they started floating on the river.

Malti tried to take her mind off the raft so she started a shaky conversation.

"You have lived in a city all your life, how come you know things like making rafts and what rope to use? I could never build anything remotely like that."

He looked at her with warmth, "Perhaps this comes to me from some past life. The mere touch of nature ignites something like a new life in me. My veins crackle with energy; every bird flying in the sky, animal, gust of breeze, all give me an invitation to joy--a joy that seemed buried and lost. Really, I don't feel this joy in anything else, not in music that moves my heart, not in philosophy that sends my intellect soaring high. This is like finding me all over again like the joy of a bird returning to its nest."

The raft shook, turned sideways, sometimes at an angle, sometimes whirling in a circular movement but stayed together, floating swiftly on the current.

Malti broke the silence.

"Do I ever feature in your life?"

Mehta reached out and took her hand in his.

"Yes, you do. Many times. Like a whiff of fragrance, a shadow of my imagination--coming, going, appearing, disappearing. I run to hold you in my arms but you vanish the next instant."

"Did you try to find out why it seems elusive?"

"Yes, I have tried to understand. Quite a few times."

"What did you realise?"

"That the foundation on which I want to build my house is unstable. It's not a mansion, just a humble cottage, but you do require a stable ground on which to build it."

Malti drew her hand away from his, acting hurt. "This is an unfair accusation. You always look at me as if you are testing me all the time- you have never looked at me with love. Don't you realise women don't like to be evaluated; they only like to be loved. Evaluation sifts goodness and weaknesses. Its job is to locate ugliness in beauty. Only love will reveal beauty in what seems ugly. I love you, therefore I cannot believe there could be something bad in you. But you measure and evaluate me so you find me fickle, unstable and god-knows what-else and keep running away from me. Do you know why I appear fickle and unstable? It is because I have not found the love that will make me committed and stable. Had you surrendered to me as selflessly and totally as I have to you, you would not make these needless accusations against me."

Mehta was amused. "Are you sure you never tried to test me?"

"Yes."

"In that case, you made a mistake."

"As if I care..."

"Don't be sentimental, Malti. Before we commit ourselves to love, we always test the other it could be involuntarily, sub-consciously, but we all do. I must admit - initially I perceived you in the manner I looked at other women- flirtatiously and for entertainment. And if I am not wrong, you too did not consider me more than another toy to play with for some time."

Malti cut him short. "You are wrong. I never considered you entertainment, of all things! The moment I saw you the first time I knew..."

Mehta replied, "Again the same soppy sentimentality. I dislike mushiness on a serious issue like this. If you fell in love with me the moment you lay your eyes on me, it only implies that I must be extremely good looking, if nothing, for women necessarily do a lot of background research before they decide to fall in love. Didn't they hold *Swayamvars* to select the best match for themselves in earlier times? The same practice continues even to this day though under some other name or form. I tried to present myself before you as I am so that I could delve into your soul. The more I entered within your spirit the more treasures within your heart. I confess I came to you, searching for little more than casual entertainment but I have stayed on to this day like a devotee. Whether you found anything in me or not, I do not know."

They were close to the other bank of the river. Wading into the water, they reached the sandy shore and sat down to rest on it. When Mehta spoke again it appeared there was no break in the conversation. "And today I have brought you here to ask that same question."

There was a slight tremor in Malti's voice as she said, "Do you need to ask it to know my reply?"

"Yes, I want your reply because today I will reveal to you that part of me which you haven't seen and which I have kept hidden from you. Okay, let's suppose I marry you and later cheat behind your back, how will you punish me for that?"

Malti was taken aback. She was quite surprised, confused as to what he was trying to ask or say. "What sort of a question is this?"

"It is very important for me."

"I don't think there is a possibility of such a thing happening."

"There is nothing that cannot happen in this world. The greatest sage can err and fall down in an instant."

"Well, I will try to search for the cause of that mistake and try to remove it."

"What if my 'mistake' turns into a habit?"

"Then I really don't know what I will do. Probably, swallow some poison and pass away into the night."

"Fine. But if you ask me the same question, I might have a very different response."

"Tell me," said Malti with growing consternation.

Mehta said forcefully and with full confidence, "I will first kill you and then kill myself."

After a few seconds, Malti smiled and broke into a laugh but her body shivered at the same time. Her laughter conveniently masked the icy cold feeling in her spine.

"Why did you laugh?" Mehta asked.

"Because I cannot imagine you could be so violent."

"No Malti, I am a total animal when it comes to it and I am not ashamed for it. Words and expressions like 'spiritual love', 'selfless love in which one negates oneself for the other', 'love that rejoices in the beloved's joys and surrenders his soul for the lover's pleasure'- they mean nothing to me. These are empty, hollow words. I have read stories in which lovers give up their lives for the other but I will not call that love. It could be service, sacrifice- but not love for sure. Love is not a placid cow but a ferocious lion that will not allow anyone to come near what it claims as its own."

Malti looked straight into his eyes and said- "If love is a ferocious lion, I'd rather remain away from it. I will avoid it. I really thought it was a gentle cow. I consider love to be above doubts and suspicions. It has nothing to do with the body as it is ultimately a spiritual feeling. There is no space for doubts and suspicion in love. Come to think of it, perhaps violence is definitely the result of doubts and suspicion. Love is a surrender of the soul. In its temple you can gain its blessings only with the attitude and approach of a devotee, not an inquisitor conducting an evaluation."

She stood up very straight and took steady, swift steps towards the river as if she had suddenly found her way. She felt a tingling energy coursing through her body. Even in her independent and bold existence, she had always perceived a certain weakness which constantly disturbed her equilibrium and rankled her deep inside. Her mind was always in search of an anchor on which she could rest her oars and face the world head-on. She failed to find that her courage was in her own being. She was attracted, almost desperately, to profound intelligence and impeccable character. She was like water- taking on the shape of whatever receptacle she poured herself into. She had no form of her own.

Her attitude was that of a student appearing for an exam. A student can love books- it's quite possible that love can be spontaneous- but it is definitely centred on those pages or sections which could be the examiner's favourites. The student's primary effort is to pass the examination; gaining knowledge for its own sake comes a distant second in his priority. If he comes to know that the examiner is very generous and discounts mistakes heavily, or is totally blind to errors and just wants to pass his students in their exams, then it is quite possible he doesn't turn to his books at all. All of Malti's actions so far were dove tailed to please Mehta. Her aim was to win his love and trust and consequently ascend the throne in his heart. But so much like the student who wasn't comfortable with the idea of earning the examiner's commendation, over a period of time, by becoming an expert in the subject, she too didn't have the patience to grow silently into the realm of his trust by proving her sincerity over time.

But seconds ago, by rejecting her feelings, he had shaken her up. She had only spoken the truth when she said she had fallen for him the moment she met him. He appeared as the most capable and accomplished amongst all her acquaintances. She held confidence and courage of convictions in a man in high esteem. According to her, wealth and glamour were toys for the intellectually imbecile. They were little playthings which indulgent boys broke at play. She did nurse a weakness for beauty and was yet to get over her distaste for ugliness. But lately, only cerebral intensity could impress her as only in its intellectual support could she channelise confidence and faith in herself. Mehta's intellectual prowess and sharp mind had left an indelible mark on her. In him, she had found the inspiration to be strong and independent in spirit. She discovered a new goal in life. By planning and working towards that goal of bringing herself close to him and tasting success on the way, in that endeavour, in so many little ways, she dreamt of the time when they would be together. And her confidence was growing every day.

But today she was frozen midstream. Mehta had brought her to the verge of love's ample grace and then placed before her a strange ideal which wrenched it from the pedestal of devotion and sacrifice and smashed it against the floor of ordinary pragmatism, where hate and envy and lust reigned supreme. Her refined intelligence refused to accept what she heard and her faith in Mehta cracked and splintered- like a disciple, accidentally discovering his *guru* in secret passion. She saw that Mehta's fine intellect was edging the soft footfall of love towards a baser instinct and blinding his eyes to an uplifting flight of delight. Confronted by this discovery, her heart sank like lead.

Seeing her readiness to return so soon, Mehta sounded a little contrite and almost ashamed, "Wait, let's sit here for some time."

Malti did not look at him when she said, "No, I think we should go back. It's quite late."

❁❁❁

31

Rai sahib was riding his luck big time. All his three wishes had been fulfilled and he was amply sated with his life. The court case had gone in his favour; he had won the election comprehensively and was consequently promoted as a Home Member as well. Compliments and congratulatory messages were pouring into his mail box every day. The post office was humming with wires that kept arriving for him in a steady stream. With the honour that came his way following the election, he had firmed up his position as the foremost *Taluqdar* of the area. The respect which he commanded earlier was consolidated further as local newspapers carried entire supplements on his life story, in a bid to outdo competing papers in ferreting out great and unknown facets of his personality. His debts had risen steadily but he wasn't too worried about that any more. He could easily pay off all debts simply by selling a small portion of the huge fortune that he now presided over.

Rai sahib found himself floating on a realm much beyond his wildest imagination. So far, he had a palatial mansion in Lucknow, now he owned one each in Simla, Mussoorie and Nainital. Owning a mansion in those hill resorts was vital as it was below his dignity to check into a hotel or stay as a guest with any member of the local royalty during his trips to those places. Most well-heeled people possessed bungalows in these resorts; so it was necessary in keeping with his status that he should have some of his own as well.

Fortunately, he didn't have to construct bungalows and go through the pain and irritation that accompanies such projects. There were enough on sale and he immediately bought the best one available. A retinue of attendants, gardeners, cooks and watchmen were selected and appointed to look after and manage each bungalow in every town. The biggest achievement of all was totally unanticipated.

On His Majesty's birthday, Rai sahib was honoured with the title of *'Rajah'* thereby leaving him with little else he could wish for.. A lavish party was thrown to celebrate his title. It was the mother of all parties and broke all records of sheer glamour and extravaganza. When the moment arrived and the Governor formally presented the title to him, every pore of his body tingled with pride and dedication to the *Raj*. This was life! He was stupid and silly to sully his image by associating with the wimps fighting for some elusive freedom. He regretted falling for their slogans of idealism that led him to jail and spoilt his image in the official's eyes. The same Deputy Superintendent of Police who had arrested him earlier stood smiling gratuitously at him, perhaps apologetic for his previous follies.

However, his greatest moment came when his erstwhile enemy, Surya Pratap Singh sent him a proposal for the marriage of his son with his daughter. The joy he felt at this was far above what he felt on becoming the Minister or after winning the court case. Those were significant but minor milestones, this was a crowning glory beyond belief. The same Surya Pratap Singh who considered him a scrawny mongrel, was reaching out to him with a marriage proposal for his son. This was truly unbelievable! Rudrapal was studying for his post graduate degree- he was a bold lad, an idealist who was supremely confident in himself, almost haughty in his demeanour. He was also a major flirt, proud of his youth yet amazingly lazy and detested his father's pelf, position and power.

Rai sahib was in Nainital when the message was delivered to him. He was delighted beyond words and despite not wanting to push or hurry his son into accepting the proposal, he knew that even his youthful idealism will find the chance of a liaison with Surya Pratap Singh's family, too hard to resist. It never crossed his mind that Rudrapal could have a differing opinion.

He sent his acceptance of the proposal to Surya Pratap Singh and promptly made a call to his son. Rudrapal heard what his father said and replied with a brief- "No."

Never before in his life, had Rai sahib felt so intensely disappointed and vexed at the same time.

"You have any particular reason to refuse this offer?" he asked.

"You will know about it soon enough."

"I want to know right now."

"But I don't want to tell you right now."

"You will have to tell me. You will not disobey what I command."

"I cannot let your commands decide what my conscience wants to do."

Rai sahib turned soft all of a sudden and said- "Son, for the sake of an elusive idealism you are pushing yourself into a corner. Have you paused to consider what this alliance will do to your social standing? This is Godsend opportunity for you. If our family were to settle an alliance with any girl from that family, I would consider myself blessed; this girl is Surya Pratap's daughter and he is whom we all look up to. I come across that girl every other day. I am sure you must have seen her as well. I have yet to see a girl more accomplished, beautiful and gentle than her. I don't have long to live, you have your entire life before you. I don't want to push you into anything. You know my views on marriage, I am so liberal and forward looking about it. But I consider it my duty to correct you when I see you are not ready to see reason or go the right way."

Rudrapal's reply was terse, "My views on this issue are clear to me and I know they are not going to change for your convenience. I really don't see them changing anymore."

Rai sahib was truly irritated at the boy's obstinacy. He roared in anger- "It seems you have taken leave of your senses. Come home immediately, we have to talk this over. Don't delay it for a moment now. I've given my word to Surya Pratap."

Rudrapal shrugged his shoulders and said, "I am sorry. I am not ready to make that trip home right away."

The next day, Rai sahib went to see his son himself. Both were ready and armed with their arguments and pronouncements. On one side was a lifetime of experience, replete with compromises and adjustments while on the other stood raw idealism-, obstinate, proud and merciless.

Rai sahib hit out at what he perceived was the core issue, "Tell me upfront, and be honest with me. Is there a girl in your life?"

Rudrapal was unmoved. He spoke without batting an eyelid, unflinchingly- "If you are so keen to know, I think you should be told. She is Malti Devi's sister, Saroj."

Rai sahib was devastated, "Oh! You mean that girl?"

"I am sure you know her."

"Only too well," said Rai sahib, "But have you seen Surya Pratap's daughter?"

"Yes, I have. She's quite an eyeful."

"And yet...?"

"I don't give any value to physical beauty."

"I pity your intelligence. You know what sort of woman that Malti is? Will her sister be any different?"

Rudrapal raised his eyebrows and spoke angrily, "I think we should not talk any further on this topic. But I just want you to keep this in mind, if I get married, it will be to Saroj and no one else."

"Not as long as I live!"

"In that case, after you are gone..."

"Oh! So this is what it has come to?"

Rai sahib's eyes moistened. His life was crumbling in a heap around him. His position as a minister, the royal title and great name in society turned into wilted flowers from yesterday's party. When his wife passed away he was no more than thirty six. He could have re-married and led a comfortable life all over again but he refrained from it despite insistent friends and relatives. All for his children. He would see their innocent faces and vow to devote his time solely to bringing them up well, even if it meant depriving himself of the marital pleasures of a second marriage.

All through his life he gave everything towards caring for his children. He poured all his love for them and today, his son spoke to him with so much venom in his attitude? He was clearly taken aback and wondered if he had done the right thing in focusing his energies solely on property, wealth and power. If his own son was so hostile towards him, then why should he sweat it out for temporal achievements? He wasn't going to live forever so he might awas well just sit back and relax. So many of his ilk gloated in their self indulgent pastimes and lead satisfied hedonist lives. He could also take a leaf from their book.

Actually, he forgot that the pains he took so eagerly was not so much for his sons as for himself and his personal glory. Or it could be put in another way-- maybe he was doing it as an industrious person for whom continuous engagement was the only option for life. Maybe he was a person who could not satisfy his soul's cravings without an indulgent lifestyle.

Yet the hurt he felt deep within himself due to his son's behaviour, soon manifest itself in no mean fashion. Those for whom we toil and suffer become our first victims over whom we want to exercise a subtle control. We desire to lord over their heart and mind; even as we feel it is actually for their own good. Often we identify so deeply with their goals that they sometimes appear as projections of our own ideas. Or maybe, it is the other way around. The greater the toil and suffering, the more severe is the desire to exercise control over the objects of our affection. That is why if there is an opposition to that control, it mutates into the form of a violent retort. Rai sahib was afflicted by a growing urge to throw a spanner in the works and upset whatever plans his son had for his marriage with that girl. He was ready to take the help of police and other symbols of control and authority that he was familiar with towards that end. In short, he was willing to take recourse to extreme steps, if need be.

In a rasping voice which conveyed the image of a sword being unsheathed, he said, "Yes, your marriage will take place when I am no more. And please remember I am not dying tomorrow. I intend to stay around for quite some time."

Rudrapal responded with a staccato of verbal shots, "May God be kind to you- may you live long. I am already married to Saroj, for your information."

"That's a lie!"

"Not at all. And I have a certificate to prove it."

That was the last straw and Rai sahib was hit where it hurt most. The hate in his eyes was unmistakable. An enemy normally attacks those sore points which are most vulnerable. This was a blatant assault on the essence of his life, an attack on the soft corner in his heart in which he had stored the cumulative affections of his life. A strong gale had uprooted his life from its roots. Rudderless, he felt absolutely crippled and helpless. Despite the backing of the entire police and law machinery of the state, he felt totally powerless because of his stubborn and incalcitrant son. Use of force was a last recourse and luck had contrived to wrest that ability from him as well. Both his son and Saroj were adults. Also, Rudrapal was the rightful heir of his own estate. Other than an emotional connect between them, he had no control over his son's affairs directly. If he knew what fate had in store for him, he wouldn't have gone the extra mile to fight for and build the estate. Litigation and sundry legal expenses had made him poor by almost a few hundred thousand rupees. Such a waste; this life! Now the best bet in his opinion was to lie low and be nice to that boy. A little brush on the wrong side and he could be in deep trouble. Rai sahib was quick to realise his shaky position. Oh, this was terrible! How his life had been ruined!

Rudrapal had left. Rai sahib hailed his car and sped straight towards Mehta's house. He had some hope that Malti would pay heed to Mehta if he tried to reason with her. Perhaps Saroj might also appreciate his words, especially, if he weighted his arguments with the jingle of money. He was ready to part with twenty thousand or so if it was any help.

When Mehta heard what he had to say, he made a straight face and stared blankly at him.

"Well, this is about your prestige, isn't it?"

Rai sahib missed the sarcasm and leapt at it. "Exactly, it's about my prestige alright! Do you know Raja Surya Pratap Singh?

"I do and I have also met his second daughter- she isn't half as good as her elder sister."

"But my son is so smitten by the other girl. He has gone blind"

"So let it go! Why are you so agitated about it? Let him sort out his life himself."

"I can't, Mehta. It so hard to reject an honour that has dropped into your lap. I can dump half my estates and wealth for a social standing like that. If Malti Devi desires otherwise, things can turn out differently. If a 'No' comes from their side, Rudrapal might cry his eyes out for a week but as sanity returns to him it will be business as usual. This is not about love, it's all about his personal whims, ego and idiosyncrasies."

"But Malti will not be moved unless she is silenced with material gifts."

"I will give whatever she wants. If you say, I will appoint her in-charge of the Duffrin hospital."

"Well, imagine if she loves you; do you think she will agree with what you ask of her for just that reason. By the way, ever since you became a Minister, her opinion about you has altered considerably."

Rai sahib tried to read Mehta's face for any hidden implications in his words. The smile on his face was a giveaway and Rai sahib got the message alright. Pained by the unspoken jibe, he said, "Is this the time to make light of my hurt? I thought you, of all people, will at least empathise with me and offer the right advice and here you are making fun of me! I am hurt. Unless they have gone through pain, no one realises what it means to be in my position today."

Mehta replied with all seriousness, "The issue you have brought to me defies serious consideration least of all by someone like you. You can be concerned about your marriage; not that of your son. Please! It beats me to think how you could be responsible for your son's affairs, especially, when he is not a minor and can make his own decisions. He should know what's good for him. I do not think marriage, like any other affair of the heart, has anything to do with social prestige and similar considerations. I am not sure how far it is correct but I have heard that Raja sahib cringes and crouches before the local constable in his locality and sucks up to him, will you call that prestigious? Ask any petty shopkeeper or man on the street and he will tell you, in choicest words, what he thinks of the Raja sahib you are so impressed with. You consider that something to be proud of? Go home and relax. You won't get a better daughter-in-law than Saroj."

Rai sahib was not impressed and objected to Mehta's statement. "But isn't she the sister of that Malti woman?"

Mehta's hackles rose, "Is being her sister something to be ashamed of? You have never understood Malti, nor ever tried to understand her. I was also guilty of that error of judgement but now I realise she is one who comes shining through her travails. She reveals her true talents and greatness in times of need. She is like a strong and silent warrior who exhibits his prowess in times of crisis and not in fiestas for cheap publicity. Aren't you aware about Khanna's plight?"

Rai sahib shook his head in a gesture of sympathy. "Yes, I heard about it and have often thought of paying him a visit. It's just that my schedules keep me terribly occupied. That fire in his mill has ruined him, what a shame!"

"Yes. He is surviving on the sympathy and charity of his friends. To make matters worse, Govindi is unwell for months. The poor woman sacrificed her health and life for her ungrateful husband who treated her so bad. Now that frail woman is ill, almost dying. And Malti, the one who wouldn't nurse princes or royalty even if they paid her a fortune, now sits at her bedside all night. It is Malti who is taking care of Govindi's kids. I didn't know she was capable of such maternal love which I now realise was dormant in her. You know the sort of person I am, completely wooden and unfeeling and hardly sentimental, but my heart warms to Malti as I see her personality in a new light. For the first time I realise how varied, indescribable and complex humanity can be. If you would like to see it for yourself and meet her, I am ready to accompany you there."

Rai sahib was circumspect. "If you cannot empathise with me, I wonder if Malti will understand what I am going through. It will create unnecessary embarrassment for all concerned. But I am sure you don't need a reason or ploy to visit her. I thought you had cast a spell over her."

The smile on Mehta's face was one of longing and possibly regret at lost opportunities.

"All that is now a dream. She has no time. I hardly see her any more. A few times that I did, I gathered she wasn't too pleased to meet me. Now I hesitate barging into her presence. That reminds me, today there is a function at the Ladies gymnasium. Would you like to attend?"

"No, thanks," Rai sahib said sounding none too pleased, "I have no time for all that. I have my own problems to attend to. I am worried what will I tell Raja sahib? I gave him my word."

With these words he rose and walked slowly towards the door. The knot he had come to unravel had tightened still more. His mind had gone blank. Mehta walked him to the car and sent him off.

Once he was home Rai sahib had barely picked up the daily newspaper when he noticed Tankha's card on his desk. He hated Tankha and had sworn not to see his face again but his present state of mind called for someone to hear him out, patiently. He wanted a sympathetic ear, if nothing. Perhaps Tankha could at least offer that sympathy. He instantly called for him to be led into his chamber.

Tankha walked in softly, almost guiltily, wearing a morose expression. Almost bowing down to the floor he said, "I was on my way to Nainital to seek an audience with you, sir. My good fortune that I find you in town. I hope sir, you are fine and in good spirits?"

After that opening sentence, he broke into a verbose glorification of Rai sahib's eminence, completely whitewashing his earlier intemperate words and behaviour with him. "What a great job you have done with your Home Membership, sir! It's incomparable. You are the talk of the town, wherever I go. This position is made just for you, sir"

Rai sahib looked at him with distaste. What a slimy, shameless man he was. One who would lick the dust off a horse's shoe, if it helped him. He was so unreliable and a crook of the highest order but he did not feel angry at him. On the contrary, Rai sahib felt pity.

"What are you doing these days?" he asked.

"Nothing at all, sir. I am without work. That's why I have come to meet you. I am in deep trouble, sir. You know Raja Surya Pratap very well, sir. He doesn't care for anybody. One day he began criticising you before me. I could not tolerate it for long. I told him that you are my lord and I can't listen to his tirade against you. And that was it! He blew his top. I didn't lose my cool and merely saluted him and returned home quietly. I was very clear in my mind. He might be a man of wealth and luxury but the respect which Rai sahib commands is beyond him. The world respects a man's inner strengths and greatness, not his wealth. The world acclaims your greatness, I know that very well."

Rai sahib played along, "Oh! You must have enraged him no end?"

Tankha preened and turned more expansive. "Sir, allow me to speak my mind. Well, somebody might not like this at all, but I must speak the truth. Why should I fear when I am so secure at your feet? The truth is, many people are totally jealous of you. They curse you all the time. Their moods are dark and minds full of envy ever since you became a Minister. They conveniently forgot to pay my salary for the last so many months. Actually it's not for them to be giving. They will go to any extent to rob those who work for them tirelessly. Nobody is safe with them. Even in broad daylight, women..."

He was cut short by the sound of a car coming to a halt in the driveway. It was Raja Surya Pratap who emerged from the car. Rai sahib went up to receive him warmly and feeling honoured by his visit, almost bent down in obeisance.

"Welcome! I was about to come and look you up, Raja sahib!"

This was the first time Raja Surya Pratap had graced his house with his presence. What an honour!

Tankha crouched on his chair like a wet and whipped cat. What was happening? Raja sahib had come to Rai sahib's house? Had they made up and become friends? He wanted to stoke the fires of hatred in Rai sahib so he could bask in its warmth but he realised the tables had turned. Something had gone seriously awry in his planning but he was still hopeful that the smouldering embers of their earlier rivalry would not extinguish overnight.

Raja sahib lit his cigar and gave Tankha a cold stare.

"Where did you disappear, Tankha? You took the payment for that party from me but the caterers have not received the money yet. They are after my life, badgering me for payment. I think this is a clear case of cheating. If I want I can pack you off to jail in a second."

Then he turned to Rai sahib and said, "I have yet to see a man more dishonest than this guy. I swear to God, Rai sahib, I would never have stood against you in the election had this scoundrel not misled and pushed me into the fray. He cunningly swiped a hundred thousand rupees from me and talked me into fighting the election. This scoundrel bought a bungalow from that money, he also bought a car and splurged on a prostitute who he has set up in a love nest. With all these trappings of the decadent rich, he has now started cheating everyone left and right." He paused and looked at Tankha angrily and snapped at him. "To act rich you must have a legacy; cheating is not the option. But your legacy is your propensity to cheat, you miserable man."

Rai sahib scowled at Tankha. "Why are you silent, Tankha? Why don't you say something in your defence? Raja sahib has usurped your salary, why don't you question him about it? Please get up and get out of this house and don't show me your wicked face again. Spoiling relations between two people and trying to make money by playing one against the other is an easy though slimy way to get rich quick but the pros and cons of this vocation are very dangerous. I hope you will remember this."

Tankha did not lift his eyes. He rose and slunk away like a guilty dog that runs with its tail between its legs on being caught in a place where it is not meant to be.

After he had gone, Raja sahib wanted to know whether Tankha was bad mouthing him.

"Indeed, he was. But I shut him up."

"He is a bad one."

"Absolutely."

"He can create differences between father and son, husband and wife. It's a relief he got a sound lesson today."

The discussion soon turned to Rudrapal's marriage. Rai sahib was in a state of mild panic as if he was being set up for target practice. He wondered if there was any escape for him. He was in a dilemma, how should he tell Raja sahib that he had no control over his son. But Raja sahib was already aware of everything. Rai sahib was spared a lot of trouble for which he heaved a sigh of relief.

"How did you hear about it," he asked Raja sahib.

"Rudrapal sent a letter to my daughter which she handed over to me."

"Young men these days have nothing better to do. They only know how to indulge their whims and fly free, unrestrained."

"Yes, I know they can be whimsical but I want to tell you that I have a cure for those whims. I can see to it that the girl, who's trapped him, disappears from the scene and no one will ever know where she went. In a few weeks, his whims will be under control. There is no point trying to make him see reason..."

Rai sahib shivered. Such a thought had crossed his mind but he had not allowed himself to dwell on it. Both men came from the same stock of cavemen. Rai sahib had covered himself with elegant clothes and sophistication whereas that primal instinct survived in Raja sahib in its stark naked form. Rai sahib could not resist underlining his human approach to the issue.

Almost embarrassed, or at least conveying the impression that he was, he said, "But this is the twentieth century, not the middle ages. I don't know how Rudrapal will react if anything untoward happens to her, but from a human and legal angle..."

In a flash, Raja sahib cut him short at the first whiff of a pacifist argument, "You go around blowing the trumpet of peace and humanity, can't you see it is brute power that rules the roost everywhere? It overshadows all talk of humanity. Why do you think nations are preparing to go to war? Wouldn't they resolve differences in summits, if it were so easy? As long as man exists, his animal instincts will continue to dominate his existence."

The argument grew from an academic discussion to a serious difference of opinion. The result was that Raja sahib left the place in a huff and Rai sahib also left for Nainital, the very next day.

On the third day, Rudrapal left for England with Saroj.

Their relationship, cold at the best of times, turned icy. Rudrapal's advisor and consultant was no other than Tankha. On behalf of Rudrapal, he filed a case of hedging of accounts on his father. An injunction of ten lakhs was imposed on Rai sahib. The pain of financial squeeze was not half as bad as the sorrow of finding his name besmirched in public. More hurtful than the spoiling of his reputation was the shattered dream which was blown up by none other than his own son. He nursed hopes of an obedient son; the illusion was snatched from his hands by the sudden turn of events, rather mercilessly.

But if he thought his cup of woe was overflowing he was in for another shock. His daughter and her husband's strained relationship erupted into an unseemly spat. Like other ordinary Hindu girls of her generation, Meenakshi was also a meek, quiet girl. She was betrothed to the man selected for her by her father. There was no love between the two. Digvijay Singh was a debauch and drunkard. Meenakshi suffered in silence, keeping books and periodicals as a tool to entertain her lonely days. Digvijay was about thirty years old and quite well educated, though extremely haughty and proud of his lineage. He was no softie and was averse to spending money, preferring to make amorous advances at poor women and girls from the lower castes. His friends were just hangers-on who fawned on him in submissive respect and he loved the attention. Meenakshi could not bring herself around to respect such a man. From the magazines which she devoured with zest, she learnt of women's rights and soon started visiting Ladies Clubs, frequented by rich women. They always talked about independence, gender rights and women's emancipation. Some called it liberation. The tenor of the discussions was such that it reeked of a secret society readying itself for a rebellion. Most ladies didn't get along well with their husbands. Like many modern women of their times, they were well educated and nursed a burning desire to break free of their husbands' vice-like grip on their freedom. A few young girls in the group considered marriage an affront to their individuality and were in search of those rare jobs that would also befit their station in life.

One of those free thinking women was Miss Sultan who had recently returned from England with a Bar-at-Law degree. She worked ceaselessly and zealously to offer legal advice and counsel to women who lived under *'purdah'*. Meenakshi took her advice and filed a case for maintenance from her husband. She balked at the idea of living with him under one roof. Actually, she did not lack money and could have led a comfortable life at her father's home, but this was an excellent opportunity to humiliate her husband which she didn't want to let go. In retaliation, Digvijay Singh charged her with immoral conduct. Rai sahib tried his best to soothe frayed tempers but Meenakshi was in no mood to relent. Though Digvijay's charges were thrown out at the first hearing, the court passed a decree against him and she won her case for maintenance, the humiliation the court battle caused to her rankled deep in her heart. She lived separately in her own house and participated enthusiastically in the socialist movement, but the hurt festered like a wound that refused to heal.

One day she took a whip and stormed into her ex-husband's house. His buddies were gathered there in full force to enjoy a dance performance. The performer was a woman of easy virtue who was prompted by lure of easy money. Meenakshi stormed into the party and created mayhem in the raucous celebrations like a furious she-demon venting her ire on hapless male predators. Lashed by the stinging whip, revellers ran helter skelter for dear life. The revellers did not want to mess with a friend's estranged wife and took to their heels. When Digvijay Singh was left alone, she rained several lashes on him. Caught totally unawares, he fell on the floor, exhausted and severely bruised. The prostitute cowering in a corner was petrified, visibly shaken, scared that she was next. Before Meenakshi could raise the whip she rushed forward and fell at her feet, weeping copiously- "Spare me, my lady! I won't set my foot at this place again. I am innocent."

Meenakshi gave her a look of disgust and said, "Yes, of course, you are innocent. You know who I am? Now get lost! Don't dare come here again. We women are mere objects of entertainment; it's not your fault."

The prostitute fell at her feet again. Relieved at her easy escape she grew emboldened enough to shower her with blessings- "May God be merciful and bless you with all happiness!." The terrified woman ran out and went home without losing a moment.

After that incident the estranged couple thirsted for each other's blood. Digvijay Singh carried a revolver with him, vowing to shoot her the moment he set his eyes upon her. She moved around with two burly wrestlers as her bodyguards and Rai sahib grew increasingly introverted as the edifice of his dreams, ambition and happiness crumbled bit by bit each passing day. So far, his hopes and aspirations had spurred him on with a zest for life. With that door closed, his mind sought solace in spiritual pursuits which he always considered a greater truth. The new properties he had acquired slipped from his possession before he could pay off the loans he had secured to buy them. As a Minister, he did receive a decent income but it barely sufficed to maintain the costs of living it up in the style expected of his position. Hence, he was forced to take recourse to arm twisting ways of attachments, seizure of properties and *challans* on the local population---all instruments of exploitation which he abhorred. He did not like putting his constituents to hardships. He pitied them but was completely helpless when confronted by his needs.

He suffered because neither worship nor devotion soothed his troubled mind. He sincerely wanted to forsake attachments but they clung to him with hooks of steel driving him insane with the diverse pulls of suffering, remorse, humiliation and guilt. How could his body cope with the troubled soul living in it? His health deteriorated despite every effort to insulate his body from illness. Every day exotic feasts were prepared in the family kitchen but his staple diet consisted of listless boiled vegetables and lentil soup with a few *rotis,* off and on. The lofty ideals of civilised upbringing still lived in his heart. But his mind consoled him with the excuse that as a government's representative and people's functionary of the district, he had to perforce turn to cunning and some extortion with a straight face because his position in society demanded pomp and show, howsoever superfluous. And his defeat lay in the folds of that notion.

32

Once out of the hospital, Mirza Khurshid found a new project to keep him occupied. A laid back reclusive existence was alien to his nature. And what a project it was! He was creating a drama company consisting of prostitutes from the city as its performing artistes.

In his hey days, his life was one continuous high of rollicking good times. Lately, confined to a hospital bed for the better part of a month, a firm determination to uplift those women from their sorry state had caught his imagination. He had contemplated on the commissions and omissions of his youth and he felt the time was ripe to give back something to those who had entertained him so profusely in the past. Utter remorse gripped his mind when he reflected on that life. If at that time he had the understanding and maturity that he possessed presently, imagine how many lives and morals he could have saved and delivered! He could have relieved so many girls of their poverty and miserable lives but like a fool he had not looked within himself more dispassionately.

There is nothing novel about the fact that our compassion and sensitivity is heightened when confronted by grave personal suffering. Who doesn't bemoan the follies of his youth? Alas, if that time is utilised in securing knowledge and doing good deeds, the present would be so much more relaxed and peaceful. It had also dawned upon him, rather painfully, that when you die there are few who weep for you. There are few whom you can call your own. An incident from the past flashed before his inward eye constantly when he was recuperating at the hospital. Once as he lay struck with malaria in a small village in Basra, a certain village lass had gone the extra mile to take care of him. After he recovered and offered her money and a few ornaments in appreciation of her attention and care, she had merely lowered her tear laden eyes and shook her head in a silent refusal of the gifts.

The nurses at this hospital were efficient and organised, but where was the love and involvement that dripped from the clumsy and awkward attempts of the village girl years ago? That angel of love lay buried in some inaccessible corner of his memory all these years. When he was leaving Basra, he promised to come and look her up again but once back, he soon forgot about her completely. The few times he did remember her, the emotion was of pity, never of love. God knows what happened to her and where she would be after all those years but lately the vision of her lithe, laughing, peaceful and humble personality danced before his eyes day in and day out. Had he married her, life would be so much more organised and simpler! The regret and guilt of the injustice he meted out to her, expanded into a reaction of service and sympathy for every character that belonged to her tribe. When the river threatened to overflow its banks at its prime, rays of light barely entered its frothy, muddy and swift currents. It was dismissed and lost in its raging flow. Now that the flow was steady, tranquil and almost still, beams of sunlight were touching the river bed and lighting up its depths in a soft glow.

Mirza sahib sat in the veranda under the thatched roof of his cottage, this quiet spring evening with two young actresses from his theatre company chatting aimlessly, when Mehta arrived unannounced. Mirza promptly extended his hand to him and said, "Great to see you, Mehtaji, I am waiting with the perfect paraphernalia to welcome you!"

Both girls smiled coyly at Mehta who felt embarrassed, blushing to the roots of his hair. Mirza nodded at the girls to leave and motioned him to be comfortable on the soft cushion and bolster on the floor.

"I was about to pay you a visit myself," he said, "The project I wish to go ahead with cannot be accomplished without your assistance. You have to stand behind me, goading me on."

Mehta smiled broadly and said, "Bookworms like us can contribute little to the projects you undertake, Mirzaji. You are senior to me, you have greater experience and have better knowledge of the ways of the world. You can impress everybody; if I had a fraction of your abilities I would have done wonders."

Very briefly, Mirza Khurshid outlined his new plan. His contention was that women enter the flesh market solely for two reasons, either they are not given proper security and shelter in their homes for whatever reasons or because they are forced into it by abject poverty. His theory was that if both these problems are tackled, few women will demean themselves in this manner.

Like other thinking men, Mehta had given a great deal of thought to this subject and had concluded that upbringing and cultural influences, along with an unrestrained desire for good life are the real motivations that pull certain women towards that profession. This difference in the outlook and understanding of both friends grew into a debate as both dug into their stands.

Mehta clenched his fist and jabbed it in the air. "I can see you have not given enough thought to this subject. One can find scores of ways to eke out a living. But unbridled desires will never be satiated easily. For that you need money. And still more money. And one takes the easy way out. Unless there is an overall change in society that encourages conspicuous consumption, such drama companies won't do any good."

Mirza twirled his luxuriant moustaches as he made another point. "But I insist there is nothing more to it than earning a living. I agree it varies from person to person – for a labourer, making a living means basic food and a thatched roof above his head. For a lawyer it might mean a bungalow, car and a retinue of servants. Man does not live by bread alone; he needs a number of things as well. It's no fault of women that they desire many material things."

Had Mehta paused to reflect on what they were saying, he might have realised they were pushing the same arguments albeit in different words but in the impatient heat of debate, logical comprehension of the subject is often the first casualty. His temper rose as he growled, "I beg to differ, Mirza sahib. As long as there are wealthy men with surplus cash in society there will be prostitutes as well. If your drama company meets with any success, which I seriously doubt, you won't draw more than a handful of such women into it and that too for a very short period of time. Not all women have theatrical talent- just as not all men can compose poetry. For once, even if we assume they stay on with your project, I am sure; the space they vacate will be filled up pretty soon. Unless you strike at the roots, plucking leaves is of no avail if you actually want to denude a tree. One often hears of some amongst the filthy rich who give up their wealth and pursue a spiritual life of self abnegation, sacrifice or charity but the world of the rich remains untouched. It survives strong as ever."

Confronted by Mehta's obduracy, Mirza felt sorry and somewhat saddened. An educated, well read and intelligent man, how could he hold such views? Is changing the structure of society a child's play? Society is a product of centuries of evolution. Should one give up any effort and wait for Armageddon? Shouldn't efforts be made to remedy the situation and save these young women from becoming fodder for the lust of men? Why shouldn't a fierce beast be encaged so that despite its sharp teeth and talons, It is rendered incapable of harming anybody? Is it any good to wait till the beast takes a vow of non- violence?

Rich men may burn money on the streets Mirza couldn't care less. If they wanted they could go ahead and drown themselves in a sea of liquor, collect innumerable cars as trophies of their affluence and string them around their neck, they could build as many charity homes, mosques he was least bothered. But they should not wreck a helpless woman's life. That was intolerable. He was determined to clean the flesh market to such an extent that the rich scoundrels' gold coins would go begging for takers. Didn't die hard drunkards quench their thirst with nothing but water when there was a picketing of liquor vends?

Mehta laughed at Mirza's foolishness - "Perhaps you should know there are countries where they don't have prostitutes. But the wealth of rich men magically creates novel ways of entertaining their baser desires."

Mirzaji was amused by Mehta's thick headedness. "Oh yes, sir, don't I know that too well? I am fortunate enough to have seen quite a bit of the world but this is Hindustan. This is not Europe."

"Human beings are the same in any country."

"Then you should also bear in mind that every society has an essential spirit that is exclusive to it. Purity and chastity is the essence of Hindustani culture."

"You can sing your glories for your ears. I am sure it sounds good."

"You are so fond of criticising wealth but never lose an opportunity to speak highly of Khanna. What do you have to say to that?"

Mehta's aggressive stance softened considerably. He was a picture of politeness as he said, "I have started speaking for him only now when he is released from the clutches of ugly riches. If you observe his present condition you will probably have sympathy for him. Moreover, what can I do to promote him? At best, I can cluck my tongue and make sympathetic noises, what with my books and academic work bearing down on me. The real support for him has come from Miss Malti who has actually saved him. I could have never imagined a human heart could be capable of so much sacrifice. You should go and pay him a visit one of these days. I bet you will be delighted to meet him. Today what he needs most is a few kind words of comfort."

Grudgingly, Mirza acquiesced to go and look him up. "If you insist, I will go. I will even go to hell if you recommend it but what was that about you and Malti? I heard you and Malti are to be married. There is a strong rumour to that effect."

Mehta seemed to blush as he spoke. "I am praying hard. Let's see when my prayers are answered."

"Oh come on man! She loves you so much."

"I had the same idea but when I extended my hand towards her I realised she is loftier than I thought. She is beyond my reach; I am not worthy or capable of reaching up to her level. I am praying to her to descend from her pedestal. Now-a-days she barely speaks to me."

With these words he stood up to go, laughing, trying to act as if he was about to burst into tears.

"When do I see you again?" Mirza asked him.

"You must exert yourself next time. It's your turn. But please go and look up Khanna soon."

"Sure. I will."

From his window Mirza watched as Mehta walked to the gate. His stride was slow, the usual brisk spring in his steps was absent, as though he was weighed down by some terrible burden.

❁❁❁

33

Mehta was no more the examiner, now he was the one appearing for the tests. Doubts that Malti might not be interested in him anymore, gnawed at his heart. For quite a few months she had not come over to his place and when he gathered the courage to visit her, she wasn't home. When Saroj and Rudrapal's affair was in full bloom she came over to his house, seeking his advice every other day often twice in a day, but after they went to England her visits ceased completely. She didn't remain at home either, which led him to speculate she was trying to avoid crossing his path, almost trying to wrench her attention away from him. The book on which he was working seemed to be stuck in limbo as if he had hit a writer's block and all his intellectual prowess had atrophied.

He was discovering, much to his consternation that housekeeping was never his strong point. He made a little over a thousand rupees a month but hardly saved anything. His meals were humble; the only concession to indulgence in his life was his car which he drove himself. He blew a sizeable part of his income in buying new books, another part in odd donations to charities, in helping poor students with their studies and the remaining portion of his earnings went towards upkeep of his garden which was a passion. He doted on his garden procuring new varieties of exotic plants from foreign countries at equally exotic rates, transplanting them in his garden and taking care of them diligently. More than a hobby, it was almost an obsession. The way he splurged on his plants, one would think it was an intellectual stimulation he couldn't do without.

But lately, his mind was wandering from his precious plants even as the condition of his house turned more sloppy than usual. He ate sparingly but food bills remained intact. His jacket had seen a few chilly seasons but he stayed with it all through the cold wintry days. He didn't bother to get a new one. At times, he ate his *daal* without frying it in butter. He didn't remember when was the last time he had bought a can of *ghee*. He didn't question the cook for he worried the man might take it as if he was being questioned for his integrity.

After four unsuccessful attempts at meeting Malti when he finally succeeded on the fifth, she saw his unkempt jacket and could not hold herself back any longer.

"Will you spend the rest of winter in this jacket?" she said, "Aren't you ashamed strutting around in this rag?"

Malti was not his wife but she was so familiar and close to him that her query had a normal tone to it which only someone very intimate acquires over time.

Mehta replied without any sign of embarrassment, "I can't help it, Malti. I don't seem to have any money to buy a new one."

Malti was quite surprised. "You earn a thousand rupees a month and you don't have enough money to get a new coat stitched? I have never made more than four hundred in my life and I live comfortably within my means and actually save a neat amount as well. I wonder what you do with your money."

"I don't waste a single *paisa* on frivolous pursuits. You know I am not a spendthrift."

"OK. Take money from me and get a new suit today."

Mehta felt a trifle shamed at this. "Oh, no! I'll get a new one stitched soon. I promise."

"When you come here next you must arrive dressed like a nice gentleman."

"That's a very tough stricture!"

"So it should be. With people like you, strictness is the only way to get things done."

However despite his brave words, his empty wallet did not inspire a visit to the tailor. Going back to Malti for a loan was an ordeal he'd rather not face; it was far better to squirm at his predicament in isolation. But there was more to come. A new problem knocked at his door one fine day. Of late, he had defaulted on paying his house rent which piled up at seventy five rupees every month. When the landlord failed to get his rent despite repeated requests, he sent a legal notice to recover it. Now a legal notice really cannot make money appear out of thin air. The notice period went by with no sign of recovery of dues. Pushed to an extreme, the man filed an appeal for eviction. He knew Mehta was a decent gentleman but the poor fellow could not do more than give a grace period of six months to Mehta to pay up. Mehta did not plead anything against the eviction notice and a unilateral court order was served to him to vacate the premises. As soon as the landlord obtained the ruling in his favour, the clerk issuing the notice hurried to inform Mehta about it in advance. He took this step because his son was studying in the university and was one of the beneficiaries of Mehta's benevolence. As luck would have it, Malti was present when he walked into Mehta's house with the news.

"What eviction notice are you talking about? Why is he being evicted?"

"It is about non-payment of rent. I thought I must inform sir about it. It's no huge figure, merely five hundred rupees. I can sit on it and delay any action on it for ten days while sir organises the amount. I will keep that fellow running from pillar to post during that time."

When the clerk left Malti spoke in a harsh voice, "So things have reached to such a head? I am amazed how you are able to write your books and treatises! You have not paid the house rent for six months at a stretch and you are blissfully unaware of it?"

Mehta lowered his head in shame. "It's not as if I am ignorant about it, I am unable to save money to pay it off. I don't spend a single *paisa* frivolously."

"Do you keep accounts of your expenses?"

"Of course I do. I pen down every figure that I earn; the income tax fellows will hang me if I don't."

"And what about the amount that you spend?"

"I don't have any account of that."

"Why?"

"Why should I write that down? It's such a bother!"

"Then how do you write these volumes of books?"

"That's easy; I don't do anything special for that. I simply pick up my pen and start writing. I can't open my account file and keep scribbling in it all the time."

"Then how will you repay what you owe to the landlord?"

"I will borrow from friends. Perhaps you can lend me some amount."

"I can but only under one condition and that is you hand over all that you earn to me and I have full control over where to spend it."

Mehta's delight was obvious and written all over his face. "Wow! If you take that responsibility, it's simply wonderful. I will dance on the streets in relief!"

Malti paid the due amount right away and the very next day forced Mehta to vacate that bungalow. She offered him two large rooms in her bungalow. She organised his meals in her kitchen. Mehta's possessions were sparse but his books took a few trips of the car to be transferred to his new living quarters. Both rooms were now full of books and little else. Letting go of his garden pained him immensely; but Malti left the entire lawn in the backyard for him where he could mess around with as many pots and plants as he pleased.

Mehta was relieved but Malti faced a Herculean task in managing his income and expenses. She could see that his income was more than a thousand rupees but it was going into secret donations and scholarships, almost in its entirety. No less than twenty to twenty-five boys were pursuing their school and university education solely on his support. An equal number of widows were also benefitting from his largesse, every month. She was in a fix about how to cut these expenses. She realised the blame would lie at her door and she would face severe flak from all sides. She felt irritated with Mehta, at herself and more so with the freeloaders who had no qualms about shifting their responsibilities on the shoulders of a simple, generous man. Her ire was compounded by the fact that a large number of those feeding off him did not deserve such charity. One day she confronted Mehta on this subject.

Mehta heard her dispassionately. "You have full rights to decide whom to give and whom to refuse. You don't need to ask me about it. However, you will have to answer them if they have any questions."

Malti felt her bile rise. "Sure! Why not? You get all the bouquets and I take all the brickbats. I fail to understand your logic in supporting this system of charity as you call it. The terrible way in which such gestures have crippled humanity and robbed it of its self respect, is unparalleled; perhaps it has harmed society more than injustice. I think possibly by provoking a reaction and revolt, injustice has done a favour to society."

Mehta nodded and said, "I think so too."

"If that is so, why do I see such a difference between your ideas and actions?"

By the third month, Malti had disappointed a lot of people. She turned away some amongst the list refusing to pay any further; politely offering regrets and excuses to a few and a good piece of her mind to others.

Mehta's budget came out of the red but a sullen guilt cast a shadow over him. When Malti came up with a saving of three hundred rupees, by the third month, he didn't say a word but his respect for her fell a few notches. A woman should be an embodiment of charity and sacrifice. Those were a woman's greatest assets; the very fabric of society depends on these two significant sentiments. The propensity to save and conserve was a disgrace, it might be a necessary evil but something to be sorry about, nonetheless.

The day his new suit and a brand new watch were delivered to him, he hesitated to step out of his room into the streets for about a week in sheer embarrassment. Acquisitions of any kind and putting oneself first were a crime in his eyes.

Malti wanted to arrest his easy ways and tried to put down his wasteful spending with a heavy hand, she questioned his ideas of charity but in her own life, she gave freely of herself, her time and her generosity when it came to her profession. She refused to make house calls for rich patients unless they paid her fees promptly but for the poor, she not only not charge any fees but provided them free medicines herself. Both loved self abnegation and a denial of their personal self. The difference between them was that while Malti lived her life both inside the house and outside it, Mehta's life was devoted to the world outside, home meant little to him. He felt responsible for nothing in his personal life, whereas Malti's life was tough; she felt a responsibility, a bonding which she dare not break, not that she ever desired to. She felt secure and comfortable within that bondage and it inspired her to do better. Observing Mehta at close quarters, she realised she could not tie this free animal to the confines of a cage. If she did, he might snap and snarl at her. He might get facilities and orderliness in the cage but his hankering for wide open spaces would suffocate and throttle him. For Mehta, domestic life was a peculiar unfamiliar world- confining and synthetic, a world strange and forbidding, whose customs and rules were totally alien to him.

He observed the world from outside and was confronted by all sorts of wrongs and injustice. Whatever he saw seemed to fester with evil but when he went up close, dived into its depths, he discovered that beneath that evil were several layers of beauty, grace, love and sacrifice struggling to make their presence felt. He perceived patience and at the same time realised that though these qualities lived and breathed under the cover of overpowering evil, they were rather rare virtues frail and hard to detect easily. Buffeted by the throes of doubt and despair of that revelation, when he saw Malti, rising like a divine vision from that darkness, he lost all reserve, turning almost frantic in a bid to secure her for himself, hidden safely from prying eyes. His sharp intellect did not grasp the simple truth that fanatic attachment is the nursery of destruction. Can a ruthless, independent emotion like love be expected to cower and accept taming under duress? Love needs complete freedom, complete trust, and total responsibility. It seeks its nourishment from within itself to unfold and grow. It needs space and light. It is not a wall on which someone can pile bricks, lay them with cement and build an edifice. It is a living thing and within its bosom is an immeasurable energy to grow and expand.

Since the day Mehta has moved into this bungalow, he found umpteen opportunities to meet Malti. His friends assumed this arrangement was the first step before marriage; its formalisation was either a matter of time or going through rituals. Mehta shared that belief as well. If Malti had rejected him forever, why would she still care for him this way? Maybe, she was giving him time to think about it. So he would definitely take this opportunity she had thrown at him. He had given deep thought to it and realised he felt incomplete without her. Externally, she appeared a woman of the world engrossed in its mores but intrinsically, the same zest for life was the actual fount of her energy and resolve. Also, lately the situation had changed. Earlier she was the seeker and now she was the sought and it was Mehta who was seeking her. After he got her reply to the question he posed to her, his attraction towards Malti was growing steadily and ever since he came to live so close to her, it was virtually galloping. The dark letters marching across the pages were a blur from a distance; now they were legible, replete with comprehensible meaning.

Incidentally, in another development, Malti had appointed Gobar as a gardener to tend to her garden. Once on her way from a house call, as she was driving back all alone, her car stalled, having run out of petrol. She was in a fix, stuck in the middle of the road with no petrol station in sight and no one around to lend a helping hand. It was October and with an early onset of winter, the night was quite chilly. There was not a soul in sight and she kept cursing her servant for not being available when she required him most. Who would push the car to a petrol station at this time of the night?

As luck would have it, Gobar was passing by and he eased her predicament by pushing the car up to the nearest petrol station.

Malti was pleased and asked him if he was unemployed and looking for a job.

Gobar accepted the offer happily. His salary was fixed at fifteen rupees, the job was to tend her garden and take care of the plants. He had ample experience of looking after a garden and was some sort of an expert at it. He earned more at the mill but his heart was not on it, therefore he pounced on the opportunity that fell into his lap.

The next day, Gobar was at her house and on the job. He was given a room in the servant's quarters. Jhuniya moved in as well with the baby. When Malti would come to the garden, she always found Gobar's son Mangal playing in the mud. On one such occasion she offered him a candy. That was all the child needed to become familiar with her. After that as soon as he saw her coming, he would trail her and keep pestering her till she delved laughingly into her bag and gave him a sweet.

One day, she didn't see him in the garden and enquired about his whereabouts from Jhuniya who told her he was down with fever.

"Why didn't you tell me about it?" Malti was concerned, "You should have brought him to me."

Mangal lay listlessly on the cot. Malti found the room to be so damp and dark with so many mosquitoes buzzing around that she couldn't bear to stand there for more than a minute. She rushed back to get the thermometer and was worried to see he was running high temperature. The child was not inoculated; she worried it could be smallpox. If he stayed in that dingy damp cell, his fever was bound to spiral up.

Suddenly he opened his eyes and seeing Malti standing next to him, he spread his arms, expecting her to lift him up. She took him in her arms and started patting his back gently, rocking him in gentle movements.

The baby felt comfortable and secure in her arms. He took his thin fingers, hot and flushed with fever to her neck and started playing with the pearl necklace around it. Malti took the necklace out of her neck and put it around the baby's neck. Despite the high fever, Mangal's childlike selfish instincts were quite alive. With a prized possession in his hands, he suddenly didn't want to remain in her lap anymore. He sensed a danger of losing the toy, thus making Jhuniya's more desirable and safe in these circumstances.

Malti was amused. "See! He's so clever!"

Jhuniya tried to admonish him. "Give it back, son. It belongs to *memsaab*'"

The boy clasped the necklace firmly with both hands and looked at his mother angrily.

Malti said, "Keep it, Mangal. I don't want it back." She promptly returned to her bungalow and moved her stuff from the spare living room. Jhuniya took little time shifting her meagre possessions into that room and ensconced herself comfortably into the new living quarters.

Mangal stared at the heaven he was transported into with wide, curious eyes. He saw a fan hanging from the celing, a number of electric bulbs, yellow and multicoloured what's more, there were attractive bright pictures on the walls too! He stared at all the fancy objects with unblinking eyes till Malti clapped gently for his attention, lovingly- "Mangal!"

He smiled shyly at her a smile that sought to convey he was speechless and unable to react; if she had anything to say, he was willing to listen.

Malti gave a long list of instructions to Jhuniya and on her way out asked her if she had any female relatives back in her village who could come to help her out at this hour. She told her to send for someone and put Gobar on the job right away. "I am afraid this looks like smallpox. Tell Gobar to go to his village and bring someone over for a few days to help you. Where is your village? How far is it?"

Jhuniya gave the name and address of her village and said it shouldn't be more than seventy or eighty miles from the city.

Malti remembered Bellari. She wondered aloud if it wasn't the same village which had the river barely half a mile away.

"Yes Ma'am, that's the one. But how do you know?"

"Once we went to that village. We stayed at the house of a man called Hori. Do you know him?"

"He is my father-in-law, *Memsaab*! You must have also met my mother-in-law!"

"Yes, of course. She seemed to be a very intelligent woman. She talked quite a bit. Tell Gobar to go down immediately and bring his mother here."

"He won't go."

"Why?"

"Well, there's some reason."

With no one to assist her, Jhuniya had to sweep, wash and scrub the room, cook for her family and mind the child all day. She cut short lunch with odd snacks and cooked the only meal in the evening when Malti returned home and sat near the child. Despite her repeated requests, Malti didn't allow her to sit with the child in the evening and all through the night. Wracked by fever, when Mangal extended his arms towards her, wanting to be carried in her lap, she readily lifted him and walked around the room, hushing him to sleep in a soft, gentle voice. On the fourth day, the disease manifested itself in right earnest. Malti inoculated all residents of the household herself and Mehta included. Gobar, Jhuniya, the cook in her kitchen, she spared none. The first few blisters were small and few, suggesting smallpox but the very next, they grew in size like grapes and in a few days, they fused together to become huge frightening bubbles of disease.

Mangal groaned with inflammation and itching caused by the blisters and stared at Malti with helpless sad eyes. The groans of pain escaping his lips sounded like those of an old man; the way he stared at people, acquired a mature and elderly look about it. In just a few days, pain erased his childish bearing, making the little boy almost grown-up in his responses. His juvenile understanding somehow latched on to the notion that if there was a saviour, it was Malti. The moment she moved out of his sight for a second he would turn restless, settling down into silence only when he saw her again. His discomfort increased at night, forcing Malti to stay awake for long hours but not once did she complain or display signs of irritation. However, she did lose her cool with Jhuniya who didn't follow her instructions because of her lack of intelligence and since she was a little slow on the uptake.

Both Gobar and Jhuniya had more faith in country medicines and faith healers than Malti's medications but they felt powerless. To make matters worse, despite having given birth to two children, Jhuniya's mothering skills left much to be desired. She would lose patience with Mangal if he acted unreasonable. The moment she got a little respite from work, she sprawled on the floor and dozed off. Gobar was scared to enter the room and would hover outside the door to enquire about Mangal's health. His health was not the same after that incident at the mill. He felt exhausted very soon after minor exertions. Earlier when Jhuniya went cutting grass and selling it to the cattle shed owners, he had regained some colour in his cheeks but strenuous work in Malti's garden had taken its toll on his health. Watering rows of plants, tilling, hoeing, removing weeds, tending to the cows, and milking them were telling on his health. He did not have the heart to shirk work since Malti was so kind to him. When Mehta himself was in the lawn every day, examining each plant and soiling his hands, Gobar could not avoid working a single day. His body was shrivelling up but the garden was blooming.

Mehta too was getting fond of the child with time. One day Malti pushed the child in his lap and goaded him to pull Mehta's moustaches which Mangal proceeded to do with gusto. He chortled with delight and cackled and was thrilled with the 'pull his moustache' game. His tiny hands pulled at the moustache hard but Mehta seemed to like it as he himself volunteered for the game once or twice every day.

When he was down with smallpox, Mehta was seriously disturbed. He went to see him in his room and stared at him for long intervals with worry lines furrowing his forehead. The child's suffering bruised his tender heart. He wanted to go the extra mile if it that could ease the boy's pain. But his limitations depressed him. Malti touched the child gingerly carrying him in her lap, patting his head on her shoulders, feeding him milk from the bottle, constantly playing with him, diverting his attention from the pain and suffering. Her affection for the child elevated Malti in Mehta's eyes. She appeared like a Goddess of maternal love and not a mere seductive nymph. Her outward demeanour of a lady of the world appeared as a camouflage to protect her real identity and the loving affection of a mother.

It was one o'clock at night. He heard Mangal crying. Malti might have fallen asleep; she was awake half the night. If the door was not bolted from inside, he could try to go in and look up the child. He tip toed to the room and peered in. Malti was sitting on the chair with Mangal in her arms. Probably, the child had a bad dream for he was crying continuously as she rocked him to and fro. She shushed him gently, showed him pictures on the wall all the while talking in a gentle cooing tone. The sight of Malti's intense caring and love for the child moved him immensely. He wanted to go in and hug her. An avalanche of unspoken words of love hovered on his lips!

Thoroughly captivated by the emotions surging in his heart, he called out to her, "Malti, will you open the door, please?"

Malti slid the bolt open and gave him a quizzical stare.

"Where is Jhuniya? Didn't she hear him cry? He seems to be in pain."

"It is the eighth day today. There will definitely be some discomfort."

"Then let me hold him. You rest for a while."

Malti smiled and said he might get irritated if she lets him go.

Mehta insisted- "You think I am good for nothing?"

Malti gave the child to him. As soon he came into his lap, Mangal stopped crying. The innate sense of the child sent a direct message to his brain. This new person who he was holding was not a woman, he was a man who might not be so sensitive to his tantrums. He might leave him alone, drop him or put him aside in a dark corner and go his way. He might even prevent any other person from trying to comfort him.

Mehta smiled victoriously- "See that?"

Malti smiled back at him. "Yes. Where did you learn this art?"

"I learnt it from you."

"But I am a woman! And women can't be trusted."

The barb found its mark. Mehta grew hot under the collar. "Malti, I pray to you with folded hands please forget what I said to you. You do not know how sorry and ashamed I am about whatever I said to you."

"Honestly, I have actually forgotten all about it."

"How do I know that you really don't hold anything against me now?"

"We live in the same house, eat together, laugh together, talk to each other isn't that proof enough?"

"Will you permit me to say something?"

He bent down and placed a quiet Mangal on the cot and looked at her with pleading eyes, as if his life depended on her what she was about to say.

Malti was moved by his demeanour and said, "You know only too well there is no one closer to me than you in the whole world. I gave myself up to you a long time ago. You are my guide, my angel, my guru. You don't have to seek my permission to say anything, just say what you want. When I had not met you, when I didn't know who you really were, my life was wasting away in a selfish and misguided world. You gave me stability and the intelligence to realise the rut I was in. I am indebted to you deeply. I will tell you why I took your words to heart. I was hurt because I didn't expect you to think like other men. At least you were different and you would know I am not the person everybody thinks I am. I know I am responsible for whoever I was but I was sad to realise that you doubted I couldn't change even after I found love from a person, as precious as you. That was so unjustified. I don't know if you will understand how contented and proud I feel at this moment. I suddenly do not want anything more after I have found your love. Your love will suffice me for life. I don't need anything else."

As she spoke, Malti felt a burning desire to draw him in an embrace. All that she dreamt for was right before her. The bliss she thought to be elusive and distant was so close; she just had to reach out and touch it. Every pore of her body shook with a trembling happiness. The joy sweeping through her soul glowed, softly on her face. Mehta thought he saw an ethereal light. Who was this woman before him? She couldn't be human! In one brief flash, the moment transcended small everyday things. Even special, rare feelings.

Jhuniya woke up and sat upright, stirred from sleep and Mehta left the room abruptly. For two weeks after that night, he did not come across Malti in private. She avoided meeting him alone but her words kept echoing in his mind. Those intoxicating words that filled him with hope, humility and joy.

In two weeks Mangal recovered and was up and about, regaling everybody with his antics. The disease had left its imprint on his face in pock marks. Malti bought sweets and distributed amongst children in the neighbourhood. She also offered obeisance at temples where she had prayed for his recovery. She experienced for the first time a curious happiness in doing something for someone else. She felt as happy as Jhuniya and Gobar. The quality of her happiness was better than what she had ever experienced in her life. Previously, there was a constant hankering in her mind. She never felt satisfied but lately, her longing had evolved like flowers that turn into fruits. What delight can a bungalow give her when squalid hamlets cried for attention in the neighbourhood? Breezing down the roads in her car was not a high any more. A little boy like Mangal had opened doors of bliss she never knew existed.

A few days later Mehta developed a terrible headache. It was a migraine attack. When she heard about it, Malti went to him and put her hand on his head and asked him since when he was suffering from the pain.

Sensing her soft hands, Mehta felt the pain vanish magically. He said, "I had this headache since yesterday. It was bad and nothing like I had suffered earlier but now that you put your hand on my head, it's gone! Your touch is magic!"

Malti gave him a medicine and advised him to take it immediately and made to leave the room.

Mehta insisted that she stay awhile.

"Won't you stay for two minutes?"

"I have an appointment. I've got to see a patient."

"Ok, fine. Go."

Mehta made such a face that she turned back from the door and said, "Very well. I am here. Tell me?"

"Nothing much. I just wanted to know why you have to go see a patient at this hour so late in the night."

"It is Rai sahib's daughter. She's in bad shape. She was worse; better now."

After she had gone Mehta could not sleep. He was confused, wondering how a mere touch could cure his headache. This was no mean feat. It was some special power or blessing. Malti had become a radiant star for him. She was no more an object of love but an object of veneration. The happiness which Mehta wanted to experience in love turned deeper and embellished with feelings of faith and sublimation. Faith is essentially a giving emotion. In its initial stages love always seeks and demands its rights. It wants some return but soon it evolves into a faith and a need to give and surrender whatever one possesses to the object of its affection.

Mehta had completed his book on different philosophies. It was a book in which he had done a comparative study of differing philosophies of the world and had tried to present a composite view of the human seeker. He dedicated the volume to Malti. The day the first printed copies arrived from England, he presented one to her. Seeing her name on the first page inside the cover, she was both surprised and saddened.

"Why did you do this? I am not worthy of this honour."

But Mehta didn't agree. "But I think you are," he said, "in fact you are worth a hundred times more."

"Hundred times? Me? Someone who is steeped in her own self?"

"I will consider myself blessed if I get a quarter of your dedication and humility. You are the epitome of sacrifice and beauty."

"I and sacrifice? Allow me to be honest with you. Not once have I felt a desire for service or sacrifice. All my endeavours are based on what pleases me. I don't sing because I want to make the world happy but because it makes me happy. The only reason I give medical help and service to the poor is because it makes me happy. In some way, it satisfies me and my ego. Don't put a halo around me, please. The way you are going, the next step would be incense sticks and glorification as some Goddess!"

"I have felt that way for a long time, Malti. And I will continue to pray at your altar till you answer my prayers."

Malti was in a jovial mood. "Very well. And once your prayers are answered, out goes the Goddess to the dump heap!"

Mehta did not laugh. "In that case it will mean the end of me as well."

Malti did not want to prolong the charade. She spoke seriously with a grave face, "No, Mehta, I worked on this question for months and have now reached a conclusion. I have decided it is better if we remain together as friends and not as husband and wife. The former is a much happier situation to be in. You love me and you trust me. I am pretty confident that you will risk your life to save me if I am in any trouble. In you, I have found a partner with whom I feel completely secure. I love you equally and I trust you too. I don't see there is anything I will not do for you. I sincerely pray to God to make me steady in my commitment to you. Do we need anything else to satisfy our souls? Is there anything else we would want to make us feel more whole and complete within ourselves? What more do we need? By restricting our lives in domesticated bliss and cramping our souls in constricted cages called home, will we ever wing it to the freedom of the skies? I think our cloistered life will only restrict our growth, nothing else. I agree there are people, though few and far between, who wear these shackles voluntarily and yet continue on their forward path of self discovery. I realise that family and love that thrives along with the sacrifices made within home and hearth has its significance. But my spirit does not measure up to that critical test. As long as there isn't any feeling of belonging, of 'me' and 'mine'- there won't be any illusory attachment to life. There won't be any pulls of selfishness as well. The day we fall in the trap of attachment, we fall into bondage. Then immediately the circumference of our humanity shrinks to encompass only our little nest. We are saddled with any number of new responsibilities and all our energies are directed to handle them. I do not wish to imprison the soul of a thinking and talented human being like you in this cage. So far, your life has remained a sacrifice- an oblation in the sacred fire of life, where selfishness is present, but only in faint traces. I am not willing to douse that fire or feed any dormant selfishness. The world needs passionate practitioners like you who burn so bright that the universe feels the warmth of your kindness and understanding. There are scary clouds of superstition, religious fanaticism and hatred that are shutting off the light of reason from people's lives. The world is groaning under the weight of injustice, fear and oppression. You have heard those screams. You are responding to those signals of distress. If you will not listen who will come forward to hear those cries? Like other weak-kneed, false individuals amongst the multitudes you cannot afford to close your eyes and ears. If you do, it will throttle your soul. Use your intelligence, utilise every bit of your knowledge, push your awakened humane self to move faster on that path. I promise to follow right behind you. Please help me make my life meaningful by allowing me to walk beside you. This is what I want from you, this is what I beg of you. If your heart ever wanders into the muck of worldliness, I assure you I will try my best to keep you from straying. And God forbid, if I fail in my attempts, I promise you I will move away from you, even if it breaks my heart in a million pieces. I don't know where that will take me or what will be my future or where it will all end for me. I might float away like driftwood and who knows which shore I will land ultimately but I am sure of one thing- I won't end up in an illusory bondage. Now tell me; order me and I will do as you say."

Mehta listened to her in rapt attention with his head bowed. Each word entered his heart, knocking everything around, waking his inner eye to realms he had not imagined. The thoughts that played on his mind in flickering images vibrated like the truth of life in his heart. He felt alive, bright and awakened. When we encounter significant moments in our lives, it is marked by a spontaneous return to impressions from our childhood. Old memories from his boyhood days sprang into his consciousness. He remembered in a flash how he would leap into his widowed mother's lap as a little boy and feel he were king of the universe. Where are you, mother? Come and see how your truant son has grown. Bless me. Your obstinate son is born again; he is getting a new life.

He caught hold of Malti's hands and spoke in a trembling voice- "I accept your decision, Malti."

In the silent room, they held each other in a tight embrace, misty eyed.

❁❁❁

34

Siliya's son was two years old. He introduced his own peculiar language in the village and blabbered non-stop, unmindful if anyone deciphered his utterances or not. There were no vowels in his language, the pronunciation of the alphabets was weird, mixed up and extremely entertaining for the villagers who doubled up in laughter at his baby talk. Passersby would stop to ask- "Hey Ramu! How does a dog bark?" and Ramu would raise his chubby face to the skies and go bow-wow-wow. Another would ask about a cat and he would go 'Meow, meow' and snap at his audience with baby fingers turned into chubby claws for effect. He was a jolly kid. He wouldn't rest for a moment, ever ready to go out and play any time of the day or night. He disliked being carried around in someone's lap. His best hours would be the ones he spent under the mango trees, rolling in the mud, making little mounds of earth and running headlong into them. He disliked the company of children his age. He probably thought they were imbeciles and not up to his standard. If someone asked him "What's your name?" He would say-"Lamu" instead of Ramu.

"What's your father's name?"

"Matadin."

Who's your mother?"

"Chhiliya."

Ramu and Rupa were great pals. They got along well. He was Rupa's little toy. She washed and bathed him, oiled his hair and lined his eyes with kohl, making his round, dark eyes still more pronounced and dark. Dhania scolded her for messing around with the boy but she was hardly bothered. Playing with rag dolls as a little girl had taught her mothering and she could not wait to practise it on a real baby.

In their backyard, Siliya had built a straw hut in which she lived with her baby, since she couldn't stay in Hori's house as a guest forever.As for Matadin, a few hundred rupees was all it meant for the *pundits* of Benares to reconvert him into a full-fledged Brahmin. An opulent fire sacrifice was held to mark his purification, hundreds of Brahmins were invited to the feast and he was sprinkled with holy water and cow urine to dispel the germs of pollution.

In a strange way, the ceremony did have an effect. His heart went through a churning and regret at his actions, thereby burning quite a bit of the negativities in his mind. The blazing fire lit up the dark corners of his sensibilities and exposed the shaky foundations of his ritualistic practices. He started hating religion. He threw away his *janeyu* and balked at his priestly duties. He observed that though he was ritually declared 'purified', few people actually ate from vessels he had touched. They did consult him about auspicious dates and astrological charts but kept a careful distance from him.

The day Siliya's baby was born he drank himself to delirium and made a fool of himself, twirling his moustaches, priding himself that the baby must look like him. But he could not actually go and see the newborn infant. Three days later, he came across Rupa in the fields. He asked her if she had seen his baby.

"Yes, of course," she said, "he has large eyes and curly hair on his head and stares unblinkingly at everyone."

The infant's image, as described by Rupa, was framed in his heart. He picked her up in his arms, raised her high and put her on his shoulders. Unmindful that she wasn't a little baby anymore but a growing young girl, he swung her around and kissed her on the cheeks happily.

Rupa collected herself from this sudden assault of his delight and said, "Come, I will show you the baby. He is right there in our backyard." Matadin didn't accept her offer and turned his face away, overcome with emotion. That night when the village slept, he crept up to that hut and lingered outside stealthily, listening to the baby cry. There was such music in that sound.

After that, he dropped by at Hori's house on one pretext or the other when Siliya was away to work and steal furtive glances at the baby. Dhania would smile at him and coax him to pick up the baby in his arms, admonishing him when he kept his distance. He would leave a few coins for Siliya with Dhania and leave as quietly as he came. As the baby grew, so did Matadin's outlook and vision. Every day he perceived a new way of looking at his life and future. Now he had an aim, an ambition, and a goal to strive for. A new sense of responsibility came over him. He became more disciplined and serious.

Once when he dropped by at Hori's house, he discovered that Dhania was away. There was no one in the house except Rupa who also scampered out hearing kids shouting, laughing and playing. He was all alone when he saw the baby in the courtyard, kicking his little feet in the air, all alone under the blue sky. Matadin couldn't hold himself back. He lifted the child and hugged him close to his chest. He looked into the baby's eyes and felt a strange mix of delight and fear. The baby's frank inquisitive stare seemed to nail him. He thought he saw an accusation in those dark baby eyes. How could he sully God's gift with his unclean hands? Quietly he placed the baby back in his cradle as Rupa walked in. Shortly thereafter, he went out of the house.

A few months later, the village was lashed by a hailstorm. Siliya was not home, she was away at the market selling freshly cut grass to whoever would buy it. Rupa was busy playing inside the house. Ramu was able to sit on his own and crawl a few steps unescorted. When he saw the white hail stones in the courtyard he chuckled gleefully, thinking they were some sort of new candy. He crawled on all fours into the courtyard and swallowed a few of them, playing and chortling merrily despite the cold. That night he had high fever. The next day, his condition deteriorated into pneumonia. The third day, he died in Siliya's lap even as she sat hugging him close, wrapped in whatever rag she could find at home.

Despite his absence, the baby remained the focus of Siliya's life. Her breasts would ache, heavy with milk, bringing tears to her eyes. After toiling all day when she pushed her breasts into his mouth for the baby to suckle, she was infused with an energy which the infant passed into her. She sang songs to him, building fantastic dreams of elaborate kingdoms where Ramu was the presiding deity. Now-a-days, after returning from work, she wept quietly, straining her imagination, wondering where the little foundling had gone. The village mourned with her. Such a bundle of joy he was! He had gone into the arms of God. His popularity didn't grow faint with his death. On the contrary, it grew still more real and strong. His memory proved to be durable, more attractive and alluring as his physical presence.

Something had snapped inside Matadin that fateful night. The emotions which he kept well reined had burst into the open. Curtains stretched across windows are meant to shield homes from sun and wind. During storms, they are of little use. It's prudent to fold them and put them aside for they don't mean anything at that time. He had held the dead child's corpse on both of his outstretched palms and carried it all alone for the last rites to the edge of the river which had narrowed to a shallow ribbon of water. For the last eight days he could not straighten his hands for the ache in his biceps. That day, he didn't flinch or hesitate for a moment.

No one spoke a word to him. Those who did gossip among themselves were all praise for him and spoke highly of his courage and commitment.

Hori said, "That's like a man! One should always stand by one's partner, in times of distress."

Dhania made a face and grimaced, "That is some partner! He irritates me no end. Is he a man?"

It was one month past since the baby died. Siliya had picked up the threads and started working in the fields again, cropping grass and weeds. It was late evening and the moon was out already. She had collected the fallen sheaves of barley in the field and bundled them in her basket when she saw the moon resplendent and white in the sky. A horde of painful associations formed in her mind and her breasts turned wet with milk. She bent her head low and wept quietly, relishing both the relief and pain that comes with weeping. Hearing a movement behind her, all of a sudden, she was startled and turned to look over her shoulder. It was Matadin. He appeared from the shadows and stood in front of her.

"How long will you weep for him, Siliya? Your tears won't bring him back", he said to her and broke down as he spoke, his body shaking in sobs.

Siliya's first reaction was to curse him but she was stumped. Surprised by this unprecedented display of emotion, she said, "How come you're here?"

"I was passing this way when I saw you and came over."

"You could not even play with him," Siliya said quietly with a note of regret.

"No Siliya. I did."

"Really?"

"Yes."

"Where was I? Why didn't I see you?"

"I came one day when you had gone to the market."

"Didn't he cry when you picked him up in your arms?"

"No! Actually he started laughing and chortling."

"Don't tell me!"

"Yes, it's true!"

"You were with him just once?"

"Yes. I played with him only once but I saw him almost every other day. I used to see him sleeping on the cot. It was such a joy to see him."

"Yes, he had taken after you. He resembled you so much."

"I feel bad I took him in my arms that day. God punished me for my sins."

Siliya's eyes had the glint of forgiveness as she picked up the basket and got up to make her way back home. Matadin stood up as well and started walking beside her.

"Now I sleep in Dhania's veranda. I can't bear to sleep in that desolate hut."

"Dhania tried to reason with me so many times."

"Did she?"

"Yes, she did. Every time I met her she tried to make me understand what was right..."

As they neared the cluster of houses Siliya said, "Ok, now you take the other road from this crossing or else the other *pundits* will see you."

Matadin lifted his chin up as he said, "I am not scared of anyone."

"If they throw you out of their fold where will you go?"

"I have got my own house now."

Oh really? Where is it? This is news! I didn't know about it."

"Come, let me show you."

They started walking again; Matadin led the way and Siliya followed him curiously. They reached Hori's house. Matadin walked behind the house and stood in front of the door of Siliya's hut and said, "This is our house."

For a second Siliya was silent, then she smiled weakly. Her tone reflected a quaint mix of surprise, disbelief, sarcasm and sorrow when she said, "This is the house of a *chamarin* called Siliya."

Matadin reached forward and slid open the loose bolt on the door. He said- "This is a temple of a goddess."

Siliya's eyes lit up but she said, "Well, if it's a temple; you'll go in, offer worship and go back."

Matadin lowered the basket from her head. There was unmistakable tremor in his voice as he said, "No Siliya. As long as I live, I will stay here and take care of you."

"Oh come on. Liar!"

"I swear on you. I am serious. I heard that Pateshwari's younger son Bhunesar was acting fresh with you one day and you gave him a good tongue lashing?"

"Who told you?"

"Bhunesar told me himself."

Siliya struck a match and lit the oil lamp. In its dim light Matadin saw an earthen pot, next to it was a fire oven with a few brass utensils stacked around it, washed and cleaned. In the centre of the hut a bundle of hay was spread on the floor. That was Siliya's bed, close to it stood a small, lonely baby cot. Lying topsy-turvy near the cot were a few mud elephants and horses with either an ear missing or a head broken. Without its general, the army had disintegrated. Matadin sat down on the hay. A sharp line of agonising pain went through his consciousness in slow motion. He wished he could cry.

Siliya put her hand on his back gently and said, "Did you miss me any day?"

Matadin held her hand and pressed it close to his chest. "You were in my thoughts all the time. Did you miss me too?"

"I don't know. Half the time the only thing I felt was anger for you."

"You never felt pity for me?"

"Never."

"Then why did you scold Bhunesar..?"

"Shut up. Don't talk rot. But I am scared and worried, whatever will the villagers say?"

"The ones who are good will say 'it is his sacred duty' and those who aren't good mean nothing to me."

"And who will cook your food?"

"My sweet princess, Siliya!"

"Then how will you remain a Brahmin?"

"I don't want to be a Brahmin. I want to be a *chamar*. The one who follows his sacred duty is a Brahmin; the one who does not is a *chamar*."

Siliya bent forward and threw her arms around him.

❁❁❁

35

Hori's health was deteriorating with each passing day. Buffeted by the ups and downs in his life--where downs outnumbered the ups--he clung tenaciously to hope. Every time he lost on one front, it spurred him on to fight ahead. But of late, he found himself at that stage of life where his confidence was completely shattered.

Like a deposed monarch in his bad days, he fortified himself within his last bastion, the three *'bighas'* of land that he owned, trying his best to cling to that last piece of his self respect. Despite utter penury, missed meals, hardships and abuse, he had not let go of his land. Unfortunately, lately the threat of eviction from that land was quite palpable and real. For the last three years, he had defaulted on paying the *lagaan* and Nokhe Ram had sent a notice for dispossession of the land, a few days ago. The land was slowly and steadily slipping away and a life of hard labour stared at him menacingly. "If that's the will of God, so be it! What's the point in cursing Rai sahib? After all, his survival also depends on people like me.' thought Hori. Half of the families in his village were faced with similar problems; they were all on the verge of being dispossessed of their fields. To hell with it! He won't suffer any worse than the others. He was not destined to be happy- or why would his only son forsake him?

Deeply engrossed in his thoughts, that evening Hori didn't notice Pandit Datadin till he came right up to him and said, "What's the latest about your notice, Hori? I am not on talking terms with Nokhe Ram these days. I am out of touch with what's cooking. I understand its only fifteen days for the eviction to be effective?"

Hori pulled a cot for him. "Well, he knows best. He is the one with money. If I had the money it would be another story. I didn't waste any money, I didn't spend much but what can I do if it's a meagre harvest which doesn't fetch a good price either. What can a peasant do?"

"But you have to protect the memory of your forefathers and save the land you've inherited from them. How will you survive if you lose that?"

"It's God's will? Who am I to question what He's ordained?"

"There is a way out. If you are willing to listen, I will suggest it to you."

Hori's dull visage lit up with anticipation of hope.

"Oh! That would be a blessing! I know only you can guide me. I had given up all hope. Tell me!"

"There's no reason for you to give up hope. You simply have to realise that a man's duty varies according to time and circumstance. In better days, his responsibilities and attitudes are quite different from those when he hits bad times. When he is doing well, a man may be charitable and giving; when luck is against him he can be reduced to beggary. In difficult circumstances that can as well be the wise thing to do. When our body is healthy and fit we sit down to eat only after washing and cleaning ourselves and saying our prayers properly; in illness we do not care for such observations. That is acceptable and right in those circumstances. There is such a wide difference between our castes, but in the holy city of Jagannathpuri, we sit and eat together as there is no discrimination there. When he was going through turbulent times Lord Ram ate the leftover berries of Shabri, a low caste woman. He also vanquished Bali using deceit. Even the greats break rules of propriety and dignity when in trouble, how are we expected to be any different? I assume you know about Ram Sevak Mahato?"

"Of course I do," said Hori. Datadin's lecture had evidently not inspired him.

"Well, Ram Sevak Mahato is my spiritual follower. He has done well for himself. He earns a good income from agriculture and has a flourishing money lending business too. His wife passed away quite a few months back. He has no children. If you are open to marrying Rupa to him, I can talk and pursue the matter with him. He will listen to me and take my advice seriously. Your girl is not a child anymore and these are bad times and no one is safe. If anything goes wrong, it will unnecessarily create fresh problems. This is a good opportunity. The girl will be married off and your fields will be saved from being auctioned as well. Besides, you won't have to spend a fortune which you will have to cough up for a regular wedding."

Ram Sevak was at best three or four years younger to Hori. Suggesting his name as a groom for Rupa was such a disgrace. His little girl married to that old stump? Insults were nothing new to Hori, but this one cut deep. Had he hit such bad times that he is told to sell off his daughter and worse, find himself tongue tied unable to refuse outright? He lowered his head in shame.

Datadin waited for a moment and said, "So what do you say?"

Hori gave no direct reply. "I will think about it and let you know," was all he said.

"What is it that you have to think about in this case?"

"I have to talk to Dhania first."

"Are you OK with the proposal or not?"

"Let me think about this, *Maharaj*. Such a thing has never happened in my family.

I have to worry about its impact on my family's name and reputation."

"Very well, take your time but get back to me within a week. Don't delay for so long that you keep ruminating over it and they initiate the dispossession process!"

Datadin went back. He did not foresee any problems with Hori. It was Dhania who might prove difficult. She had tremendous airs; she was the one who'd rather die than give up without a fight. But if Hori put his foot down she might come around. After all, land dispossession is as bad a disgrace to family honour as any.

As soon as Datadin left, Dhania asked Hori the reason for his visit.

"Nothing much, he was enquiring about our case."

"I am sure he came to merely click his tongue in sympathy. It's not for him to offer solutions. Will he offer to give a hundred rupees to solve our problem? No, never!"

"Neither do we have the face to ask for it."

"Then what's the point in coming to us?"

"He had come to talk about Rupa's marriage."

"With whom?"

"You know Ram Sevak? He suggested his name."

"I have not seen him though I have heard about him quite a bit. But isn't he too old?"

"He's not old. He is middle aged."

"Didn't you give him a piece of your mind? Had he made the suggestion to me, I would have given him something to chew on for the rest of his life."

"I didn't lose my temper but I did refuse him. He kept repeating it won't cost us a *paisa* and our fields will be saved as well."

"Why don't you put it straight? In so many words, he was suggesting we sell our daughter to that old man."

Dhania had made her point but Hori's opposition to the idea grew weaker as he reflected on the proposal. Family name and honour exercised him as much as it did Dhania but those struck with a terminal illness often turn callous to their own sensitivities. His attitude towards Datadin's proposal was obviously not of acceptance but his mind was not totally averse to the idea. What did age have to do with it? Life and death was matter of fate. Old men live for long, young men die in the prime of their youth, it's all about destiny. If Rupa was destined for happiness, she would find joy anywhere; if providence was against her, she won't find joy in any situation. Moreover, there is nothing in this proposal that smacks of selling one's daughter. Whatever money he took from him would be a loan which he would repay as soon as he could. There was no shame in taking a loan. Well, if he was rolling in wealth he would have definitely found a younger, more eligible groom for Rupa, probably organised a lavish wedding with sumptuous feasts and given away gifts and dowry to make anyone envious. But if God had clipped his feathers it was foolish to attempt to fly. People would smirk, no doubt, but would they ever offer to help? No! Then why should he worry about their reactions? The problem was that Dhania would not accept it easily. She was such a stubborn woman at times. What with her lame song and dance about family honour and stuff. This was no time to worry about honour; one should worry about staying alive. If she was so fond of social prestige, would she cough up five hundred rupees to preserve it? Where was that kind of money?

For two days they hardly exchanged a word on this subject again. However, they did mention it to each other in oblique ways.

Dhania would say, "A perfect wedding is when the bride and groom complement each other."

Hori would reply-"Marriage is not another name for enjoyment. Marriage is about sacrifice."

"Oh! So it's about sacrifice?"

"True, only if you have the patience to realise it. If being content with whatever situation God leads us to isn't a sacrifice, what else is?"

The next day Dhania came up with yet another aspect of marital bliss. What worth was a marriage unless there was a father-in-law, mother-in-law along with a number of brothers and sisters-in-law, not to talk of uncles and aunts in the husbands' family?

Hori countered that with, "They are not a gift; they are a liability."

Dhania was unimpressed. "You come up with weird theories! How can a new bride live alone in a household with no one from the family for company?"

"Well, when you came to this house you had not one but two brothers-in-law plus a father-in-law and mother-in-law. What joys did you get out of living with such a huge family? Do you have an answer to this?"

"Is everybody like that in every family in the world? "

"Of course, people are the same everywhere. Do you think in other families they aren't any different? Do you think everybody is an angel? One poor bride and so many to lord it over her! How many can she please at a time? In a large family someone or the other will definitely not be too happy with her. Ideally, a girl should live in a nuclear family."

The discussions would cease at this point but the scales were gradually tilting against Dhania.

On the fourth day none other than Ram Sevak Mahato himself arrived at their doorstep. Accompanied by his barber and another assistant, he came astride a fine breed horse in a style befitting a rich landowner. He must have been around forty as was obvious from his salt and pepper hair but his body was fit and there was a visible glow of good health on his face. As compared to him, Hori appeared ancient and haggard. He was on his way to attend the court regarding some case and was looking at escaping the heat of the sun by resting at their place for the afternoon. The weather was quite hot and the wind was so searing, it could scald the skin.

Wheat flour and *ghee* was procured from Dulari sahuain's shop and steamy poories were fried for the three guests.

Datadin also dropped by to pay his compliments to the visitors.

"How's the court case going, Mahato?" he asked.

Ram Sevak puffed up his chest. His attempt at mock humility failed miserably; not that he was really keen to sound humble.

"You see, *Maharaj*," he said, "in the position that I am, there is always one or the other litigation to attend to at any given time. There is no point being meek in today's world. There are courts, police and the law but none will come to our assistance when we need them most. It's a free for all everywhere! No one is ready to spare the poor and the weak. God forbid, I hope you don't presume I am trying to speak in favour of dishonesty and cheating! Oh, that's a bad thing, yes, it is. But not fighting for your rights is a bigger evil. Isn't it? Why should anybody tolerate injustice? Peasants are cheap fodder for anybody these days. The poor chaps dare not forget to grease the palms of the village *'patwari'*; they are in trouble if even the peon of the *zamindaar* is not looked after well. And what should one say about the constable or police? They are pompous sons-in-law who want you to stand in attendance when they condescend to visit the village. It's the poor peasant's duty to welcome them with gifts and offerings or in one stroke they can lock up the entire village. Everyone is tweaking the peasant, whether it's the minister, his deputy, the zonal chief, the law enforcement officer, the collector or any other official. The peasant must bow to their lordships. Right from organising supplies, milk, poultry, butter, *ghee* for them they are expected to come up with almost everything. Aren't you facing the same situation, *Maharaj*? Everyday there is a new official to please! Now-a-days we have a new doctor sent by the higher-ups to check on the health of cattle, another comes by every week to drop some medicine in the wells. There are officials and inspectors for everything little thing. One to examine the boys in school, one for the canals, another for the forest land, one for the toddy shops, a rural development inspector- God! The list is endless. What's worse, even the priest from the church expects good treatment or he threatens to lodge a complaint. And if you think all these innumerable inspectors and officials do any good to the people you are totally mistaken. The other day there was a call from the *zamindaar's* house for a contribution of two rupees per family. It was in aid of a party to be thrown in honour of a visiting dignitary. The peasants refused and guess what happened? They were all fined for insubordination! The functionaries of the government are as bad as their masters. They don't care for the poor man- they'd rather side with the high and mighty. Do they have any concern for the families of poor peasants? No, sir, not at all! They care two hoots. This is all due to our meekness and cowardice. I made an announcement in my village – exhorting everyone neither to pay taxes for irrigation rights nor give up working in their fields. I told them not to take it sitting down- they could arrest us if they want- we must stand firm. Fortunately they responded positively to my call. When the *zamindaar* met such resistance, he retreated quietly. Had he evicted all peasants from their land who would have tilled the fields in his area? In today's world if you are a softie you are finished. If the baby doesn't bawl out loud, even mothers don't bother to feed him milk."

Ram Sevak left late in the afternoon, leaving Hori and Dhania suitably impressed and awestruck. Datadin's formula had worked perfectly.

"What do you say?" he asked them.

Hori nodded in Dhania's direction, "Ask her."

"I want to know from both of you."

Dhania said, "Well, he is a little old, alright; but if you men think it's okay, then it's fine by me too. Whatever is destined shall come to pass for sure but I do agree he is a nice man."

As for Hori, he was totally sold on the idea. His confidence in Ram Sevak was similar to the willing trust weak men have on others with an aggressive streak. His imagination had already taken wings. If a person with such a strong attitude were on his side, his life would be a song.

After calculating an auspicious date from the almanac, the next important step was to inform Gobar about the wedding. Whether he came or not was his lookout; they had to do fulfill their duty. He hadn't cared to look back after he stomped out of home but they should at least let him know.

Gobar decided to return home as soon he received the letter. Jhuniya was not too keen but kept her mouth shut, sensing the tricky situation. A brother not attending his sister's wedding was unusual. It was something unheard. The stigma of not being around for Sona's marriage was already something they could barely live down.

Gobar was feeling very contrite. "It's not fair to be so detached from one's parents. We might have disagreements and we can afford to live without their support as we can fend for ourselves now but how can we forget that it's they who brought us up and made us what we are today? We should be patient even if they appear unreasonable at times. Incidentally it's such a coincidence! For the last few days I was missing them. I don't know what got over me that day, I shouldn't have got mad at them. It's all your fault! I had to leave my folks just for you."

Jhuniya snapped back, infuriated by the accusation. "Now don't drag me into it. Don't try to pass the blame on me. You were the one itching for a fight. I lived with *amma* for so many months we never had any arguments."

"No. The fight was about you."

"Okay. Agreed, it was about me; but I also left my folks just for you!"

"Oh yeah! As if your folks were withering away for you! Your brothers thought you were a liability, their wives hated you. Your father would have roasted you alive!"

"All because of you!"

"Say what you like but this time we must try to be nice to them. They should also feel happy and get some respite from their dreary life. We should take care that we do nothing against their wishes this time. *Dada* is such a nice man, he never scolded me. *Amma* did beat me up a few times but always gave me something nice to eat later on. She did beat me at times but did her best to make me smile afterwards."

They informed Malti about their decision to go home and the reason why it was so important for them to leave as soon a possible. Malti not only gave them permission to go but also gave a spinning wheel and bracelet as gifts for the bride.

She wanted to attend the wedding too but certain patients in her care required her constant attention so she excused herself. She did promise to do her best to come for the wedding, if only for a short while and packed a bundle of toys for their baby. Hugging and kissing the child profusely, she wanted to compensate for the days he would be away from her but the child, totally unconcerned, was thrilled with the idea of a journey to a home about which he didn't have the vaguest idea. For him 'home' was a magical house in some distant fairyland.

When Gobar reached home and saw the state of his house, he was shocked. One part of the house was in shambles, ready to crumble any moment. A sickly bull was tethered to the door. Dhania and Hori were overjoyed to see him but Gobar was feeling depressed. Was there any point in saving a house that was in such a bad shape? He worked for others but at least he could afford two square meals a day. He reported to just one master but here every other person in the village lorded over his folks. This was slavery and that too without any rewards. They had to toil day and night and had to give all that they earned to others just because they owed them money. They were left with nothing for themselves. Only *dada* could handle and bear such misery! Gobar wouldn't have survived a single day in this wretched place.

But Hori was not alone in his misery. There was not a single peasant in the village who didn't have a similar story to tell. They walked like zombies, toiled and struggled like helpless vermin as though agony and misery was their destiny. Their lives were wasted, with no sign of relief, joy or hope.

It was the time for harvest but none in the village wore a smile. The granaries were loaded with freshly harvested crops but that didn't bring cheer to their lives. More than half of it would be handed over to the money lenders and their touts; the remaining would go straight to the homes of a large number of other bigwigs. The future of the peasants was one dark hole, a yawning bottomless pit of despair.

They didn't have a way out. Their desire for life itself was dull and insipid. Huge mounds of garbage piled up at their doorstep, an unbearable stink surrounded it but their nose had turned immune to the stench. Their eyes were listless and dead. Often jackals come in from the forests close by and wailed mournfully at night but they made no efforts to chase them away. They ate whatever they could lay their hands on with ease. Their cattle moved their snouts away from the fodder pits unless it was the right mix but the peasants did not have the luxury of choice. Taste didn't mean anything to them. They simply needed a few morsels to subdue their hunger. They would cheat and thieve at every step; for a fistful of rice they could bloody another's nose. Their depravity touched new lows each passing day where shame and honour meant little and man was completely unconcerned with whatever future held for him.

Since his childhood, Gobar had grown used to such a life in the village. However, after four years in the city, he looked at it in a totally new light. He was thrown into the company of people who could read and write and got the opportunity to attend quite a few political speeches and campaigns. Now he realised that he had to draw his destiny with his own hands. He had to utilise his intelligence and discretion to overcome personal weaknesses and difficulties. No invisible power would descend from heaven to solve his problems. Life in the city had evoked emotions which he never felt before. The arrogance and obstinacy which marked his life earlier was gone and he had turned humble and enterprising. He questioned his dithering and doubtful nature that prevented his mindset from rising above narrow, short term thinking. He had heard that self defeating sorrow and procrastination bound one to misery. Unity and co-operation amongst people was a bond that released individuals from the confines of selfishness. By coming together with others one could form a greater bond of humanity. Such ideals had given wings to him on which he soared above himself, perceiving the world and his country in a new light.

When innocent and trusting people come unscathed through the rollercoaster crests and troughs in life, they are more often than not filled with humility and compassion. Today, he eagerly volunteers to do any odd job his father did around the house. He wanted to repent for his belligerence and bad behaviour. He told his father to relax and let him labour for the rest of his life. For so many years, his parents had toiled without a moment's respite; now it was his turn to wipe the sweat off their brow. When Hori heard him say that his heart overflowed with joy and blessings. His old frame seemed to revive the strength of his younger days and a firm conviction dawned in his heart—he would never burden his son with his debts. It was the boy's time to revel in the joys of youth; Hori could handle pain alright. He was used to it. Moreover, it was not up to him to pass his time in the backyards of a retired life of spirituality. It was the shovel and sickle for him; not a life of quiet contemplation of God. That would not bring him any peace, for sure.

Gobar said, "I think you should allow me to send you some money every month so that you pay off the debts. How much is the total amount?"

Hori shook his head vigorously. "No, son! Don't bother about that. I will manage it here; you aren't earning so much that you should add this new burden on your head. Times will not be the same forever. See, Rupa will soon go to her new home. We don't have any other pressing expenses except paying off the debts. You stop working yourself up about it. Take care of your health. If you take care of your health today, it will help you later on when you are older. Stop worrying about me. I am quite happy as I am and rather used to the life I lead. Don't bind yourself to a life of toil in the fields. One day you will make it good in life. You have a fine master who you should serve well with dedication. She is already here. I have seen her. She's such an angel, really!"

At that moment, Datadin came in and took Hori aside. Pulling out two hundred rupee notes from his pocket, he thrust them in his hands and said, "You took my advice; that was really good, I appreciate that. See, you have successfully achieved two things in one stroke. Your daughter is married comfortably with no expenses and you have saved your ancestral property as well. I did the best I could to help you, now it is up to you to manage your life."

When Hori accepted the money with trembling hands, he could not raise his face to look Datadin in the eyes. Not a word escaped his lips. He felt he was sinking in a deep hollow in the ground. After thirty years of continuous struggle with life, this was the first day he felt completely vanquished. He felt utterly defeated and crushed with a decisive finality as if he was pulled into the village square to be abused and spat upon by any passersby. He was screaming in agony, 'come brothers, look at this miserable wretch. I am at your mercy. I have been singed by the heat of June and frozen by the icy winds of December. Slit open my body and you will discover how the blood runs dry in my veins. Take a look at my bruised and battered body, scarred with innumerable wounds. Ask me, did I ever have a single moment of respite under the shade? Do I look as if I have lived one day without pain? And now- to top all that such a vicious humiliation! Come, see how my insensitivity survives since I am not dead yet. What a coward, disgraceful and lowly creature I am!' His confidence battered, blinded and bruised with time had already cracked and splintered; today it crumbled all around him with a finality he had never felt before.

Datadin stood up to go and said, "So I will take your leave now. I suggest you hurry up to Nokhe Rams' house right away. Why delay things?"

Hori said, "Sure, I will definitely go to him, *Maharaj*. But please remember- my reputation is firmly and solely in your hands."

36

It was revelry all the way for two full days in the village. There was music and singing that local bands played in high decibels and amidst drama and tear jerking scenes, Rupa was given an emotional farewell and dispatched to her new home. Not once during the festivities did anyone notice that the father of the bride did not step out of his house. He kept to himself and avoided any public appearance. Meanwhile, since Malti had kept her promise and come over for the wedding, the number of visitors and guests was more than usual---as much to attend the festivities as to see the special guest. Women from neighbouring villages made it a point to drop by to pay a visit.

Gobar won the goodwill of everybody with his polite behaviour and had the entire village eating out of his hand. There was no house left where stories of his humble and exceptional conduct were not narrated in admiration and awe. Bhola almost fell at his feet while his wife offered him *paan* and a rupee as a gesture of respect and promised to look him up if she happened to be in Lucknow any time. She noted his address and studiously avoided any mention of her financial help to his father during Sona's wedding.

On the third day, when Gobar was ready to return to Lucknow, he confessed before Hori and Dhania, the guilt which was tormenting his soul. Eyes brimming with tears, Hori said, "Son, out of selfish attachment to my land, I have committed a crime and I have to carry this terrible burden on my shoulders. God will punish me for my sins. I don't know what awaits me in the future!"

Gobar didn't flinch; his face was calm and he was completely composed when he reassured his father. "You have committed no crime, *dada*. But I agree with you that we should pay back Ram Sevak's loan. What could you have done after all? I have turned out to be a no-good son for you, your fields yield nothing worthwhile, nobody will give you a loan, there's barely enough food in the house to last over a month, could you have done any better in such a situation? If you hadn't saved your land and property, you would be left with nowhere to stay. It's better to trust one's fate when pushed in such a corner and do whatever appears sensible. I don't know how long this injustice will continue. All talk about reputation and honour is a farce for those who can't manage two square meals a day. Had you also snatched other's properties, trampled over them and swindled their money, you would also be known as a 'nice' and 'respectable person' like everybody else. You clung to certain morals; this is your punishment for it. If I were in your position, I would either be in jail by now or might have been hanged soon enough. I would have never tolerated working like crazy- only to fill the coffers of others, all the while starving myself and my kids. I wouldn't have taken it lying down even if it meant walking into trouble."

Dhania was not keen to send Gobar's wife back to the city with him. Jhuniya herself wished to stay on for some more time. Finally, it was decided to let Gobar return alone.

Next day morning Gobar left for Lucknow at the crack of dawn. Hori walked him to the outskirts of the village. He had never felt more affectionate for his son as he felt now. When Gobar bent down to touch his feet, he was choked for words as though he won't see him ever again. But his soul was bubbling with pride and joy. His son's reverential attitude and love had enthused him with energy; it made him feel larger than life. A few days ago, his life was covered under a dark, gloomy cloak of despair which obscured his vision of the road ahead. Now he saw a brightly lit highway of enthusiasm instead.

Rupa too was perfectly happy at her new home. The state in which she passed her childhood was one in which money and its lack was the theme song every day. She nursed scores of desires that wilted long before they took the form of yearning. Today she was reliving all those desires. In her eyes, her husband was not a middle aged person but a man with personality. He was a husband and his youth or advanced years made no difference to her wifely feelings. Her attitude as a wife and woman was not built upon her husband's looks, features or age; it came from a deeper foundation based on pristine traditions which could only be shaken by nothing less than tremors of cataclysmic proportions. Her effervescent youth was an inward delight to her soul; she would make herself up and take time dressing herself up for her own pleasure.

For Ram Sevak, Rupa was a housewife, busy and engrossed in household work. She was careful not to cause him concern or embarrass him by any exposure of her youth. Granaries full of grains, long winding tracts of agricultural fields and herds of cattle tethered at her doorstep prevented her mind from suffering any notions of lack or incompleteness.

However, she had an intense desire to find ways to bring cheer to her parent's drab life. She spent a lot of time wondering how to rid them of their poverty. She still retained strong memories of the cow that had come into their lives as a guest and left them crying, as if bereaved. Instead of healing over time, those memories had survived and grown still more poignant and real. Her new home was still a novelty for her to which she had not grown comfortably familiar with, despite knowing it did belong to her now. In her mind the old ramshackle hut was her real home; its inhabitants were the only people close to her heart. Her joys and sorrows centred on their ups and downs. The satisfaction of owning a herd of cattle tethered behind her courtyard was nothing as compared to the thrill and exhilaration she felt on seeing the lone cow in her old home so many years ago. She was sorry her *dada* could not fully realise his dream of owning his own cow till this date. She never forgot how happy he was and how he beamed when they brought that cow home. After the unfortunate manner in which she died, they could never manage to buy another one but she knew Hori's longing was very much alive and as intense as it was years ago. She decided to take one of the healthier, well bred cows with her on her next visit to her parents and leave it with them. Better still, why wait? She could send it across with one of the men taking care of the cowshed. The only thing remaining was Ram Sevak's permission which came instantly the minute she asked. The very next day, a man was despatched with a cow to Hori's house. He was given clear instructions to let her father know that the cow was being sent so little Mangal could have fresh milk to drink every day.

Hori was keen to acquire one though he was not in a tearing hurry. But with Mangal in the house, they did need one rather urgently. Buying a cow was his priority number one and he had decided it would be the first thing he'd do as soon he came into some money. As luck would have it, a city contractor had arrived at the village and needed labourers to break stones to produce gravel for construction work. When Hori heard about it, he was one of the first to rush and sign up. At five *annas* per day he felt it was not a bad bargain. If the job lasted two months it meant enough money to at least afford a cow.

He hammered away at the stones all morning till late afternoon, returning home towards the evening- all weary and tired but without a frown or trace of regret upon his face. He carried the same enthusiasm to work the next day, busying himself in breaking stones to build his future. At night he sat at the spinning wheel, making coarse rope often as late one o'clock in the night. His enthusiasm infected Dhania who instead of preventing him from over exerting himself, joined him in the spinning. Ram Sevak's loan had to be paid back; a cow had to be bought. Gobar was so concerned that they had just got to do it.

It was twelve o' clock and they were still at the wheel, spinning non-stop. Dhania turned to Hori and said, "You must be sleepy. Go and rest! you have a long day ahead and have to wake up early."

Hori turned his eye skywards and said, "I will go to sleep when I have to. It doesn't seem more than ten o'clock at the moment. Why don't you go? I think it is you who should take a break."

"I take a break in the afternoon. There's ample time to stretch my back in the day."

"I also take time off in the afternoon and relax under a tree. I am fine."

"It sure must be blistering in the day; the heat is too much, isn't it?"

"Not really! It's quite shady under the tree, it's not hot at all."

"But I worry for you. What if you fall ill?"

"Don't be silly. Only those with time on their hands can afford to fall sick. I am determined to have, at least, half of Ram Sevak's amount ready with us when Gobar comes here next. He will bring something too. Together we will be able to pay off Ram Sevak and begin life afresh with no debts dangling above our heads like a sword."

"I guess so. By the way, I am missing Gobar so much this time. He has turned so nice and polite I can't believe it."

"True. The way he touched my feet when he was about to go! It's amazing."

"When Mangal arrived from the city he was such a healthy, bonny child. Here we can hardly offer him little more than mere *rotis*. He must get a good diet with plenty of milk. The moment I get paid the first thing I'll do is buy a cow."

"We could have bought a cow long back had you listened to anyone other than yourself. It was tough to fend for your own family; did you have to take on Puniya's responsibility as well?"

"What could I do? All said and done, I am still bound by my obligations and duties. I know Heera wronged us. But someone had to look after his wife and kids. Who do they have other than me? Do you realise what they would have gone through if I had not come forward to help? Spare a thought for them, Dhania. Despite this, Mangru filed a case against them do you realise how heartless the world is?"

"If she hides money and cheats people what else can you expect?"

"Don't talk nonsense. That's utter rubbish. It is tough making both ends meet. You think someone in her state can stash money on the side?"

"Whatever! But it's so curious about Heera. He simply disappeared."

"My heart says he will be back one day. He will return."

It was getting late. Ultimately, they put the ropes aside and went to sleep. Early morning when Hori rose to get ready to leave for work, the first sight that greeted his eyes was Heera standing right before him in flesh and blood. Long scraggly hair, his clothes in tatters, face dry and sunburnt, his body was emaciated and he seemed to have shrunk in height. When he saw Hori staring at him, he rushed and fell at his feet.

Hori hugged him close to his chest, "What happened to you Heera? You've grown so weak! When did you arrive? Are you ill?"

For Hori, his younger brother Heera was the same little orphan boy he had vowed to protect. He was certainly not the man who had poisoned Hori's cow. The thirty odd years separating the little boy from the haggard man who stood before him evaporated, in an instant, as if the little boy had just stepped across all those years in one gigantic stride, completely erasing everything that transpired in between.

Heera stood silent, sobbing inconsolably.

Hori took his hand and said, "Why do you cry, brother? We all make mistakes; it's no big deal. Where were you all these years?"

When Heera spoke, his voice came from the depths of loneliness and remorse, "What can I say, *dada*? Perhaps fate spared me; I was destined to see you once again. I live to see this day. I had gone mad. My sins bore down on me. All my waking hours and even while I slept, that cow seemed to stalk me wherever I went. She was before my eyes, constantly, every moment. I went crazy. I was locked up in a madhouse for five years. They released me six months ago. I begged on the streets, scraping for morsels to survive. I didn't have the guts to come here. How could I face the world? But my heart dragged me here. I steeled my heart and gathered the courage to come to you. In my absence, my kids, you took care..."

Hori cut him short. "You shouldn't have run away. We could have palmed off five or ten rupees to the constable and hushed up the matter. What worse could have happened? Nothing."

"I will forever be indebted to you, *dada*. As long as I live."

"I am no outsider, brother. I am one of your own."

Hori was a happy man. All the tribulations and disappointments of his life lay vanquished and squirming at his feet. Who says he has lost the battle of life? His embattled and shattered weapons of defiance were now his flags of triumph. This exhilaration; this pride; this delight; and this elated confidence, were they signs of a defeated soul? Within the petty setbacks and defeats strewn along his life lay his victory. His back was erect, chest pulled out, puffed in pride. There was a glow on his face. The success of his efforts and struggles had come to manifest itself in Heera's contrite words of gratitude. There could be a hundred, possibly two-hundred mounds of grains spilling out of his granary; under the loose stone in his courtyard, he might have stashed a thousand, even five thousand rupees but could any of those possessions given him the heavenly delight that was bursting out of every pore of his being at that moment?

Heera stepped back to take a good look at his brother. "You've grown so thin, dada!"

Hori laughed and said, "Is it my age to grow fat and healthy? Only those people grow fat who do not have worries of debt, payments or a reputation to live up to. To be fat in this age, one has to be totally shameless. One has to trample over a hundred others to grow fat. There is no fun in such a life. Real happiness is when everyone around you is equally healthy. By the way, have you met Sobha yet?"

"I met him last night, *dada*. It was from him I learnt that you not only took care of your own family but went all out to take care of those who hated you. Sobha wasted his life and sold all his land. God knows how they'll manage in future."

Later that day when Hori went out to work, he felt slightly under the weather. His body was not fully rested and last night's fatigue was getting to him. But his steps were quick and light and he walked with the haughty air of one who feels invincible.

By ten o'clock, the hot winds blew so fast and furious that by noon it was like fire raining on the roads. Hori lifted baskets of crushed stones and pebbles from the stone quarry on his head and emptied them on a truck waiting by the roadside. When it was time for the afternoon break he was extremely tired. He was surprised this was the first time he felt so fatigued. Every step he took seemed laboured and heavy. His wiry frame was scalded by the heat. Exhausted, he didn't bother to munch the bundle of food he carried in his pocket for lunch. He spread a towel that doubled as the shirt on his back and stretched himself in the shade of a tree. He slept briefly but his throat was parched. He knew it was not advisable to drink water on an empty stomach so he tried his best to postpone quenching his thirst. But the heat in his body showed no signs of following his diktat. He couldn't bear it any longer. Another labourer sat close to where he lay, munching on his crumbs. There was a pail of water next to him. Hori staggered up to it and downed a pitcher of water and lay down again. Within half an hour he threw up, vomiting hard as a death-like pall fell across his face.

The man stopped munching to look at him. "Brother Hori? Are you alright?"

Hori's head was spinning but he said, "Its nothing. I am fine."

Before he could finish his sentence, he vomited again and his hands and feet went cold all of a sudden. He blacked out as his eyes closed but a host of images from his life scrambled to his mind's eye. They were flickering visions of memories, scattered and incoherent, in no particular chronological order. They flashed before him like a dream with no logic---incongruous, unrelated, grotesque and disjointed. He saw his mother and himself as a small boy rushing into her lap. Then he saw Gobar had come home and was bending down to touch his feet. The scene changed abruptly. Now it was Dhania, dressed as a young bride, in a red bridal saree, serving him food...

Then it was the picture of a cow that looked exactly like Kamadhenu---the celestial cow of the Gods. He milked her and was looking for Mangal to feed him when suddenly the cow turned into a Goddess and...

His fellow worker was calling out to him, "Hori, come on lunch time is over. Pick up your basket. Time to get back to work."

Hori was quiet. He was flying in and out of distant lands. His body was burning with high fever, yet his hands and feet were cold. He had had a heat stroke.

The man sprinted to Hori's house on the double. Within the hour Dhania hurried to where Hori lay under the tree. Sobha and Heera followed behind her, carrying a cot they strung on their shoulders to carry him home.

When Dhania touched Hori's skin, she was stunned. Her face turned ashen.

Her voice trembled as she called out to him, "What's happened? How are you feeling now?"

Hori opened his eyes to look at her as his pupils moved in vague directions.

"Good, so you are back, Gobar? I have got a cow for Mangal. There she is, look!"

Dhania had seen the face of death. She recognised it. She had seen her come on tip toe, softly and also like a tornado, howling and wailing. Her mother-in-law died before her eyes. She had seen it all; her father-in-law breathed his last, her two sons had died in her arms when they were babies and so had scores of people in the village. She received a jolt as though someone had knocked her down. The base on which she had built her life had shifted precariously but no, this was not the time to hurry to conclusions, it was just a heat stroke. This was time for patience and presence of mind. Her fears were unfounded; he was unconscious because he had had a heatstroke.

She bit her lips to keep tears in check, "Look at me. Come on, look at me. I am right here! Don't you recognise me?"

Hori surfaced for a moment. Death was close; the pyre was about to be engulfed in flames. But what was that? The smoke had stopped billowing out. He stared at Dhania as the corners of his eyes crinkled with pain and two tear drops rolled down the sides. "Forgive me for all my faults Dhania. I am leaving. We could not get the cow. Now all this money will go for the last rites. Don't cry Dhania. How long do you want to hold me back? Everything is lost. Let me die."

His eyes closed yet again. Heera and Sobha had come with the makeshift stretcher. They lifted Hori on the cot and hurried home.

The news spread within minutes. The entire village crowded outside his house. Hori was lying on the cot in the veranda. Probably he saw what was happening, maybe he understood it all, but his tongue refused to move and form words. The tears flowing from his eyes were mute testimony of his helplessness, they spoke of the difficulty in breaking through the bonds of attachment. What was attachment but regret of not holding on to what one can never hope to secure for oneself? There is no attachment to duties that are realised or promises that are fulfilled. Bonds of attachment are for those whom we leave unattended or whom we leave midstream. It is for unrealised dreams and ambitions which we still aspire to attain.

She knew it all but Dhania continued to clutch at fidgety shadows of hope. She was weeping silently but scurried around the house like an automaton, roasting green mangoes over a flame to make *Panna,* the cure for a heatstroke; rubbing and massaging husk on his body to cool the rising temperature. What could she do? There was no money or she would have sent someone to fetch a doctor.

Heera said to her in a choked voice- "Steel your heart, *bhabhi*. It's time for Godan. *Dada's* slipping away!"

Dhania turned a disapproving look at him. How much more would she have to steel her heart? Would she have to be told or reminded about her duties to her husband? Her partner for life was leaving was she not worth anything except beating her breast at his loss?

A few other voices rose from the crowd, "Yes. You must donate and gift away a cow. It's high time."

Dhania stood up like a robot. This morning she had sold the last bundle of coir rope for 20 *Annas*. She brought the coins and placing them in her husband's cold palm, and then she addressed Datadin who was standing in front of her, "*Maharaj*, there is no cow, no calf, no money in the house. This is all we have. This is his Godan."

She fell on the floor, weeping bitterly.

❁❁❁

POPULAR SCIENCE

9496 A • Rs. 120/-

2215 S • ₹ 165/- Available in Hindi also.

2214 S • ₹ 165/- Available in Hindi also.

8716 T • ₹ 160/-

8733 D • ₹ 195/-

9660 K • ₹ 295/-

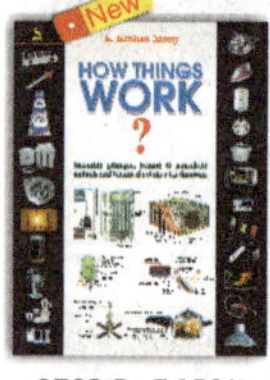

8702 B• ₹ 150/-

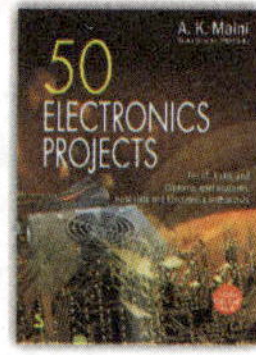

6678 D • ₹ 195/-

6679 A • ₹ 150/-

QUIZ BOOKS

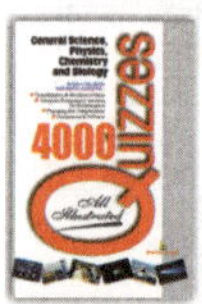

8965 D • ₹ 150/-

7726 K • ₹ 120/-

7727 L • ₹ 120/-

7723 F • ₹ 100/-

9412 C • ₹ 150/-

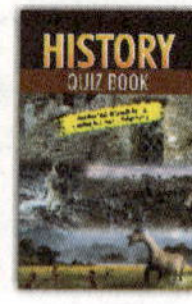

7753 G • ₹ 120/-

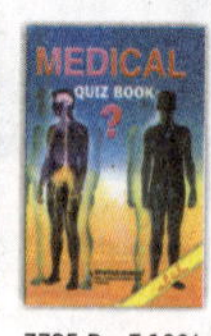

7725 B • ₹ 100/-

7722 E • ₹ 120/-

NEW RELEASES

8767 C • Rs. 120/-

0019 R • Rs. 160/-

8762 P • Rs. 140/-

8764 T • Rs. 160/-

- Over 900 Illustrations
- Over 800 Pages
- 890 Articles
- Four Volumes

Set Code: 4514 S

Set 4 Vols.: ₹ 780/-
Each Vol.: ₹ 195/-
Available in Hindi & English both

This Library is must for every student *of a* School *or a* College

Also equally useful for everyone else

Price: ₹ 600/-
Contains 4 books of ₹ 150/- each

4 Books of the Library

Miscellaneous

9497 B • ₹ 120/-

9783 H • ₹ 150/-

9680 B • ₹ 295/-

9686 H • ₹ 120/-

SELF-IMPROVEMENT

New

698 R • ₹ 195/- 9498 C • ₹ 180/- 9490 H • ₹ 175/- 9464 R • ₹ 80/- 9096 B • ₹ 150/- 5614 E • ₹ 150/- 4008 J • ₹ 150/- 9026 D • ₹ 120/- 9786 M • ₹ 195/-

491 J • ₹ 100/- 8885 D • ₹ 150/- 9081 D • ₹ 150/- 9091 B • ₹ 120/- 9060 B • ₹ 195/- 9684 F • ₹ 195/- 8928 D • ₹ 80/- 9449 A • ₹ 195/- 9788 R • ₹ 195/-

MANAGEMENT/JOB/CARRIER/BUSINESS & PROFESSION

All Time Bestsellers

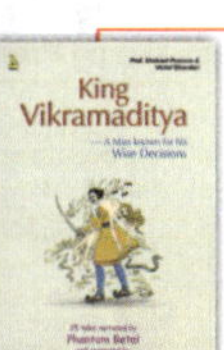

9461 K • ₹ 150/- 5338 A • ₹ 135/- (with CD) 8979 A • ₹ 135/- 9406 B • ₹ 150/- 9672 G • ₹ 150/- 9682 D • ₹ 120/- 8729 T • ₹ 120/-

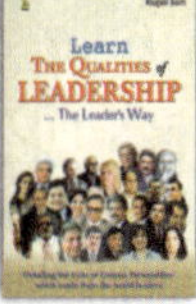

9697 P • ₹ 195/- 9313 D • ₹ 150/- 5623 B • ₹ 250/- 9439 L • ₹ 150/- 5441 D • ₹ 195/- 8883 D • ₹ 150/- 8735 F • ₹ 150/-

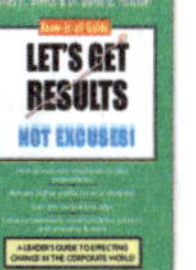

4018 D • ₹ 150/- 9079 B • ₹ 195/- 4005 E • ₹ 195/- 5643 B • ₹ 120/- 9431 C • ₹ 175/- 8990 C • ₹ 96/- 9763 P • Rs. 195/-

5618 D • ₹ 120/- 5640 C • ₹ 120/- 5615 D • ₹ 150/- 8972 C • ₹ 80/- 4001 A • ₹ 150/- 5646 A • ₹ 225/- 4017 D • ₹ 150/-

PERSONALITY DEVELOPMENT

8748 E • ₹ 195/-

9666 A • ₹ 150/-

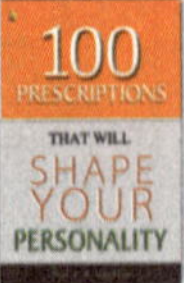
9678 R • ₹ 195/-

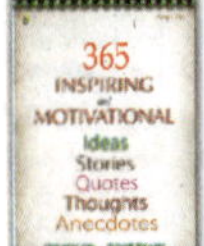
9670 E • ₹ 240/-

9696 M • ₹ 220/-

9070 B • ₹ 195/-

9028 D • ₹ 175/-

5641 A • ₹ 150/-

9450 B • ₹ 195/-

9088 C • ₹ 195/-

9667 B • ₹ 150/-

8966 E • ₹ 100/-

5639 B • ₹ 80/-

9466 T • ₹ 96/-

9973 B • ₹ 110/-

9981 B • ₹ 96/-

8868 D • ₹ 120/-

9487 E • ₹ 150/-

STUDENT DEVELOPMENT

9090 A • ₹ 220/-

9668 C • ₹ 150/-

9071 D • ₹ 165/-

8731 B • ₹ 100/-

9495 R • ₹ 175/-

9455 C • ₹ 150/-

5622 A • ₹ 120/-

9967 C • ₹ 120/-

2241 J • ₹ 100/-

94441 S • ₹ 195/-

9654 D • ₹ 100/-

9652 D • ₹ 120/-

8962 A • ₹ 150/-

9089 D • ₹ 135/-

4016 D • ₹ 160/-

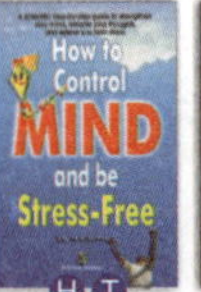
4009 K • ₹ 150/-

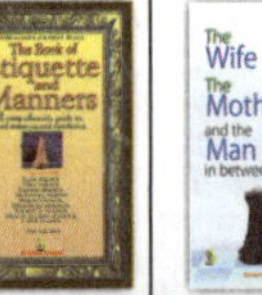
8997 B • ₹ 120/-

4010 L • ₹ 100/-

9787 P • ₹ 100/-

2244 D • ₹ 80/-

PARENTING

9906 J • ₹ 250/- (HB)

8261 D • ₹ 180/

9674 J • ₹ 220/-

9784 J • ₹ 150/

9594 K • ₹ 80/-

8917 D • ₹ 120

9458 G • ₹ 80/-

9438 B • ₹ 150/

9065 A • ₹ 80/-

9994 E • ₹ 120/

ALTERNATIVE THERAPIES

8882 F • ₹ 215/-

8983 E • ₹ 100/-

8836 D • ₹ 135/-

9935 F • ₹ 120/-

5637 D • ₹ 96/-

8889 D • ₹ 100/-

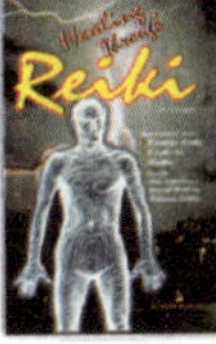

8842 D • ₹ 100/-

8941 A • ₹ 100/-

GENERAL HEALTH

9075 C • ₹ 225/-

8747 D • ₹ 150/-

9940 D • ₹ 150/-

8859 G • ₹ 80/-

8877 A • ₹ 150/-

8847 M • ₹ 100/-

8870 D • ₹ 100/-

9950 B • ₹ 120/-

9902 F • ₹ 120/-

COMMON AILMENTS & DISEASES

8891 D • ₹ 120/-

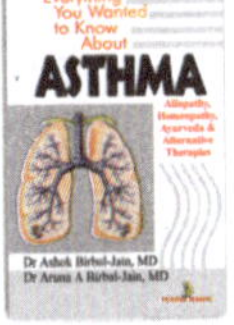

8281 A • ₹ 100/-

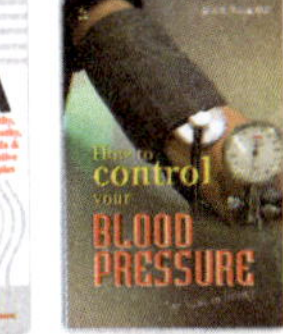

8094 D • ₹ 120/-

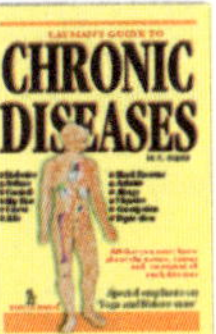

8848 D • ₹ 150/-

8276 A • ₹ 96/-

8888 D • ₹ 96/-

8908 D • ₹ 120/-

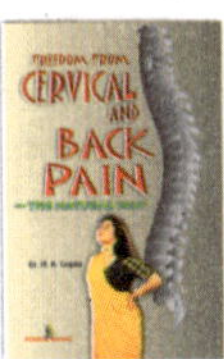

8878 B • ₹ 80/-

SLIMMING & FITNESS

8277 B • ₹ 120/-

8875 K • ₹ 120/-

9445 A • ₹ 150/-

DIET & NUTRITION

9941 D • ₹ 100/-

8904 D • ₹ 150/-

8985 B • ₹ 120/-

8968 G • ₹ 120/-

8271 C • ₹ 96/-

9037 D • ₹ 150/-

HINDOOLOGY / RELIGION / SPIRITUAL BOOKS

9873 C • ₹ 60/-

9770 E • ₹ 150/-

9453 A • ₹ 250/-

4179 A • ₹ 295/- (HB)

4138 B Rs. 250

4177 B • ₹ 250/-

9997 C • ₹ 80/-

4181 C • ₹ 195/-

9984 E • ₹ 399/- (HB)

4130 B • ₹ 120/-

9811 P • ₹ 120/-

9585 A • ₹ 96/-

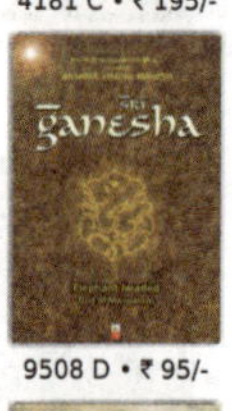

9508 D • ₹ 95/-

9989 D • ₹ 96/-

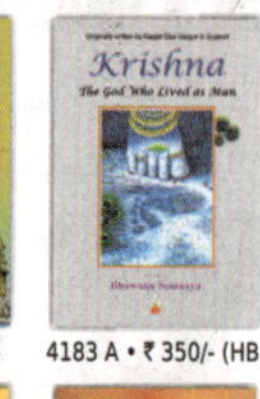

4183 A • ₹ 350/- (HB)

9504 D • ₹ 100/-

9540 D • ₹ 150/-

9513 A • ₹ 195/-

4126 B • ₹ 96/-

9812 R • ₹ 120/-

9504 D • ₹ 100/-

4124 A • ₹ 120/-

4190 C • ₹ 160/-

9509 A • ₹ 150/-

4152 B • ₹ 96/-

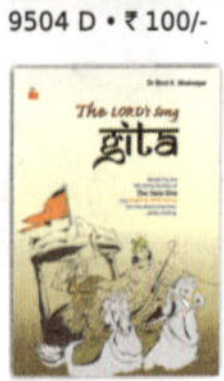

4188 A • ₹ 160/-

4132 D • ₹ 100/-

9987 E • ₹ 150/-

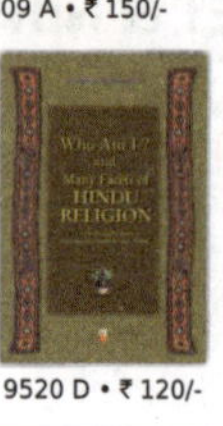

9520 D • ₹ 120/-

4134 B • ₹ 80/-

4182 D • ₹ 96/-

9405 A • ₹ 195/-

COMPUTERS

7712 K • ₹ 165/-

7711 J • ₹ 120/-

9768 C • ₹ 175/-

7766 A • ₹ 120/-

HOME MAKING / GRILLS & RAILINGS

3111 E • ₹ 175/-

3107 F • ₹ 88/-

3106 E • ₹ 100/-

3105 D • ₹ 100/-

3108 G • ₹ 150/-

3104 M • ₹ 100/-

ASTROLOGY/VASTU/HYPNOTISM/PAMISTRY

9871 A • ₹ 240/-

9693 H • ₹ 195/-

9671 F • ₹ 195/-

2127 D • ₹ 250/-

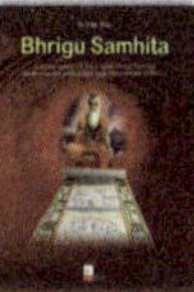

4177 C • ₹ 295/-

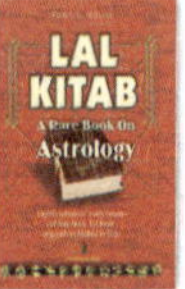

9086 A • ₹ 295/-HB

2116 D • ₹ 150/-

8259 D • ₹ 88/-

2109 F • ₹ 150/-

2112 D • ₹ 120/-

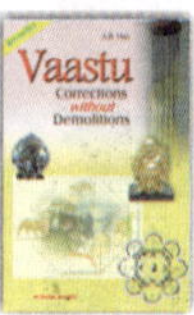

3110 B • ₹ 120/-

2133 B • ₹ 96/-

8899 D • ₹ 195/-

8925 D • ₹ 96/-

2132 A • ₹ 150/-

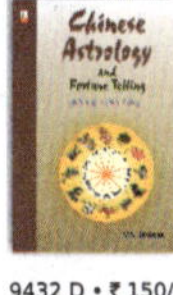

9432 D • ₹ 150/-

2120 D • ₹ 150/-

2109 F • ₹ 100/-

ENGLISH IMPROVEMENT

97540 D • ₹ 175/-

5541 C • ₹ 196/-

6651 E • ₹ 195/-

9448 D • ₹ 175/-

9056 A • ₹ 125/-

5538 D • ₹ 100/-

PERSON & PERSONALITIES

9669 D • ₹ 120/-

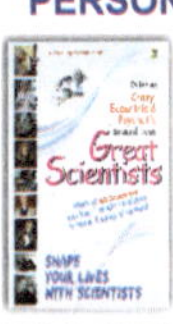

9825 E • ₹ 150/-

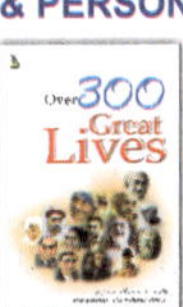

2113 D • ₹ 195/-

9764 R • ₹ 100/-

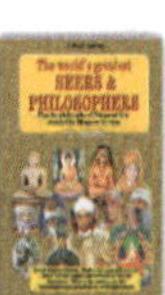

8991 D • ₹ 120/-

BODY/BEAUTY CARE

8093 D • ₹ 150/-

9986 B • ₹ 150/-

8971 B • ₹ 120/-

9922 F • ₹ 120/-

8865 F • ₹ 120/-

JOKES HUMOUR & SATIRE

2342 C • ₹ 100/- 2343 D • ₹ 100/-

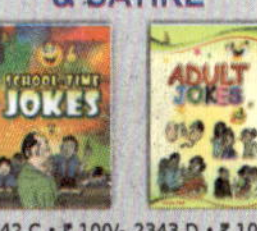

2341 B • ₹ 96/- 2318 A • ₹ 96/-

2330 B • ₹ 96/- 2319 B • ₹ 96/-

FICTION

Set Code SH 001

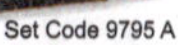

Set Code 9795 A

Set Code 9752 B • ₹ 550/-

SAYING/QUOTATIONS/ PROVERBS

9474 F • ₹ 170/- 9789 A • ₹ 150/- 8999 D • ₹ 80/-

9953 A • ₹ 100/- 8947 E • ₹ 100/- 8890 D • ₹ 150/-

5512 A • ₹ 150/- 8963 B • ₹ 80/- 9425 A • ₹ 60/-

FUN, FACTS, MAGIC & MYSTERIES

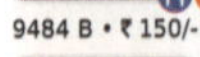

9484 B • ₹ 150/- | 2275 D • ₹ 120/- | 9479 M • ₹. 120/- | 9470 B • ₹ 100/-

2208 M • ₹ 100/- | 9816 D • ₹ 100/- | 2247 F • ₹ 100/- | 2250 A • ₹ 110/-

2211 F • ₹ 100/- | 9457 E • ₹ 150/- | 2237 M • ₹ 100/- | 2335 A • ₹ 80/-

2243 L • ₹ 100/- | 9775 M • ₹ 100/- | 9985 A • ₹ 80/- | 5110 A • ₹ 80/-

2337 C • ₹ 100/- | 2336 B • ₹ 100/- | 2331 C • ₹ 100/- | 9977 B • ₹ 100/-

YOGA & MEDITATION

8269 A • ₹ 195/- | 9998 D • ₹ 150/- | 8939 D • ₹ 96/-

9958 S • ₹ 160/- | 9087 B • ₹ 195/- | 2118 F • ₹ 120/-

8901 D • ₹ 150/- | 8099 D • ₹ 80/- | 9025 D • ₹ 80/-

HOMEOPATHY, AYURDEDA

9446 B • ₹ 150/- | 8887 D • ₹ 195/- | 8270 B • ₹ 195/- | 8923 D • ₹ 195/-

8010 D • ₹ 96/- | 9094 E • ₹ 96/- | 8944 D • ₹ 175/- | 8948 A • ₹ 120/-

WORLD FAMOUS SERIES

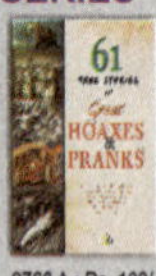

9472 D • ₹ 100/- | 5164 E • ₹ 100/- | 9483 A • Rs. 100/- | 51107 • ₹ 100/- | 9766 A • Rs. 100/- | 9489 G • Rs. 100/- | 9761 M • Rs. 120/-

World Famous Mysterious Objects
True Stories of Mowglis and other Wild Childrens
World Famous Treasures (Lost and Found)
World Famous WARs & Battles
True Stories of Mystic Places
World Famous Adventures
World Famous Military Operations
World Famous Spy Scandals
World Famous Spies & Spymasters
World Famous Crooks & Con Men
True Stories 81 Weird Humans
True Stories of Great Explorers
World Famous Strange Mysteries
and many more......

LOVE, ROMANCE & SEX

9602 B • Rs. 125/- | 8260 D • Rs. 96/- | 8266 D • Rs. 80/- | 8278 C • Rs. 100/- | 8916 D • Rs. 120/-

MORAL, WISDOM & FAIRY TALES

9677 P • Rs. 150/- | 9486 D • Rs. 250/- | 8967 F • Rs. 80/- | 9077 E • Rs.120/- | 9563 N • Rs. 125/- | 2289 D • ₹ 96/-

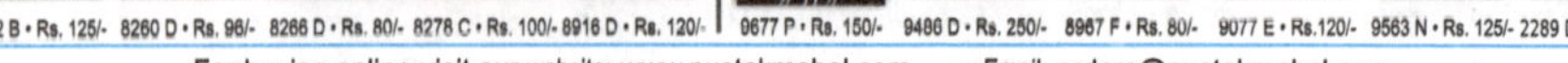